THE CAMP

CHATEAU #2

PENELOPE SKY

HARTWICK PUBLISHING

Hartwick Publishing

The Camp

Copyright © 2021 by Penelope Sky

All rights reserved.

"The difference between treason and patriotism is only a matter of dates."

-Alexandre Dumas

The Count of Monte Cristo

CONTENTS

ONE

PUNISHMENT

THERE WAS NOTHING LEFT.

The cabins had turned to ash.

The coke on the tables had burned too.

A camp that had stood for a decade was now a graveyard. Some of the guards lived. Some had died. Most of the women got away, except a few we retrieved. The guards rode down the path lit by torches and rounded up the ones who'd fled. If they resisted, they were shot.

I sat on a wooden bench that had survived and looked at what was left of the camp.

And that wasn't much.

The night had passed, and now it was morning. The sun shone down, highlighting the damage.

The damage *she* caused.

My hands still shook in anger. My veins popped out of my arms. My entire face hurt because the muscles were so fucking tight. There were seldom times in my life when I got this angry.

This might be the worst.

I wanted to kill her.

I stared at where she lay in the snow…and almost did it.

I was too angry to kill her. Was that possible?

The guards had ostracized me because they recognized her running through the camp with her sister. They didn't know I'd helped her escape, but they knew I'd helped her in the past, so they spat on me as they passed.

Horses were audible as they approached, galloping through the patches of snow and the hard earth. There were several, an entire entourage.

I kept my hands on the ground, not in cowardice but indifference.

The horses neighed as they came to a stop.

His boots thudded against the ground as he got off his horse. Then the footsteps came toward me, thudding louder and louder as they came near. Then they stopped.

I looked up to see my brother standing over me.

He wore the exact same expression as I did when I looked at Raven.

Like he wanted to kill me.

One of the guards found a chair from somewhere and placed it behind him so he could take a seat if he wanted.

He didn't.

I didn't rise to my feet or speak a word. I had no defense for the events that had transpired last night. If he decided to kill me, I would accept that decision. After all, this was entirely my fault.

I should die.

After minutes of angry silence, he lowered himself into the chair. "Leave us."

The guards all stepped away to give us privacy. There was nowhere for them to go since not a single building had survived. They just walked farther into the clearing full of snow and ash.

He stared at me, wearing his bomber jacket, jeans, and thick boots. His hair had been shaved, so he was bald with a shadow on his head that matched the one on his jawline. With wide nostrils and lips that quivered with rage, he looked at me with more than anger.

Shame.

When he spoke, his voice was surprisingly quiet. "Everything I built is ash—because of you."

I held his gaze.

"Because you helped her."

I gave a slight nod but didn't apologize.

"You didn't just humiliate yourself. You humiliated me."

I had done everything for that woman—and she'd stabbed me in the back. The one time I dropped my guard, the one time I had empathy, the one time I felt human…blew up in my fucking face. Both of my hands tightened into fists because I was so fucking mad. I started to breathe harder, the headache returning because the vein in my forehead stuck out so far.

He studied my reaction. "The humiliation isn't enough. The anger isn't enough. I must punish you."

I'd betrayed my brother, the only family I had left in the world, for a woman who'd gutted me like a fish. My softness had callused into stone. My kindness had turned into blood lust. If I ever saw her again, I wouldn't be able to resist putting a knife to her throat and watching her choke on her own blood.

"You will pay me for everything I've lost."

I relaxed my fists because my knuckles had started to ache.

"You will rebuild this place with your bare hands—and your own money."

I had already assumed.

"You will work day and night to get this done as quickly as possible so we can resume normal productivity."

"Where will productivity—"

"This place will be better than it was before."

I stared at my brother's face, seeing the disgust in his eyes.

"I will bring that cunt back here to work. She will pay for what she's done with her body, her blood, and her spirit."

She deserved worse for what she'd done to me. "Kill her."

He shook his head slowly. "She doesn't fear death. She fears this place. That's why she burned it to the ground—because it's in her nightmares. Her punishment will be to live this nightmare forevermore."

Just the thought of seeing her again made my stomach flood with acid. All she'd had to do was live. But she chose to throw it all away. She chose to betray the one person who kept her alive all that time.

That wouldn't happen again.

"I won't kill you—because you're my brother. But I will punish you to satisfy the men who want me to kill you."

I expected nothing less.

"Anything you want to say before I start?" He pulled out a knife from his pocket and held the hilt between both hands, his eyes slightly down, patiently waiting for me to speak my final words before the torture commenced.

I shook my head.

He got to his feet and turned to his men. "Hold him down."

TWO
EXECUTIONER

WINTER TURNED TO SPRING.

Months passed, and we rebuilt that place.

It was tough work because we couldn't get shipping trucks out there. All the essentials had to be carried in wagons, and while that became easier as the snow disappeared, it was never simple.

I rarely left the camp, unless I had other business to attend to.

Fender and I hardly spoke during that time.

He was still angry with me.

I was angry with myself.

I didn't spend my free time thinking about the woman who'd made a fool out of me, but the humiliation had left a deeper scar than the one my brother gave me. It was a part of me now, an integral piece to my puzzle. I was bitter, angry, and spiteful.

I wished death upon her.

After everything I'd done for her…everything…she did that to me.

How fucking stupid was I?

I actually felt like shit for what had happened to her, to her sister, to the women who had to hang from the noose every week. I questioned the camp altogether, considered another way of doing business without the loss of lives.

But then she reminded me why it could never change.

Why it should never change.

The camp was built in a similar fashion as last time, the same foundation of cabins scattered throughout the field between the cover of trees. But this time, we built a wooden fence around the perimeter.

No one was escaping this place again.

Fucking no one.

When Raven was returned to the camp, I would make sure she stayed there for the rest of her life.

The camp was completed by late April, before the summer season hit. It would be too hot to work in those conditions, so we busted our asses to get everything done before that time. The surviving guards didn't speak to me, seeing me as a traitor, but they didn't try to harm me…probably because my punishment had been sufficient.

But I never dropped my guard because a knife could slice into my back at any moment.

It was unlikely they would kill me because my brother would slaughter them all.

But if it looked like an accident…maybe they would.

Once the camp was completed, Fender came for a visit.

On horseback, with some of his men, he entered the camp, strong and bulky in the saddle. He looked around as he held the reins, scanning the wooden cabins, the clearing where the new prisoners would work all day, and then he stopped his horse in front of us.

The prisoners were locked in the cabins, so there was no reason to hide our faces. We wore work jeans and t-shirts with sweat on the backs of our necks. Fender was dressed similarly, and when he threw his leg off the horse and landed on the ground, the thud from his body was loud.

He moved forward and looked around, taking his time examining everything.

I waited outside with the guards as he went into the cabins, the bunks, the weapons room, and the clearing to inspect everything with his highly trained eye. He wanted this place exactly as it'd been before—but better.

Some of the guards looked at me, making it clear if Fender didn't like it, the blame would be mine alone.

Alix, the one with the dark beard who tried to coerce Raven into a blow job, stared me down with malice in his eyes. The other guards disliked me, but he particularly hated me. "The boss doesn't like it, it's on you, Romeo."

That was my nickname now—Romeo.

Because I was a fucking pussy.

Fender returned, scanning the area before he finally placed his gaze on mine. His brown eyes were the same, but his were innately furious. Even when he laughed, he looked livid. He stared at me for the first time since that night, really stared at me. The other times we had been in the same room, he'd ignored my existence.

Like he was ashamed of me.

He gave his approval with a slight nod.

Alix narrowed his eyes on my face, as if he'd hoped Fender would hate it so I'd be cut again.

"We'll get our first drop tomorrow. The girls will get back to work." Fender looked at the clearing where the tables were prepared, exactly as they'd been before. There was a new noose hanging on the wooden pole, ready for the first victim. There was no snow, but the ground would still bleed red. "More workers will be delivered to the camp throughout the week." He moved toward me, his boots thudding against the earth with his muscled weight. His arms didn't even swing by his sides because his posture was still so rigid. It was hard for him to look at me because I still made him so angry. He stopped right in front of me, so he could speak quietly enough for only me to hear. "I'll personally retrieve that cunt."

I didn't blink.

He waited for me to argue, as if the past few months would have given me a change of heart, as if I would stick out my neck for her again, humiliate myself to keep her out of this place. It was a test.

I passed.

"Help her escape again…and I'll kill you." His gaze burned into mine, ferocious.

I knew he wasn't bluffing. He would grant no more mercy—even if our blood was the same.

He turned away and raised his voice so the other guards could hear. "We need a new executioner." He turned back to look at me, like he would nominate me for the role as an opportunity to prove my loyalty to him, to everyone. "I think Magnus—"

"I'll do it." Alix's eyes gleamed with mirth, as if nothing would make him happier than putting on that mask and butchering innocent women who were in the wrong place at the wrong time. They went to the grocery store alone at night. They rode the metro alone after a long night at the office. Just regular women…who should have taken a different route home.

I kept a straight face, but my lungs relaxed when Alix volunteered because no amount of anguish would make me want to take on that role even once, let alone every week. It'd been offered to me before, but I never volunteered myself. Now, my brother put me on the spot, but Alix came to my rescue without even realizing it.

Fender accepted the offer. "Then let's get to work." He headed back to his horse with his men to leave the camp. After he got into the saddle and grabbed the reins, he gave me a final look before he rode off. "No one escapes this place. No one."

THREE
THE CAMP

Every time a wagon arrived at the camp, it was full of bound women.

They were assigned their cabins and put to work instantly.

Since we had to start over and establish obedience with the frightened girls, we had a Red Snow every day until the group of women became so afraid they stopped fighting, stopped talking back, and then they became the quiet and submissive group we wanted.

They were officially traumatized.

Years ago, I'd told Fender that the Red Snow was an unnecessary maneuver to establish obedience, that there were other things we could do to maintain control, but Fender dismissed my suggestions.

Eventually, I stopped asking.

I once told Raven that after the first time, she would get used to it.

That was a lie.

I never got used to it.

I was in the main cabin when I heard her screams.

I'd recognize them anywhere.

I sat at the table in front of the TV, blankly staring at the screen, listening to her yell and scream as she fought to be free. It was quiet and distant, but the sound became louder, right in my ear, like my mind filled in the sound from memory.

My hands automatically tightened into fists, not from rage at her treatment, but from rage over what she did to me.

I gave her everything.

Fucking everything.

I pushed the chair back with my legs, and I jumped to my feet. It was an out-of-body experience, the way I threw the door open and descended the stairs of the porch to the earth below, seeing red in my vision because I was still furious—even after all this time.

My body would be forever mutilated…because of what she did to me.

She was on the ground with her hands bound, Eric's heavy boot resting on her back to keep her pinned. She tried to squirm free even though there was absolutely no chance of escape. She tried anyway, like an idiot.

Eric kicked her in the side.

She groaned then stilled, the air forced out of her lungs.

"Now, if you'll be a good little bitch, I'll free your wrist and take you to your beautiful suite." Eric stared down at her, returning his boot to her back to keep her in place so she wouldn't writhe anymore. "That sounds nice, huh?"

She breathed hard, furious and in pain.

I walked across the ground and slowly approached where the guards were gathered, looking at the woman who had killed our own, who had torched this place to ash and tried to burn us alive. They all stared down at her with ferocity in their gazes. They would probably kill her…if Fender hadn't instructed them to torture her by keeping her alive instead.

I stopped near her head, looking down at her dark hair, her face turned away so she couldn't see me.

The guards looked at me, as if they expected me to save her ass.

Eric cut the rope that bound her hands. "Ready to go, Your Highness?"

She was still for a second, just breathing on the ground, like she was afraid to rise and meet her fate.

I'd never seen her look so weak.

She finally placed her palms against the earth and pushed herself up, wearing the camp outfit she'd been dressed in before she arrived. It was a black tank top and loose waterproof pants. Her arms shook as she got up and slowly rose to her feet. She looked around at the guards, obviously recognizing Alix. Then she turned to look at me, as if she expected another nameless face. But then she stilled, her eyes rigid and fixed in place, her breathing nonexistent.

I couldn't describe this rage. It made my blood boil, my chest ache with every breath, made me breathe like a knife had punctured one of my lungs through my back—because she'd stabbed me. Affection had spoiled into hatred, and I could honestly say I hated this woman, that I wanted every bad thing to happen to this woman—because she deserved it.

She started to breathe again, looking at me with eyes that slowly started to water. "Magnus—"

My body instinctively reacted to the sound of my name, the name she only knew because I'd shared it with her. She humiliated me further, right in front of the guards who had no respect for me after I let a wet pussy control my dick. Both of my hands reached out to her throat, and I grabbed her tightly, choking her with a grip so hard I thought I might snap her neck.

Her hands immediately went to my hands, and she tried to pull them off.

I slammed her down onto the ground and continued to choke her, right on top of her so I could watch the life leave her eyes, watch her suffer so my suffering would be more bearable. I pushed her head into the earth, my hands about to pop her skin. "Don't speak to me. Don't look at me. And don't you ever say my fucking name again." My hands released her throat, and I got back to my feet, breathing through my anger, feeling the adrenaline leave my heart and circulate everywhere else.

She rolled onto her stomach and heaved into the ground, gasping for air, coughing as she felt her neck with her fingertips.

The guards stared down at her.

I didn't do it for show. I didn't do it to earn back the respect I'd lost.

I did it…because I fucking wanted to.

FOUR

WAR BEGINS

I wasn't her guard anymore.

The position hadn't been offered to me intentionally, but even if it had, I wouldn't have taken it.

I was no one's guard.

Now, I was the leader of the camp, overseeing day-to-day operations, managing the cocaine that came in and out. Every single ounce was closely monitored, and I had to make sure the prisoners weren't stealing any to snort in their cabins, and I had to make sure the guards weren't doing it either.

I wasn't certain when I would leave again.

Fender knew I didn't want to be at the camp, which was why he kept me there. He wanted me there —with her.

I went to the clearing and examined the completed cocaine packets. They were preweighed in certain amounts and organized because it was much easier to give to our street distributors in their desired increments. Some clients wanted more, some wanted less.

I never bothered to look at her.

Despite the heat, we still wore the same outfits. It was easy for us to recognize one another, but for the women, it created confusion. And they never really knew when they were being watched.

When I felt a stare on my face, I lifted my chin and looked across the clearing.

She stood at the table, her next box ready to be carried when a spot opened, and she stared at me openly. Her dark-brown hair was flat now that she was back to her life at the camp. She had no hair accessories like she did at her apartment, so her long strands hung down her body in disarray. Her skin was fairer than it used to be because being indoors had lightened her complexion. Her eyes were blue and innocent, like a porcelain doll that had been sitting on a bookshelf in her office. The longer she stared, the more her breathing increased. Her eyes held emotion that was easy to read because I was so accustomed to every little reaction she made.

I dropped my gaze and ignored her.

She meant nothing to me now—absolutely nothing.

I stepped into the cabin that held the break room, where the guards stopped for snacks and water throughout the day. It was right next to the clearing, so they could come and go and use the restroom if they needed it. It was also the place where we kept some weapons, like the bows and arrows, so they were easy to retrieve if a fight broke out.

It was evening now, after dinnertime, and I stepped inside to see the guards sitting at the table, their hoods down, beer and snacks on the table, along with a pile of poker chips. My companionship had been disowned, so I never expected an invitation to join. They'd once respected me as the next in command, but now they spat on me as they passed.

Alix's eyes immediately shifted to me, the cards held in his hands. "Look, one-nut chuck."

The guards snickered at his joke.

I ignored him and entered the weapons room to make sure everything was where it was supposed to be. They'd put a bolt on Raven's door so she wouldn't be able to lock-pick her way out of there again. I accounted for everything and walked back out again.

Alix spoke to me again on my way out. "You think that cunt would still suck your dick with half a sac?"

In another scenario, I would just shank him for speaking to me that way, especially in front of the others. But I was the one who'd fucked up. I was the one who'd cost us everything. If I fought him, it would only make the others hate me more.

I took the steps to the ground and headed back to my cabin.

"Hey, asshole." Alix's voice erupted behind me.

I stopped but didn't turn around. The lights from buildings cast limited illumination in the darkness, but I could picture him clearly in my mind far better than I could ever see him anyway.

"I asked you a question."

I slowly turned around and stared him down.

Alix came down the stairs, in dark jeans and a t-shirt, grinning once he had my attention.

The rest of the guys moved to the porch—to witness whatever was about to happen.

Alix slowly came toward me, his boots kicking up little clouds of dry earth in his path. There were patches of grass, and soon the place would be covered in vegetation as the final bits of springtime cold faded.

His taunts enraged me, but again, I couldn't be that angry.

I was the one who had betrayed them for a woman who had so easily betrayed me.

He came closer and closer, stopping just feet in front of me. "Does it feel different? When you fuck a woman?" Alix already despised me for all the times I'd helped Raven in the past. But now, his hatred was beyond the stratosphere. He would never stop this shit.

I could fight him, but even if I won, I still lost. I turned around and continued to walk.

"Do you come less?"

The guys on the porch snickered loudly.

I kept going.

His footsteps sounded behind me. "I'm talking to you, asshole."

I walked at a normal pace because I wasn't running from my enemy. I was simply indifferent.

Then his footsteps became quicker, telling me he was right behind me.

I quickly pivoted and steadied his arm, which held a blade that had been pointed at my back just seconds ago. I twisted it away, kneed him in the balls, and then slugged him in the stomach.

It happened too quickly for him to respond.

I twisted his elbow then pulled the knife out of his hand before I kicked him in the chest, and he fell back—landing on his ass.

He groaned when he landed, the dirt flying up into the air.

I approached him, holding the knife in my hand.

He looked up at me—furious that I'd humiliated him in front of everyone.

I threw the knife down, making the blade slice into the soil next to him, the hilt up so he could grab it. Then I extended my hand to him.

He stared at me, nostrils flared.

I handed his ass to him to remind him who he was dealing with. Then I asked for a silent truce, wanting this problem to go away, for the camp to return to its normal operations. I'd kill him if I had to, but if I did, the other guards would hate me more. Earning respect and giving mercy was the only way out of this predicament.

He looked at my hand then spat on it.

I dropped my hand, disappointed but unsurprised.

He got to his feet and grabbed the knife at the same time. After a final hostile stare, he returned the way he came.

I walked to my cabin—as if nothing had happened.

FIVE

THE NOTE

I WAS THE MOST HATED MAN IN THE CAMP.

I took it in stride, didn't complain to Fender, and brushed it off.

My door was always locked and bolted shut, and I always looked over my shoulder because there was always a target on my back. When I went to the clearing during the day to do paperwork, I felt her look at me again.

There was no chance of us speaking because she was never near me. I was never tempted to enter her cabin for a late-night conversation. If I came anywhere close, I might kill her.

I wasn't sure how I didn't choke her to death.

But I lifted my chin and looked at her anyway.

Her face was black and blue.

One eye was swollen shut because a fist had beaten her so badly. Her cheek was cracked with a scar that would be there forever. Her neck was even bruised, like she'd been choked then punched, and then choked again. Dried blood was in both corners of her mouth because she had no mirror to know what she looked like. She almost looked unrecognizable.

I felt nothing.

I looked down and got back to work.

I was there when the girls were dismissed.

I told the guards to carry the packaged cocaine to the storage facility so it could be put on the wagons tomorrow morning. With my clipboard in hand, I walked off, headed back to my cabin to get the information logged so Fender could access it.

"Magnus."

I stilled at the sound of her voice. It took me a second to turn around and look at her, caught by surprise because I hadn't expected her. Alix wouldn't stab me in the middle of the day with everyone gathered in one place, so it was the one time I felt safe.

She was still bloody and bruised from her beating the other day, and up close, she looked even worse.

I pulled down my hood so she could see my face.

See how much I didn't care.

She flinched at the hostile look in my gaze.

"Leave. Before I kill you—"

"I'm sorry." Her eyes watered and quickly turned into tears.

Her guard realized she'd run off, so he marched toward her to retrieve her. She'd be punished for what she did.

But she didn't care about the consequences. "I don't regret what I did…but I'm sorry that I hurt you." Tears dripped down her cheeks. "I'm so sorry—"

"I'm not going to help you."

Her eyes tightened into confusion. "I know…I'm not asking. I just needed you to know—"

Eric grabbed her by the throat and yanked on her. "You run from me, bitch?" He pulled her away then grabbed her by the hair, dragging her across the ground until he released her. Then he kicked her. "Up. Come on."

I stood and watched.

She pushed herself to her feet slowly.

Then he pushed her again, making her fall back down.

He did it over and over, watching her get up, move a couple feet, and then he kicked her again.

I headed back to the cabin as if nothing happened.

I left with the wagons in the morning.

I didn't concern myself with Raven's treatment. Whether I was there or not, her punishment would be the same. She wouldn't be killed because Fender had decided death was too good for her.

It took us the entire day to reach the end of the road and get the product on the trucks. It all happened quickly, barely taking a few minutes, so no one would notice from the main road. The doors were shut, and then I got into the back with the rest of the guys.

My outfit was discarded, and I put on jeans and a t-shirt.

I sat on one of the pallets and leaned against the wall, drinking a bottle of water as we started our long journey to our processing facility in the middle of Paris. The outsides of the trucks were marked with a fictitious food delivery logo.

Baker's Dozen Baguettes.

But the real world knew who we really were.

Carcass.

Gilbert answered the door and let me inside, addressing me in French. "It's been a long time, sir. How are you?" He was the only person in this world who treated me with respect, other than the lower henchmen and Parisian distributors.

"Fine."

Gilbert led me farther inside, in his customary black tuxedo, walking slightly ahead so he could guide me where I was allowed to wait. "His Highness will be down in a moment. Is there something I can get for you while you wait? Glass of wine?"

"Something stronger, Gilbert."

He nodded then excused himself.

I looked out the back windows to the lush gardens, the long pathway that carried through the acres of land into the French countryside. The hydrangeas blossomed in colors of purple and blue, and pink roses were dispersed everywhere. The gardens had been maintained for hundreds of years, most of the plants receiving better care than hospital patients. This place was a legacy and had more value than a person's life.

I stood there, remembering the last time I was in that room.

Raven was with me.

I'd stood there and asked my brother for a favor so ridiculous that I felt stupid for asking, but I did it anyway. I even took it a step further and used our shared blood to get what I wanted, when I'd never done that in our entire lives.

I regretted that…deeply.

Gilbert brought the short glass to me. "He'll be down momentarily." He gave a slight bow before he excused himself from the room.

I drank the whole thing in a single gulp then held the empty glass at my side.

Booze, money, women…couldn't drown out this shame.

His footsteps sounded behind me. "You've nearly recouped our losses."

I kept my gaze out the window. "The women are working longer."

"You've negotiated more product?" He came to my side, looking out the window with a glass of scotch in his hand. He was shirtless and barefoot, in his sweatpants.

It was difficult to get our contacts in Colombia to deliver more cocaine because it was risky to put it on the airliner, even just an extra palette. But I convinced them to do it...after a few attempts. "Yes."

"What's the fee?"

"No fee."

He slowly turned his head to look at me.

I kept my eyes ahead.

"How did you manage that?"

I shrugged. "Persuasion."

He faced forward and drank from his glass again. "I'm impressed."

I wanted to earn back his favor, to erase the shame I had brought to our family name. I'd made him look weak in front of his men because he wouldn't kill me. I wanted to make up for that—to everyone. "With the new production schedule, we'll make fifty percent more than we were before on a regular basis. I'm trying to figure out a way to secure more, but it's complicated."

He took another drink then wiped his mouth with his hand. "How are the men treating you?"

I wasn't a snitch, so I kept my mouth shut. "Fine."

"Negotiating that increase in product will increase their salaries, so they must have granted you some forgiveness."

Not even a little bit.

"You've definitely earned some from me." He turned away from the window and looked at me.

I turned to meet his gaze, to look my brother in the eye, seeing the brown eyes and facial features that were bestowed upon us both.

"How's the cunt holding up?"

I knew exactly who he referred to. "I wouldn't know." I had no interaction with her, and when I wasn't with her, I didn't think about her.

He seemed to believe me, either because he had a source on the inside keeping tabs on me, or because my word was still good enough. "I don't understand your fascination with her. Melanie is beautiful, petite, quiet…and she's the ugly one."

I gave no reaction to his words. I didn't even respond because I didn't know what to say. All I knew was that I disagreed with that statement entirely. Beautiful women were plentiful for powerful kingpins like us, but there was something about Raven that attracted me beyond the physical desires of the flesh. Melanie never registered on my brain because she blended in with everyone else. But Raven was a bright and shiny beacon that I could see even with my eyes closed.

Fender took a drink of his scotch then looked out the window again, like he didn't expect me to explain. He just wanted to insult me, to insult my choices on another level. When footsteps sounded behind us, he turned to look.

I did the same.

Melanie stood there in an expensive blue dress with earrings dangling from her lobes, her hair pulled back elegantly. Her skin was slightly tanned, as if she'd been lying by his pool for several weeks. Her makeup was done in a sultry way, like she was ready for a photo shoot rather than an evening around the estate.

Fender didn't tell her to leave. He stared at her then raised his hand, silently beckoning her close with his fingertips.

She obeyed.

I hadn't expected to see her there because Fender hadn't mentioned her. When he went to take Raven away after the fire, he must have taken Melanie for himself. The request I'd made was now void because of everything that happened.

His arm moved around her waist, and he looked at her in a way I'd never seen him look at a woman before. His hand gripped the material of her dress in a tight fist, a possessive hold. He corralled her to him, bringing their lips close together so he could look at her like a priceless piece of art that he owned. He switched from French to English. "A glass of wine, beautiful?"

"Please," she whispered.

He gave her a soft kiss before he released her and walked away.

It was completely out of character to retrieve something himself instead of asking his butler to do it.

Melanie came closer to me, glanced over her shoulder to see where he was, and then loosened her closed fist to reveal a small piece of white paper. "Give this to my sister." She spoke in a whisper, her voice shaking like she was afraid she would be caught any second.

I stared at her coldly.

"Please…"

"No." I owed her nothing.

She grabbed my hand and shoved it into my fingers. "Please…" Her eyes watered, like this note was life and death. "I know you don't owe me anything, but please. She didn't want to hurt you like that, but she couldn't live with herself, knowing those girls were still there. Trust me…it killed her to do what she did. You meant a lot to her."

I kept my fingers clenched in a fist so I couldn't take the paper.

"Have you seen her hands?"

My eyes narrowed at the question.

"The wood from the roof was on fire, but she still pulled it off you. She's got third-degree burns because of it. She saved you. The executioner stood in her way so she couldn't get to you, but she didn't run. She fought for you."

I remembered being knocked out, but I had no recollection of anything else.

"I'm begging you…"

Even if that were entirely true, that Raven had executed some ridiculously heroic feat, it didn't matter. "The only reason I was under that burning building was because she set it on fire." I spoke in a normal voice because I didn't care if she got caught trying to slip me this note. "That means nothing to me."

She breathed harder, her wet eyes forming tears that became so heavy they dripped down her cheeks.

Fender's footsteps became audible from the other room.

She forced my fingers apart and shoved the paper inside. "If you knew what she said about you when you weren't around, you would take this note. So please. Please." She wiped her tears away quickly so Fender wouldn't notice. She pushed my closed hand into my body. "Please."

Fender's footsteps became loud once he entered the room. "I had to go down to the cellar to get your favorite." He carried the glass to her, his arm moving around her waist after he handed it to her.

She gave me one final look before she turned into him and kissed the corner of his mouth. "You didn't have to do that."

He kissed her on the neck before he released her. "You know I'd do anything for you, beautiful. Now, let the men talk business. I'll join you for dinner soon." He kissed her again before he turned back to me.

She gave me one final pleading look before she walked away, her heels slowly tapping against the tile.

Fender turned back to me, oblivious to the tension in the room because he couldn't think straight when it came to her. "Now that is a woman worth fighting for." He grabbed his scotch again and took a drink.

I almost told him what had transpired, but something changed my mind. My fingers kept the small piece of paper in my grasp before I slipped my hand into my front pocket. "I've never seen you this way with a woman." I didn't ask him for details, didn't ask for any specific kind of response.

He stared at me for a long time, his brown eyes still and focused. The silence continued as if I hadn't spoken at all. "Because this is the first time it's happened."

When I was in my car and safe behind the tinted windows, I pulled the note from my pocket and read it.

Sister,

I've gone back to him. I think in enough time I can convince him to let you go. Just hang tight, okay? I'll get you out of there...I promise.

I love you.

-Melanie

SIX

THREE VERSUS ONE

I RETURNED TO THE CAMP.

I walked through the clearing and felt Alix stare at me, his head turning to watch me as I passed. My week in Paris obviously hadn't subdued his anger. Even armed with a weapon, he couldn't overpower me. He might be bulkier, but I was quicker, and the stronger fighter didn't necessarily win.

If he tried again, I'd kill him this time.

Fender had dropped his palpable hostility given the progress I'd made, so I had his favor again. If I killed one of the guards, there would be no repercussions. The other guards would hate me more, so I'd rather not, but I wouldn't put up with Alix's bullshit much longer.

I stared at him as I passed, so he would know I was aware of his stare, that he could try again if he wanted.

But I'd knock him on his ass again.

I checked the packaged coke on the table and ignored the other stare that landed on my back. Her blue eyes pierced into me, silently asking me to turn around and meet her gaze. She pleaded, her energy traveling through the air and absorbing into my skin then bloodstream. But I ignored it.

The note was in my pocket.

But I wouldn't give it to her.

It was late in the evening.

I sat at my desk against the wall, my TV on. My laptop was open, and I worked on the spreadsheets that I had to catch up on after my week-long absence because Fender didn't trust anyone to do the numbers right other than me. They could falsify numbers, take a cut for themselves, and we'd look like idiots.

My thoughts started to trail away as my gaze turned unfocused on the screen.

It was almost midnight, and I was tired.

But my hand reached into my pocket and pulled out the note that had been opened and crumpled many times. I studied the feminine handwriting, listened to the sound of Melanie's voice in my head, the way she quietly pleaded. Her tears shone brilliantly under the light of the chandelier. She'd returned herself to a monster to save her sister. Back and forth, they made sacrifices for each other.

I crumpled the note again and threw it in the wastebasket next to my desk.

I would tell Fender the truth the next time I saw him.

He'd keep Melanie anyway, but at least he would know that her affection was false. She was manipulating him…the way Raven had manipulated me.

I closed my laptop, turned off the TV, and then got into bed.

It was a clear night, the moon so bright through the window that I had to turn over and look the other way.

My eyes went to the wastebasket, highlighted by the moonlight. The paper was the only thing inside, sitting at the bottom, crumpled and forgotten.

When I closed my eyes, I still saw the image in my head.

I still saw it sitting there.

I opened my eyes and looked again, thinking about the way Melanie had pleaded with me, the way she cared for her sister…the woman who sacrificed everything to keep her safe. Raven wasn't even supposed to be here, but she'd come voluntarily because she'd follow Melanie anywhere.

I sighed and sat up, sitting at the edge of the bed in just my boxers, staring at the wastebasket in fury.

I didn't owe that bitch anything.

I'd already rescued Melanie from Fender once.

I'd already gotten Raven out of this camp.

I did my part and had nothing to feel guilty about.

But after a few seconds, I rose to my feet, got dressed, and put the note back in my pocket.

Then I left my cabin.

It was quiet out because we didn't post guards on patrol. The cabins housing the women were bolted shut now, so no one would be able to break their way out. The high fence was around the perimeter, so there was no escape, even if they could get out of their cabins. So, I was alone.

No one would know what I'd done.

I approached her cabin, unlocked it, and then opened the door. My hand flicked on the light, and I turned to look at the bed, assuming she would be asleep. But she wasn't there. I stilled at the sight before me.

A noose was around her neck, tied to the beam across the ceiling. Her wrists were bound behind her back, and she balanced on a flimsy box on the ground, which was uneven and shaky. One wrong movement, and she'd lose her balance…and hang herself.

She couldn't speak because the rope was too tight. All she did was stare at me, her eyes pleading for help. She lost her balance for just a second, as if she recognized me even though my hood was up.

I knew the guards were giving her a rough time, but I'd never imagined this.

I shouldn't care.

She was here because she *chose* to come back.

But I couldn't just turn around and leave her there.

I pulled out my knife, cut the rope around her wrists, and then removed the noose around her neck.

She quickly hopped off the box and moved to the other wall, breathing hard as she ran her fingers through her hair, processing the trauma in silence.

I pushed my hood down and returned my knife to my pocket.

She slid down to the floor, her arms wrapping around her knees. She rested the back of her head against the wall and looked at me, her face still bruised from the beatings she received on a daily basis. There was no way she didn't regret her decision now. She must have realized how pointless it all was. Most of the girls had gotten away, but new ones had quickly replaced them. "They'll know you helped me."

"I don't care." They already hated me anyway.

When her breathing returned to normal, she gave me that same emotional look she wore in the clearing, like she would do anything to get a minute of my time. "I'm so sorry—"

"You will never earn my forgiveness—stop asking for it." It was difficult to be around her because just looking at her made me angry. Her blue eyes shone the same way they did when we were in bed together, that emotional connection still there. I regretted sleeping with her. I regretted giving so much of myself to her…sacrificing so much. Her brown hair, full lips, and slender neckline had no effect on me anymore. "The only reason I'm here is to give you this." I pulled the note from my pocket and threw it at her because I didn't want to be anywhere near her. If I were in arm's reach, I might choke her harder than that noose would.

She picked it up off the floor and slowly unfolded it. Then her eyes shifted left and right as she read the short message. "Oh my god…Melanie." Her eyes immediately watered before she clutched the note into her tight fist. "No…" A small breakdown took place, a loud sniff echoing in the small cabin, tears shaking on her eyelashes before they fell down her cheeks. "You saw her?" She turned back to me. "How did she look?"

She was dressed in the finest things money could buy. Designer clothing, priceless jewels, under the protection of the biggest kingpin in all of France. And he was a handsome guy, always getting the attention of beautiful women without having to pay for it. "A lot better than you do." I moved to the door to leave.

"Magnus, wait." She got to her feet. "Please—"

I closed the door and bolted it shut.

Her voice sounded through the door. "It was real…"

I stilled at her words, flashbacks coming into my mind, images from the two passionate nights we'd shared. I could still hear the raindrops hit her bedroom window. I could still taste the sweat in the valley between her tits. I could still feel her nails in my back, the pressure nearly breaking my skin. But I also remembered the nights when we just stared at each other, the conversations that unfolded even in the direst circumstances. Beautiful women came and went in my life, but moments like those…never did.

I did my job and kept to myself.

The women worked longer hours because of the increased amount of daylight. The days were getting warmer, the vegetation growing bigger, and the wilderness came to life with green leaves, flowers, and creatures from the forest. Sometimes coyotes would howl to the moon in the middle of the night.

I didn't have a single ally in that camp because they'd all turned against me.

But still…I didn't snitch.

I had too much pride to make a single complaint.

But I could never drop my guard because the knife was constantly at my throat. My eyes were always in the back of my head. The guard must have told the others that Raven had been freed from her noose because the hostility was even worse than before.

I ignored it.

I went to the communal cabin to do my checks, and I instantly knew something was off. The guys weren't seated at the table as usual. There was no one there, all the lights off. But it was too early for them to be in their cabins.

I could feel it.

Then the footsteps sounded behind me.

I quickly ducked then threw my body hard into Alix's frame, knowing exactly where he stood based on the slight creak of the floorboards. He fell back and rolled down the stairs, groaning as his back thudded against the hardness.

The other guards emerged from the room behind me because it was an ambush.

"Get that piece of shit!" Alix pushed to his feet.

I ran down the steps then kicked him in the face before I jumped over him.

Alix spat out blood then got to his feet, facing me with a whole new level of ferocity. He pulled a knife from his pocket and spun it in his palm. "Get him." He spun the knife again. "And I'll cut off the other half of your sac."

Eric, Karl, and Nathan came toward me, their hoods down, all carrying blades like they were going to slice me into little pieces.

I pulled out my own knife and held my ground. I didn't turn and run because that would result in a knife in the back. If I was going to die, I'd do it on my own two feet. But I wasn't going to die. If it were them or me…it would be them.

"You let your little girlfriend go." Alix stepped toward me, moving over the grass, stalking toward me like a lion in the savanna.

"She's not supposed to be killed."

"And she wouldn't die," he said. "If she just stayed on the box." He chuckled.

The rest of the guys chuckled too.

"If I die, Fender will hang all of you."

"Who said anything about dying?" Alix took another step forward. "We just think you aren't man enough to have any balls at all, not even one." He rushed me, his heavy mass sprinting.

I ducked under the knife and kneed him in the balls like last time. Then I tripped him over my knee, making him fly through the air and land on his head, knocked out at the collision. Eric came at me next, and I redirected his knife into his thigh, making him cry out loud, the blood dripping down his leg to his boot. He collapsed and yanked the knife out by the hilt.

Karl hesitated and backed up. He lowered his knife.

Nathan did the same.

I walked toward them, wanting to carve their mouths off their faces because I was furious.

They backed away farther, tripping over their own feet in their hurry to scurry away.

Eric continued to howl loudly, his teeth clenched tightly together as he gripped his flesh wound. Blood dripped onto the dirt.

I walked back to them, taking my time as I stood over them.

Eric looked up at me, nostrils flared, breathing through the pain.

"You should get to the infirmary if you don't want to bleed out." I extended my hand to help him up.

He hesitated before he took it.

I pulled him to his feet.

Then I punched him so hard in the stomach he lost his entire breath. "Don't." I hit him again. "Fuck." Again. "With." Again. "Me."

He fell to his knees, breathing through the pain I'd just caused.

Alix had woken up with a jolt, and he quickly climbed to his feet.

I kicked him in the back until he fell again.

When he got up, I did it again. "I can do this all night, Alix."

This time, he stayed down, blood still dripping out of his mouth from the kick. He turned over onto his back and looked up at me, his chest rising and falling quickly, soft groans accompanying his breaths. But he looked up at me like he still wanted to kill me.

"No more mercy, Alix. Try this shit again…I'll kill you."

SEVEN
ULTIMATE SACRIFICE

ERIC WAS IN THE INFIRMARY FOR A FEW DAYS. HE couldn't walk because the blade had pierced his muscle so badly that he couldn't hold his weight anymore. Nathan and Karl steered clear of me like they thought I might decide to finish the job. Alix stopped staring at me every chance he got.

When I saw them in the evenings, they pretended I didn't exist.

I hoped that was the end of it.

But I wasn't stupid enough to assume anything.

A week passed, and my time at the camp was repetitive and uneventful. Alix did the execution every Friday, and I was never around to witness it. I tried to work out a bigger distribution with our Colombian partners, but the cargo hold simply wouldn't allow it. I tried to think of another shipment route, perhaps by a cargo ship. They could dock in Spain, and our guys could meet us somewhere near the French Alps. It was risky, but Fender wanted to grow this business more, to be richer than we already were.

I didn't glance at Raven again.

She always tried to look at me at the clearing, but I ignored her.

The only reason I'd cut her down in her cabin was because I was already there, but I wouldn't go out of my way to check on her or intercept danger in any way whatsoever. I shouldn't have even delivered that note, but it would have haunted me if I hadn't.

I went to the clearing at midday when the girls were eating. They sat together at the tables, eating in complete silence so they wouldn't be punched in the face, or worse, hung. I went to the product table and made my notes on the spreadsheets. I meticulously checked everything that was there so people wouldn't try to steal. The best way to keep people honest was to make it impossible not to be honest.

One of the guards yelled unexpectedly. "What the fuck is she doing? Get her!"

I turned, assuming Raven was the culprit. She was probably doing some stupid stunt to escape.

But she sprinted right at me, panicked. "Move!"

What the fuck? Stunned, I just stood there.

It all happened so fast.

She crashed into me, making me fall onto the table.

I rolled and hit my head, confused.

A collective gasp sounded from the women in their seats.

I turned to look, seeing Raven standing there, a knife buried deep in her stomach.

She swayed slightly, her legs growing weak, and then she fell to the ground.

Alix stood there, staring down at her like he was surprised by what had happened too. His hand was bloody.

I immediately righted myself and looked down, still in shock.

Alix spat on her. "That worked out better, if you ask me."

I finally understood what had happened.

Alix had come up behind me to stab me, knowing this was the only time of the day when my guard was down, and Raven had seen what he was about to do…and tried to help me. "Fuck." I hopped off the table and leaned down over her. Her shirt was already wet with the blood seeping from the wound. A puddle was growing on the dirt beneath her.

"Leave her." Alix stood over me.

I scooped her into my arms and carried her away.

Alix walked after me. "Let that bitch die!"

Revenge was the last thing on my mind right now. "Stay with me."

She turned limp in my arms.

"I said, stay with me!" I ran with her to the cabin that housed the medical supplies. Up the stairs and through the door, I carried her to the table in the center of the room. I laid her flat then shouted out the door. "Daniel!" I came back to the table, unsure if he would help me since he hated me along with everyone else.

I worked like no one was coming.

I lifted up her shirt and saw the bloody gash. "Jesus."

Her eyes were still open, and she breathed hard, the color leaving her face right away. She shifted her gaze to me, like she knew she was going to die.

"You aren't going anywhere, Raven. What's your blood type?"

"I…I don't know."

I pulled out the universal bag, stuck a needle in her vein, and started to give her blood.

Then Daniel appeared in the doorway. "What the fuck happened?"

I couldn't believe he'd actually come. "She's been stabbed. She's bleeding out." I covered the gash with gauze and tried to keep her alive.

Daniel got to work, putting on gloves, pulling equipment over so he could find where her internal bleeding was.

Raven continued to breathe hard.

Fuck, she wasn't going to make it.

I set up her vitals while Daniel worked, staying quiet so he could concentrate.

I knew the cut was too deep. There was no hope. But I came to her side and looked down into her face, letting her see my confident expression so she'd stay calm. "It'll be alright." I lied to her face.

Daniel pulled out his suture kit. "Get on gloves."

I did as he asked.

"Here." He grabbed my hands and positioned them, keeping the wound open.

He leaned over and got to work.

"What are you doing?"

"She's bleeding through her intestine. I've got to patch this up now, or she's gonna die."

I held part of her stomach to the side so he could work, my eyes moving to her face.

Her face became paler, and her eyes closed.

"No."

She opened them again.

"Your eyes stay on me, alright?"

She gave a slight nod.

Daniel worked quickly.

I stared at her, hearing the beep of the monitor increase because her heart rate spiked from loss of blood.

"Okay." Daniel straightened. "Release her."

I pulled my hands away.

He moved to a different position and sutured the outside of her wound.

Her heart rate slowly started to normalize.

I released a deep sigh of relief.

Daniel finished then cleaned up the blood on her stomach.

"Thank you." I stared at him, grateful that he hadn't turned on me like the others would have.

He nodded. "It's my job."

"You can ask me for anything at any time, and I'll oblige."

"I know." He pulled off his gloves and tossed them in the garbage. "I'll give her some antibiotics and some pain meds. We'll keep the machines going to monitor her vitals. She should live." He washed his hands then got another IV going. Then he into the cabinet and pulled out a vial of antibiotics so he could inject it into her IV.

I continued to stand over her, unsure what to do now that everything had been done. That was when I noticed the insides of her palms. They were covered with dark third-degree burns. They were on her wrists too. I could see where the heat had burned her skin to the bone, the destruction that would leave permanent scars, the cost of saving my life from that burning building.

Daniel moved to the door. "I'll check on her every few hours." He walked out.

She was still conscious, but her eyes were getting heavy. Color had returned to her face, and her low blood pressure started to rise.

I stared down at her. "What the fuck were you thinking?"

Her eyelids lifted a little higher. "I wasn't…"

"Yeah, that's pretty obvious." I was furious. I could have taken that knife much better than she could. I was stronger, bigger, not some slender, vulnerable woman who was already dealing with other injuries.

Her eyes turned heavy again, like she couldn't stay awake.

I couldn't get back to work and leave her here alone. Alix might finish the job.

She took another deep breath before her eyes closed. "Please don't go...don't leave me here." Her hand slowly moved to mine on the edge of the bed.

I let her touch me. "I won't."

She fell asleep instantly...because she trusted me without question.

Daniel retrieved my things from my cabin so I wouldn't have to leave her.

Even if I were gone for just two minutes, that would be enough time for Alix to come in here and give her another knife to the stomach.

I worked on my laptop through the day and into the night. There was food in the cabinets, so I made a meal out of that. When I had nothing else to do, I sat in the chair and just stared at her.

It had all happened so fast that I wasn't entirely sure what had happened at all.

Alix must have meant to stab me in the back, probably right in the heart so I'd die then and there.

She saw him unsheathe his blade and did the only thing she could do to stop it.

She pushed me out of the way. She probably didn't intend to take the knife herself, but that was how it happened.

She saved my life.

I'd be dead right now if it weren't for her.

But I didn't know how to feel about that.

I'd already done so much for her, had suffered so much for her, that this still didn't make up for her betrayal.

She was out for a long time, at least nine hours. She opened her eyes and took a deep breath, immediately panicked because she couldn't see me in her line of sight. It was dark in the room, and everything probably came rushing back to her.

"I'm here."

The second she heard my voice, her body relaxed. A deep sigh escaped her lungs.

I got to my feet and stood over her so she could see me.

Her eyes narrowed on my face, studied my expression, and then she reached out her hand for mine.

I pulled away.

Disappointment filled her eyes.

"I'm glad you're alright." My deep voice drowned out the sound of the monitors. "But it doesn't change anything." I would be there until she was back on her feet. I'd look out for her until she was back to full health. But after that…she was on her own.

When she breathed, it was with a hint of pain. "Are you okay?"

"I'm not the one who got stabbed."

"But still…"

I knew she was genuinely asking. "I'm fine."

"Why did he try to kill you?"

The question made me angry because she had absolutely no idea the shit I had to deal with. "You."

The pained look on her face was so raw that I felt it too.

"Everyone wants me dead—because of you."

"Magnus—"

"I don't want to hear your apology ever again. It's meaningless. You made your decision—and you have to live with it." I wanted to storm out, but I didn't because there was no way to know if she would be safe. My anger didn't combat my obligation. I would stay until she was ready to walk away. "I will be here until you're well again. But that's only because you saved my life—and now I owe you." I moved back to the chair and sat down so she couldn't look at me. I stared at one of the screens, not interested in looking at her face again.

She was quiet for a long time, the monitors beeping and filling the tense air with their obnoxious sounds. Her blood pressure cuff tightened until it beeped and released the air. The new reading appeared on the screen.

She broke the silence with a weak voice. "I did it because I care about you...because I'd die for you."

I closed my eyes and clenched my jaw, refusing to feel anything again. I refused to get caught up in that bullshit again. I refused to feel empathy, compassion, kindness. I only felt bitterness and spite.

"I understand why you feel betrayed, but you know I did the right thing."

"The *right* thing?" I got back to my feet and looked down at her, getting angry. "You're back to where you started. Literally."

She didn't match my emotion because she was too weak. Her eyes watched mine for a while. "But I freed those girls—"

"And they were replaced by a new batch. Nice work."

She shifted her gaze away, like that knowledge truly pained her.

"This place will never go away. Girls will die and be replaced by new ones. It'll be here after you're gone, after I'm gone. You can burn the place to the ground, but it will just be replaced. This is bigger than you, bigger than me, and it wasn't worth your life to challenge it. Your sister belongs to the man I saved her from, and you're back in the same captivity. Fucking stupid."

"If I had to do it all over again, I would."

I clenched my jaw in irritation.

She shifted her gaze back to me. "You know I did the right thing, Magnus. You know you respect me for trying. You know that the reason *this* is here…is because I have a heart, and so do you."

I held her gaze and felt my heart sink to my stomach.

"I had to do the right thing, even if that meant betraying you. And I know this is difficult to believe…but I'm still loyal to you. I will do anything for you, not because you saved me, but because… you deserve to have someone look out for you too. Liberating this camp took precedence over you because it's bigger than either of us. But I will take a knife to the stomach over and over, as many times as necessary, to keep you alive."

I looked away, refusing to acknowledge the sincerity of her gaze.

She moved her hand to mine.

I pulled it free. "You have no idea what your betrayal has cost me." I looked at the monitor and felt my body shake in anger. "You have no idea the humiliation I've suffered because of you. The one fucking time I allow myself to feel something, it bites me in the fucking ass. I will never make that mistake again."

"Why don't you just leave?"

"I can't."

"Why—"

"Because I can't." I stepped back from the table. "Don't speak to me again. When you've recovered, I will be indifferent to you once again. The guards can do whatever they want—and I will let it happen."

EIGHT

SUCKED BACK IN

AFTER A FEW DAYS OF REST, DANIEL DISCHARGED her from the infirmary.

She was young and healthy and bounced back from the injury fairly quickly. The wound closed, there was no infection, and she was able to walk out and return to her cabin. The second Daniel said she was ready to return to her normal duties, I walked out without looking back.

I hadn't gotten my tasks done like I was supposed to, so I was behind. I had to work my ass off to catch up and hope Fender didn't notice.

After I asked Raven not to speak to me, she didn't.

So, we never spoke again.

I didn't owe her a goddamn thing. I'd saved her life so many fucking times—so she was still in my debt.

I'd warned Alix that I would kill him if he made another attempt.

Now I had to make good on my word.

I went to the communal cabin that night with my blade in my pocket. If he was sitting there and playing poker with the guys, I'd hold him down and slit his throat. The mess would remain behind until someone else cleaned up because I certainly wouldn't.

When I walked in, that exact scene was in front of me.

Alix sat on the other side, holding the cards in his hand.

I shut the door behind me and pulled out my knife.

Alix immediately got to his feet. "Truce."

"Truce?" I actually laughed because it was fucking ridiculous. "I asked for a truce twice—and you ignored it. I may only have one ball left, but you're the pussy who couldn't kill me three fucking times. You're gonna sit in that chair, and I'm going to slit your fucking throat. Anyone who resists me will get the same fate."

None of the guys moved. Word had spread that I was outnumbered four to one, and I still prevailed.

Alix held up his hand. "Magnus, come on—"

"Come on?" I snapped.

"We'll forget what you did if you forget this. That's fucking fair."

I wanted life in the camp to return to normal, when all the guards didn't despise me. If I killed Alix, they would still hate me. But if I let him live…I wouldn't have to sleep with one eye open. I sheathed my blade and returned it to my pocket.

Alix immediately looked relieved. "You want in?" He sat down and grabbed his cards again.

The guys looked at him then looked at me.

It was hard for me to pretend nothing happened, that they hadn't turned against me so ruthlessly for the past month. But the quickest way to leave it behind was to move forward. I opened the fridge, grabbed a beer, and took a seat. "Deal me in."

My routine became normal once again.

The guards stopped ostracizing me. They spoke to me like nothing had happened at all, like the camp hadn't burned to the ground because of my stupidity. Whenever I worked, they would step in and help me like before.

It made my life a lot easier.

Raven went back to work on the line, but I never directly looked at her to see if she was struggling.

I returned to my indifference—as I promised.

In a couple weeks, I would return to Paris, which I'd been looking forward to. The repetitiveness of the camp could be mentally exhausting at times. The food was always the same, there were no eligible women around, and you couldn't get a good glass of wine. Now that I had earned the forgiveness of the camp, I knew Fender's full pardon would follow soon afterward.

I joined the guys for a round of poker that night. Chips were in the center, cards on the table, and the empty bottles of beer continued to cover the surface. Some of the guys smoked cigars, but I'd never been a fan of the taste it left in my mouth.

The guys threw their final bets into the pile.

Then it was just Eric and me.

Despite the permanent scar on his thigh, he seemed fine with me. He looked at his cards before he laid them down. Two pairs.

I dropped mine. A royal flush.

Eric groaned. "Motherfucker…"

I scooped the chips into my arms and pulled them to my side of the table.

"You've got the best poker face I've ever seen." Nathan drank from his beer.

I shrugged then added my cards to the discard pile.

"Where did you learn that?" Eric asked.

"Experience." It was a lie. I had a great poker face because I was perpetually indifferent to everything. It didn't really matter if I won the hand or not. I was already rich. More money wouldn't make me richer—that was how rich I was.

Screams sounded from outside.

The guys all stilled before glancing at the door.

Because it was coming this way.

It was a woman—screaming at the top of her lungs.

The door burst open, and Alix dragged her inside by the hair. "Scream all you want, bitch. Make the wolves howl."

She only had her black top on. She was completely bare on the bottom, a dark bush of hair between her legs. She fought against him as hard as she could, her dark hair flying about, her blue eyes panicked with streaming tears.

I watched her being dragged across the room.

She looked at us, her eyes settling on me for a moment, sheer terror in her gaze.

Time slowed down, just for a moment.

Alix dragged her away. "Come on, you'll like it. You may not like the guys after me, but…" Their bodies thumped against the walls and the floor as they made it to one of the unoccupied bedrooms. Her screams continued and became muffled when the door closed.

The guys turned to me, like I might do something.

I grabbed the deck of cards and shuffled. "Another round?"

They all looked slightly surprised, but that wore off as they drank from their beers and ate their pretzels.

I could still hear her screams.

My hands shuffled the cards as her face was imprinted in my mind.

Tears dripping down her cheeks.

I'd never seen her cry out of fear…only sorrow.

No. I wouldn't help her.

I'd never seen her look that terrified.

No. She's not my problem.

Her screams were still loud as she continued to fight a hopeless battle.

No.

She'd accepted her Red Snow with her head held high. She accepted a knife to her stomach without shedding a tear. She took my whip lashes with barely a sound. But this…was the thing she hated most.

No.

I started to deal the cards.

Her screams continued.

I stopped halfway, my eyes on the table, thinking of the way she'd looked when she brought me coffee in the morning, a new woman with her hair and makeup done. There had been affection in her eyes, like she wanted to take care of me. "God fucking dammit…" I slammed the cards down and got to my feet.

The guys all stilled as they watched me leave the front room and move down the hallway.

Her screams grew louder and louder the closer I came. I started to move quicker, afraid I'd waited too long. "Get the fuck off me!" I pushed the door open and found her on her knees at the edge of the bed, her hands tied behind her back while her head was forced into the mattress. Alix had his face between her legs, smelling her. Her face was turned to the doorway, and she went silent when she saw me. The look of relief on her face was indescribable. She closed her eyes, and the tears fell to the sheets as her lips quivered. She choked back a sob.

"Stop."

Alix straightened and looked at me, his pants gone. "What?"

"Get off her." Seeing it with my own eyes made me sick to my stomach. It was like being stabbed in the gut, taking the knife that had originally been meant for me. When Alix didn't move, I raised my voice. "*Now.*"

He struggled to obey, angry at my orders but also wanting to keep the civility between us. "What the fuck, Magnus? What the hell happened to—"

"Don't make me ask again."

She continued to whimper on the bed, his fingers deep in her hair.

He finally moved away from her.

She sobbed harder once she was released, her tears shining in the light from the hallway.

He got to his feet, his hard dick hanging there. "I said we'll forget your crimes—not hers."

I could look the other way when her face was black and blue. I could look the other way when she had a wound in her stomach as she worked. I could look the other way when a noose was secured to her neck in her cabin. But I couldn't look away for this. "Walk away, Alix."

He was furious, like a bull that just saw red. But he didn't fight me. He grabbed his bottoms and pushed past me as he left the room.

I knew I'd just relit a fire I spent weeks putting out.

I pulled out my knife and freed her wrists.

She moved off the bed and onto the floor, her wrists red and scarred because she'd tried so hard to get free. Tears still fell down her cheeks because she wouldn't stop sobbing. She heaved like she couldn't get enough air into her lungs.

I watched her…getting sucked right back in.

Her arms covered her chest even though she was clothed from the waist up, and she shivered as if she were cold when she was just traumatized. Her tears glistened in the light, and she rocked herself gently, having a complete breakdown.

It was so fucking painful. My jaw clenched to keep a stoic expression, to keep all sympathy outside my body. But it was a fight I couldn't continue anymore. I hadn't thought this woman was capable of breaking like the others...and it was disturbing to see it happen. "I won't let them do that to you." My voice escaped as a whisper in an attempt to calm her.

Her eyes finally shifted to me, red and puffy. "I knew you would save me..." She crawled across the space between us and moved into my chest, her arms circling my neck and her face pressing into my shirt. Her eyes soaked the material instantly, and her fingers yanked on the shirt as she tried to pull me closer, like I was the only thing in the world that could put her back together.

My arms wrapped around her, and I cradled her close to me, sitting on the hardwood floor next to the bed, listening to her cry against me. My hand moved up her back, feeling the bumps through her shirt from the scars I'd given her. "I'll always save you."

NINE

ONE PROBLEM, ALL PROBLEMS

AFTER SHE WRAPPED HER BOTTOM HALF IN A TOWEL, I took her out of the communal cabin, walking past the men whose favor I had just earned a week ago, and back to her cabin across the camp.

Sniffles still sounded behind me because even though she'd calmed down, she still wasn't herself, with her steely gaze, an unbreakable posture, a woman who believed in triumph in the face of defeat.

I knew the tormenting would never stop.

If Alix didn't try again, it would just be someone else.

She was the woman who'd cost us the lives of men we used to know, and the torture had escalated from physical pain to something much more sinister. It would just keep happening until they completely crushed her spirit.

I unlocked the door, and we stepped inside.

She immediately took a seat on the edge of the bed, still wrapped in the towel from the bathroom. Her arms crossed over her body like she was still cold, and her gaze was downcast, her eyes open and still, as if she was reliving it all over again.

"Grab your things."

She slowly lifted her chin to look at me. "What?"

"I said, get your things." I kept my voice controlled and soft since she was sensitive right now. What I really wanted to do was snap my fingers and get her to move quickly, so no one would see what was about to happen.

"Why?" She got to her feet and looked at me, her face so puffy from her tears, she looked like she'd just taken a beating.

"Because you're going to stay with me. Now, come on."

She inhaled a deep breath when she heard what I said, like she couldn't believe it.

"If I leave you here…" I didn't need to finish the sentence to make my point. "Do as I ask."

She nodded then dropped the towel, not caring that I could see her naked bottom half. She pulled on her underwear and her pants then gathered what few possessions she had. It was just a couple items that she stuffed into her pockets. Then she turned back to me, emotional all over again, but for a different reason.

"I can't let you go, but I can keep you safe while you're here." I walked out.

She followed behind me a second later.

I locked the door even though there was no point. Just a habit.

We crossed the camp until we reached my cabin. I unlocked the door and let her go first.

She stepped inside and looked around, seeing the small desk against the wall with a laptop, the TV on the stand against the wall, the twin bed in the corner under the window, and the bathroom.

I didn't want to share my space with her like this, but I had no other choice.

She moved to the chair in front of the desk and took a seat. She was in a dreamlike state, like she was still in shock. She glanced at her hands before she raised her chin and looked at me again.

I stared back.

The moonlight came through the window and made her eyes shine. "Now what?"

It was late, and I had a long day tomorrow. "We've got to sleep." I pulled my shirt over my head and tossed it in the hamper in the corner. My jeans came next because I couldn't sleep unless I was in my boxers. If it made her uncomfortable, that was too bad. "You can stay up and watch TV if you want. Just keep it on low." I pulled back the sheets and lay on the small bed, which was already too small for just me. I missed my king-size in Paris, having all the space I could need. I lay on my back and stared at the ceiling.

She stayed in the chair, her eyes looking out the uncovered window.

I was tired, but I couldn't sleep, not when she was sitting in that chair, looking out the window. Someone had just tried to rape her fifteen minutes ago. It would be impossible to wind down and drift off so quickly. "Do you want to talk about it?" I could see her face turn slightly in my peripheral to look at me.

She stared for a while. "No."

"Touch my laptop or my phone, I'll throw you back to the wolves. I may have helped you, but I won't liberate you. I built this place to make it impossible to escape, so I suggest you don't bother."

She was quiet.

"Do you understand?"

Her voice came out quiet, afraid. "Yes…"

I turned my head to look directly at her.

She shifted her gaze away, like it was too hard to look at me. "Should I sleep on the floor?" She stared at the hardwood at the foot of the bed. There was a rug, but it would still be rock hard against her sore body.

"No." I pushed the sheets back.

She turned back to me. "You want me to join you?"

"If you sleep on the floor, you'll hurt your back. And I'm not sleeping on the goddamn floor."

She gave a slight nod before she got up and started to undress. She turned around and pulled off her shirt, revealing her bra underneath…and the scars.

I quickly looked at the ceiling again.

She dropped her pants next and stood in just her underwear. "I don't have anything to wear…"

"Take a shirt out of my top drawer."

She moved to the dresser and grabbed the one on top. It was a short-sleeved gray cotton tee. She pulled it on, and it fell down her body to her thighs, covering the scars that made me sweat with disgust.

She approached the bed and looked at me, as if she expected me to move over.

"I sleep close to the door."

She got on the bed then crawled over me, settling into the narrow spot right against the wall.

The bed was not made for two people.

There was no way for us to lie together without touching each other. I couldn't lie flat without being on top of her slightly, so I turned on my side and faced my desk, the sheets around my waist, my eyes open and looking at the light and shadows in the room.

She was still after she found her position. Based on her breathing, she was wide awake and alert.

So was I.

She sat up and closed the curtains over the window, bringing the bedroom into darkness. "What will happen to you tomorrow?"

All the damage I'd finally fixed was gone. I had to start over…because I was weak. "That's my problem, not yours."

"Your problems are my problems…just as my problems are your problems."

I walked her to the clearing—like I was her guard again.

I *was* her guard again.

She didn't speak to me or look directly at me. She was submissive, which was completely unlike her. She was always strong and fierce, but all those qualities had faded. She shone in bright colors, but now, she was muted gray.

I didn't like it. "Nothing will happen to you." I looked at the side of her face, seeing her eyes down. "I promise." I'd never made a promise to anyone in my whole life, but I made one to her…and she didn't even ask me to.

She slowly turned to look at me. "I know."

When we reached the clearing, she walked away and headed to work, keeping her head down, like if she were small enough, quiet enough, no one would notice her.

Alix walked up to me right away.

My eyes glanced down to his hands, expecting to see a blade.

He carried nothing.

He stopped in front of me, getting so close to my face that his breath fell on my cheeks.

I didn't back away because I wasn't intimidated. Even if he had a knife and I had nothing, I'd still kick his ass.

He kept his voice low so everyone else couldn't hear, but the threat was unmistakable. "The boss is going to hear about this. What will you do, then?"

"She's a prisoner all the same. But now, she's my prisoner."

When he was this close to me, it was easy to see his features inside his hood. He gave me an incredulous look. "It doesn't look like you treat her as a prisoner."

"What I do with her is none of your business." I was concerned what would happen when Fender came to the camp for a visit. He would see what I'd done—and he'd definitely have an opinion about it. "Guards keep prisoners for themselves. What I'm doing is no different."

"It's different if you let her go."

"I'll never let her go." She may have softened my heart once again, but I would never allow her freedom. My life would be forfeit if I did. When my brother made that threat, I knew it wasn't idle.

Because he honored every threat he made. It didn't matter if I was his brother. That wouldn't be a strong enough reason to keep me alive.

Alix studied me, like he didn't believe me.

"We continue our truce—and you stay away from her."

He gave me a glare before he stepped away. "Whatever you say, Romeo. You found a woman who's happy licking one ball instead of two…" He returned to his post.

My eyes shifted back to Raven.

She was staring at me, like she was afraid for me.

I'd survived this long. I'd be fine.

I found any excuse to stay out of the cabin.

When the workday was over, I locked her inside then found something else to do. I had dinner alone in the communal cabin, did my evening checks at the camp to make sure everything was in order, and then I went back to the communal cabin later in the evening. There was a living room with a TV, so I sat there and watched it, a scotch in my hand to wash away the aches from the long day.

Footsteps sounded on the other side of the wall as the guards filed in. Chairs scraped against the hardwood as they got in their seats around the table to play a few rounds of poker.

I didn't make a sound. The TV was on, so they obviously heard it, but they probably assumed it was someone else on the couch.

Beers were opened, a bag of chips popped as it was ripped open, and then the poker chips clattered on the table.

"What are you going to do about Magnus?" Eric's voice was easy to recognize. It was raspier than the others, like he always had a sore throat.

Alix took a long time to answer. "Nothing."

"That's a first," Nathan said with a laugh.

"The boss will take care of him." Alix wasn't his usual jovial self. He was quiet, as if the mention of my name made him simmer with anger.

"You think?" Eric asked. "Magnus burned this camp down to nothing, and the boss let him live."

"But he mutilated him," Nathan said. "I think I'd rather take death than the knife."

"He won't let him off easy again," Alix said. "She's supposed to live here forever, to be tortured every day, to work until her body gives out. She's not supposed to receive special treatment."

"She's still working every day," Eric said. "So, I'm not sure if she's getting much special treatment."

"I can't fuck her, can I?" Alix snapped. "That's special treatment."

"Must be jealousy," Nathan said. "Because Magnus never cared about the beatings we gave her."

No, not jealousy. It was just fucking disgusting.

"Or maybe it's because she took that knife for him," Eric said. "She may have saved his life. Of course, he's going to feel indebted to her."

That wasn't it either.

Eric spoke again. "If he tells the boss you tried to kill him, he's going to kill you."

It was quiet.

For a long time.

The game continued, poker chips clattering as they were thrown in the center pile. A hand dug in a chip bag. Obnoxious munching sounded from teeth.

Alix spoke. "Magnus is a lot of things, but he's not a snitch."

Did I catch a tone of respect in there?

He spoke again. "But she killed our guys. She let our prisoners go. She humiliated us. She doesn't deserve to sleep soundly in that cabin. The boss knows that. He won't let it slide."

When I entered my cabin, she was on the floor against the bed, watching TV. She was still in her work clothes because she didn't have anything else. Her knees were up and against her chest. Her eyes immediately darted to me once I stepped inside.

I locked the door behind me then carried the tray of food to her.

She eyed it before she took it.

She didn't get her dinner until late in the evening because I stayed out of the cabin until bedtime. I didn't want her to be raped, but I didn't want to spend any extended time with her. I moved to the desk and opened my laptop. Since she was blocked by the bed, I used my fingerprint identifier to see if she'd touched my laptop while I was away. I did it every single day—and she hadn't touched it.

I would hide my laptop, but there was nowhere I could put it without her being able to get to it anyway.

I was surprised she hadn't tried to use it, but I also would have been surprised if she did anything to jeopardize my generosity. She'd broken my trust, and she could never earn it back now. My guard would always be up.

She ate quietly in front of the TV, not making conversation with me, like she knew I was avoiding her.

I shut the laptop then stepped into the bathroom to shower. I locked the door behind me, got under the hot water, and took my time, hoping she'd be finished with dinner and ready to go to sleep.

So we could not talk.

I dried my hair afterward then returned to the bedroom in a new pair of boxers.

She was in bed like I hoped she'd be. Her hair was styled now because she'd been using my comb and hair-dryer, so she looked more refreshed than the other girls. She probably couldn't resist it, having nice hair. In a horrible place like this, you needed any little thing to make you feel better.

Even I hated this horrible place.

I turned off the lights then got into bed beside her.

Now, I was perpetually uncomfortable, sharing the bed with someone when it was designed for a single person. Our cabins had AC, so it kept it cool. Without it, this would be unbearable. I was at the edge, trying to stay as far away from her as possible so her body heat wouldn't touch my bare skin. I hated listening to her breathe, but I'd have to get used to it. A week had passed, and I still wasn't used to it.

But putting her back in her cabin wasn't an option.

Her voice broke the silence. "Magnus?"

I didn't respond.

"You should just send me back to my cabin…"

I stared at my desk.

"Because when you leave, they're gonna get me anyway."

I released a loud sigh because it was true. Why suffer this proximity when my absence would expose her to all the cruelty again? Now that I'd taken her away, they'd want her even more, just out of spite. I felt like a lone wolf trying to protect a pup from an entire pack. The second I was gone, they would rip her to pieces. "Then I won't leave."

She was quiet.

That sounded like a terrible plan too, but I didn't have any other option.

The mattress shifted as she came closer to me, her chest pressing against my back, her arm wrapping around my waist. Her face moved to the back of my neck, her warm breaths falling on my skin at a quickened rate. Then she kissed the back of my shoulder, pulling me closer to her.

I pulled her arm off my body and pushed her away. "Get off me."

She stilled, stung by my reaction. "You don't want me?"

"No."

She was quiet again.

I just wanted to go to sleep…and do this all over again tomorrow.

Emotion cracked her voice this time. "He didn't… He didn't rape me."

I threw the sheets off and sat at the edge of the bed, wiping my palm across my face in irritation. "You think that would matter to me?" My arms moved to my thighs, and my bare hands rubbed together. "Don't misunderstand my intentions. I helped you because I couldn't abandon you. But I don't desire you anymore. I desired the woman that I trusted. You are not that woman anymore." I rose off the bed and stepped away, needing space so I wouldn't throw my fist through a wall.

"I am that woman—"

"You fucking humiliated me." I turned back around and stared her down, seeing her eyes well up with new tears. "You have no idea what they did to me. You have no fucking idea how they tortured me!

Why the fuck would I want you when you sent me to the guillotine? Why the fuck would I want you when you weren't there for me when I was there for you?" My shouts became so loud that the guards in nearby cabins probably heard them. "A man protects his woman against everything—but she also protects him. You fucking abandoned me."

Tears dripped down her cheeks, and she bowed her head, like she couldn't look at me.

"No. I don't fucking want you." I couldn't look at her, so I turned away and faced the wall. The cabin was too fucking small for me to go anywhere other than the bathroom, but I refused to cower away in the room where I took a shit every morning.

She cried quietly.

Melanie told me Raven had fought against the executioner to get to me. She lifted the burning rubble off my back to save me, giving her hands scars she would carry the rest of her life. I'd seen them myself—so I knew it was true. But that wasn't enough to make me forgive and forget. She took that knife for me, but that still wasn't enough to make me move on. Nothing would make me move on. "I let you live here so Alix and the others won't do the unspeakable. But that's it. My invitation means nothing more than that. So, you keep your mouth shut and be as invisible as possible. Touch my laptop or do anything stupid, and I will throw you back outside. Got it?"

She got out of bed, still crying, and went into the bathroom. The door locked—like she thought I would go after her.

I went back to bed and tried to go to sleep. Her tears were slightly audible through the door, so I grabbed the remote, turned on the TV to drown out the sound, and forced myself to go to sleep.

TEN

PLAYTHING

A WEEK PASSED, AND WE DIDN'T SPEAK.

I spent my nights at the communal cabin, drinking beer, playing poker with the guys, watching TV. I'd begun to bring her dinner right after the workday so she would be asleep by the time I came to the cabin for bed.

It started to become a routine.

She was my silent roommate.

Sharing the bed with her was always uncomfortable. I'd have to lie in the same position so I wouldn't touch her. In my sleep, I would roll over the other way, and once I touched her, I'd wake up and roll back the other way. Sometimes, I went right back to sleep…and other times, I was awake for an hour.

The guards didn't ask me about Raven. They didn't mention her at all.

When I played poker with the guys, Alix was quiet. But his silence was better than his perversion.

The day arrived when Fender returned to the camp.

He came at sunset.

The double doors to the perimeter opened so he could enter on horseback, four guys flanking either side of him, guns hidden under their clothes to protect him from an unexpected ambush.

I walked down the steps of the main cabin to the grass then waited for his approach.

When he came closer, I realized Melanie sat behind him on the horse.

I was surprised he'd brought her.

She must have convinced him to, in the hope of seeing her sister.

Fender stopped, and instead of getting off the horse first, he took Melanie's hand and helped her down, his entire focus on getting her to the ground safely.

Her curled hair was pulled back, she wore heavy makeup, and she was in skintight jeans, knee-high flat boots, and an olive-green t-shirt. Diamonds were in her lobes, she wore an expensive necklace, and she looked like French royalty even when she was dressed casually. She pulled off her riding gloves.

Fender came next, landing on the ground and handing the reins to one of the horse masters. When the other guards realized the boss had entered the camp, they came out of the communal cabin to look at him.

I pushed my hood down to look at him.

Fender walked over to me, Melanie staying slightly behind him. His brown eyes were locked on to mine, and he looked at me the way he used to, like we were brothers. My crimes seemed to fade more and more with every passing week as our profits soared. In his eyes, I'd made up for my stupidity, and I'd suffered enough for it.

He stopped in front of me in a gray t-shirt that fit his muscled frame tightly. A shadow was on his jawline because the hair never went away, no matter how often we shaved it. It was there by the evening. We were the same height, so his stare could pierce right into me. "Brother."

I gave no reaction, but the affectionate term affected me deep down to my core. It was in front of this cabin where he'd mutilated me with a knife, but I understood that it was just business, that it was the only way to keep me alive. It was no different from when I whipped Raven until she collapsed. "Brother."

He extended his hand to me.

I paused before I took it, my hand gripping the inside of his elbow, just as he did to me. Then he brought me in, giving me a quick embrace with a pat on the back. I did the same before I stepped back.

All the guards saw.

I nodded to the cabin and stepped aside so he could walk inside.

He moved up the stairs and through the door.

Melanie came to me next, her blue eyes identical to her sister's. She looked at me affectionately, like she wanted to convey her gratitude for not ratting her out. But she couldn't speak, so she touched me subtly on the arm and kept going.

I'd thought I was loyal to my brother, but now I wasn't so sure where my loyalties lay.

I walked in behind them and shut the door.

There was a large dining table against the wall and a seating area with two couches facing each other. Melanie took a seat on the couch, sitting straight with her knees together, a woman so beautiful and elegant, it was hard to believe she'd ever been a prisoner here. A life of fine things had turned her classy, making her appear like a member of the aristocracy. Her hands moved to her thighs, and she sat there quietly.

I sat on the other couch and didn't look at her.

Fender went to the cabinets and poured the drinks. He made himself a scotch, while retrieving a bottle of water for Melanie.

My eyes moved back to her face, seeing an ocean of emotions. There was relief, guilt, anxiety...but no fear. If she was pretending to feel affection toward Fender, she wasn't just fooling him but also me. She went back to him to save her sister, but maybe she did it for herself too.

Her hair was a shade lighter than her sister's, and she had high cheeks and full lips. Their similarities were noticeable. There was no denying she was a woman of exceptional beauty, but there was something inherently boring to her appearance…at least to me. She was a simple woman with simple thoughts…blandly unremarkable. When I looked at Raven, I saw a complex woman with a fire that never burned lower than an inferno. She was intelligent, resourceful, resilient…fearless. Like she was a priceless work of art, I could stare at her forever and always find something new to admire.

Fender sat on the couch beside Melanie and handed her the water bottle.

"Thank you." She twisted off the cap and took a drink.

His large hand moved to her thigh, gripping the tight material of her jeans. "It's time for the men to talk, beautiful." He nodded to the next room. "Wait for me."

She slowly placed the cap back on the bottle before she obediently did as she was told.

I stared at my brother and watched him drink his scotch. "I'm surprised you brought her here."

"She wants to see her sister."

"And you'll allow it?"

He swirled his glass even though there was no ice. "Haven't decided." He took another drink then held the glass between his thighs.

The guilt started to crush me. I should tell him that Melanie's affection wasn't genuine. But I also knew he would want her, regardless, and I wasn't entirely sure if my initial assumption was correct anymore. Melanie wasn't brave like her sister. Would she really make a sacrifice like that if it were truly so horrible? Unlikely.

"Operations are going well."

"Yes."

"What did Renata say about an increase in shipments?"

I shook my head. "Not possible by plane. But we're considering delivery by cargo ship. They dock in

Spain and drive through the Alps to meet us here. It's just far riskier."

"We're untouchable—so I don't see the risk."

"There's no risk of the police or the governments. But our competitors…there's always a risk there." We monopolized the industry, but once secrets got out, that would change. If anyone knew this camp was here, they would burn it to the ground and kill us all. "Don't let arrogance turn to complacency."

"It's not arrogance—greed." He took another drink then set it on the table. "And you know how greedy I am."

There was never enough money for Fender. He wanted more money, more power, but he'd already reached the top of the hierarchy. "Trying to figure out how to make it work. But if it's too risky, we'll have to accept what we have."

He gave a slight nod. "When you leave in a few days, take care of it."

Now that this conversation was happening in real-time, I realized there was no way I could ask Fender if I could stay at the camp indefinitely. He would lose all respect for me because the request was absolutely ridiculous. I was an essential part of the operations of the camp, but I had responsibilities outside the facility. To abandon those duties for a woman was ludicrous.

His eyes shifted back and forth as he looked into my gaze, as if he noticed my subtle hesitation. "What is it?"

I could say nothing and leave Raven here. But if I did...I knew what would happen to her. She'd be raped by every guard here. Alix would be ruthless every time, bringing her into such darkness, I wouldn't be surprised if she gave up and took her own life. That was an outcome I couldn't accept. I would never sleep well again. I would never be able to get the acid out of my throat. It would be a different kind of agony, a mental pain that would never heal. "I've taken Raven as my own." I had to word this correctly, to make him understand, to make him allow it.

His eyes immediately narrowed.

"I want to take her with me."

Slowly, his features tightened and changed, as if he couldn't believe the words coming out of my mouth. His eyebrows furrowed in anger. His nostrils flared even though he hadn't taken a breath. "What the fuck is it with this cunt?" He raised his voice, maniacal instantly.

"I'm not asking for her freedom. I'm asking for her to be bound to me—the way Melanie is bound to you."

Once I mentioned the woman who'd claimed his heart, his anger simmered down.

"When I leave, she comes with me. When I return, she's back to work with the other prisoners." I could never tell him I was doing this to protect her from the guards. He would stick a knife in my heart for my weakness. "I want her to be mine. That's all."

He studied me for a long time, his hostile gaze burning holes in my face. "I don't understand your fascination. What about Stasia? She's far more beautiful. What about all the women in Paris? You can have any woman you want, and this is who you choose?"

"Yes."

He shook his head slightly.

"But it's not monogamous. It's not affectionate. She betrayed me, so I want her at my beck and call whenever I wish. She's mine to use. She will make up for what she did to me. That's all." I refused to sacrifice my personal life to put up false pretenses. I'd bed the women I wanted because I wouldn't bed her. I just needed to take her with me to keep her safe. She could never earn my forgiveness. She could never earn my affection.

My brother studied me, his anger slipping away further. "She's your plaything?"

I nodded.

He bowed his head slightly as he considered the request, his eyes on his glass on the table.

If he said no, I'd have no choice but to leave her here.

He lifted his gaze again. "If she escapes...I'll cut off the rest of you and watch you bleed out."

If Raven betrayed me again, I'd be dead. I shouldn't risk anything for her, but it was the lesser of two evils—because I couldn't abandon her. I couldn't trust her, but I also couldn't live with myself knowing what happened to her every single time I left. It would kill me. "I understand."

"It doesn't matter if you let her go or she betrays you. If she's out, it's your head."

I nodded again. "I know."

He clenched his jaw slightly and shook his head. "I'll never understand it, but I'm not going to try anymore. If this is what you're into...so be it. I grant your request." He grabbed the glass, finished the scotch, and then slammed it down again before he rose to his feet.

I couldn't believe I'd done it.

I saved her.

"Beautiful." He raised his voice slightly, with a hint of affection.

The door opened, and she came back in, her eyes on him like there was no one else in the room. Her petite frame had an hourglass shape, a flat stomach with large breasts. She had long, slender legs. She wasn't the type of woman I usually saw my brother with. He generally detested American women. But there was something different about this one.

Just as there was something different about Raven.

His arm circled her waist as he brought her close. "We'll have dinner then go to bed. I have a lot of things to do tomorrow."

"Can I see her?" The words flew out of her mouth like she'd been holding them back since they got there. "Please." Her arms circled his neck, and she brought her face close to his, using his obsession to get what she wanted. "I just want to see my sister… please." She leaned in and gave him a gentle kiss on the lips.

His hands squeezed her ass before he stepped away. "Take her to the cunt's cabin. Give them five minutes. Nothing more."

"Thank you, *amoureux*…" She called him her lover, then moved in to kiss him again.

He gave her a final embrace before he walked out of the cabin.

Melanie covered her face for a moment, instantly emotional at the prospect of seeing her sister.

I got to my feet. "Let's go."

"What were you saying? I know you were talking about Raven, but I couldn't make anything out."

I didn't answer her and headed to the door. "Haven't I done enough for you?"

She followed behind me and didn't ask again.

I guided her out of the cabin and to mine across the clearing. My key moved into the lock, and I opened the door. "I'm not going to give you longer than five minutes, so don't ask." I stepped aside so she could enter.

She stepped inside.

Raven dropped something and gasped. "Oh my god…"

Melanie broke down into tears. "Sister…"

They came together and embraced.

I watched them for a moment, seeing the way they both cried as they shook in each other's arms, the raw emotion that flowed out of them both, like this little moment was a gift from God.

I shut the door until it was only cracked, and I lingered outside so I could listen. I didn't trust Raven anymore, so if they were plotting some foolish attempt to escape, I needed to know about it.

"I only have five minutes…" Melanie sniffled.

"I just can't believe you're here…" Raven spoke through her tears.

"I asked him to bring me so I could see you."

"Melanie…" She sniffled loudly. "You shouldn't have gone to him. I never would have wanted you to do that."

"It's fine. It's not so bad."

"Not so bad?" she asked incredulously.

Melanie dodged the question like she didn't want to talk about Fender. "Your cabin…why does it have a laptop and a TV?"

"Oh…" Raven's excitement fell. "It's not mine. It's Magnus's."

"Why are you in his cabin?"

"Because it was the only way he could protect me from the guards." She burst into tears again, either from gratitude or terror.

"He still cares about you," Melanie whispered.

Raven didn't verbally respond.

I stared at the crack in the door, unable to see them.

Melanie lowered her voice, as if she hoped I wouldn't hear. "He was talking about you to Fender, but I couldn't figure out what they were saying. I asked him, but he wouldn't tell me."

"He was probably telling him that I'm in his cabin. Thought it would be better to come from him instead of the other guards."

"Maybe…but it seemed like more than that."

Raven was quiet for a while. "Does he treat you well?"

"Yes, he does." She spoke again, changing the subject a second time. "I'm gonna get him to release you. Every time I bring you up, he cuts me off. So…I just need some more time with him."

"You don't need to do that—"

"It's not like I can leave anyway, Raven. I'll keep working on him. I know I can get him to let you go…eventually."

She was wrong about that. Even if he loved her, married her, had a family with her, he would never change his mind. Fender wasn't like me. He was stubborn. If he made a decision, he would never change it. After everything Raven did to this camp, he would never let her go—ever. Honestly…I couldn't blame him.

Raven sighed quietly. "Thank you, Melanie."

"I told you we shouldn't have come back to the camp."

"I would have done it anyway, and I know you would have too."

"I told Magnus that you saved his life," Melanie whispered. "But I'm not sure if he believed me."

Raven took a deep breath. "It doesn't matter. He won't forgive me."

"He will. The fact that he's still protecting you… He will."

She started to cry again. "You don't know him like I do. He's a good man, so he'll be there for me…but what we had… It's over."

"I didn't know you felt that way about him."

"I…I didn't know either."

I kept my stare in place, refusing to feel anything for her, to react internally to what she said.

"He told me he was tortured because of what I did." Her voice shook, like she could feel the pain she didn't even know I'd experienced. "He told me the guards turned on him. One of them tried to kill him, and I didn't know what to do…so I tried to push Magnus out of the way…and the guard stabbed me instead."

"Oh my god." Clothes started to rustle, like Melanie was looking for the wound. She must have found it because she said, "Jesus…"

"It doesn't hurt anymore. I'm fine."

"And he still won't forgive you?" she asked incredulously.

Raven was quiet for a long time. "I have a feeling what he went through is much worse."

It'd been more than five minutes, so it was time to end this. I pushed the door open. "Come on."

Melanie stood in front of her sister, their hands clasped together. She didn't turn away because she wasn't ready to let Raven go. She started to cry again, like it was too hard to leave her sister there.

"Don't make me ask again."

Raven cupped her cheeks and forced a smile through her tears. "I'll be okay, Melanie."

Melanie released a shaky breath. "I love you…"

"I love you too." Raven hugged her tightly, supporting her like she was the mother and Melanie was the child. "We will get out of this someday. I truly believe that." She rubbed her sister's back and gave her a kiss on the forehead.

Melanie nodded then pulled away. She didn't say goodbye before she walked out of the cabin.

I locked the door behind her then escorted her to my brother's cabin, walking in front, ignoring the sound of her sniffles. By the time we got to the cabin on the other side of the clearing, her tears had been silenced.

I nodded to the door at the top of the stairs before I turned away.

She reached out and grabbed me by the arm. "Wait."

I twisted out of her grasp because I didn't want her to touch me.

With watery eyes, she stared at me. "Thank you… for protecting her."

I gave her a blank expression because her gratitude meant nothing to me.

"The only reason I could walk out of that cabin is because I know you'll keep her safe."

ELEVEN

BOIS DE BOULOGNE

Alix didn't attack me, but I knew he was pissed off.

He'd expected my brother to punish me for my actions.

Not only did he pardon them, but he agreed to let me remove her from the camp. Once Alix knew that, he would probably lose his shit.

Fender was only there for a day to see the state of the camp with his own eyes. Melanie stayed in his cabin and wasn't permitted to visit her sister again. I didn't tell Raven what I had asked of my brother because I dreaded the conversation.

She and I didn't talk, not even after she saw her sister.

We continued to pretend the other didn't exist. She faced the wall while she slept and I faced the other way, so we never touched throughout the night.

I looked forward to leaving the camp just so I would have my own bed again.

I hated sleeping with people, even with my lovers. It could be a king-size bed and she could be on the opposite side, but I still hated it. The touching, the breathing, the closeness, I hated it. I always moved into another bedroom when the sex was over. They were used to it and didn't ask any questions.

I hated being asleep with someone else in the room.

I just couldn't do it.

I did it now because I had to. And I did it once before…because it was different at the time.

The night before I departed, I told her the plan.

She was on the floor watching TV, so I grabbed the remote and turned it off. I sat in the chair at my desk, turned sideways so I could look at the bed.

She got to her feet and looked at me, knowing I wanted her attention.

I nodded to the bed. "Sit."

She did as she was told. She sat at the edge and looked at me, fidgeting with her fingers like she was afraid I'd decided to throw her out of the cabin. She'd been quiet as a mouse, staying out of my way like she feared I would have a change of heart and abandon her. She stayed silent and gave me all the time I wanted to speak.

I looked at the floor for a while, unable to believe what I was about to say. Before she came to the camp, my life was routine. It was ordinary. Nothing unusual happened. But then she came in, like a fucking storm, and destroyed everything. "I'm leaving tomorrow."

She inhaled a deep breath, a painful breath, like she pictured her fate in my absence. The emotion happened instantly, the fear entering her tight features and making her eyes slightly wet. The Red Snow wasn't the subject of her nightmares. That was being forced against her will, for someone to desecrate her body when there was nothing she could do to stop it. Death was a dream in comparison.

"You're coming with me."

Her head lifted to look at me, her hands stilling in her lap. "What?"

"I'm not freeing you. You will remain a prisoner. Try to run, and I'll kill you. If you betray me and escape, my brother will execute me. If you want to repay my kindness toward you, you won't do that to me."

She breathed hard, as if she couldn't believe the truth.

"You will accompany me while I'm in Paris. When I return to the camp, you'll go back to work like the others. I couldn't ask Fender if I could stay in the camp indefinitely, so I asked if I could take you with me…just as he's taken Melanie for himself. It was the only solution I could find."

She stared at me in her stillness, like she couldn't believe anything I'd just said.

"Don't make me regret this."

She nodded. "I won't try to escape. I promise."

I looked away and felt the bitterness flood my mouth. "I wish I could believe you." I'd have to lock her in the house while I was gone, handcuff her to the bed or something. All she needed to do was walk out of the place and disappear. I'd hunt her down again eventually, but if I didn't do it quick enough before Fender found out, I'd lose my life.

"If running results in your death, I won't do it."

I still wouldn't look at her. "I know you. I know you'll do everything you can to save your sister, the women who are prisoners now, and no amount of loyalty to me will change that. These are your words I'm echoing back to you."

"I know, but things are different now."

I lifted my head and looked at her. "Why?"

"Because I knew you wouldn't be killed when I burned the camp. Now, you will…and I can't let that happen. You're a prisoner to this place as much as I am."

I shifted my gaze back to the floor. "You're wrong about that."

"You don't agree with the rules of this place, but you stay. There's a reason why. You just haven't told me what it is."

We left the next morning.

I helped the men load the wagon with the prepared product so we could leave the camp and make it to the end of the road before sunset. I left Raven in the cabin while I helped the loaders, but that meant she didn't report for work with the others.

I made my way back through the clearing.

Alix watched me.

I walked past him, knowing there would be trouble.

"Where the fuck is she?" He followed behind me.

I kept going, moving out of the clearing and toward the cabin.

"Asshole, I asked you a question."

My knife was in my pocket if I needed it.

"The only reason she shouldn't be at work is because she's dead. So, tell me she's dead." His footsteps quickened.

I turned around and faced him before he came too close.

He pulled his hood down so I could see how angry he was.

"I'm taking her with me."

"What?" His voice was so loud, it echoed off the surrounding trees.

"She's still a prisoner—just in a different place."

"Are you fucking kidding me with this shit?" He got in my face, spittle flying from his mouth.

"The boss agreed to it. Let it go."

"After what she did, she just gets to leave?"

"She'll return and get back to work." I turned and continued to walk.

He grabbed me by the arm.

I spun around and quickly threw his arm down. "Stop this."

"You're such a traitor." He spat on me.

I let it get on my clothes and didn't wipe it away. "I've kept my mouth shut about your behavior up until this point. But if you don't keep your shit together, I will have you killed. This is his decision. You're just pissed off that you can't fuck her. During your time off, spend your money on a nice whore." I turned away.

He followed me. "No. I'm pissed that she killed our men—"

"Who enslaved and killed innocent women." I turned back around. "Stop changing the narrative. We're the villains here. She did what anyone else would do…if they had the balls."

He stood still, staring at me like he couldn't believe a single word that flew out of my mouth. "Are you one of us? Or one of them?"

I didn't know how to answer that question anymore. "I'm loyal to my brother. Always."

He spat at my feet. "Doesn't seem like it." He turned around and walked off.

I watched him go before I moved to the cabin to retrieve her.

She was sitting on the edge of the bed when I opened the door. In her work uniform and with no possessions, she immediately turned her eyes to mine when she saw me.

I nodded. "Let's go."

She got off the bed and joined me.

I took her to the gate through a different route so we could avoid the clearing. The guards already knew she wouldn't be reporting to work and the women obviously realized it too, but it was smart not to flaunt her existence.

"The guards won't punish you for this later?"

I wasn't afraid of them. Unless they came at me with a gun, they couldn't defeat me. "No."

"Are we riding to the chateau?"

"No. Wagons."

"Oh."

"There's no reason to hide the path since you obviously already know it…"

She turned quiet.

We reached the wagons.

There were three altogether. There was a driver in each one. I would be the driver for the last. "You can lie in the back if you want or sit up front with me. Makes no difference to me." I climbed to the front and grabbed the reins.

Instead of taking the back, she climbed into the spot beside me. "May as well enjoy the view."

We traveled down the narrow path, three wagons in a row. In the springtime, there was much more to look at than white fields and heavy branches with piles of snow on top. The cold and dry air didn't sting the eyes when you gazed, so you could take in the scenes all you wanted.

That was what she did.

We passed a river to the right, and later on the left was a small pond with lily pads drifting on top. Deer were visible on the other side, drinking from the water, wiggling their ears as they kept their eyes on us. Hawks passed in the skies, the world alive in the warm water. Hunters searched for food, and prey stayed hidden in the brush.

Raven didn't make conversation and spent her time appreciating the wilderness around us. It must have made her think of her journey across the river in the opposite direction because she asked, "How's Rose?"

I looked at the wagons in front, all spaced out with several feet in between in case one of the horses made an unexpected stop. The drivers didn't turn around to glance at us, and they seemed too far away to hear the question. I didn't want to be seen talking to her, not when I was already the camp's most hated man. "She's fine."

"You kept her?"

"I told you I would, didn't I?"

"Yes, but—"

"You betrayed me," I said bitterly. "I'm the kind of man that keeps his word." I turned to look at her. "Even if the person I gave it to doesn't deserve it."

Her blue eyes dropped like the insult truly affected her. Her sadness seemed sincere, and the words she'd shared with her sister had been packed with such raw emotion that she seemed to tell the truth.

Didn't change anything.

"It was really nice to see Melanie." She looked ahead, sitting on the edge of the seat so there was plenty of space between us. She did whatever she could to stay out of my way, pressed up against the bedroom wall at night so her presence would be nearly forgettable.

"I didn't arrange it. That was her."

"I know…just saying."

My hands held the reins, but the horses were so well behaved that it wasn't necessary. They knew the route better than we did. They even knew to avoid the bumps in the road so the wagons wouldn't shake.

"Is he good to her?"

"We don't discuss such things."

"But what do you think, based on what you've seen?"

"You can't change it, so what does it matter?"

She gave a pause. "It matters to me…"

I looked at the road ahead, knowing we had another hour to go before we reached the hidden clearing where the vehicles were stored. "He never addresses her as Melanie. He always calls her 'beautiful.' When I was at his estate and she walked into the room, instead of getting his butler to fetch her drink, he did it himself. When they came to the camp, he made sure she got off the horse safely and onto the ground before he dismounted. He's gentle when he touches her. I've never seen him be that way with a woman in my entire life."

Raven was quiet as she processed that. "He loves her."

"I don't know."

"Every time I asked about him, she changed the subject. I don't know why she wouldn't just tell me that."

"Because she feels the same way."

She turned back to me, incredulous. "Not possible."

I didn't argue because I really didn't care anyway.

Her eyebrows furrowed in anger. "She would never feel anything for someone like that. Maybe there's Stockholm syndrome going on, but no, Melanie would never care about the man who owns this place."

I kept my eyes on the road.

"She wouldn't…right?"

I didn't care either way.

"Magnus?"

"What?"

"Do you think that's true?"

"I've only seen them together a few times, so I'm no expert. Believe it or not, but dissecting people's emotional feelings isn't my hobby. I can read Fender well because I know him, but I don't know your sister. Maybe she's pretending… I have no idea."

She faced forward again.

"I know you live a virtuous life and see the world in black and white, but other people see shades of gray. Most women would want to be the one who earns Fender's affection, regardless of his criminal enterprise."

She turned back to me. "Why?" There was a hint of disgust in her voice.

"He's rich—"

"Money means nothing. Having a soul is the only currency that matters."

I turned to her. "Can I finish?"

She faced forward again.

I turned back to the road. "He's rich. He's power-ful. And he's handsome. Melanie was in this camp for almost two months, and now she's underneath the man that has everyone in his pocket. Nothing could hurt her ever again. That's the dream, right?"

She shook her head. "I disagree."

The wagons rolled across the hard ground and little pebbles in the road, and the horses started to turn as we came around a bend to avoid a large tree. "You slept with me, didn't you?" I was the man who kept her alive. I was the only man powerful enough to keep the others away.

She slowly turned her head back to me, her features immediately etched into an expression of pain. "That's totally different…"

"Is it?" I kept my face forward.

"Yes. We're different. You're nothing like him."

I shook my head. "You give me more credit than I deserve."

"Really?" she snapped. "Because I don't think you give yourself enough."

After the wagons were parked, the truck pulled up and the back was quickly thrown open. The guy didn't get out of the driver's seat because his job was to pull away the instant we were finished.

We hustled to get the drugs out of the wagons and into the back of the truck.

Raven just stood there.

I turned around and stood at the edge of the truck, seeing her petting one of the horses. "Get your ass moving. Now."

She stilled at my command, her hand still on the horse's nose, but she didn't argue. She moved to one of the wagons and started to help us load the back. It was a lot of product, but we could get it loaded within three minutes. I pulled down the door, pounded my fist into the metal so the driver could hear, and then hopped off.

He drove away.

The horses were given food and water and a break before they would turn around and head back to the camp. My car was covered in a brown tarp, hidden in an enclave we'd made in the trees, so it was impossible to spot from the road. I pulled the tarp off and tossed it aside. "Let's go."

She eyed the car for a moment, recognizing it from the last time I drove her to Paris. There was a brief hesitation before she got inside.

I started the engine, and we pulled onto the road. I drove far past the speed limit because I would never be pulled over, even if another driver called and reported my license plate. That number would be entered into the database along with instructions to disregard it.

It'd already been a long day, and now we had a long drive to Paris.

She looked out the window and watched the scenery as we passed. "Where do you live?"

"Paris."

She rested her head against the leather headrest, her eyes heavy like she might sleep on the drive. "You know what I mean."

"I live at the edge of Bois de Boulogne."

She turned back to me. "I'm sorry...what is that?"

"It's a park. It once belonged to the royal family, but Emperor Napoleon made it public in 1852. It's ten minutes away from the Eiffel Tower."

Her eyes filled with a slight look of excitement. "Can you see the tower from one of your windows?"

I turned my eyes back to the road. "Yes."

She turned back to the window and relaxed. "That's nice…" She got comfortable and closed her eyes, her arms crossing over her body like she was cold from AC. "I can't wait to see it."

When I glanced at her, her eyes were closed, and there were bumps on her arms.

I turned down the air and turned on some music so she wouldn't have to listen to the engine roar every time I accelerated.

IT WAS TECHNICALLY AN APARTMENT, BUT IT FELT more like a small estate. I enjoyed solitude at my estate in the countryside, but I also enjoyed the hustle of the city, the nearby bars, the brilliant view of the Eiffel Tower over the large pond right outside the front of my property.

I thought she would like it…which was another reason I decided to stay here.

I drove slowly down the road around the pond and approached the apartment.

Her eyes opened when the car slowed down. She blinked a few times before she sat up and looked at the landscape around her. The perimeter of the pond was lit with subtle lights, and white Christmas lights were wrapped around the surrounding trees even though the holidays were long gone. The tower stood in the distance, and she stared at it like it was a beacon of hope.

I opened my private gate remotely then pulled into my driveway where my garage was. There were buildings down the line, my neighbors having the same view that I did. Every morning, the residents left their homes and jogged around the park before walking to work in the heart of the city.

Her expression told me everything. "Oh my god… this place is beautiful."

I closed the garage behind us, and then we stepped into the elevator. The ground floor had no access, to make it impossible for robbers to get inside. I hit the code, and we rose to the entry level of my apartment.

When the doors opened, she stepped inside and looked around, seeing the grand entryway, the intricate moldings on the wall, the flecks of gold across the ceilings, the Parisian style windows and the hardwood floors. She immediately went to the window and looked outside, gazing over the pond and to the tower nearby.

I stopped and stared at her back, seeing the way she appreciated the city that had been so cruel to her. She worshiped it like it was her home, when she was really a long-term tourist. Her previous life had been permanently taken away from her, but the love in her heart was unstoppable.

I moved farther into the house. There was a sitting area on this level that I never used, along with guest bedrooms that were also never used.

When she heard me walk away, she followed me. "This place is…gorgeous." She looked at the lights that extended from the walls and lit up the artwork above. Her fingers moved to the intricate gold leaves that were embedded in the wall. Then she examined the traditional Parisian furniture, the Turkish rug, the ancient statues.

Most of the women I brought here didn't extend a single compliment, like they were trying to impress me by not being impressed. "This is your room." I opened one of the guest bedrooms, which had a view of the park and the tower. There was a pile of clothes for her on the bed to wear during her stay.

She looked at the open window for a moment before she looked at the clothes. "How did these get here?"

"My property manager."

"What's a property manager?"

"Someone who manages all my homes and prepares them for my arrival on a whim's notice." I turned away and walked back into the sitting area and to the stairs. It'd been a long day. I was tired and hungry.

She came after me. "Where are you—"

"This is how this is going to work. I've armed the place with an alarm, so if you try to leave, I'll know. You won't get far, and when I get to you, I'll drown you in that pond right outside. Got it?"

Her expression immediately fell in disappointment. "I told you I wouldn't run—"

"That means nothing to me."

She stilled at my hostility.

"There's food in the kitchen. Help yourself." I turned to the stairs.

"What about you?"

"I have a kitchen up here." I moved halfway up the stairs and turned back around. "Don't come up here. It's off-limits."

"What if I need something?"

"You're on your own." I moved the rest of the way and made it to the third floor. The lights were already on because my manager had readied it for me, and since I was starving, I immediately went to the fridge and pulled out the dinner prepared for me. I scarfed it down because I was so hungry, washing it down with a vintage bottle of wine, and then I showered and went straight to bed.

When I woke up the next morning, I put on my running shorts and shoes to run in the park. I walked down the stairs to the second landing, and she must have been listening for the sound of my steps because she came out of her bedroom. She was in the clothes Miranda had picked out based on my description of her, wearing a simple floral dress. Her hair was done, she wore makeup once again, and she looked like a different person once she was back to a normal life.

I ignored the way she stared at me and headed to the door toward the elevator.

"Where are you going?" She followed after me.

"A run."

"Can I come?"

I turned back around. "The only reason I brought you here is so the guards won't tear you to pieces. Don't get in my way. Don't bother me. I want you to pretend you don't exist, alright? There's a TV, a kitchen, books in the library. Don't speak to me again." I headed back to the elevator.

"You saved me just to lock me up in here?" she asked in disappointment.

I turned back to her, immediately furious. "Would you rather I have left you there?"

Her eyes shifted back and forth, slightly afraid of my anger. "Don't mistake my question as a lack of gratitude. I just want to go outside. Please let me go outside. I promise I won't run."

"You've been outside every day for six weeks."

"Not the same and you know it. I can keep up with you."

"I highly doubt that."

"Let me try."

My hands moved to my hips, and I stepped closer to her, my bare chest already starting to sweat from the anger. "I want to come and go as I please. I don't want to be interrupted. If you annoy me too much, I might just leave you there next time." I turned around and hit the button on the elevator.

"Magnus...you can trust me."

I stared at the doors and waited.

"If I make a promise, I keep it."

I listened to the mechanism as the elevator was pulled to my level.

"I would never compromise you—"

"You already did compromise me. You already betrayed my trust." I stepped into the elevator and turned around to look at her. "And once that happens, you can never get it back." I hit the button, and the doors started to close.

She stood there the entire time, her eyes filled with emotion. "I saved your life… That has to count for something."

The doors closed, and I started to move to the ground floor. "How many times have I saved yours?"

She stayed out of my way after that.

I set the alarm every time I left so I would know the second she tried to run. I thought about bringing men over to watch the elevator so she couldn't try, but I didn't like having anyone in my homes besides Miranda and myself. If Raven ran for it, there was no doubt I would find her.

But would I find her before Fender found out?

That was the problem.

I got dressed, grabbed my keys and wallet, and headed downstairs to depart.

She came out of her bedroom, wearing pajama shorts and a spaghetti strap top. It revealed a lot of skin, showing how toned her legs were from working every day at the camp, her flat and strong stomach just beneath the hem of the top. Her bathroom was full of various beauty supplies because if I had to bring Raven here every time I returned to Paris, I wanted to make sure she didn't ask me for anything. Her hair was in soft curls down her body, the first time I'd seen it done that way. There was no denying her beauty, and sometimes, that magnetic pull I felt for her drew me in.

But I severed it.

"Where are you going?" Her nipples hardened through the thin fabric of her top, like she was cold or scared.

I didn't look directly, but I could see it in my peripheral. "Work."

"Work where?"

Just like that, she ignited my fury. "There's obviously a misunderstanding here if you think you have any right to ask me anything."

Her blue eyes shifted back and forth as she looked into my face, her eyelashes thick from the makeup, the bright color even more vibrant in this lighting. "I'm not being nosy. I just…" She dropped her chin for a second. "Look, I know you're angry with me and you don't trust me, but…if this is going to be a long-term thing, we should talk to each other—"

"Why?"

"Because we can't just—"

"Yes, we can. The only reason I brought you here is to save your ass—literally. Make no mistake, you're still a prisoner. You're just a prisoner here instead of there. Change of location, that's all it is." I turned to walk to the elevator.

"Are you doing anything dangerous?"

"I only do dangerous things." I hit the button for the elevator.

She came up behind me. "Just…be careful."

I glanced at her over my shoulder before I stepped into the elevator. "You're the one who should be careful."

When I arrived at the estate, they patted me down for guns then allowed me inside.

I came alone because I was fearless.

They were the ones that wanted something from me—after all.

I moved through the impressive grand entryway, past the butler, and into the parlor where I'd meet the infamous Napoleon. Rich from blood diamonds in Africa, he wanted to be a distributor to that continent, which meant he needed a big cut of product from us on a regular basis.

He had men and butlers throughout the house, perhaps to show his status, but the parlor was empty except for him. He didn't rise from his chair to greet me. "Magnus." He nodded to the couch in front of me.

I took a seat directly across from him.

His hand rested on the top of his cane, which had a diamond in the pommel. He wasn't my age, but he was too young a man to be helpless without a cane, though a life in the fast lane resulted in injuries that never really healed. "What's your poison?"

"The same as yours."

He snapped his fingers, bringing a butler into the room. "Open a red. Barsetti Vineyards."

The butler retrieved the bottle, opened it in front of us, and poured two glasses.

We were silent during the process, nothing but eye contact.

The butler left the bottle behind and disappeared.

I took a drink then set it down.

He didn't touch his.

"How much product do you want?"

"Africa is a big place…"

"We're loyal distributors, so we can't back out of commitments with other clients. I can give you what we have, but it won't be enough for a continent that size."

"Can't you get more?"

I relaxed into the leather couch, crossing one ankle and resting it on the opposite knee. I took my time answering the question, always keeping my cards to my chest, regardless of how innocent the question seemed. "Like I said, Africa is a big place. We'll never get enough product to satisfy such a large area. We can negotiate a specific amount—and nothing more."

"Is that why you haven't moved your enterprise into Italy? Because you don't have enough?"

This was starting to feel like an interrogation—and I didn't like that. "Italy is already claimed by the Skull Kings. Pointless to break into that market. France is our territory, and we respect the territory of others." Italy had an extensive underground criminal underworld, and for us to cross the border and infiltrate such a place would be an undertaking unworthy of our time. If Napoleon wanted to compete with other kingpins in Africa, we had nothing to do with that. Our hands were clean.

Napoleon stared with his steely gaze, watching me with a poker face nearly as good as mine. His wine was untouched, and he gripped his cane like he might need it to fight me off if this conversation didn't go the way he wanted.

"If you want to be a dealer, we have rules. Abide by those rules, and we don't have a problem."

Silence.

"Are you still interested?"

"Very."

I didn't ask how he intended to smuggle the drugs into Africa because it was none of our concern. Once he paid for the product, the transaction was finished. "I will take your interest into consideration. You can expect a phone call with our answer." I rose to my feet. "Thank you for the wine."

"Your answer?" he asked, slightly amused. "Didn't realize there was an application process."

I stared down at him, seeing his crossed legs, his navy-blue suit rising up and revealing his maroon socks underneath. "We don't accept just anyone. It's the reason we've been in business so long…"

I sat on the couch and watched Fender walk into the sitting room, his black sweatpants low on his hips and his bare chest in view. A scotch was in his hand, and he took a drink as he sat across from me. "How'd it go?"

"I don't like him."

He held the glass in his hand. "You don't like anyone, Magnus."

I was more than cautious; I was paranoid. Trust was impossible to earn from me. They could say all the words I wanted to hear, but the content of the conversation meant nothing. It was the energy in the room. Betrayal had a scent, had a spirit, and I certainly felt it in Napoleon's company. "I don't trust him."

"Why?"

I shook my head. "He asked questions I didn't appreciate."

"Such as?"

"Why we haven't crossed the border into Italy."

"Maybe it's because he intends to." He took a drink. "Wish him luck."

"I don't think—"

Melanie's voice interrupted us. "Fender?"

I looked at my watch and saw the hour. It was almost midnight.

He looked up at her. "Yes?"

She stilled when she saw me on the other couch. She was in one of his shirts that fit her like a blanket. Her hair was down, and there was no makeup on her face. "I woke up…and you weren't there." She spoke to him but stared at me.

"I'll be up in a minute."

She lingered. "Is she here?"

I nodded.

She turned to Fender. "Can I see——"

"Go to bed." His affectionate tone was gone and replaced by one of a dictator. "I'll be there in a minute."

She didn't argue and walked away.

He shook his head when she was gone. "All she ever talks about is her obnoxious sister. Maybe I should kill her, so I don't have to hear about her anymore —from either one of you." He shot me a glare before he drank his scotch.

I didn't take threats from him lightly. "You'll lose her affection and never get it back."

He looked into his glass with no reaction, but he seemed to have come to the same conclusion because he didn't snap at me. "I hope you're enjoying her."

All I did was nod. We'd been there for a week, and we'd barely exchanged a few words. I kept her at a distance because my resentment had never faded away. I was spiteful. I held grudges for decades.

"I'm sure the guards weren't happy."

"They'll get over it." I knew I'd have to deal with Alix when I returned…might even have to kill him. Fender would be furious to lose another executioner since it was a difficult job to replace, so I would avoid that if possible. "I think we should pass on Napoleon."

"You pass on a lot of partners, Magnus."

"For good reason. All it takes is one bad seed…and we lose it all."

"Yes, but now that we've increased our production, we need to sell it to someone to distribute. Napoleon would work in Africa, so he wouldn't infringe on any domestic territory. We won't saturate the market and upset our current clients."

I knew he would say that. "I felt like he was trying to get information from me."

"By asking about Italy? Again, he might have his own eyes on it."

I shook my head. "I really don't think so."

He swirled the contents of his glass before he set it on the table between us. "Sleep on it for a few days."

"I've made my decision."

"He's too great a partner to pass up without concrete information. We'll look into him."

"We won't find anything because it's impossible to discover intention."

"Magnus—"

"I think he's trying to figure out how much coke we're getting in an effort to deduce how we're getting it…so he can come in and steal the business from us."

He stared at me. "Our Colombian partners would never betray us."

"Betrayal can be bought. The diamond business is just as lucrative as ours. He has the money. He could be trying to acquire our assets to take over France, Africa, and maybe Italy."

"No one can take over Italy. They'd be stupid to try."

I shook my head. "And maybe he's stupid enough."

Fender relaxed into the chair, his neck resting on the back of the couch as he looked at the ceiling, thinking it over.

I rubbed my hands together as I leaned forward, waiting for the thoughts he was collecting.

He leaned forward again, releasing a quick breath. "We'll think it over."

He never overrode me, and I knew he was only doing it now because of greed. "Fender, we're already richer than most countries combined. No reason to risk all of that for just a little more—"

"I didn't say I'd accept him as a partner." He got to his feet and left the living room. "I said I would think about it." His footsteps faded as he walked farther away. "You can let yourself out."

THIRTEEN

THE EIFFEL TOWER

WHEN I WALKED IN THE DOOR, SHE WAS THERE.

Sitting on the couch in front of the TV, she quickly jolted upright when she heard me, like she'd been trying to stay awake until I returned but had fallen asleep in front of the mindless entertainment on the screen.

I looked down at her, seeing even more of her long legs because her shorts rode up while she lay on the couch. One of the straps to her top came loose and fell down her shoulder.

She ran her fingers through her hair to pull it from her face in a way she never did at the camp and got to her feet, the sleep making her eyes heavy. The makeup was gone from her face, but her eyes were still much brighter here in Paris than they ever were at the camp.

"What are you doing? You have a king-size bed, a TV, and a view of the tower in your bedroom." I was tired from my evening because the frustration drained me. Fender was a genius mastermind who'd put this business together when we were still practically kids, but his success turned him arrogant, and that arrogance made him greedy, and that greed made him stupid.

"I wanted to make sure you came home." She stood up and pulled the strap back up her shoulder before she crossed her arms over her chest.

"And if I didn't?"

She wore a blank look, like she didn't know what to say.

"You would have walked out of here free." I moved to the stairs so I could go up to my room and get in the shower.

"No, that's not what I would have done."

I stilled at the bottom of the stairs, my hand on the railing. I should just keep walking, but something about my foul mood made me stay. I was tired but I was also frustrated, and I just wanted to get that out. I turned around and looked at her.

"I vaguely remember where Fender lives. I would have gone there and told him."

My hands remained on the banister, and I stared her down, annoyed by that answer.

"You act like you don't trust me, but I know you do."

I dropped my hand and walked back to her.

"You know I would do everything in my power to save you. I've already proven that to you." She lifted up her shirt, revealing the long scar that was the exact length of the blade she took for me, the blade that almost claimed her life.

I stopped in front of her and stared her down, my eyes shifting back and forth as I looked into her eyes, seeing the innocence of her gaze, the way she looked at me like I actually mattered. No other woman ever looked at me that way...like they really saw me. To everyone else, I was just a fat wallet and a powerful man. I was just a pretty face with a strong body. I was the ultimate prize. She didn't care about any of that. In fact, she hated all that stuff about me. She liked the deeper parts of me, the things I did in secret that no one knew about.

She was still, waiting for me to do something or say something.

I did neither.

"You're in a bad mood… Why?"

"Shitty night."

"What happened?" She didn't step back despite our close proximity, but she kept her arms over her chest, her breathing quicker than usual, like my nearness made her heart pound a little harder.

Instead of walking away, I answered. "I met with a potential partner. Didn't like him."

"Okay…"

"I told Fender my concerns, but he didn't see the merit. Still wants to consider him."

She didn't ask about her sister. "Why does that bother you?"

"Because his greed is masking his logic."

She studied my face, her eyes absorbing my features like she was trying to understand my feelings as well as possible. "You really care about him."

"Why does that surprise you?"

"Because he's a monster…"

My eyes drilled into her face. "You don't know him."

"I don't need to know him. Turning innocent women into slaves and then executing them will never be okay…*ever*. I know you agree with me, so why don't you do something about it?"

"I never said that."

"Then say it now." She challenged me, turned into the fierce woman who rode out into the storm without fear.

I could walk away whenever I wanted, but I stayed rooted in place.

She started to breathe a little harder, her eyes forming a wet sheen. "Tell me…"

"You don't know me—"

"I know you in every way that matters." Her voice was immediately loud, like she couldn't take this emotion anymore. "It's not what we do in the presence of witnesses that matters. It's what we do in secret that no one knows about. That's how you know who you really are. You have risked yourself for me because you said I deserved to be free. You saved my sister because it was the right thing to do. Even after what I did to you, you still protect me when you have absolutely no obligation. Yes, I fucking know you! So, why do you allow this to happen? Why?"

It was impossible to turn away when her eyes shone like that, when she looked at me like I was her hero —when I was everyone else's villain. "I tried to talk him out of the Red Snow. I told him that kind of punishment was unnecessary, and we would just lose workers that we spent time and resources to capture. But he told me without it, there was no way to keep the women in line. When we tried it, he was right. The women were slow, lazy, and useless. The threat of a whipping or a beating wasn't enough to scare them."

"Why do you have to take these women at all? Just hire people to do the work."

I shook my head. "It doesn't work either."

"Why? You make so much money off these drugs that you can afford to pay for labor——"

"That's not the problem. There's no way to make sure they aren't a spy."

"A spy?"

He nodded. "There're a lot of men out there who would kill to figure out how we are doing this. Our operation is unique, and if they knew where we operated and how this enterprise is run, they would take it from us and kill us all. Getting the product all the way from Colombia is impossible with all the new international regulations. We can pay off European governments, but not all governments. Taking these women is the only way it works because people assume they're trafficked, and no one bats an eye over it."

She shook her head, her eyes watering more.

Her reaction made me feel like shit. "There are two different worlds in this reality. There's the one you know, and there's this one. Trust me, I want to keep it separate. I want to deal with our own kind and never cross that barrier and involve innocent people. But Fender is right—it doesn't work any other way."

Two tears dripped down her cheeks. "There is *always* another way."

There was nothing more I could say on the topic, so I didn't. I just stood there and watched the emotions run through her, watched the inevitable pain drown her in sorrow.

She wiped her tears away then dug both hands into her hair as she took a breath, bringing herself back to calmness. She dropped her hands and her gaze, looking at the floor.

"I'm sorry." The words came out of my lips on their own, like I had no control. It just happened… like all the other things just happened when she was next to me. She pulled out a side to me that I tried to forget, a weakness that I buried over and over, but it always rose from the depths.

She lifted her chin and looked at me again, her eyes taking in my gaze. "I know you are…"

When I walked downstairs, she wasn't there.

Days had passed since our conversation, and she hadn't tried to speak to me again. She spent her time in her room, never questioning my whereabouts as I came and went. It didn't seem like she was angry at me…just disappointed.

Her bedroom door was open, so I stepped inside to see her sitting in the armchair that faced her window, looking at the Eiffel Tower over the tree line. A mug of coffee was beside her. She twirled her hair with her fingertips, unaware of my presence because she wasn't paying attention.

I stared at her for a while, noticing the way the natural light highlighted her beautiful skin, her bright eyes. "Want to go for a walk?"

Her fingers stilled in her hair, and her eyes suddenly focused. She dropped her hand and turned in the chair to look at me. "Are you talking to me?"

I suppressed my grin as much as I could. "Come on." I nodded to the door and stepped away.

She was already dressed in a dress and flats, so she stepped out a moment later, still in shock because she couldn't believe this was real. "Where are we going?"

I shrugged. "You want to get a coffee and walk to the Eiffel Tower?"

Her eyes opened even wider. "Uh…fuck yes."

This time, I did grin before I headed to the elevator.

"Why are you doing this?" She followed me.

"Do I need a reason?" The doors opened, and I stepped inside.

She joined me. "No…but I'd like one."

The elevator carried us to the ground floor, and then we stepped outside.

I shrugged. "I don't have any plans today."

That seemed to be a good enough reason for her, so she stopped the interrogation. She moved to the gate and looked at the pond through the iron bars, like she wanted to climb over to reach it.

I unlocked it, and then we walked together down the path.

Whenever she was outside in the city, she was a different person. Her shoulders were relaxed, her eyes were open and vulnerable, and she touched everything, like the wall, the petals of a rose, anything.

A couple passed us on the sidewalk, holding hands.

She smiled and waved. "Hi."

They flinched at her greeting then kept walking.

"What are you are doing?" I asked, my eyebrows furrowed.

"It's just so nice to see regular people, to know that this world is still here." When we left the park and headed to the area where the shops and cafes were, she glanced over her shoulder once more. "I've never been over there before. It's so beautiful. I feel like I'm back in time hundreds of years…"

I walked beside her, my hands in my pockets, seeing the way men looked at her as they passed. Miranda had picked out all the clothes and seemed to know what would look nice without actually seeing her. Today, she was in a lavender dress, tight around her waist with a slight flare. Her eyes were on everything, oblivious to the men who glanced at her as they passed. If she was plotting her escape, it didn't seem like it.

She stopped outside a coffee shop. "Oh my god, can we go here?"

"Sure."

She moved inside and looked around, like she'd been there before. "I used to come here all the time…" The barista made a coffee at the machine, and the person in line ordered a couple of muffins before they walked out. "Shit." Her eyes fell.

"What?"

"I…I don't have any money."

I studied her face, seeing the genuine surprise in her features, like she didn't expect me to take care of her. She would never escape at this point, so she would never have money again, but she still didn't expect anything from me. "I can buy you anything you want, whenever you want."

She hesitated, as if she didn't want to accept my money. She'd taken care of herself for a long time, took care of her sister even when she should have taken care of herself, so once she was out in the real world, she immediately reverted to that identity. "I have money at my apartment. It should still be there… I haven't been gone that long."

"We'll go by and collect your things some other time. For now, order."

There was another look of sadness in her eyes at my words when she realized she would lose that apartment for good. But she accepted it quickly then moved to the barista. "Can I get a white mocha, please? Ooh…and one of the blueberry muffins."

The woman looked at me next and spoke in English. "And for you?"

I spoke in French. "Just a black coffee." She took my money and gave me the change.

When I looked at Raven, she'd already taken a big bite of her muffin with a look on her face that implied it was the best thing she'd ever eaten. "Oh wow…" Her sorrow was quickly erased by the sugar rush. She ate the entire thing before her coffee was even ready.

We left minutes later and walked down the sidewalk and headed to the tower.

When we reached a wine bar, she stopped. "This is where we were…when the guys took us." She stopped at the window and looked inside then turned to an invisible car that was parked in her mind. "They were in this ugly brown car. I tried to warn my sister…but she was so stubborn."

"No. She was stupid." I started to walk again.

She joined me at the same pace.

"After everything you did for her, you'd think she'd listen."

"She's just… I don't know. Some guys were giving her attention, and it just messed with her head."

"You still make excuses for her when you know the truth."

She looked down at her coffee, where she'd left a lipstick mark. "I'll always make excuses for her."

I drank my coffee then looked ahead. "You said you intended to live here permanently?"

"Yeah, when I graduated."

"And do what?"

"I was hoping to be a professor."

"Why not go back to America?"

She shrugged. "Because I love it here. I came here to have my own identity apart from Melanie. But honestly, it's such a beautiful place. When I got here, I knew I would never leave. They could throw me out, and I would just keep coming back…"

"Did you have friends?"

"I did…"

"What did they say when you were back?"

"They were happy I was home. They believed my story. They were already in their next semester and I wasn't, but we still spent a lot of time together. When I disappeared again, I'm sure they went to the police and told them everything I had said. But that won't go anywhere."

No, it wouldn't. "How did your mother pass away?"

"An accident. She worked two jobs, so she was tired a lot. She fell asleep at the wheel…"

It was such a sad story that I didn't know what to say.

"Her name was Rose."

I turned to look at her, understanding the meaning.

"The horse reminded me of her…that's why I named her that. I know it sounds stupid, but I almost feel like my mother's spirit was in her, carrying me to safety, taking care of me one last time."

I didn't believe in shit like that, but I didn't say it. "It's not stupid."

"It's not?" she asked quietly.

"Not if it makes you feel better."

She stared at the tower for a long time, her coffee cup in the garbage because she'd finished it.

I stood beside her, letting her enjoy the sight for as long as she wanted. I got tired of treating her like a prisoner and wanted her to feel good again, to get some fresh air before we had to return to the camp.

"I'm getting hungry. We should head back." She turned her back to the structure and walked away.

I walked beside her. "You want to eat somewhere?"

She halted and looked at me in surprise. "Seriously?"

"Why not?"

"Because…do you eat out for lunch?"

"Why would I have an apartment here if I didn't?"

"I just…can't picture you going to a café for lunch, like a normal person."

I continued to move forward. "You can pick."

Her mind immediately kicked into overdrive. "Oh my god, there's this cute little place——"

"Sure."

"Really? This is, like, the best day of my life…in a long time."

I tossed my coffee into the bin that we passed.

We went to the café and got a table outside under the umbrellas. People passed on the sidewalk nearby, and the pots around us had red geraniums blooming in fullness. People spoke in French around us, all locals.

She held the menu right up to her face, like she couldn't decide what to get. "Jesus, I could eat everything…"

The waitress came over and addressed us in French. "What would you like?"

"A bottle of water for the table and two glasses of Bordeaux."

She walked away.

Raven lowered the menu. "What did you say?"

"Ordered some drinks. What do you want?"

"Uh…I don't know. What are you getting?"

"Steak and frites."

"Ooh…I think I'm going to get the ravioli."

When the waitress returned, I ordered for us both in French. She took the menus and left.

Raven looked around for a while, watching the people at nearby tables, the flowers that bloomed in the pots, the pedestrians on the sidewalk. When she'd taken it all in, she looked at me. Her gaze settled on mine, and she hardly blinked as she regarded me, her bubbly joy slowly simmering down into the intense expression she usually gave me. "I feel like I'm in a dream or something."

I grabbed the glass and took a drink.

"Just last week, we were sleeping on this tiny bed in the middle of nowhere—and now we're having lunch in Paris. I've seen those brown eyes look at me so many times, but never like this."

I held her stare, ignoring the world around us and just focusing on her.

She dropped her gaze and grabbed her wine. "I don't want to go back…" It was a whisper so quiet that I wasn't meant to hear it.

But I did.

We entered the apartment, the sunshine coming through the windows and filling the room with light from the beautiful afternoon. I intended to go upstairs and work on my laptop and just be alone.

But her hand grabbed my wrist.

I stilled at her touch but didn't turn around.

"Thank you…for today." Her fingers stayed on me, gently pulling me toward her so I would turn around.

I turned around and looked down at her, her hair curled in a pretty way, her eyes bright even though the sun wasn't shining on her face anymore. There was sincerity in her gaze, like taking her outside for the afternoon was equal to the other things I'd done for her. I couldn't bring myself to acknowledge her gratitude because it was a bit sickening that it was something she needed to be grateful for. I turned away again.

Her hand squeezed my wrist so I wouldn't go. "Do you forgive me?" Her voice turned desperate, like she hoped for something more now that we were back at the apartment, now that I hadn't been a complete ass to her.

I didn't turn around to face her completely.

She waited, her fingers still clamped onto my skin.

I didn't know the exact reason I'd taken her out that afternoon. It was an impulsive decision that I didn't make until I saw her sitting there looking out the window. Like all the other times I'd done something for her, there wasn't any thought put into it. It was just instinct. I pulled my hand away and headed to the stairs. "No."

FOURTEEN
STASIA

THE VALET TOOK MY CAR, AND THEN I ENTERED THE estate, joining the crowd of women in their fancy dresses and the men in their tuxedoes. A flute of champagne was handed to me, and I took it even though I didn't drink that piss.

I made small talk with people I didn't want to make small talk with.

These parties were the bane of my existence.

They just reminded me how corrupt the world really was.

The president invited us.

We donated money to his causes and his campaigns, and in turn, he looked the other way about our enterprise. We were even friends, if friendship was a real thing. After long and meaningless conversations about the weather, the changes to the Republic, and the immaculate estate that entertained us, I eventually found Fender.

With his arm around Melanie, he spoke to someone I didn't know, his hand holding a flute of champagne even though he hated it too.

Melanie was in a black cocktail dress that barely had a back or a front. She was the trophy that Fender wanted everyone to know he had. With heavy makeup, her curled hair pulled back to reveal her face, and her bare skin in all the places the dress didn't cover, she stood there with a diplomatic smile, being an accessory more valuable than a watch or a ring. She noticed me, and her fake smile quickly dropped when we made eye contact.

I came to her side and greeted her with a nod.

She looked slightly past me, as if she hoped her sister would be behind me. "You didn't bring her?"

"Why would I?" She was my prisoner, not my woman.

Fender finished his conversation before turning to me. "Stasia is looking for you."

I'd forgotten about her.

"Who's Stasia?" Melanie asked.

I didn't answer.

Neither did Fender.

"Have you come to a decision about Napoleon?" I asked, hoping he took my gut instinct seriously.

He nodded. "It's fine, Magnus."

I couldn't hide my annoyance. "It's not the right choice."

"It doesn't matter if it's the right choice or not." He quickly turned on me, raising his voice like he didn't care if anyone overheard. "It's my choice. Maybe I would value your input more if your decisions didn't cause me to lose my entire camp, nearly all of my workers, and some of my guards."

Melanie looked at the floor like she was the one on the guillotine instead of me.

Fender stared at me with a fiery gaze, like he dared me to respond.

"I'm just looking out for you—"

"If you wanted to look out for me, you would have let that cunt die the first time." He walked away and pulled Melanie with him.

I stared at the spot where he'd just been, looking at the wall now that he was gone. I brought the glass to my lips and took a drink even though it tasted like garbage. I just needed to get something down to wash away the bile flooding my mouth.

A hand grabbed me by the wrist and dragged me away.

My eyes moved to the brunette woman in front of me, pulling me down a hallway and into a deserted room full of vintage wine, an overflow because the cellar down below couldn't hold it all.

"What is it, Stasia?" I pulled my hand free once we were alone and looked down at her. Even in heels, she was still substantially shorter than me.

She had dark hair that was almost black, green eyes that were confident and playful, and full lips that were the perfect seal around my dick. She flipped her long hair over her shoulder. "*What is it, Stasia?*" she asked, mildly incredulous. "An odd way to greet the woman who lets you come in her mouth." She crossed her arms over her chest, wearing a red cocktail dress with a single strap over her shoulder, short to reveal her nice legs all the way to her thighs.

"I... This isn't the best time."

"Fender piss you off again?"

He always pissed me off. "Something like that."

A soft smile moved on to her lips as she came back toward me, her hands flattening against my chest so she could feel my hardness underneath. She crept closer, our noses touching, and then she kissed me, her hands sliding down to the front of my pants. With her full lips, she kissed me hard, pausing after the first embrace to savor the taste, and then she kissed me again, breathing deep like she liked it.

I kissed her back because it was muscle memory at this point.

Her hands undid my pants so she could have me. "I'm a little hurt that you've been here for a week and haven't called..."

When her hand moved underneath my boxers, I pulled away.

Both of her eyebrows rose in surprise. "What's gotten into you?"

I zipped up my fly and fastened the button. My thumb automatically went to my mouth to wipe away the lipstick she'd undoubtedly left there. My hands settled into my pockets next, and I kept my distance.

She crossed her arms over her chest and cocked her head as she regarded me. "Magnus?"

"I didn't call because I didn't want to." I stared her down, eyes burning with fire, my voice ringing with authority.

Her playfulness evaporated when she realized this was serious and not just a mood swing. Her lips fell into a frown, and the confidence left her gaze. "I don't understand…"

"There's nothing to understand. We were fucking—now we aren't."

"We've been fucking for months, so that's a bit abrupt, don't you think?"

I looked at the wine display on the wall. I didn't deny her just because I was in a bad mood, but that definitely made my reaction harsher. The second her lips were on mine, it felt weird, like she'd never kissed me before. I didn't like it. Felt a little sick, truth be told. She wanted me because I was rich, powerful, and good-looking. It was an investment, getting into my pants and then my heart so she could have everything that came with me. It made me angry…because she didn't know me at all. She didn't know who I really was. "Not really."

Her eyes narrowed farther. "A man only turns down sex with a beautiful woman for one reason…he's already getting sex from another beautiful woman."

That wasn't the case with me.

She waited for me to look at her.

I shifted my expression to her face.

"I thought you didn't commit."

"I don't. I've just lost interest, Stasia. Don't read too much into it."

She came closer to me, strutting as she moved across the hardwood floor, her heels tapping. "Men don't lose interest in women who look like me. So, the reason your dick is still in your pants is because it's loyal to someone else. Interesting. Who is she?"

I held her gaze and saw the jealousy, anger, and betrayal swirl in her eyes. I was the big catch she wanted to reel in, the man she wanted to take care of her, the man to buy her everything she wanted. And once her plan failed, she was furious. I turned away to leave. "No one." I never promised her anything. It was her mistake to assume she could be what Melanie was to my brother. "Like I said, you're reading too much into it."

FIFTEEN
FORGIVENESS

I HAD TO RETURN TO THE CAMP IN A FEW DAYS— with Raven.

I wasn't excited about it. I'd always hated going to the camp, but now I loathed it. The guards hated me, it was hot, and now I had to share what little space I had with the woman who betrayed me.

I'd be there for a month before I got to leave again.

I sat in the living room upstairs, drinking scotch while sitting in front of the TV, my mind slowly slipping away. I was in my sweatpants without a shirt, ready for bed but too lazy to actually get up and walk into my bedroom.

Out of the corner of my eye, I saw her figure emerge into the darkness. Her body was highlighted by the light of the TV, becoming brighter the farther she moved into the room. Then she stilled when she knew I saw her.

I sat up on the couch and looked directly at her. "I told you not to come up here."

"I wanted to talk to you." She moved in front of me, blocking the TV behind her.

"You can talk to me all you want—downstairs." I grabbed the remote and turned off the screen.

"I tried, but you just walk away—"

"Because I don't want to talk to you." I threw the remote down and got to my feet, leaving my glass of scotch on the table to be finished tomorrow morning. "I still don't want to talk to you."

She didn't move.

The longer I stared at her, the angrier I became. I didn't like her in my space. I didn't like her walking up here like she had every right to do whatever she wanted. Whenever I was kind to her, she pushed me for more.

"Do you really want to do this for the rest of our lives?"

I stared at her blankly.

"Because I don't."

The silence suddenly became louder, like a buzzing in my ears, but her words had so much weight... and I didn't understand them. "Do what?"

Her eyes changed, like she was surprised I didn't understand her riddles. "You need to forgive me, Magnus."

My body tensed all over.

"Let it go."

I took a breath, my nostrils burning as the air rushed out like hot smoke.

"The entire reason you feel this way about me is because I care about people. You saved me because I didn't deserve damnation. Going back and trying to liberate the women I left behind is completely in my character, so you weren't surprised. I'm sorry that it complicated your life, turned everyone against you, but let's not forget what the situation is here." She stepped closer to me. "You work at a camp that enslaves innocent people…and I'm an innocent person. To assume I wouldn't try my hardest to help those women is naïve. I stand by what I did, and I would do it again…and you respect me for it."

Flashbacks of that night came back to me, the smoke that rose into the nighttime sky, the screams from the women as they fled, the shouts of the guards as they tried to get to the fire extinguishers in one of the cabins that was already in flames.

"You need to forgive me, just as I've forgiven you."

"Forgiven *me*?" I whispered. "For what?"

"For being part of such a heinous operation."

"I didn't ask you to forgive me——"

"But I do. Because I see who you really are, Magnus. I know you're a good man who would never hurt anybody. You're just in a bad situation, for reasons I don't understand because you won't share them with me."

My hands moved to my hips, and I stared at her in my upstairs parlor, seeing the way her emotional eyes pierced into me as if she demanded something from me. "What do you want from me?"

There she stood in her little shorts and top, her hair pulled over one shoulder, looking at me like she never looked at anybody else. Her expression was full of sheathed affection, as if I were a person who meant the world to her. It was similar to the way she looked at her sister, but with more substance. "I want you to let it go. Because if this is going to be our lives for…the foreseeable future…I don't want it to be like this. I don't want my face pressed against the bedroom wall so we don't touch. I don't want you to snap at me every other second. I don't want you to lock me up because you think I'm going to run and get you killed. I want…*us*."

Maybe she had no idea I'd stood right outside the bedroom door and heard the entire conversation between her and her sister. I knew exactly what she wanted, but I hadn't given it to her because I was so furious at the way she'd betrayed me. But it was getting more difficult to hold on to my anger…especially when I believed every word she said. I fell right back into the place I used to be. "I'm not going to let you go, no matter what we are."

"I-I didn't expect you to." Her emotional voice broke with sincerity. "I know you can't."

My hands left my hips and hung at my sides. The lights along the walls were dimmed, so while the room was dark, they were still bright enough to cast a glow that distinguished her beautiful features, her high cheekbones, her kissable lips, her starlike eyes.

She came closer to me. "The last time we saw each other outside my apartment, it was so hard to watch you go. I've never felt pain like that...like I was losing a piece of me that would leave me crippled until I got it back." She looked up into my face, open like the centerfold of a book, letting me read every page in any order I wished. "The time I lived in Paris with Melanie, there was never anyone else...because none of them were ever right. I'd go on a date, see your face, and then go home...alone. I've never, in my life, had a connection like this with a man...and I miss you." She closed her eyes for a brief moment, steeling the emotions that flew out of her heart as well as her mouth. She looked at me again. "Please let it go...and be with me."

There was an initial jolt of anger because I wanted to hold on to my bitterness because it was all I'd had to survive these last few months. Sometimes it was easier to suffer the world angry than calm. It was a defense mechanism, and I was angry all the time, had always been angry...since I could remember. But this woman made me different, brought me back to an innocence I hadn't known in over a decade. She brought out the best in me, made me risk everything for the first time in my life, and she saw all my flaws but never forgot my good qualities.

Her hands reached to my arms, her fingers giving me an affectionate squeeze. "Let it go..."

The sound of her gentle voice released the tension in all the muscles of my body. She was the light that led out of my prison, and I slowly followed it until I reached the world outside...and it was beautiful.

My hands left my sides and moved around her waist, wrapping around her possessively, my skin burning when I finally got to touch her the way I wanted. They locked in place as I crushed her against me, my mouth finding hers and giving her the kiss I'd wanted to give every single time I looked at her lips. I pulled her tighter once I felt our bodies come together, my lips pausing to breathe.

Her hands slid up my arms until they stopped. She pulled away slightly and looked at my mouth, breathing hard even though I'd only kissed her once, an embrace that ended as quickly as it began.

Then she moved into me abruptly, her arms hooking around my neck to bring me back to her, anxious to kiss me again. "Magnus…"

The resentment and rage fell from my body as I kissed the lips I'd never stopped thinking about. They were full and so soft. I pulled her bottom lip into my mouth before I came back to her and gave her my tongue this time.

Hers greeted me with a sexy swipe, a hot breath.

My hand left her back and moved into her hair, digging underneath the curls, and I supported the back of her head as I crushed her lips to mine. My hand covered both her cheeks, and I dug my fingers into both sides, feeling her petite size in my grasp. The longer I touched her, the more the ice thawed in my extremities, and the passion leaped to life like a burning hearth that just had another log thrown on top.

But her desire was even greater than mine. She cupped my cheek as she kissed me, devouring my mouth like she needed to pack in every kiss to make up for all the ones we missed. Her fingers moved up the back of my neck and into my hair, pulling on the strands as she kept my mouth on hers.

Both of my hands moved to her ass, and I lifted her into me, our faces level so she could continue to kiss me as I carried her into my bedroom. Her hands were still in my hair, and she breathed against my mouth like she was the one doing all the lifting.

I got her on the edge of the bed and pulled down her shorts and panties in one swoop. She used to have hair between her legs, but now it was shaved clean. Hair or no hair, it didn't matter to me. But I liked seeing her in greater detail than before.

She pulled her tank top over her head and revealed her perky tits underneath. They were full, round, beautiful. Her nipples were hard as if she was cold, when this room was already an inferno.

My shirt was pulled over my head, and I watched her reaction to me, like she liked my ripped physique, liked the sight of my two hard pecs and the valleys and grooves of my abs. Her brown hair was behind her on the bed, and her lips were slightly parted as she breathed through her desire. Her pale cheeks were flushed with heat, and her eyes were so anxious, like she wanted this more than I did, like she wanted me inside her as soon as possible so she could finally feel better.

I dropped my sweatpants and boxers, my cock hard and more anxious than her hungry kisses. There was a slight drop in heat because I knew there would be a reaction to the change in my body.

But it was dark, and she was so deep in the moment she didn't notice.

I moved on top of her, pressing her into the mattress and the sheets that I'd left a mess when I'd woken up that morning. My heavy body pressed her beneath me, and I looked at her, seeing a woman who had never wanted me more.

Her legs wrapped around my waist, and she pulled on my hips, anxious to feel me, another second too long to wait. Her eyes were already watery with desire, her parted lips panting, and her hands dug deep into my hair as she pulled my face to hers, wanting my kiss to burn her mouth once again.

She moaned at my touch, like she hadn't already kissed me, like it was the first time all over again.

My hand directed my dick inside her, and I paused the second I felt her wetness cover my throbbing head. It smeared all around me, coated me like a bottle of lube had been poured right on me. I kept going, kept sinking, moving into her wetness and tightness, breathing harder the more I felt her, every nerve in my body firing off and giving me unspeakable pleasure.

She moaned loudly when I was inside her, her lips hesitating against mine like she needed time to feel this, to treasure how good I felt deep inside her. Her fingers left my hair and dragged down my back, giving me her sharp nails like she knew I was man enough to handle it.

I hadn't even started to thrust, and I already felt defeated.

She breathed against my mouth, labored and heavy, her hand holding on to the back of my neck. "Fuck…" She pressed her face into my cheek, her eyes closed, just breathing with me. Our bodies were connected, but nothing happened…and it was somehow the most passionate moment of our lives.

I started to move, holding myself on top of her so I could look into her beautiful face, see every reaction she gave, like I was the only man in the world she wanted. Our connection started almost instantaneously. When I'd thrown her out of that wagon and she talked back to me, I'd known she was different. And every moment after that…our connection grew. Now, we had this.

Whatever the fuck this was.

Her body squeezed my length right away, and the tears flowed from her eyes as she gave an animal-like moan. Her head rolled back, and she panted and groaned as if she were in pain, her nails clawing at my back as her hips automatically bucked against me. Just like the other times we were together, her climax was nearly immediate, like all she needed was me…and it sent her to the stars.

I thrust into her harder, moaning because it felt so good to get lost so deeply that I had no awareness of the outside world, of the weather or time. It was just us, two people free of the chains that bound us both, finding something good in each other.

Her hand moved to my ass, and she gripped it with her small fingers, pulling me deeper into her, wanting more of my length even though there was nowhere for it to go. Her head rolled back, and tears sprouted in her eyes, this time from pleasure and pain. "Yes…Magnus."

SIXTEEN
DISFIGUREMENT

THE INSTANT WE WERE DONE, I PULLED ON MY boxers to hide myself from her.

She lay there for a moment, her eyes closed like she was too tired to move. She lay in the moonlight coming from the window, her beautiful figure highlighted, her strong legs long and sexy. Her tight stomach had a scar from the knife she took, but her skin was still beautiful because it showed everything she had survived.

She had more scars than I did.

I pulled back the sheets from the head of the bed and got underneath.

She was at the foot of the bed, and she turned over to look at me. "That better not be it." She crawled up the bed, her ass in the air, her nice tits shaking as she came to me. She pulled back the sheets and lay beside me.

I'd come inside her three times. I couldn't do it again—at least, not right now.

She immediately snuggled against me, her arm banding over my chest, her leg hugging mine. She closed her eyes like she intended to sleep there.

I got out of bed then scooped my arms underneath her.

"What are you doing?"

"Taking you to bed."

"This is my bed." She moved away from my hold and shifted back.

I let her go and straightened.

She stared at me, visibly confused by the sudden change in atmosphere.

I turned to walk out.

"What are you doing?"

"Sleeping in another bedroom."

"What the hell, Magnus?" She came after me and grabbed my wrist so I would turn back to her.

I looked down at her hurt face. "I don't like to sleep with people."

"You sleep with me all the time."

"Only because I don't have another choice. But I really don't like it."

She released my wrist when she understood it wasn't personal. Naked, she crossed her arms over her chest, making her tits even perkier, the nipples hardening because she wasn't surrounded by my heat or the sheets. "You slept with me at my apartment."

"That was…different."

"Why?"

I stared.

"You said you would let it go."

"I did—"

"Not all the way. You trusted me then, and I need you to trust me now."

"You asked me to forgive you. Nothing about trust was ever mentioned."

Her eyes narrowed. "You do trust me."

"Not yet."

"You wouldn't have taken me out of there if you didn't. I could have just screamed and made a scene. You've left me alone with your laptop, and I could have gotten online and told everyone about the camp and asked them to trace my location. You know I would never compromise you, so stop acting like you think I would. Your life is my life—and I would never risk it."

I believed her when I shouldn't.

"I bluntly told you I was going to the police when you released me. You didn't care."

"I didn't think you were going to liberate the camp—"

"Then you underestimated me," she snapped. "I never told you I wouldn't do everything I could to destroy that camp. I didn't give my word and take it away. I'm giving you my word now—and that means something."

My body was still coated with sweat from the time we'd spent locked in the heat of passion. It was like a vacation, a moment away from reality. But now we were back to the real world.

"You aren't telling me something…"

I dropped my gaze slightly.

"Why won't you sleep with me?"

I kept my eyes averted, reliving a horrible night that was so vivid in my memory, it felt like it had happened yesterday.

She studied me, her hand gently moving to mine, like she could read the emotion in my eyes.

"I just…don't like being unconscious when other people are around."

"Why?"

"Because I'm afraid someone is going to shoot me in the back of the head." My eyes turned back to her.

She was motionless, her hand still holding mine, and she looked at me like she didn't know what to say. "That's very specific…"

"It is."

"Well, we both know that's not going to happen
with me—"

"I still don't like it—"

"We're going to go back to the camp and have to
sleep in that tiny bed together, so it's unavoidable.
You may as well get used to it, may as well embrace
it, because if someone really came in to harm you,
it would be two against one…not one against one."
She came closer to me, close enough for a kiss. "I'd
die for you, and you know that." Her arm moved
around my neck, and she brought our foreheads
together, making me give and receive affection that
I never had before. "Now, let's go to bed." She
kissed me before she pulled away, her hand giving
mine a gentle squeeze.

I hesitated, standing my ground.

Then she gave me a subtle smile, a comforting stare,
and another tug.

This time, I joined her.

When I woke up the next morning, she was gone.

I immediately stiffened in panic because I'd never set the alarm, and if she left hours ago and took the cash out of my wallet, it would take forever to find her. I sat upright in bed and felt my heart pound.

Then she stepped inside, carrying a mug of coffee. "Oh good, you're awake." She gave me that bright smile and affectionate gaze as she carried the coffee to the nightstand. Steam erupted from the surface, immediately filling my bedroom with the aromatic smells of freshly brewed coffee. "It's not hot chocolate with marshmallows, but I have a feeling you wouldn't like that anyway." Her hair and makeup were already done, so she'd been up for a while. She was in one of my t-shirts, which she must have taken out of my dresser, the one with a loaded revolver inside.

And she did nothing.

I sat up in bed, feeling the panic slowly circulate out of my blood as I returned to calm.

She sat at the edge of the bed and studied me. "Everything okay?"

I glanced at the coffee then held her gaze, seeing the innocence in her eyes. She had absolutely no idea all the thoughts that had just swirled through my head because escape was truly the last thing she thought about. "Bad dream."

Her eyes softened before she leaned in and pressed a palm to my chest and a kiss to my lips. "It's because I wasn't here to chase them away." She rubbed her nose against mine before she kissed me again.

I closed my eyes and felt that same rush of emotion enter my throat whenever she kissed me. It wasn't sexual, had never been sexual, even the first time I'd asked to be with her in her old cabin. It'd always been more than that, always raw and emotional, and that was why I wanted it again…and again.

She pulled away and left the bed. "I'll let you get to work…or whatever it is you do in the mornings."

Fender and I hadn't spoken since that party.

Just when I thought things were good between us, they weren't. I thought he'd forgiven me for my mistake, but in reality, he would never forgive me. He would always throw it in my face the instant I did something he didn't like.

It was like a permanent scar.

But perhaps that was fair...because I didn't regret it anymore.

I'd do it again.

I texted Fender. *I'm heading out tonight. Is there anything you need me to do before I leave?*

His response was immediate. *Your job.*

I sighed and set the phone on the table.

His message popped up again. *Or is that too difficult for you?*

I knew I should just let it go, but I couldn't. *Asshole, I'm just trying to protect you. But if you don't give a damn, I'll stop trying.*

If you wanted to protect me, you wouldn't have allowed some cunt to burn my fucking camp.

Different issue, Fender. Napoleon is bad news.

I'm in charge. Not you. So fuck off.

This time, I threw my phone at the wall.

Footsteps sounded a moment later as Raven came upstairs to investigate the noise. She stopped and looked at the phone on the floor against the wall and then at me on the couch. Instead of asking a million questions, she picked up the phone from the floor then sat beside me. She set the phone on my thigh.

I didn't touch it. I sat with my face propped against my closed knuckles, staring at the TV without really paying attention to what I was watching. I clenched my jaw then chewed the inside of my cheek, so angry but with no outlet to express it. Sometimes I wanted to beat the shit out of my brother.

She tucked her feet under her ass and propped up her body to look at me.

"I don't want to talk about it."

"I assumed."

I didn't look at her.

She scooted closer to me until we were side by side. When I didn't resist her, she rubbed her hand across my chest then pressed a kiss to my neck.

I didn't give a reaction, but I liked it.

Her hand moved underneath my shirt, and she came closer to me, rubbing the hard muscles of my core as her lips continued to kiss my neck, her small tongue gliding over the warm skin, making me breathe hard, making my dick stiffen in my jeans.

Her hand undid my jeans then dragged them down along with my boxers, so my cock came free.

I thought she was going to get on top of me.

But then she moved her head down.

I pulled her away from me then got to my feet, pulling up my jeans and my boxers to hide my disfigurement. I didn't want her to see it, but she would have to see it eventually. I didn't want to relive that moment, and I didn't want to hurt her either. I moved to the other couch and sat down.

She slowly sat up and stared at the side of my face since we were perpendicular to each other. She scooted to the edge of the couch and rested her hands on her knees. She was quiet, as if she didn't know what to do in this moment.

I didn't know what to do either. My arms rested on my knees, and I leaned forward, looking at the hardwood reflecting the sunlight coming through the window. "We're going back to the camp tonight."

She didn't protest. "But that's not what's wrong."

"I don't want to talk about what's wrong."

A long stretch of silence passed. I sat on one couch, and she sat on the other. Then she left her couch and came to mine, taking a seat beside me, like she somehow knew something was coming. She pressed a kiss to my neck then rested her chin on my shoulder while her hand moved to my thigh. She always sprinkled me with affection, and I fucking loved it. It felt so good to have a woman's touch like that, to have her devotion because I earned it.

"I have to tell you something." I kept my voice steady because that was the only way to have this conversation. Just get it over with. Put it out there then move past it. "I wouldn't share it with you... but you're going to find out anyway."

She pulled away slightly, but her hand remained on my thigh. "Okay..."

"I told you I was tortured after…" I kept my eyes on the floor, but I could see her movements in my peripheral vision.

Her breathing increased, and her fingers loosened against my jeans. Her energy changed, subtly panicky, like she wanted to run but there was nowhere to go.

I got to my feet, unfastened my jeans, and turned around. I could just tell her what happened, but she would see it at some point, and I'd rather just get it all over with now.

Now, she looked confused, like she had no idea what I was about to show her. She'd been with me last night, but it was too dark to notice anything, and we were both distracted by the moment.

Then I pushed my pants and boxers down.

My cock was soft, so it was easier to see the difference.

She spotted it instantly, her eyes watering like a dam had broken behind her gaze, and she covered her mouth to stifle the scream that wanted to burst from her lungs. Like it was too ghastly to confront, she dropped her chin and covered her face with both hands, her body suddenly heaving with the sobs that took her over. "No…" She broke down in front of me, overcome with so much pain that she couldn't process it all. "Oh my god…"

I pulled up my pants then stared at her, watching her grieve for me. Her heartbreak would have been revenge to me months ago, but now I just felt sick. Her pain was worse than the pain I'd actually had to endure when it happened.

I moved to the seat beside her, then wrapped my arm around her, comforting her the way I did after Alix had her half naked and bent over on the bed. This woman didn't shed a tear often, so when she did, it was real…it was horrific. I pulled her into me and rested my chin on the top of her head as I listened to her wail.

"I'm so sorry…"

I closed my eyes, hearing the ring of truth.

"I'm so…" She couldn't finish because she was overcome with tears.

I could relive the memory and feel the flood of hatred overwhelm me, but I didn't. I didn't hold on to the past. I didn't hold on to what she'd done to me. We'd taken cuts for each other, our bodies mosaics of scars because of everything we'd done to protect the other. That was when I realized there was no act more loyal than that, that we would literally do anything for each other...and that was beautiful. "I forgive you."

SEVENTEEN

GUARD DOG

SHE DIDN'T WANT TO LEAVE.

She took a long time to get ready, even though all she needed to do was put on her uniform. She didn't need to do her hair and makeup. There was no preparation at all, but she still took forever.

When I walked into her bedroom to hurry her up, I stopped and watched her.

She sat in front of the window, seeing the lights of the Eiffel Tower in the darkness. She stared without blinking, as if she were saying goodbye to the structure that acted as a monument to her heart.

I gave her a few minutes.

She must have known I was there because she said, "I don't want to go to the camp, but I don't want to leave this place more, if that makes sense."

It did. "We'll be back in a month."

"A month is a long time…"

"I know. I don't want to go back either."

She turned to look at me. "Then why do you?"

Even if I could, I'd never leave her there by herself. "Because I have to." I stepped away from the doorway because this conversation couldn't continue. "It's time to leave. Come on." I walked to the elevator and hit the button so the doors opened.

She joined me, her head slightly down, still depressed after I'd shown her my mutilation. Her eyes were puffy even though hours had passed, like she shed tears when she was in private because it continued to haunt her.

We got into the elevator and then the car and began the long journey back to the camp.

She was quiet for much of the drive, like she didn't feel like talking as much as I didn't feel like it. But hours later, she said, "What do you think will happen with the guards…since you took me away?"

"They'll be mad. But they're always mad at me."

"Will they try to hurt you?"

With one hand on the wheel, I kept my eyes on the road. "Probably. But I don't care."

She turned her head to look at me. "How do you not care?"

"Because they can't kill me."

"Because Fender is your brother?"

"No. Because every time they've tried, they failed."

"Every time they've tried—"

"Don't worry about me." I didn't want to continue this. "I'm more worried about you."

She looked out the window again.

"I'm going to give you one of my blades. If Alix or anyone else tries anything, kill them."

She turned back to me. "But then they'll know you gave it to me—"

"They should have assumed I would give you something in the first place. That's their fault." Alix was furious the day I left, and I wasn't sure when his next rotation was, so he'd probably be there when I got back. He might not try to kill me because that was clearly pointless to attempt, but he might hurt me more by going after her. I was afraid the rest of them would corner me and Alix would go after her alone…and finish what he started.

I'd rather die than let that happen.

"If I kill one of the guards, they'll kill me."

"No, they won't." Fender would be pissed off at me, but he was already pissed off at me, so I didn't care anymore. "Do what you've always done—everything you can to survive."

She slept through the rest of the drive and then woke up to ride horseback with me. We rode through the night with her arms around my waist, holding the bright flashlight so the horse could see where he was going.

We made it to the cabin at sunrise, and after locking up the horse in the stables, I escorted Raven to her post to continue her job like she'd never been gone. The guards were there, their faces hidden, but their gazes unmistakable.

I didn't give her any special treatment in public, so I turned away and walked off.

I went into the main cabin, collected all the data I'd missed, and got back to work.

None of the guards spoke to me.

It was like I never left.

When I went to my cabin, it was exactly as I left it. But I added another bolt to the inside to make sure no one could get through if she was in there alone and I was elsewhere. My time was split between catching up on everything I'd missed and fortifying the place to keep her safe. My obligation to her was even more intense than it had been before, and I quickly felt gripped by an identity crisis.

Because I really didn't know who I was anymore.

At the end of the workday, I escorted her back to the cabin and gave her dinner.

She must have been hungry because she sat on the floor in her work clothes and immediately started to eat.

"I'm going to be out for a while."

She turned to me and finished chewing her food. "Where are you going?"

"I've got a lot to catch up on."

"Okay. I'm really tired, so I think I'm just going to go to sleep." She turned back to her food. She hadn't been the same since I'd told her what happened to me. It'd been a day and a half, but since she hadn't had a full night of rest, it felt like the same day.

I came closer to her and withdrew the sheathed blade from my pocket. I'd taken it from the weapons room, but they wouldn't know it was missing. Even if they did, I'd deny it, and there would be no punishment. If they tattled to Fender, it would just annoy him because he had more important things to do with his time.

She stared at it for a moment before she took it.

"Keep it on you at all times when I'm not around. You remember how to hold it? Like I taught you?"

She nodded and slipped it into her pocket.

"When we have time, I'll teach you how to fight."

"I'd never win against someone like you or Alix. You're too big."

My eyes narrowed on her face. "Don't say that shit again."

She stilled at my words.

"The bigger fighter doesn't necessarily win. They'll underestimate you, and if you hit them where it counts, it'll give you enough time to run. I've never seen you give up, so don't start now. It's not the woman I know. It's not the woman I…" I cleared my throat. "Just don't act like that."

"I'm sorry. I just… It's been a hard day." She bowed her head and looked down at her food as she moved it around with her fork.

I knew she was sad to be back here and she was disturbed by what I'd told her that morning, so I gave her a free pass. Wordlessly, I left the cabin and locked the door behind me before I went back to work.

The product wasn't shipped out when I wasn't there because I was the only person Fender trusted not to steal. We timed my departures with large deliveries, so nothing had to leave the camp until I returned. That meant I searched every cabin belonging to the guards, along with the common areas. I took the dogs while the guards were in the clearing, letting the dogs sniff out every place since they were better searchers than I was.

I never found anything.

The guys were either loyal or smart.

After I did my checks, I went into the communal cabin.

The guys were gathered around the table playing poker.

They didn't acknowledge me.

I didn't acknowledge them.

I went into the weapons room and did my checks even though a blade was missing—that I'd taken.

I headed to the front door when I was done.

"Got your own little whore now?" Alix looked at his cards as he addressed me.

I didn't just walk off like I normally would. This time, I faced him, ready to gauge his mental state.

He placed his cards on the table and won the hand. "You know, I had my eye on her first, if your memory serves you right. She should be mine, not yours."

"I didn't choose her—she chose me."

He lifted his gaze and looked at me. "Because you bend over backward for her like a pussy."

"Because I do things for her, just like the rest of you do things for the prisoners you sleep with."

He pulled the chips he won toward himself. "Escape is not something we give to any prisoner."

"She's here, isn't she?" It would make my life much easier if Fender would let me remove her from the camp but keep her as a prisoner. Every time I brought her back here, it would ignite their fury again. But I understood why Fender couldn't cave...because he'd risk losing control of the entire camp.

"In your cabin, with a fucking guard dog."

I was her guard dog, and I'd protect her with my life. "Let this go, Alix. The only reason you want her is because you can't have her."

"Exactly." He grabbed the deck of cards and started to deal. "And there's nothing I can't have."

When I returned to the cabin later that night, she was asleep.

She was against the wall like nothing had changed, her body straight and taking up the least amount of room as possible. From underneath her pillow, the hilt of the blade poked out because she slept in just her underwear since it was much warmer there than in Paris.

I stared at her for a second before I looked at the laptop.

It was untouched.

It was hard for me to trust her because I wasn't a trusting person, but I knew she wouldn't betray me again. I needed to learn to trust the one person who really had my back…and that was Raven.

She was the only friend I had in the camp right now.

And since things were bad with my brother, she felt like the only friend I had in the world.

I showered then returned to the bedroom.

She was awake, lying on her back with heavy eyes, like she'd been stirred from sleep by my entrance.

There was no way to truly be quiet in such small accommodations, so it was inevitable. I pulled on a fresh pair of boxers then sat at my desk, looking through my email to make sure Fender hadn't sent anything over.

I felt her stare on my back. "I didn't mean to wake you."

"It's okay. How'd it go?"

I shut the laptop and didn't confide any details. "Fine." I left the chair and came to bed. It was a twin-size because the cabins were too small for full beds. Fender was the only one who had a bigger bed because he had the biggest cabin, even though he was almost never there.

I lay on my back and looked at the ceiling. I was tired because I hadn't slept in thirty-six hours. Coming back to the camp was always difficult because we had to arrive in the evenings so no one would follow us.

She came close to me, her arm hooking over my stomach, her face on my shoulder.

I didn't cuddle, but I didn't ask her to move. I assumed she wanted to cuddle after sex because that was just how women were, but she cuddled now even though we were both too tired…and depressed.

She pressed a kiss to my shoulder then closed her eyes.

My hand moved over hers on my stomach…and I fell asleep.

EIGHTEEN
BULLET TO THE SKULL

A WEEK HAD PASSED.

Three more to go.

I'd never counted down my time to freedom in the past, but now that I had something to look forward to, I wanted time to rush by in a matter of seconds as opposed to weeks. I didn't want to have to look over my shoulder all the time.

"Why don't you kill him?" Raven leaned against the wall on the bed with her head turned to the TV. She was snacking on nuts, not because she was hungry, but bored.

I sat at the desk with my back to her, working on my laptop. We still didn't talk much, even though we were confined together in the small space, because there was nothing to say. We were both waiting for time to pass so we could go back to Paris…and have a somewhat normal life. "It'd piss off Fender."

"You could just replace him with someone else."

"Not really. It's hard to get guards we trust. We can't hire just anybody."

She turned quiet, her teeth cracking the nuts in her mouth.

Alix and the guys hadn't tried anything, but I didn't drop my guard. I knew it was only a matter of time.

"What if you killed him outside the camp?"

My eyes froze on the words I was reading.

"When he rotates out, you could kill him, and no one would suspect you."

I leaned back against the chair because it wasn't the worst idea.

"Where does he live?"

"Nice."

She continued to eat the nuts. "What do you think?"

It would fix my problems, except it would create new ones. "Fender would want to investigate who killed him, and if it had anything to do with the presence of this camp. It would worry him, and I'd have to lie to him and mislead him…"

"So?"

"I won't lie to him." I wouldn't put him on a false trail and waste his time. I wouldn't make him feel insecure about this camp when there was no need to.

It was quiet, but the energy in the room had changed.

She spoke again. "Why are you so loyal to him?"

"Because he's my brother."

"If my sister were a murderer, I wouldn't be loyal to her."

"I doubt that."

"If she was hurting innocent people, damn right. Does he have something on you?"

This conversation was going in a direction I didn't want to take. "What are you watching?"

She paused. "Did you seriously just try to change the subject?"

"Yes." I raised my voice slightly. "Because I don't want to talk about this." I shut my laptop.

"Now—or ever?"

I stared at the wall, my thoughts turning dark. "Ever...preferably."

We became domestic partners who developed a routine.

She showered after work, and I showered in the evenings.

Sometimes we ate dinner together, but most of the time, we didn't.

In the evenings, she watched TV, and I worked on my laptop.

She didn't ask me questions I didn't want to answer.

She hadn't initiated sex, and neither had I.

My attraction to her was undeniable, but being in this place curbed my arousal. I suspected her abrupt change in desire was a result of my mutilation. It made her sick to her stomach, and she couldn't look at it again, not because of the scars or the appearance, but because it was directly her fault.

I didn't take it personally.

I got out of the shower that night then walked naked into the bedroom to grab a pair of boxers from the drawer. Another week had passed, but we still had two more weeks to go. I didn't hide my nakedness from her. She could look away if that was what she wanted. I turned to the bed when I was clothed.

She sat up against the wall, wearing one of my t-shirts that fit her loosely. The deep look in her eyes suggested she had something to stay.

I stood next to the bed, waiting for her to speak her mind.

"It's not that I don't want you. It's not that I think less of you. I just…feel so terrible every time I think about it." Tears welled up in her eyes instantly, and she sniffled then wiped them away before they could fall. "It's like this wall that I can't climb because I know when I see it, I'll…think about what happened." She took a deep breath then stilled her emotional response, getting herself under control.

I continued to stand there, to watch her process all the ways she felt about it. "There's no pressure—if that's what you're worried about."

"There is pressure…because I miss you." She spoke about me like it was an unstoppable need, like I was water to her throat, air to her lungs. "I've wanted you since I've had you. I've wanted you since my apartment. I've always wanted you…"

Women had seduced me, had turned me on with the things they were willing to do to earn my attention, but a woman had never talked about me like her desire was such an intricate part of who she was. It was a need that satisfied other parts of her body, parts I didn't even touch. "Then have me." She chased away all the stress on my shoulders, made me feel like we were in my apartment in Paris, like we weren't even part of this world anymore. My cock was hard in my boxers for the first time in weeks, and I'd never wanted to bed her more.

She breathed a little harder as she looked at me then gave a slight nod.

I dropped my boxers and let my hard cock come out.

This time, she looked at it, but she didn't look at it with tears. She looked at it like I was just as whole as I'd been before.

"I would do it all over again."

Her eyes lifted up and looked at me, emotion returning to her gaze.

I moved on to the bed then grabbed her ankles to drag her down until she was horizontal. The bed was too small for us to be in another position except parallel to the side of the bed, so I repositioned her underneath me then pulled her panties down her long legs. She now used my razor to shave, so she was always groomed and ready for me, even though I'd desire her the same even if she wasn't.

She pulled her shirt over her head then widened her legs for me before she guided me on top of her. Her hand moved to my length, and she touched me that way for the first time, guiding my head inside her as she breathed at my entrance, her eyes on me. Then she grabbed my hips and pulled me inside her as much as she could take, her legs wrapping around my waist, a deep moan coming from her throat. "Yes…"

I walked in the door then removed the long-sleeved shirt and the cloak, eager to get it off because it was hot outside, even in the dark. I tossed it on the floor then got into the shower so I could let the cold water cool me off.

Whenever I returned to the cabin after a long day, I didn't want to talk.

Not even to Raven.

I showered and sat at the desk to drink my scotch and try to forget all the bullshit from the day.

Raven seemed to understand that without my having to explain it because she rarely spoke to me until several hours had passed. She either read a book in silence or watched TV, usually in one of my t-shirts while she leaned against the wall.

I closed my laptop then drank the rest of the scotch in my glass.

She spoke when my need for solitude was over. "Who did that to you?"

I stilled at the question, not expecting it. After we'd talked about it last week, we'd had sex every night before we went to sleep, like a couple. It was the highlight of my day, to get lost in her and forget about our miserable lives, then go straight to sleep. I had unimaginable wealth because of this operation, but I realized that didn't bring me happiness, now that I had her. I couldn't spend it on her. I couldn't give her a life she deserved. It was meaningless at this point.

I turned in the chair so I could look at her.

"It was *him*…wasn't it?"

I nodded.

Instead of tearing up, she looked angry. "Who the fuck does that to their own brother?"

"He had to punish me."

"Don't defend him. What he did was unacceptable."

"My crimes were severe. He didn't have a choice. My punishment should have been death, so this was the only way to keep me alive. If he didn't give the men the satisfaction they wanted, he would have lost control of the guards."

She shook her head, looking at me incredulously. "How can you possibly say that?"

I looked away. "You wouldn't understand…"

"Why are you so loyal to that monster?"

"It's not any different from whipping you to keep you alive—"

"Fuck off, it's totally different." She got so angry that her face turned beet red and spit flew out of her mouth.

"Keep your voice down—"

"No." Emotion cracked in her voice. "Why do you put up with him, Magnus? Why don't you stop him from doing all these heinous things? Why don't you just kill him?"

I turned back to her slowly because the suggestion was outrageous. "He's my brother—"

"He hangs innocent women—"

"Not he, himself—"

"Doesn't fucking matter. He's just as guilty."

I stared at her. "Then I'm just as guilty."

Her face tightened into a look of pain. "You're nothing like him." She breathed through the emotion making her chest rise and fall at a quicker pace. "Don't say that again. You would never do any of this shit if it were up to you. You've asked him to stop. You saved me. Don't compare yourself to that fucking psychopath." Angry tears came from the corners of her eyes. "Why do you allow this to happen? Why do you do nothing? Why do you continue to work here?"

I stared at the TV.

"Magnus… Answer me."

I tilted my chin to the floor. "You wouldn't understand…"

"Try me."

I held my silence.

"Tell me…"

"I continue to work here because I owe him."

"Owe him for what?"

I inhaled a deep breath. "For saving my life."

"You shouldn't have to owe him for that. Any brother would—"

"Shut up." I rose to my feet and regarded her. "You want me to tell you or not?"

She pulled her knees to her chest and shut her mouth tightly, like she needed to clench her jaw not to speak.

I looked away for a moment, reliving the memory, feeling the raindrops against my fingertips when my hands hit the concrete. I remembered how hard my body worked to sprint to safety. I remembered my brother's voice as he told me to run. I wouldn't have believed the story if I hadn't seen him in the flesh… standing on the porch with his gun aimed at our backs. "When I was fifteen, I was asleep in my house…"

Her eyes softened when she realized how far back this story went.

"My sister's room was across the hall, my parents' bedroom at the far end. My eldest brother's room was next to mine. I was dead asleep, drugged so I couldn't hear anything. Fender was supposed to be home before curfew, but he didn't make it on time. When he came into the house, he tried to sneak into his room, but then he heard a muffled gunshot. Assuming there was a burglar in the house, he grabbed a knife and went to my mom's room to wake her…but she'd been shot in the head."

She inhaled a deep breath, quieting her gasp so she wouldn't interrupt me.

"When he went to my sister's…she had the same fate." I could picture it all without actually having seen it with my own eyes. I still remembered the layout of that house vividly, knew how the house looked at that time of night, the lights from the city coming through the windows to light up the hall-way. "The gunman went into our brother's room, and Fender knew there was nothing he could do. The gun went off. He came to my room…and I was the only one still alive."

Tears fell down her cheeks as she pictured it in her head, mourning people who'd been dead for nearly fifteen years.

"I was drugged, so I couldn't get up. So, Fender picked me up and carried me down the stairs. He didn't make it to the door before the gunman came after him. He raised his gun and fired, but Fender got me out of the house without taking a bullet. We were young at the time and not as strong as we are now, so he dropped me on the stairs. It jolted me awake. I didn't have time to process what was happening. Fender told me to run, so I did...and we sprinted for our lives, gunshots firing behind us."

She covered her mouth with both hands to muffle her words. "Dear god..."

"Fender saved my life...and he's all I have now." I hoped that would be enough to help her understand the connection we shared, why I did nothing even though I didn't agree with the shit he did.

"Did you ever find out who did it?" She wiped at her tears, but they just kept coming.

I nodded. "My father."

She stilled in horror, like the information was too sickening to process, like she couldn't allow the words to enter her mind because they were so wrong. Her hands moved over her mouth again, and she cried quietly.

It was too hard to look at her, so I turned away. "Shit like that leaves a permanent mark that never goes away. I didn't have to see it with my own eyes, but he did. He had to discover my mother's body, my sister's, listen to the bullet leave the barrel as it killed my brother...and that's why he is the way he is. It's no justification for his actions, I understand that, but...that's why. I have more humanity because I didn't have to witness it myself, didn't have to experience that firsthand. His descriptions are my memories. It's like looking at the sun on the TV. It's not the real thing, so it doesn't do physical harm to your eyes like it would if you looked at it directly." I stared at the TV for a moment longer before I turned back to her. "I don't condone his decisions, I don't condone this camp, but he's all I have. I've tried to talk him out of it many times, but he doesn't listen. And I'm obligated to work here... because of what he risked to save me from our father. We are bound by this event forever. I don't expect you to understand that because you have no idea how it feels, but I will never move against my brother because of it. I just...can't. If I kill him, I'm no different from our father."

We didn't talk much for the next few days.

She still wanted me every night as if nothing had changed. The passion was at the same intensity, but she did hold me tighter when she slept afterward, practically sleeping on top of me even though it was too warm for that.

I expected more questions about it, but she seemed so upset by the story that she needed time to get past the initial trauma before she could talk about it, like it had happened to her.

I lay in bed beside her, half of her body on top of mine while we reclined under the sheets naked, her bare tits against my body because I'd just been on top of her minutes ago. But I could tell she wasn't ready for sleep because her breathing hadn't changed. I usually waited until she was under first before I allowed myself to drift off.

"Can I ask you something?" Her voice broke the silence, lacking her usual confidence.

I already knew what she wanted to ask about. "Yes."

She turned quiet for a while, as if she didn't want to ask the question anymore. "Do you know why he did it?"

"Money."

That wasn't sufficient for her, so she asked for more. "What do you mean?"

"My father was a count. I come from a noble line."

She stilled before propping herself up on one elbow to look down at me, like she couldn't believe what I'd confessed. Her eyes shifted back and forth as she looked into mine, having even more questions now. "That's why you have the chateau, why the butler calls Fender his Highness… You're a count."

"Fender is. I'm not."

Her eyebrows rose.

"He's the eldest sibling, so the title goes to him. But it was just a title at one point because my father pissed away all our money. Rather than confess his crimes and live with the shame, he decided to kill all of us."

"Jesus…"

"Over money." It still sounded ridiculous, after all this time. "When Fender and I ran from the house that night, we had to start over from nothing. We didn't go to the police because we knew they would just hand us back to him…and he'd finish the job. We survived on the streets and worked for money any way we could get it. It was the beginning of our criminal careers. This camp was born from that nearly a decade ago. When I told Fender we were being inhumane, his response was always, 'the world is inhumane,' and carried on." I looked at her as she leaned over me, her long hair on my chest.

"What happened to him?" She looked down into my face, her hand on my chest as she tried to comfort me.

It was a long time ago, and I didn't need to be comforted.

"We killed him."

She had no reaction, as if she expected me to say that.

"When we had enough power, we hunted him down—and shot him in the back of the head." Fender was the one who'd pulled the trigger, but I wouldn't have hesitated to do the same. "He went into hiding because he was too much of a coward to finish himself off…like the rest of us. We eventually reclaimed our noble titles and funded our family name with all the money we'd earned doing what we do. Fender didn't want the chateau, so he gave it to me."

Her fingers gently rubbed into my chest as she kept her gaze on me. Then she dropped it, watching her fingers move across my chest, her eyes carrying the grief that had been on my shoulders for many years. "I'm so sorry…about all of it."

When people said something like that in response to your trauma, it was usually just a common phrase that needed to be stated so they wouldn't seem rude. But I knew she meant it.

"I can't even imagine…"

When we'd found my father and finished the job, it hadn't given me any satisfaction. He was weak and scared, begging for his life like a blubbering idiot. He'd drugged everyone in the house so he could kill them in their sleep. He didn't even look them in the eye like a man. He was so fucking despicable. It was unbelievable that someone so pathetic had claimed the lives of people I loved. He took my family

away…my life away. What kind of men would
Fender and I be today if none of that had
happened? "Don't ask me again to kill my brother
because I won't. And I hope now you understand
why I won't."

NINETEEN

FENDER

I'D NEVER TOLD ANYONE MY FAMILY SECRET BEFORE.

Aristocrats and socialites knew because the history of our noble line was of great interest to them. Our family was brought into shame after losing all our assets, but Fender and I returned them and reclaimed what was rightfully ours. But I never told the women I was seeing, and I imagined Fender didn't either.

I told Raven because I had to.

She would never understand my situation otherwise.

As a young man without the muscle definition he possessed today, he carried me from my bed and strained his body to get me out—and could have lost his life in the process. But he saved me from a senseless death.

I'd always feel indebted to him.

But there was also this unspeakable connection between us, two survivors who were permanently angry, permanently sorrowful. No one else in the world would understand us except the other. I didn't agree with a lot of things he did, and he took almost everything too far, but he was the one person immune to my acts of vengeance.

Once we got our hands on some money, he hit the weights and bulked up into the beast he was today. His physique was a part of his defense, to know that he'd always be strong enough to carry me—even though that would never happen again. He was built like an ox, with muscles so thick that if someone stabbed him, the blade would never reach his organs.

I had an athletic build, all muscle and no fat, but I was definitely on the leaner side. I was just too active to be that bulky.

There were only a few days left before we returned to Paris. I was eager to get Raven out of there, but it also seemed as though Alix had let it go. He would have done something by now, otherwise.

She and I didn't talk about Fender or the murders of my family again. Everything that needed to be said had been said, and we went back to our quiet, domesticated life. There were a lot of things I liked about Raven, but her intuition was one of the qualities I valued most. She could read my moods without asking me a single question. She knew how to be what I needed her to be at any given time. She also didn't need a conversation to be entertained. She was perfectly comfortable just being with me, watching TV in silence, running her fingers down my chest as she lay close to me on the bed made for one.

All the women in the outside world were weak and superficial.

Raven was so much deeper.

I didn't spend all my free time in the cabin because I didn't want to piss off the guards. If they knew I was slacking, they would know exactly why, and it would be another excuse for retribution. So, I made a point to show my face as much as possible.

I stepped into the communal cabin to do my evening checks, and the guys were at the table. Every seat was filled—but Alix wasn't there. I loathed bumping into him, which was inevitable because we were required in the same area multiple times of day, so any opportunity not to look at his piece-of-shit face was a good one.

I went into the weapons room and did my checks, even though the only prisoner there who would have the balls to take anything already had a knife in her pocket and no reason to steal. The guards didn't have much of a reason either, but it was part of the routine, so I did it.

I'd just shut one of the drawers and locked it when I heard a distant scream.

I stilled, my ears straining to hear it again. It was faint, like it was far away or just muffled inside the bedroom of a cabin. My heart was steady, and it was impossible to get a spike in my pulse because I was always in a state of eternal calm, but that scream sent a tremor of fear down my spine.

I stopped what I was doing and immediately left the room to get to the front door.

The scream was louder. "Let me go!"

It was her. I sprinted to the door.

"Now!" Eric jumped on me and slammed me into the wall.

My body hit and bounced back like I was made of rubber instead of muscle. Nathan grabbed me next, Eric jumping on my back.

I twisted and threw them off, still moving toward the door because nothing was going to stop me from getting to her. "I will fucking kill you!"

Eric yanked me down, Nathan kicked my feet from underneath me, and then another guard was on top of me, pinning me to the hardwood with six hundred pounds from their body weights. Nathan pressed his knee into my back while pinning down my arms.

Her voice came loud, full of terror, full of tears. "*Magnus!*"

"Get the fuck off me! I swear to fucking god, I will kill all of you!" I pushed as hard as I could, tried to wiggle free, but it was no use. I couldn't fight the weight of three men with my hands tied behind my back. I breathed hard, spit dripping to the floor because I was so furious that I practically frothed at the mouth. Every muscle in my body burned because I continued to fight against a weight I could never conquer. The pain was excruciating, not their restraints, but having to listen to her scream, beg for me to help her, and there was nothing I could do about it. "Please…please let me go."

She screamed again. "Please don't!"

My eyes burned with a sheen of angry tears. "Eric, come on… Nathan…" I begged without shame, abandoned my pride because all I cared about was the woman I'd promised I would protect. I should have killed Alix. I should have done something instead of looking the other way. "Please…"

Then the screams abruptly stopped.

I breathed against the floor, blinking my eyes so the tears dripped to the floor along with the stream of saliva that fell from my mouth with my screams. "Let me up. Now." Their hold seemed to slacken, so I tried to jerk free, but it didn't work.

They all stared at each other then at the door.

Then a voice sounded, a voice I'd recognize anywhere, a voice I remembered in my greatest memories and some of my worst. "Let her go."

I started to breathe hard again, imagining the scene outside. Fender must have entered the camp on his horse with his guards at that moment, witnessing whatever the fuck Alix was doing to her.

The guys stopped holding me down because they recognized his voice too.

I pushed to my feet then tumbled forward slightly, my legs carrying me quicker than my body could allow. Revenge wasn't on my mind at the moment because all I cared about was the woman screaming my name. I pushed through the front door and took the stairs to the ground. It was nighttime, but the lights lit up the horrific scene in front of me.

Raven was on her knees on the ground, completely naked.

Alix was standing behind her with a knife in his grasp, like he'd held it to her throat just seconds ago.

Raven covered her chest with her folded arms and kept her gaze averted.

Fender stood there in black jeans, boots, and a black t-shirt. His guards were positioned behind him, holding the reins to his horse so she wouldn't run off until she was put in the stables. Fender faced Alix directly, staring down at him with one of those stoic gazes that could mean anything.

Alix just stood there, breathing hard, still as a statue.

I strode across the ground and headed right for Raven, pulling off my shirt so I could cover her with it.

Fender didn't look at me when I approached. His eyes were on Alix. "This woman doesn't belong to you—and you know that."

Alix was stupid enough to argue. "She's a prisoner—"

"Don't. Speak."

Alix inhaled a deep breath, a little timid in Fender's presence.

"She belongs to Magnus." Fender pulled a blade from his pocket and placed the tip right against Alix's heart, the point digging into the fabric of his shirt. "Touch her again, and I will not hesitate to slam this deep into your heart and make it stop."

Alix didn't even breathe.

I made it to Raven and pulled the shirt over her body.

The look she gave me…was indescribable. She looked at me like I was a hero, when I wasn't the one who saved her. She pulled the shirt to her thighs and clutched the fabric like it was a bulletproof vest. Silent tears still dripped down her cheeks.

Unable to resist my natural instincts, I cupped her face and brushed her tears away with the pads of my thumbs. I wanted to do more, to kiss her, to hold her, but I couldn't do that right now. I got to my feet then extended my hand to her.

She stared at it for a moment, her eyes watery but a slight smile coming through, and then she took it.

I pulled her to her feet.

Fender continued his showdown with Alix. "Magnus was punished for his crimes. He's increased shipments to distributors, lost his own pay to make up for losses, rebuilt this camp, and has atoned for those sins. If you can't let your need for revenge die, then perhaps you need to die."

Alix kept a straight face, but it was obvious he was scared, judging by the way he didn't have strength in his gaze anymore. There was no sinister smile, no confidence in his posture. His shoulders sagged, like he wanted to disappear.

Fender finally turned to look at me, to study my face. He must have seen the redness of my skin, the terror in my eyes, and deduced exactly what had happened. He turned back to Alix. "This has been going on a while, hasn't it?"

I knew Fender was talking to me.

When I didn't say anything, he turned to me again.

I kept my mouth shut.

Alix looked at me, like he knew I would throw him under the bus.

But I didn't.

Fender turned back to Alix. "He's not a snitch. Looks like it's your lucky day, Alix." He put his knife in his pocket. "I won't pretend to understand my brother's fascination with this unremarkable cunt, but as long as she is his, she's off-limits. Do you understand?"

Alix nodded. "Yes, sir."

"The only reason I won't kill you is because Magnus stirred unrest in this camp. But you're even now. Cross my brother again, and I won't hesitate to kill you." He turned behind him to see the guards on the porch of the cabin. "All of you." He stepped away from Alix and looked at me. He pretended Raven didn't exist, even though he'd just saved her from a kind of cruelty she would never recover from, and nodded in the direction of his cabin. Then he walked away.

Alix immediately walked off, likely afraid Fender would change his mind if he looked at him again. The guys went back into the cabin. I turned to Raven. "Go to the cabin. I'll meet you there."

Her disappointment was obvious, like she didn't need a cabin, but me. "There's no door…" Her eyes were still wet from her tears, cheeks red and puffy, and her fingers immediately reached out to my stomach because she wanted me to hold her.

There was nothing I wanted to do more. "No one will bother you. Wait for me there."

Fender stopped walking and turned around. "Magnus."

I wanted to cup her face and kiss her, but my brother was far more generous than I expected him to be, and kissing the woman who had destroyed his camp and humiliated us was not the smartest move. "I'll be there as soon as I can." I turned around and joined Fender, not turning back to look at her again because it was too hard. If I did…I wouldn't be able to leave. I joined his side as we walked to his cabin.

Fender didn't speak.

I didn't either.

He preferred to speak in his cabin away from the ears of the guards. He didn't trust anyone except me, and he treated everyone like they had a knife in their pocket aimed at his back…except when a pile of money was on the table.

Everything had happened so fast, I didn't know how to process it. I was held down, helpless, and if Fender hadn't made his surprise visit at that moment…I wouldn't have saved her. Not only did he show up, but he did something about what was happening, which was a great surprise. He hated Raven and couldn't care less about her existence.

We were silent as we walked into the cabin.

Fender went into his bedroom immediately to change out of the clothes he'd worn while riding horseback.

I poured two glasses of scotch and sat on the couch across from his usual seating place.

The door opened, and one of the guards delivered his dinner. He left quickly and didn't speak a word.

Fender returned to the room in just his sweatpants. He took a seat across from me and went for the scotch first. He took a long drink like it was water instead of hard liquor then set it down, wiping his mouth with his thumb afterward. Then he stared at me.

We hadn't spoken since that heavy conversation through text message. He was livid with me, telling the guards that my sins were forgotten when he'd never forgotten them. I held his gaze and stared back. "Thank you."

He had no reaction to my gratitude.

"I know you probably did it for Melanie, but——"

"No." He shook his head. "I did it for you."

I inhaled a deep breath as I stared at my only relation in the world. There were no aunts, uncles, or cousins in different places around the globe. It was just him and me, and seeing those identical brown eyes made me feel less alone in this bleak world. "Then I appreciate it even more."

"How long has this been going on?"

I shrugged in response. "You can't expect them not to hate me…after what I did."

"That didn't answer my question."

"Like you said, I'm not a snitch."

He grabbed the bottle and refilled his glass.

"I earned their respect by not getting special treatment from you. I don't want that to change now."

"But was this today enough to return to normalcy?" He took a drink, his eyes looking at me over the rim.

"Hopefully."

He set down the glass. "Because I will kill him, Magnus. I don't care how irreplaceable these guards are."

This side of him was shown so infrequently that I forgot the last time it happened. He did appalling things, but he was more than that, and I hoped Raven would realize that after what had happened this evening. "I have an idea…"

He nodded then cut into his steak and placed a large bite in his mouth.

"You didn't bring Melanie."

He shook his head as he chewed.

"Everything alright?"

"Just needed some space." He cut into his meat again and took another bite.

I didn't ask any more questions about her. "I wasn't expecting you."

"That was the point."

"I thought you trusted me."

"You aren't the one I'm worried about." He stabbed his fork into his potatoes and shoved the bite into his mouth, chewing the mouthful, bare-chested in front of me.

I watched him eat and let the silence continue.

"You leave in a few days."

"Yes."

"I'm having an event. Napoleon will be there."

I held my tongue this time.

His eyes were down, but he felt my mood. "Feel him out again."

"I doubt my impression will change."

"It won't if you continue to be arrogant."

"I'm not arrogant. Sometimes you can't see straight when it comes to money."

"And you're less greedy?" He lifted his gaze, still eating.

"Just more level-headed."

He cut into his steak and put another piece in his mouth, along with a stalk of asparagus. "We'll see how he conducts himself."

"Black tie?"

"Always."

"I want to bring Raven."

A pause ensued as he took a few more bites of his meal, his eyes trained on me. "I heard Stasia is old news."

"Where did you hear that?"

"Does it matter?"

I drank from my scotch.

"Beauty is in the eye of the beholder, but Raven doesn't hold a candle to Stasia, so I have to ask… what's wrong with your dick?"

Nothing. It'd never been better. "I don't think Melanie is as remarkable as you claim."

He grinned slightly, like he didn't believe me.

"We'll just have to agree to disagree."

He ate again. "I don't think prisoners go to fancy parties."

"Melanie would be happy to see her."

He gave a slight nod. "True."

I could go alone, but I'd rather bring her along, give her a chance to talk to Melanie.

"Do whatever you want."

I looked into my glass before I took a drink and listened to him finish his dinner. I waited until he was completely done, full and comfortable, before I said something I wouldn't have dared to say before. "I will pay for Raven…if you let her go."

He was about to grab his drink, but my words made him pull back his hand, made him sit forward with his hands together between his thighs. He stared me down with that stony face, like a slab of concrete that didn't have a story to tell. "No."

"I will pay you whatever you want——"

"No."

"She would still be a prisoner, but she would be my prisoner. When I'm here, she'll stay in my home until I return."

He rubbed his palms together as he studied me. "What part of no don't you understand?"

I kept my anger in check so my previous gratitude wouldn't be forgotten. He had already done more for me than he should. He should have killed me for releasing Raven in the first place, but he didn't. He should have denied my request to take her with me every time I left the camp, but he didn't. He should have let Alix do whatever he wanted and continued on his way…but he didn't.

"I can't let her go, Magnus. Not after what she did. I've been lenient with her because she pleases you, but her freedom is something I will never allow. Her punishment is to work in this camp until she dies. She must fulfill her debt. You said you don't want the guards to see special treatment, but if I let her go—after she killed their comrades—that would be the biggest display of special treatment ever seen. And more importantly, I don't want to let her leave. I want her to serve her punishment for what she did to me. She wormed her way into my brother's bed and turned him soft. Not only did she spite my authority by leaving, but she had the nerve to come back and burn this place…this place that I built with my bare hands. If she wanted to be free, she shouldn't have returned. But she did return, and now she'll never leave. She made her decision—she has to live with it."

The door was on the ground because Alix had chopped it down with a fucking ax.

There were holes from the blade where he'd chopped it free, shards of wood protruding. I couldn't return it to the hinges because it would serve no purpose. When I looked through the open doorway, I saw her sitting on the bed, still in my shirt, her knees to her chest and her eyes still afraid.

I stepped inside and approached the bed.

The second she looked at me, her expression changed, like she'd never been so happy to see me.

I moved to the bed beside her and leaned against the wall.

She moved into my side and cuddled close, her arm curving around my neck so she could bury her face in my shoulder.

My arm circled her waist, and I brought her close to me, holding her against me, my chin on top of her head, feeling her chest rise and fall from the deep breaths she took. I could feel the tremors of her body, feel the invisible scars that added another layer over her heart. "It's over," I whispered. "And it'll never happen again."

She nodded against my body like she believed me. "What did they do to you?" She knew the only reason I hadn't been there to save her was because something had held me back…and that unflinching faith meant the world to me.

"Three guys held me down in the cabin. All I could do was lie there and listen to you scream." It was the first time I'd felt raw fear since I was young. The last time was when I sprinted down the wet sidewalk while gunshots rang out into the night. But this was a different level of pain, listening to someone you cared about suffer like that…scream your name for rescue.

"God…" She pulled away and looked into my face, her eyes heavy and watery. Her fingers cupped my face, comforting me as if I'd suffered the way she had suffered. Her fingers brushed over the coarse hair of my stubble, her eyes on mine, like she could read my feelings so easily. "I'm sorry."

I stared at her, amazed that she knew how much that had hurt me, how much it had killed me to lie there and listen to her and feel like I'd failed her. My hand moved to her cheek then slid into her hair, pulling it from her face and holding it there, just looking at her, watching her regard me like I was the only man in the world whom she wanted to protect her.

"Is Melanie here?"

I shook my head.

"So, he did that for you."

I nodded.

"I was surprised."

"I was more surprised." My fingers gently shifted in her hair, feeling its softness. "His hatred for you is unmistakable, but his love for me...is greater." Raven trusted me to be there for her through the best and the worst of times. That was exactly how I felt about my brother because he would always be there for me...no matter what. If I let her go, I wasn't sure if my brother really would make good on his threat and kill me, but our relationship would never be the same. He might ostracize me and tell everyone else I was dead...because I would be dead to him.

She studied my gaze, seeing the emotions on my face. "I can't even imagine the conflict you must feel."

I felt it every day. I knew Fender as my loyal brother, but I also knew him as the man who did all these terrible things. I still remembered the day he conjured the idea to steal innocent women, put them in the camp, and work them until they died. The Red Snow came later. I had other suggestions that left innocent people out of it, and when he dismissed those ideas, I still tried to talk him out of it. But nothing worked. It was hell, not only to live in this world, but to participate in it...and damn myself to hell.

I tied the rope around Eric's wrists then pushed him to the ground.

He landed with a thud, directly beside Nathan, groaning at the impact against his chest.

I did the same to Karl then shoved him to the ground.

A wooden pole stood erect in the dirt. Alix had his hands tied above his head, and he was standing there shirtless, the first one to go.

Fender stood at the edge of the clearing, looking at Alix. Then he turned to me. "Have fun." He took a seat in the chair the men had brought for him, one ankle resting on the opposite knee, waiting for the show to begin.

I was tired of granting mercy.

Alix had had a lot of chances to do the right thing —but he never did.

I stared at him, ready to beat the shit out of him.

Alix held my stare and refused to show fear, refused to look weak in front of the other guards.

This seemed too easy, to just stand there and take a beating.

I pulled off my shirt and tossed it to my brother.

He caught it without even looking at it.

I pulled a blade out of my pocket and walked toward Alix.

Alix immediately flinched at the sight of the blade.

I stood in front of him and let him squirm, let him stare at the blade that could carve him like a roast on Christmas Day. Pain wasn't a sufficient punishment, not when there were worse things. I moved behind him and cut the ropes.

He dropped his hands and massaged his wrists, immediately turning around so his back wasn't to me.

Fender raised an eyebrow in curiosity but didn't question me.

I threw the knife down into the soil, the hilt sticking up. "Fight me."

Alix backed up, glancing at the guards that stood behind Fender and had come to watch the sport.

"You beat me, and I don't move on to Eric. If you don't, I fight Eric. If he doesn't beat me, I move on to the next...and then the next. So, you can either end the punishment now...or you can lose. Admit defeat, or I will beat you to death."

Fender gave a slight nod in satisfaction. "This should be interesting. Let's begin."

I rushed Alix immediately, ready to turn my knuckles bloody beating the shit out of this moth-erfucker.

He quickly dodged to the left, his eyes wide and full of fright because he hadn't expected this. There was an audience to witness the showdown, and he already knew how our previous fights had ended—even when he was armed and I wasn't.

I followed him, cornering him at the edge of the clearing. "You afraid of me, asshole?" I grinned because we both knew exactly how this was going to end. I would beat his fucking ass, and he would have to ask for mercy in front of everyone—or die. He was a fucking coward so I knew what his answer would be, and I would enjoy every second leading up to it, savor his shame as he chose life over his reputation.

That enticed him to swing.

I took the opening and punched him so hard in the face he fell back.

I was the best fighter in this whole fucking camp, but I also had rage on my side. I was fucking furious, hearing her screams in my head as she called out to me for help. He'd touched her when he had no right to. He had no right to touch what was mine. "Get up, bitch." I spat on him.

He climbed to his feet then sprinted at me.

I kicked him in the face.

He fell down again, blood coming from his broken nose.

"Is that all you got? Come on. Look, I'll give you a chance." I raised my arms and beckoned him to me. "Hit me."

With his hands in the dirt, he looked at me, blood dripping down his lips. He growled then got to his feet.

"Give me your best shot."

He pulled his arm back and punched me, making my head turn.

I took the hit and reacted quickly, slamming my fists into his stomach, his chest, his face, driving him backward because I was too fast and he was too stupid. Even after a fist to the face, I was still quicker than him, striking blow after blow.

He threw his fist back and missed because I dodged out of the way and ducked, anticipating every move before he made it because he was careless. Then I slammed my fist up and hit him under the chin, making him fall back on his ass.

I got on top of him and hit him.

Again.

And again.

Blood covered his face and splashed onto my skin with every impact of my fists against his body. I beat him hard, barely giving him a chance to breathe, punishing him with both pain and shame. I kept going, knowing he would ask for mercy in seconds, knowing he would rather live in humiliation than die.

He finally got the words out. "Okay…okay."

I pulled my fists back and straightened. "Okay, what?"

"You win."

"Bitch, I didn't hear you." I slapped him across the face. "Speak up."

Alix was in too much pain to give me a furious look, and even if he could have, his face was too bloody to show a visible reaction. He raised his voice even though it made him wince in pain. "You win."

I got off him then grabbed the knife from the ground. "Alix failed you, so you're next." I sliced the ropes around Eric's wrists and yanked him to his feet. The knife went into my pocket before I shoved him forward into the ring, where Alix still lay, on the verge of passing out.

Eric stumbled forward then quickly turned around. "You win."

My eyes narrowed at his admission. "That's fucking pathetic." I came at him with my knuckles red from Alix's blood as well as my own. "I'm gonna beat your ass anyway—and I'm gonna like it."

All four of them were beaten bloody, beyond facial recognition.

No one helped them to their feet and back to their cabins until Fender ordered it. "Get these guys to bed. Give them ice and meds. They've been punished enough." The guards helped all of them to their feet and escorted them to their cabins, leaving the clearing.

I stood there and watched them go, my body dripping with sweat, the blood creating drops of red in the dirt beneath my feet. I'd given Eric, Nathan, and Karl the same punishment as Alix because they were the ones who had tortured me more by forcing me to listen to Raven beg for my help. I'd beaten them senseless and enjoyed every second of it.

Fender left his chair and walked to me, approval in his eyes. "Practice much?"

"Only every goddamn day." I had a punching bag in the gym, and I strapped on my gloves and beat it every day. There were splits in the seams from the use after all these years.

He looked at my bloody knuckles before he looked at me again. "Did that satisfy you?"

I nodded.

"The pain? Or the shame?"

"Both."

He gave me a slight grin before he moved his hand to my shoulder. His fingers dug into me slightly, like he was proud of me for being able to fight like that, to maintain my endurance through four different men who were all my size.

But he didn't understand how much rage I had.

He dropped his hand and nodded to my hands before he walked away. "Put some ice on those."

I listened to his footsteps grow quieter as he headed back to his cabin.

I turned around, my hands on my hips, my skin shining in the light from the nearby cabin because I was drenched in sweat. "I want to leave tomorrow."

Fender stopped and paused before he turned around. "You aren't scheduled to leave for two more days."

"I know." I wanted to get out of there sooner rather than later. I wanted to get Raven to a place where she felt safe so she could shake off the whole thing.

He considered my request in silence before he gave a slight nod. "You've earned it."

TWENTY
EYES TO THE DOGS

I'D INSTALLED A NEW DOOR, SO I OPENED IT AND stepped inside the cabin.

She was there, wearing my t-shirt as she sat on the bed. Her eyes widened as she looked at me, seeing how sweaty I was. Then her eyes dropped down to my bloody hands. "Are you okay?"

"Never been better." I went into the bathroom and got under the cold water, washing away the sweat, feeling the coldness numb my inflamed knuckles. A red line trailed down to the drain, a mixture of my victims as well as myself.

When I turned off the water and opened the curtain, she stood there.

I stilled and stared at her for a second before I grabbed the towel off the rack and dried myself.

"What happened?"

I scrubbed my hair dry then stepped out of the tub. "I punished Alix and the others."

She stepped back to give me room in the small bathroom. "How?"

"I fought them."

"You fought four men?"

"I hurt them until they asked me to stop—with all the other men there to watch." I dried my body and returned the towel to the rack to be used again.

She stared at me in disbelief.

"I said if Alix didn't beat me, I would move on to Eric. And if Eric didn't beat me…on to the next guy. None of them did, so I beat each and every one of them to within an inch of their life—with my bare hands." I skipped the shave and the rest of the shower routine and went straight into the bedroom, pulling on a new pair of boxers.

She followed me.

With my back to her, I grabbed a bottle of scotch and filled the glass. "And I did that for you." I took a drink before I turned around and looked at her.

She stared at me like she didn't know what to say. "All I care about is that you're okay."

"Like I said, I've never been better." I set the glass down then walked to her. "It felt good…really fucking good." My hands moved into her hair and cupped her head, looking into her soft blue eyes that cared about my well-being more than her revenge. "We're leaving tomorrow."

Her excitement was impossible to hide. "I thought we were here for a few more days."

"I said I wanted to leave early. Need a break from this goddamn place." My hands dropped from her face as I turned back to my scotch.

She grabbed my wrist and pulled me back, wanting my eyes on her face.

I stared at her and would do so as long as she wanted.

"Thank you." Her fingers pulled me closer, bringing my body into hers so she could kiss me. It was a soft kiss, but a deep one, her hungry mouth parting my lips and giving me her tongue instantly.

Adrenaline was still in my veins, and my heart still beat a million miles a minute. High off endorphins and scotch, there was nothing I wanted more than to be between her legs, to be with the woman I'd just destroyed four men to avenge.

She pulled her shirt over her head then pushed down my boxers.

I ended the kiss and looked into her face. "We can wait as long as you want." My hands moved around her wrists and kept her still, ignoring my rock-hard cock that was right against her stomach, begging for entry. "No rush."

"He didn't have me…"

"I know." It was still traumatic for her, and I understood why.

"And when I'm with you, I don't think about anything else."

When we left the camp the next morning, I didn't take her through the gate or via a circuitous route.

I walked her straight through the clearing, right by Alix, and I gave him a cold stare as I did it. The guys had to report for work despite their injuries because they would appear weak if they didn't. And Fender wouldn't give them the option either.

Fender joined me at the wagon, which was already full of product that I would take with me. It wasn't everything, but Fender would take the second load when he left in a few days. "How're your hands?"

I lifted them, showing the wrapping that covered both.

"Must have hurt this morning."

"Worth it."

He didn't smile, but his eyes had a slight look of affection. "I'll see you on Saturday."

"Anything you want me to do for Melanie while I'm there?"

He suddenly turned cold. "My woman is taken care of."

After the way he'd intervened for Raven, I felt even worse about not telling him the truth, that Melanie was just using him in the hope of freeing her sister. But his possessive response told me his obsession was deep, and even if she felt nothing for him, he would still keep her. Might as well let him enjoy the fantasy.

Raven came from behind me and joined us, her eyes on Fender.

I had no idea what the fuck she was doing.

I turned to her, giving her a glare that told her to leave—now.

But she was too absorbed in Fender's gaze to notice mine.

Fender stared at her with narrowed eyes, the energy around him immediately menacing, like he might grab her by the throat and choke her to death right then and there.

But she held his look anyway. "I just wanted to say thank you…for what you did."

Her appreciation would mean nothing to him, and I wished she hadn't come this close to him.

He held her gaze in silence, his eyes becoming more terrifying with every passing second. His stillness was sinister, and his clenched jaw showed how hard he was working not to strike the woman I had claimed as mine. "Your appreciation means nothing to me because my intervention had nothing to do with you. My only interest was keeping my brother's dick clean. Speak to me again, and I will cut those blue eyes out of your skull and feed them to my dogs." He shook slightly, like it took all his strength not to make good on that threat.

My hand moved to her stomach, and I forced her to back away and give my brother space. "Get in the wagon. Now."

She did as she was told and walked away.

Fender continued to stare at her, his face flushing slightly, like her proximity was borderline insulting. It took a few seconds for him to look at me again, to pull his look away from the woman who had destroyed his camp and brought him humiliation. "If you want your whore to keep sucking your dick, make sure she stays away from me."

We took the journey down the path to where my car waited at the end.

She didn't speak for hours, just looking at the luscious landscape around us.

I didn't speak to her either. I was annoyed with her stupidity, and I needed time to calm down. My hands gripped the reins of the horses, my knuckles aching every time I made a fist.

She seemed to feel my anger because she waited until it was at a simmer before she spoke. "I just thought—"

"You thought wrong." I watched the road ahead.

She stared at the side of my face. "I thought if I was kind to him—"

"Doesn't work that way."

She faced forward again and sighed.

"Don't speak to him. Don't look at him. Keep your head down when you're near him."

"I'm not a dog."

"To him, you are."

She shook her head as she sighed loudly. "I know I pissed him off—"

"Just leave it alone."

She turned quiet and swallowed the response sitting in her throat. "I'll probably never be near him again, so it doesn't matter."

"You will on Saturday. Don't embarrass me again."

"*Embarrass you?*" Her head snapped back in my direction. "I was just trying—"

"I know what you were trying to do. But as you can see, that got you nowhere. Just leave it alone."

She studied me. "You're mad at me."

"Yes." I continued to avoid her gaze.

"Why?"

"Because you were fucking stupid. That's why." I turned to look at her, so she could see just how furious her little move made me. "He has bent for me many times, and the last thing you should do is get in his face after what you did."

"Wow." She shook her head. "He should be grateful I'm even thanking him given all the shit he does in that godforsaken camp. Let's not rewrite history here. He captured me, and I escaped—just as he would escape if this were flipped around—"

"This conversation is over." I looked ahead and gripped the reins in my hand. There was no point in discussing my brother when there was nothing we could do about it. We'd established the unbearable moral dilemma I had to suffer. It didn't need further debate.

She watched the scenery around her, letting the conversation die. But minutes later, she addressed it again. "Wait…what do you mean, I'll see him on Saturday?"

"He's having an event. I'm bringing you."

"An event?"

"A party."

"And he's fine with that?"

"He was when I talked to him about it…before you pulled your little stunt."

It was hard for her to swallow her retort, but she managed it by clenching her jaw. "I don't even want to go, but I know she'll be there."

"That's why I wanted to bring you." I hated get-togethers and conversations. It was all just a bunch of bullshit, rich people talking about how rich they were. Fender had a god complex, so he enjoyed flaunting his wealth and success, like it was a big fuck-you to our father...who'd been dead for nearly ten years at this point. "So, I suggest you swallow your pride and do as he asked because you'll never see Melanie without him."

She dozed off on the drive.

I listened to the radio as I drove down the country roads toward Paris, the occasional headlights coming at me from a passing car in the other direction. With one hand on the wheel, I counted down the time until we arrived at my apartment, where this long day could finally conclude.

I used to spend my time in solitude, enjoying my cabin at the camp alone, having a lover in Paris who was only there in the evenings and gone in the morning. The rest of my time was spent with my laptop, in front of the TV, or working.

But now, Raven was with me every single day.

When she worked in the clearing, I didn't have her around, but that time alone stopped feeling like a respite from her company. Her presence in the cabin didn't feel suffocating. And when we arrived at my apartment, I knew she would sleep with me tonight, even if we wouldn't have sex beforehand.

That was our life now.

Even though I was still angry with her after what happened with Fender, that anger didn't change my feelings. When someone pissed me off, our interaction was usually over for good. If a woman said the wrong thing, she was no longer my lover. But no matter what Raven did…nothing changed.

We arrived in Paris hours later, driving through the streets that were still busy despite the hour, and passed the lit-up tower before I pulled into the park and slowed down in front of my apartment. I hit the button to open the gate and then the garage and pulled into the driveway.

She woke up when the car came to a stop. "Are we here?"

I hit the clicker, and the garage door closed behind us. "Yes."

"Oh, thank god…" She stretched in the seat with her arms behind her head, making a loud yawn. "I have to pee. And I just fucking hate that place." She opened the door and ran her fingers through her hair as she moved to the elevator.

I joined her in the elevator, and we rose to the entry level.

Her eyes were heavy like she was still half asleep.

I leaned against the wall and watched her.

She sighed when the doors opened, and she went first, in a hurry. "Gotta pee…gotta pee." She went into the nearest bathroom and disappeared.

I made my way into the parlor and saw that it was meticulously clean because Miranda had taken care of it once we'd left. Groceries were in the fridge, clean linens were on the bed, and fresh vases of flowers had been placed everywhere…because she thought my guest would enjoy them.

I went upstairs and rinsed my face and got ready for bed.

I got under the sheets and plugged in my phone so it would charge, the bedroom door open because I assumed Raven would join me.

Minutes later, she did. She was in just her black thong with her hair up because she'd washed her face over the sink. She went to her side of the bed and pulled back the covers, getting in beside me, turning over to face me, and closed her eyes. She didn't cuddle with me, like she was too tired and just wanted to go to sleep.

My hand moved behind my head as I turned to study her face, to watch her sleep.

She drifted off instantly.

I was tired, but I watched her anyway, thinking about one of my conversations with Fender. I'd asked if I could buy her freedom, and he said no. I didn't have the heart to tell her that, and I didn't think I ever would.

TWENTY-ONE
OLD SCARS

I walked downstairs and found her on the couch, reading a book, fully dressed for the day, even though we had no plans. With her legs crossed, she absentmindedly reached for her coffee and brought it to her lips for a sip. She was in a green sundress, her full lips vibrant with a shade of lipstick, and the color over her eyes complemented the colors she wore.

When I reached the bottom of the stairs, she looked up at me, seeing me in nothing but my sweatpants. A night of sleep had seemed to wash away her anger because she looked at me with subtle softness. "Morning."

I nodded then went into the kitchen to pour myself a mug of coffee. I took it black, while she drank hers with a gallon of milk. I grabbed a banana off the counter and stripped it so I could eat it in a couple bites. I usually went for a run every morning, but I was too tired for that today.

She closed her book then joined me in the kitchen. Whenever we were in Paris, she looked like a completely different person in her dresses with her hair done. She behaved differently too, a lot more relaxed, and the closer we came to returning to the camp, she reverted to her withdrawn existence. "Do you have plans today?"

"I have to work this evening."

"So, you're free during the day?"

I already knew what she wanted. "We can't go anywhere today."

"Why?"

"Because—" I was caught off guard by the sound of the doorbell.

She turned to the entryway, her eyebrows raised. "Who is that?"

I pulled out my phone and fired off a text to Miranda. *Come up.* "My property manager. Assistant. Whatever you want to call her." I grabbed the mug and took a drink as I stood at the counter, listening to the elevator hum as it brought her to our level.

"Should I leave?"

"No. You're the reason she's here."

The elevator doors opened, and Miranda came into the room, carrying a long plastic bag to protect the dresses underneath, along with a few bags for the shoes and other accessories. "Good morning, Magnus." She was a few years older than Raven, always dressed in heels and a skirt, even when she brought me heavy groceries and everything else I asked for. She moved to the couch and laid down the hanger over the back, placing the extra bags on the table.

Raven was quiet, like she didn't know if she was allowed to talk.

Miranda unzipped the covering and then pulled out the two dresses. "I've got two. Pick the one you want, and I'll make the alterations." She turned to Raven. "Raven, right?"

Raven stepped forward and extended her hand. "Yes. It's nice to meet you."

"You too. So, what do you think?"

"About what?" Raven glanced back at me, like she had no idea what was going on.

I stepped forward, holding my mug in my hand. "You need something to wear on Saturday, so Miranda picked out these gowns."

"Oh…" She looked at the two gowns spread over the back of the couch. "Sorry, I just… It's been a long time since I tried on clothes."

Miranda held up the first one, classic black, which hung down to the floor with a slit that went all the way up the thigh and had an interesting array of straps at the top. "You can't go wrong with black, and while it's a simple dress, the unique array of straps the designer created for this piece really makes it stand out." She laid the dress down again and grabbed the other. "This is the total opposite. The purple color is perfect for a summer event, and the subtle texture in the fabric will give it a slight sheen under the light of a chandelier. Either one will look great on you, so there's no wrong choice."

Raven continued to stand there and stare, like she didn't know what to do. "Uh..." It seemed to be overwhelming to her.

I made the decision for her. "Black."

"Alright." Miranda returned the purple dress to the protective cover then held the black dress out to Raven. "Try this on for me with these heels so I can put the pins in." She reached into the bag and pulled out a pair of black high heels with satin bows at the backs.

Raven took everything then walked into her old bedroom and shut the door.

Miranda turned to me. She hesitated, like she wanted to ask about Raven's peculiar behavior, but she didn't. "Is there anything you need me to do while I'm here?"

"No." I drank from my coffee. "Raven doesn't get out much, so she's not used to this sort of thing."

She nodded. "You don't try on designer gowns every day."

Raven returned minutes later in the tall heels and the tight dress. She was petite, so it was a little long on her and it could be taken in around her waist, but it already looked stunning on her, especially that slit up her thigh.

Miranda got to work and put the pins in place so she could alter it and sew it back into place. On her knees, she worked, clipping it in all the right places.

Raven stood there, balancing in the high heels, looking out of place in a dress that cost me €5,000. She was confident in the uniform she had to wear at the camp, but in a Paris apartment in a designer gown, she was uncomfortable.

Miranda stood up when she was finished. "Great. Now, just take it off, and I'll be on my way."

Raven went back into the bedroom, changed, and then returned with the dress.

Miranda gathered everything, said a few final words to me, and let herself out.

When she was gone and Raven was back in the dress she'd put on that morning, she returned to her usual self. "I've never worn anything like that in my life. This is going to be a fancy party, isn't it?"

"Very." I stood at the counter and continued to drink my coffee.

She stood across from me, just the way we did in her apartment. "You think I'll have a chance to talk to Melanie in private?"

"Not sure." Whenever I saw Fender with Melanie in public, she was always right at his side. "But I'm sure if Melanie asked, he would give her whatever she wanted. And it's a big place...easy to duck into another room."

She gave a slow nod. "I haven't seen her in so long... How is she?"

"She's treated very well—from what I've gathered."

"That's good." Her gaze shifted to look out the window, the natural light coming in and lighting up her face. Her hands rested on the edge of the counter, and she got lost in her thoughts.

I drank my coffee and studied her. "What are you thinking?"

She shook her head slightly, her gaze still out the window. "That I want to see Melanie, but I don't want to spend my evening with a bunch of rich people when I can be here...with you."

Being stripped down naked and dragged into the open by a madman hadn't changed her desire for me. Her nails sliced into my skin, she breathed into my mouth, and she whispered my name like it would live on the tip of her tongue for the rest of her life. I preferred to be on top because I liked feeling those nails carve my back, liked pressing her into the mattress underneath me as I claimed her as mine, liked feeling those sexy legs around my waist. But every time she got on top of me, I couldn't believe how good it was.

She fucked me good.

That night, she moved off me then turned around, on all fours, her back arched, her ass up.

The moonlight outlined her sexy curves, the deep curve in her lower back, the perkiness of her cheeks. Her long hair stretched down the center of her back, the curls falling out as the day progressed.

But all I could see were the scars.

Even in the darkness, I could see them…because I knew exactly what to look for.

I'd held that whip in my hand and beat her with it. I'd sliced open her skin, made her lose enough blood that she almost slipped under. I'd hit her again and again and watched her body grow weak then hang from the branch. It was one of the worst moments of my life. The pain and the shame made me sick to my stomach.

I couldn't handle the sight, so I looked away.

When I didn't move behind her, she looked over her shoulder. "Magnus."

I wouldn't look at her. "I told you I don't want to look at it." My gaze was turned to the window, partially obstructed by the curtains. When we were in bed together and I opened my eyes to her bare back, I always turned the other way. I did whatever I could to pretend the scars never happened, and the only way I could do that was by not looking at them.

"Magnus…" She turned her body so she was back on the bed, lying down with her body propped up, looking at me.

Now that I couldn't see her scars, I shifted my gaze back to her.

"You have to accept me as I am."

I clenched my jaw and shook my head. "You know that's not the problem."

She crawled toward me, moving on top of me so her hair dragged across my chest as she moved. "We've both done things for and to each other that change the way we look, but we're still the same." Her hand moved over my chest, over my heart. "You did what you had to do to keep me alive."

"It still…" It still killed me.

"I forgive you." She moved her forehead to mine and rested it there, her hand over my heart, her hair on my chest. "Now, be with me." She pressed her lips to mine and gave me a deep and purposeful kiss, her mouth taking mine before she kissed me again and again, her tongue greeting mine and bringing me back to the moment. Then she pulled away, moved back to where she was, and looked at me over her shoulder.

I tried not to let the past come into that room and infect me with misery. I tried not to think about the way the whip felt in my grasp, tried not to think about the crack it made once it hit her skin. When it was just her and me, we forgot about our unfortunate existence and everything that had been done to both of us.

I leaned over her and pressed a kiss between her shoulder blades, my lips feeling the bumps over her scarred skin, the welts that had never really gone away. I listened to her breathe harder as she savored my kiss like she enjoyed it. I moved farther down her spine and to her ass, my face moving between her legs to kiss the area that was plenty wet.

She breathed harder, loud in the silence.

I straightened and placed myself inside her with a deep thrust.

She jerked forward and moaned loudly.

My hands gathered her in my arms, and I pulled her against me, my chest against her back, my arms across her tits and her stomach. I held her as I thrust, both of us on our knees on the bed, grinding together as the passion rose like heat to the ceiling.

Her hand moved to the back of my head, and she angled her body so she could kiss me as we moved together, her pants entering my mouth and filling my lungs with new warmth. Her fingers gripped the hair at the back of my neck, and she moaned as I thrust into her. "Magnus…"

One of my hands squeezed her tit, while the other slid between her legs and rubbed her clit.

She moaned louder and louder.

I could feel the scars against my chest as we moved together, feel the bumps that would never fade as long as she lived. But instead of carrying the grief on my shoulders, I saw them as a testament to her survival, of what we'd both done to get here…to have this.

TWENTY-TWO

THE COUNT OF MONTE CRISTO

When I opened my eyes and looked at the nightstand, I realized it was almost noon.

It'd been a long night.

I wiped the sleep from my eyes before my arm slid toward Raven on the bed. All I felt were cold sheets. She was always up earlier than I was, probably because she was excited to be in Paris. I got out of bed, used the bathroom, and then headed downstairs to make some coffee.

She wasn't sitting on the couch.

And the coffeepot hadn't been turned on.

I went to her old bedroom to see if she was sitting in the armchair so she could see the Eiffel Tower past the park.

She wasn't there.

My heart started to pound. "Raven?" I raised my voice so she could hear me if she was in the apartment.

Nothing.

I checked the bathrooms—nothing.

I stood in the living room and dragged my hand down my face, feeling my jaw clench, feeling the terror grip me by the chest.

Did she run?

The alarm wasn't set because it didn't cross my mind anymore.

Maybe that was what she wanted.

Did she lie to me? Was this all…a stunt?

Was any of it real?

I moved to the window in her old bedroom to look down at the gate and the sidewalk, as if she would be standing there. Did she spend all that time earning my affection for protection in the camp, building up my trust, just so she could have this moment? When we were up late so she knew I'd be asleep for hours?

Was I that stupid?

Why did I actually believe this was real?

My heart pounded harder, and the pulse was vibrating in my temples. The blood was like a drumbeat in my ears. So many emotions ran through me at once. But then my eyes noticed the woman in a dress across the street. She checked both ways before she crossed, carrying two coffees, a bag hanging off her wrist with the bakery logo on the front. She moved through the open gate and approached the apartment.

I closed my eyes and pinched the bridge of my nose.

It was real.

The elevator hummed down the hallway until the doors opened. Her footsteps came a moment later, passing the bedroom and entering the kitchen, without noticing me standing in front of the window.

With my hands on my hips, I stood in front of the window and let the anger circulate out of my blood.

She must have taken a bite of a pastry because she said, "Oh man…that's so fucking good."

I left the bedroom and approached the kitchen.

She stilled when she spotted me, half a muffin stuffed into her mouth, crumbs and blueberry juice in the corners of her mouth, eating like a pig because she assumed I was still asleep upstairs. The food was already in her mouth at that point, so she chewed it quickly and tried to get it down. "I…" *Chew chew chew.* "Didn't know…" *Chew chew chew. Mumble mumble.* "Awake…" She grabbed a napkin from the bag and tried to wipe all the shit off her face as she chewed the last of it and got it down her throat.

I stepped closer to her, my arms resting by my sides, still angry about the heart attack she'd just given me.

She balled up the napkin and left it on the counter. "I got you a muffin too, but you don't have to eat it. I'll eat it if you don't want it." When she looked at me, she realized that something was wrong, that the intense stare I gave her was a hostile one. "What is it?"

I stepped closer to her, exploding in fury. "Did I say you could come and go as you please?"

She stilled at my outburst, not anticipating this at all.

"I wake up and you're gone, and I have no idea where the fuck you went. What the fuck, Raven?"

She stepped back slightly, recovering from the surprise and turning cold. "I just went to get coffee, Magnus. What is the big deal?"

"What's the big deal?" I asked incredulously. "You didn't tell me. That's the big deal."

"Where else would I have…" Her voice trailed away when she figured out why I was so angry. Understanding entered her gaze, and that softness was quickly replaced by anger. "I told you I wouldn't run."

She'd had the perfect opportunity to wave down a cab and go in any direction, but she chose to come back, her intentions completely innocent, so innocent that if I woke up and didn't see her, the idea of her escaping wouldn't even cross my mind. I rubbed my fingers across my jawline, letting the angry high dissipate.

"You need to trust me."

I dropped my hand and looked at her again.

"I'm gonna come and go as I damn well please because I'm not going to run—and you know I'm not going to run. At least, you do now...because I've been awake for four hours now, and that's plenty of time to disappear if that's what I wanted. So, when I wake up, I'm going to walk to my favorite coffee shop and get a sugary, fattening, hot cup of coffee and as many goddamn muffins as I want, and you aren't going to say a damn thing about it. If you're gone in the evening and I'm alone, I'm gonna walk down there and get my dinner to go and eat it here because it's what I want to do. Alright?"

I stared into her angry eyes, seeing the genuine hurt she felt, like my doubt was a slap in the face. She was beautiful all the time, with makeup or without, when she was asleep or wide awake. But when she was emotional like this, there was something particularly magnetic about it. It was when I was most fascinated with her, when she spoke her mind candidly and with confidence. "Alright."

I parked the car outside her apartment, and we walked up the steps of the stoop and then the staircase inside. Like before, there were envelopes underneath the door, telling her that the rent was late.

She tested the knob, and it was unlocked.

The door creaked open.

She stared inside, saw that it looked exactly the same as before, and then stepped into the room.

I followed behind her and watched her look around at the place that must have stopped feeling like home months ago. I could feel her energy in the room, feel a past I wasn't a part of. I could picture her making dinner every night for her and her sister. I could picture her working upstairs in her office, while glancing up at the tower every time she took a sip of her coffee.

With her arms crossed over her chest, she looked around.

It seemed cruel to bring her to box up her possessions, never to return, but it was better than leaving
it behind so someone would throw it all away. Her
favorite books, family photos, keepsakes that meant
a lot to her… It would just end up in the dump.

After a long pause, she grabbed a box and set it on
the counter. She seemed to know exactly what she
wanted to take because she grabbed the things and
quickly put them inside.

I stayed by the door and watched.

She went upstairs a couple times, grabbing photo
albums, picture frames, and books. She placed them
inside and returned up the stairs.

I grabbed one of the picture frames and took a
look.

It was a woman with two little girls. Even though
the girls had the same eye color, I knew exactly
which one was Raven. She looked to be maybe five
at the time, sitting on her mother's lap with that
fiery brightness in her gaze…a shine that was still
there to this day. I put it back in the box.

She stuffed the box with everything that meant something to her, and the last thing she placed inside was a purple scarf. "That's everything."

"You don't want to take anything else?" She left behind all her furniture, clothes, and shoes. She didn't touch anything in the kitchen, except removing a few magnets from the fridge.

She shook her head. "These are the only things that matter." She pulled the box to the edge to pick it up.

I grabbed the top and slid it toward myself so I could carry it.

"I pick up boxes like that all the time at the camp."

I picked it up and headed to the door. "I know."

She placed her things in her old bedroom. It still held her new clothes and accessories, so she showered in that bathroom and set up her picture frames and photo albums. The two of us fell into a routine just the way we did at the camp, albeit it was completely different.

Whenever I was out of the house working, she spent her time walking around Paris, window-shopping with the money I gave her, buying coffees and pastries and books at the bookstore.

I never worried about her running again.

Sometimes, I worked on my laptop upstairs in the parlor, and she knew to leave me alone.

When we were together, we shared meals, went on walks, made love, stuff other couples did. It felt like a relationship, even though I'd never had a relationship like this before. There were a lot of odd things about it, given our circumstances, but the oddest thing about it was the foundation we stood on. She wasn't just my lover, and she wasn't just my friend… she was somewhere in between.

I came downstairs and saw her pull her purse over her head and onto the opposite shoulder then tug her hair free from the strap across the back of her neck. She was in a blue dress with her hair curled. When she heard me approach, she lifted her gaze and looked at me. "I'm going to the bookstore. Want to come with me?"

I read spreadsheets and emails, but that was it. "Sure."

We left the apartment then walked side by side farther into the city. The cafes and shops came into view, people sitting outside and enjoying a cup of coffee with a baguette with a side of jam. We always stood a few feet apart. We didn't show affection in public. It wasn't my thing, and it didn't seem to be hers either because she never tried to hold my hand or kiss me.

She entered the bookstore and browsed through the shelves.

"What are you looking for?"

She moved down the aisle and browsed the titles, most of them in French. "Nothing in particular. I just like the way it smells in here."

"Like dust?"

"Like fresh pages, rich details, history…"

With my hands in my pockets, I walked alongside her.

"You should give it a chance."

"I never cared for reading when I was in school."

"What did you care for?"

I shrugged. "Math, science, stuff like that."

She turned to look at me. "I didn't know that."

"Why would you?"

"I guess it makes sense. You seem more pragmatic and logical than most people." She turned back to the books. "But I think you should give it another try. You might be surprised." She stepped back so she could crane her neck and look higher up.

I left her side and walked down the aisles to see what was available, not that I would find something I liked. The books were new, but the shelves were dusty. My eyes scanned the titles, and the only time I stopped was when I was on the other side of the store.

I looked at the spine and read the title.

I pulled it off the shelf and opened the cover, looking through the words in French. I'd read this book a long time ago in school, but I couldn't remember the details anymore. I closed the book and held it at my side.

"Have any recommendations?" A woman came to my side and addressed me in French.

I stepped back slightly because I'd been so focused on the book and not my surroundings. I replied back in French. "I don't work here."

"I know…just wanted a reason to talk to you."

I gave her a blank stare before I walked away and returned to the other side of the store. Raven was still there, flipping through the pages of a book in her hand, oblivious to the world around her because the only thing that mattered was already in the palm of her hand.

When she felt my presence, she addressed me. "Find anything?"

I held up the book.

She looked away from her pages and stared at it, a slow smile coming onto her lips. "*The Count of Monte Cristo*…good choice."

TWENTY-THREE
LA PETITE AMIE

I waited in the downstairs living room, pulling back the sleeve of my tuxedo to check the time.

She was taking a long time to get ready.

I hated these social events, so I didn't care about getting there on time anyway. She could take all night for all I cared. But she wouldn't see Melanie, so it was her loss and not mine.

She finally stepped out of the bedroom, the dress fitting her like the designer made it with her in mind. Black was a great color on her, and the tightness over her chest highlighted the sexy cleavage she had. The high slit in the dress showed her toned and strong legs, the muscles prominent when she was in high heels like that.

She walked toward me and stared at my face.

I didn't meet her gaze because I was too busy looking her up and down, loving every curve. Her flat stomach looked even more petite than usual, which made her tits look even bigger. Her hourglass frame was on full display.

My eyes finally lifted to meet her gaze. "Beautiful."

All the uncertainty she'd felt in her appearance faded away at the compliment. A smile slowly came through, the confidence returning to her gaze. "I wasn't sure if I could pull this off."

I got to my feet and walked toward her, liking her in those heels because we were nearly at eye level, which was a nice change. I stopped in front of her, seeing the diamond necklace around her throat, the top of her chest, and the swell of her breasts. Her makeup was dark and smoky, giving her a sultry look that was so damn sexy. Her lips were painted dark red, the color of her blood, and I wanted to kiss it away until it was all over my lips and the corners of my mouth. "You definitely pull it off."

The front lawn was lit up with lights, a long driveway from the very beginning of the estate to the mansion at the top of the hill. It was nearly a mile just to get there. My car was in line behind the others, even though we were an hour late, because all of society was there. As we got closer to the valet at the entrance, she started to fidget.

"What are we celebrating?" she whispered, her eyes focused out the window.

I watched couples walk inside in their tuxedoes and gowns, the tall door opening to reveal a peek of the interior. Gilbert bowed to the guests and ushered them inside before he closed the door again. "Being rich."

We pulled up to the valet, and I tossed my keys at him before Raven stepped out of the car and joined me, her long dress difficult to manage as she rose to her feet. But she made it work and came to my side.

I walked with her beside me, up the stairs and to the entryway.

Her arm slipped through mine, and she came closer.

I turned to look at her, surprised at the affection.

She stilled and looked at me. "Is this okay?"

I'd never done this before, never had a woman on my arm like this. When we walked around Paris, I never held her hand and she never tried to hold mine. My arm never moved around her waist. It just wasn't natural to me. But most of the women had their arms through those of the men who accompanied them, or the men rested their hands against the women's lower backs. After a pause, I gave a nod.

She pulled me a little closer when she had my permission. "These heels are not my friend."

Gilbert greeted us and opened the door. "Sir, it's so nice to see you." Then he turned to look at Raven, a slight look of surprise in his gaze before he quickly covered it. He switched to English, knowing she couldn't understand a lot of French. "You look beautiful, mademoiselle."

She smiled. "Thank you."

I took her inside, into the crowd under the chandelier. Loud conversations echoed all the way to the top of the third floor. Waiters passed flutes of champagne, along with appetizers. Most of the people were strangers to me, socialites who had wealth passed down through hundreds of years. "I have to talk to a few people."

"And what should I say?"

"You're my date."

"I mean, what if they ask me about what I do and stuff?"

"Tell them you're a student studying literature, like you were before."

She nodded. "Makes sense."

I spoke to a few people I knew, feeling Raven on my arm the entire time. Some of the men were distributors, so we talked openly about shipments, and in this fancy underworld, people didn't care about breaking the law. If you wanted to be as rich as we were, going against the grain was the only way to do it.

Raven didn't say much, and when people asked questions, she stuck to the script.

I took her through the crowd to our next destination.

"They just talk about it so nonchalantly."

"Yeah, that's how it works." I spotted Fender with his arm wrapped around Melanie, who wore a gold gown that was cut so low in the front, the opening went all the way to her belly button.

I stopped with Raven. "There's my brother."

She saw her sister and stared at her for a while. "Wow…she looks beautiful."

"Just stand there quietly, alright?"

She didn't want to stir up that argument again, so she just nodded. "Can I talk to Melanie?"

"I'll try to get you in a room together. Just let me handle it."

She nodded.

I guided her to my brother, and once I arrived, the gentleman he was talking to silently excused himself, as if he understood exactly who I was without introduction.

Fender turned and looked at me, his eyes slightly hostile because he recalled our final conversation near the wagons. Raven was directly beside me, and he didn't give her a single glance, pretending she didn't exist.

Melanie looked at Raven.

Raven looked back.

But neither spoke.

I kept my eyes on Fender. "Is Napoleon here?"

He raised his champagne to his lips and took a drink. "Somewhere." His arm stayed around Melanie's waist, his fingers curling around to the front and coming closer to her bare flesh down the middle. She was decorated with jewels, sparkling like she herself was a diamond. It'd been months since they'd met, and Fender hadn't lost interest... which was saying something.

Melanie looked at her sister. "You look really nice, Raven."

Raven didn't speak and just gave a nod.

Fender still didn't look at Raven.

"I'm going to put the girls in the parlor so we can speak in private," I said, knowing Raven would only be able to stare at her sister if the situation didn't change.

"No." Fender pulled her closer. "She stays here."

There was nothing I could do. There was no argument I could make to entice him to let Melanie leave his side. She was the treasure no one else could have—and he wanted everyone to know it.

But Melanie stepped up. "*Amoureux*, please…" She turned into him, bringing her face closer to his, her free hand moving against his chest and resting on the black fabric of his tuxedo.

He wouldn't look at her. "You're lucky that I permit her in our home at all."

She turned his face toward hers and forced him to look at her, to see the desperation in her eyes, and then she leaned in and kissed him. "For me…"

He abandoned his prejudice instantly, his eyes softening when she kissed him like that. "Alright." He pulled his hand from her waist so she could walk away. "Just a couple minutes. Nothing more."

"Thank you, *amoureux*." She squeezed his hand before she stepped away and moved to Raven.

Fender turned his gaze on me, his affection falling once he looked at me instead of her. "Take them." He brought his glass to his lips and took a drink before he stepped away to talk to another guest.

I escorted them away from the main room and into the hallway where there was an open room with couches. I nodded inside. There was no door because it was just an extension of the grand entryway, but there was no one nearby, so they wouldn't be overheard. And even if they were, no one would care.

The first thing they did was embrace.

Melanie hugged her sister tightly, her face moving into Raven's shoulder, like a child holding her mother.

Raven held her, being the crutch as usual.

They stayed that way for a long time.

I lingered just on the outside, watching them.

Raven pulled away and rubbed her sister's arms. "That dress is so gorgeous on you."

"It's mostly the dress, not me."

Raven smiled. "No, it's not."

"You're the one who steals the show tonight, Raven. That dress was made for you."

"Well, black is my color." She smiled before she sat on the couch beside Melanie.

They were both oblivious to me because they were absorbed in each other. They just stared, like they didn't know where to start.

Raven held Melanie's hand on her thigh. "How are you?"

"No complaints. He's good to me. What about you?"

She paused as she looked at her sister, as if contemplating whether she should tell her all the shit that happened at the camp before we left. She made her decision and didn't reveal it. "Good. I really love being in Paris. Magnus has an apartment near my old place, so I get coffee in the morning and go shopping… It's nice."

"He lets you go alone?"

She nodded.

"Wow, he trusts you."

"He does." She looked at their joined hands. "It's not that I've given up. It's just…if I run, it'll put Magnus in jeopardy, and I can't do that. Does

Fender let you go where you want?"

"Yes. But it rarely happens."

"Why?"

"Because he wants to come with me every time I want to go somewhere."

"To watch you?"

"I think he just wants to be with me, actually. But he's given me one of his cars and has let me drive away before."

Raven was quiet, just watching her sister.

"I'm trying to convince him to let you go, but he won't budge."

"Yeah, I don't think he ever will."

"I don't know… Give me more time. I think he'll do it for me."

Raven dropped her gaze, like she didn't believe that would ever happen. "You know, if you were to kill him…it might fix all our problems."

Melanie's eyes widened, like the suggestion was unexpected.

"In his sleep or something."

Melanie slowly pulled her hand away from her sister's. "I…I can't do that."

"If you do, the camp will belong to Magnus. He'll let everyone go—"

"I said I can't." She dropped her gaze and stared at her hands in her lap.

Raven looked disappointed, but after a few seconds, she hid that expression. "Why?"

"Because…I can't do that to him."

When Raven started to understand the truth about their relationship, she couldn't hide the revulsion that spread across her face. "Melanie, this is the man who raped you—"

"He didn't." She raised her gaze and looked at her sister, absorbing the disgusted look directed at her. "I never said that."

"But he took you from the cabin, put you in another… He dragged his fingers against your cheek and said you tried to get away from him."

She shook her head. "He put me in a different cabin so he could be alone with me, but he never forced me. He would just have dinner with me and said he would wait until I was ready. And then…I was ready."

Raven was stunned into silence.

Melanie bowed her head again, in shame.

It was exactly what I suspected, that Melanie had never been putting on a production, that the affection between them was genuine. She went back to him to save her sister…but she also wanted an excuse to be with him again.

"Melanie…I understand we've been in dire circumstances and it's easy to grow attached to anything that's comforting, but this is the man who enslaves and kills innocent women, women that we've known. How can you possibly feel that way about him?"

She raised her chin and looked at Raven. "The same reason you feel that way about Magnus."

The anger that appeared on Raven's face happened instantly, her breathing deeper, her face flushing slightly. "They are not the same, Melanie. Magnus is nothing like that monster."

"How are they different?" Melanie questioned. "Both men don't hang the women themselves, but they both work there. How is it different? Magnus is just as guilty, and yet you look at him the way Fender looks at me."

Raven took a few breaths before she responded. "Magnus doesn't agree with the way the camp is run and has expressed that many times to Fender, but Fender ignores it. Magnus is the one who risked his neck to save us both. What has Fender done other than buy you pretty things? I'm sorry, but to compare the two men is fucking insulting. How can you feel any affection for the man who's the boss of that camp? How?"

Melanie held her sister's gaze, watery shame in her eyes. "I just… I can't explain it."

"Well, you better try."

"He's just…more than that. He takes care of me, he's good to me, he's…a man. He's not like the other boys out there, and I like that. I know it's wrong, but I can't change the way I feel. I can't kill him. I can't do it, okay? I'm sorry." Her eyes watered until the tears dripped down her cheeks.

Raven held her silence, but it was obvious that she struggled to process all of that without losing her temper. "If you don't kill him, I'll never get out of that camp. The women will never get out of that camp. Magnus will never be able to be free."

She kept her head down. "Why can't Magnus do it—"

"Because Fender will kill him. And Magnus won't kill his brother, so…"

"You can kill Magnus and run—"

"Don't say that again." Raven lost her temper, her eyes like daggers. "You know Magnus is not like him. I don't even need to say it. Lie to yourself all you want, but it won't change reality. Magnus is the hero…and Fender is the villain."

Melanie kept her gaze down and couldn't look at her sister. "Look, I'm willing to set him up for his downfall. I'm willing to sneak around and carry your secrets. I'm willing to do anything and everything to help you and those girls that are stuck there, but I can't kill him myself. I'm sorry…" Melanie started to cry.

Seeing her sister break down made Raven sheathe her anger. Her hand went to Melanie's shoulder then into her hair, tucking it behind her ear like a mother with a daughter. "Melanie, it's okay… Don't ruin your makeup."

She straightened and wiped her tears with her fingers, bringing herself to calm. "I know I can get him to set you free. I know I can…"

"But that doesn't fix the problem, Melanie. Even if I'm free, the camp is still continuing."

She shook her head. "We tried to stop it once before. There's nothing we can do."

"Melanie—"

"No, listen." She straightened and looked at her sister. "We went back and burned that place to the fucking ground, and it didn't change anything. I know you want to put an end to it, but you need to understand this is bigger than the two of us. I told you we shouldn't go back, that we had no chance, but you forced us to do it anyway. We lost our freedom because of it. I'm never going to be able to walk away from Fender at this point, so I need to make the best of it. Yes, I feel something for him, but how can I sleep beside the same man every single night and see his goodness and not feel something?" She paused to take a few breaths, her eyes filled with emotional intensity. "I know I can get him to free you, but that's the best I can do."

They spoke candidly because they didn't realize I was there, so my trust in Raven was even more solidified than before. It felt pointless to stand there when there was nothing new to listen to, so I walked away and gave them their privacy.

Napoleon walked right up to me, as if he'd been waiting for me to turn away and step into the room. His hand gripped the pommel of his black cane, and he looked at me with his stony expression. Every criminal had a specific energy, usually bad, but there was something about this guy that felt innately malevolent. "Your brother tells me you don't like me." A slow smile spread across his lips, like that was a compliment rather than an insult.

"I like you even less now."

His grin widened. "We're going to make a lot of money together. You'll see."

I wished I didn't have to see.

He gave me a slight nod before he moved into the crowd and took a drink from a passing waiter.

I watched him go, feeling that same unease in my stomach, like this guy was bad news. I'd been digging into him for a while and couldn't find any red flags, but just because I couldn't find them didn't mean they weren't there.

A new face appeared in my vision.

With long dark hair, green eyes, and a slight smile full of arrogance, she looked at me like she'd been waiting for this moment all night. "I have to admit, I'm a bit offended."

I stared at Stasia and felt the annoyance flood my body. I'd always been indifferent to her, just interested in the way our bodies felt when they were together. But the words out of her mouth always fell on deaf ears.

Her eyes glanced past me before she looked at me again. "That you prefer to be with a hag over a woman that looks like me." She flipped her hair over her shoulder and gave me a cold stare. "I guess we're all into weird shit sometimes."

My eyes never trailed away from her face, and instead of just walking away like I normally would when a conversation was displeasing, I actually said something back. "I disagree." It must have been her anger that provoked me, even though her words were so completely false that I shouldn't feel obligated to fight them at all. Stasia was just a poor loser, trying to get into my head to get my attention. "Because she's the most beautiful woman I've ever seen."

After Stasia walked away, I spotted Fender across the room—his arm around Melanie.

My eyes narrowed in confusion before I turned around to search for Raven. She wasn't there, so I returned to the sitting room to see if she was still sitting there, composing herself after the emotional conversation with her sister.

But she wasn't there either.

I scanned the room, searching for the brunette in a black dress, but there were lots of women who fit that description, and none of them was ever the woman I was searching for. The front door opened, and I caught a glimpse of Raven through the cracks between people as she left.

I had no idea where she was going.

I maneuvered around the crowd to get to the entry-way. Gilbert quickly opened the door, like he knew I had somewhere to be based on the intense look on my face. I stepped onto the main portico under-neath the twenty-foot pillars with the lit-up lawn and enormous fountain out front. I turned to the right and didn't see her. The valets were at the bottom of the stairs talking since everyone was inside and enjoying the party.

I looked to the left and saw her standing there at the very edge, leaning against one of the pillars and looking at the lights from the city in the distance. Her long hair was down her back, and her arms were crossed over her chest.

I came up behind her and stopped when I heard a sniffle. Her back rose with deep breaths, like she was doing everything she could to silence her sobs and turn quiet. Melanie looked fine, so I wasn't sure what had provoked this raw emotion. Why would she go outside when she could stay in the sitting room?

Then I remembered the way Stasia glanced behind me.

Melanie had a drink in her hand and was engaged in conversation like she'd been standing there a while.

Raven must have been behind me when Stasia decided to be a ruthless bitch.

She'd heard everything.

I stood there with my hands in the pockets of my tuxedo, unsure what to do to fix it. I could just go back inside and give Raven time to calm down on her own, but I didn't want to leave her out there alone, suffering over something that wasn't even true. There was only one thing that could bring her to tears, and name-calling wasn't it. So, this had hurt her...deeply.

I came closer to her and placed my hands on the backs of her arms so she would know I was there.

The second she felt me, she stopped breathing.

I moved until my head rested against the back of hers.

She took a few moments to slow her breathing, to return herself to calm, to get the hot tears out of her throat so she could speak. "Who is she?"

I took my time composing a response because I'd never had to give an answer like this before, never wanted to answer a lover's intrusive question. "An on-again, off-again physical relationship. We were off when I was at the camp, and then when you burned it down, we were on again…and then off when you came back." I'd always known Stasia had an ulterior motive with me, but she was easy sex, good sex, so I'd let her come back to me. "But we're off for good now."

She didn't turn around.

I waited for her to say something, to turn around and brush off what she heard.

But she didn't.

"It's not true, Raven. You know it's not."

She still didn't move into me.

My brother had made some comments, but he was an asshole, at least when it came to women. Anything less than perfect wasn't good enough for him.

Raven finally turned around, letting me see her puffy eyes, the pain still etched into her features, her ruined makeup because she had cried hard enough to make it run like black rivers down her face. "My whole life, Melanie has always been the pretty one. Every guy I liked would like her instead. If I met someone without her around, we'd hit it off...but then they would meet her, and it was always obvious they were more attracted to her than me. I've just been compared to her my entire life, and it hurts."

I'd never understood Fender's fascination with Melanie when she was so unremarkable, but I didn't say that...because Raven probably wouldn't believe me.

"When I moved to Paris, it was liberating. She was never there for comparison, and I met guys in bars and had a great time...but I always had that chip on my shoulder." Her eyes were slightly down, looking at my chin like she was too self-conscious to look me in the eye. "And then, that woman is far more beautiful than I'll ever be. And you're the sexiest man I've ever laid eyes on... I've always known that you're out of my league."

My eyes narrowed because I couldn't believe the words that came out of her mouth. "What did I say to her?"

She kept her gaze down.

My hand moved under her chin, and I forced her to lift her gaze and look me in the eye.

Her eyes started to water more, like she might cry again.

"What did I say to her?" I whispered.

When she blinked, new tears ran down her cheeks. "I'm the most beautiful woman you've ever seen…"

"And I meant it." It hurt me to see her like this, to have her ever feel inferior to a woman with half the brains, half the courage, and a fraction of her looks. Raven had a glow in her eyes that reminded me of the brightest stars in the night sky even on a cloudy night…because they were that luminous. There was no comparison, and there never had been one.

"I know…" Her hands moved to my chest, her fingers feeling the buttons of my tuxedo shirt. "It's the first time in my life that I have a man who thinks I'm the pretty one…who only notices me and not her…and I never thought that would happen."

When she blinked, her tears fell down her wet cheeks. "I don't have to compete with her. I don't have to compete with anyone. Because you see me...you really see me."

Now I finally understood why she'd come out here to be alone, finally understood what her tears really meant. They grew from heartbreak. And then they fell down her cheeks for a different reason altogether. "*Ma petite amie...*" *My girlfriend.* My hands cupped her face, and I wiped her tears away with my thumbs, cradling her face in my embrace. "You see me too."

TWENTY-FOUR
THE SLAP

TWO WEEKS AWAY FROM THE CAMP HAD NEVER BEEN enough, and now it felt like even less time with Raven. The first day at the apartment was always a rough transition. We were tired from the long journey, and the dirt was still deep underneath our fingertips because only an intense scrubbing could clear it away. But the following day...the camp felt like a distant memory.

It gave us two different lives.

The one in Paris was one...and the camp was another.

I lay on the couch with the TV on, Raven cuddled into my side in my t-shirt, one arm over my stomach while her leg was tucked between my knees. Her soft hair was always against my skin, gently tickling it, taunting me.

I hit the screen on my phone and knew it was time for me to go. I shifted gently underneath her so she would know to move aside. I took my phone with me into my bedroom and changed into my jeans and t-shirt. When I came out dressed, she knew I was leaving.

"Where are you going?"

"Work."

"When you say work, what does that entail?" She was cold without me, so she grabbed a blanket and pulled it over her legs.

"I'm meeting Fender to prepare a new distributor."

"The one you don't like?"

I nodded.

"Be careful, okay?" Every time I left, she wanted me to come back. She wanted me to be returned to her in the same condition as when I left.

I drove to Fender's place, and Gilbert let me inside. It wasn't as grand without a party taking place, but it was still a beautiful property that displayed his ridiculous wealth, wealth that hadn't been passed down through generations until it reached his hands. It had been earned in one lifetime.

Gilbert guided me out the back patio to where Fender sat at one of the tables. The rectangular pool was lit up a deep blue color, and Melanie rested her arms on the edge next to her drink, looking the other way to the lawn that stretched for acres behind the estate.

Fender didn't look at me as I joined him.

Gilbert immediately placed a scotch in front of me and silently excused himself. A cheese board was on the table, with hard and soft cheeses as well as Marcona almonds, dried cherries, and dried apricots. A long baguette had already been sliced.

I wasn't hungry.

Fender didn't touch it either.

It was probably for his muse in the pool.

He stared at her for a long time, the light from the pool reflecting on his face. "You left early."

"Raven wasn't feeling well." After our conversation outside on the portico, I took her home. Neither one of us wanted to go back inside and mingle with people who didn't matter. Her cheeks were puffy and her eyes were too red not to be noticed, and I didn't want Stasia to rejoice in her success, even though her tactics only brought us closer together.

Fender was quiet, but his silence showed his annoyance. "Napoleon and I agreed on a starting amount, a small introduction to the game. We'll see how he does and go from there."

Our conversation at the party had only deepened my suspicion, but I kept those doubts to myself this time.

"You're the one who has to work with him most of the time. Is that going to be a problem?"

I stared across the grounds, surrounded by fantastic gardens and a distinct sensation that made us feel separated far away from everything else. The city lights were visible, but they were easily blurred out by everything right in front of us. "You already know how I feel about him."

"But can you play nice?"

"I can do my job. Didn't say anything about being pleasant while doing it."

Fender grabbed his glass of wine and took a drink, his eyes on Melanie again.

"But this is a mistake, Fender."

He took another drink before he set the glass down on the table. "If we can get product through Spain, we can use Napoleon to supply the entire African continent. That's a lot of money on the table."

"If he has such a big cut, why wouldn't he just over-throw us?"

"Because he doesn't know how to get the drugs."

"Come on, Fender," I snapped. "If he really wanted to figure it out, after some time, he could. And this guy works in a whole different country. We really don't know enough about him."

When Melanie heard us raise our voices, she turned around to look at us.

"We agreed from the very beginning that we would only have small distributors, that we would keep them oppressed so they can't rise up and defy us. But by recruiting someone like Napoleon, you're risking all of that. And who the fuck names himself Napoleon? He's not even European."

Fender remained calm despite my outburst. "We're expanding. That's how it works."

"There are a lot of other ways to do that."

Melanie got out of the pool and wrapped herself in the towel waiting for her at the edge. Her hair was pulled back into a bun, with gold hoops from her lobes. She had a full face of makeup even though she was swimming.

Fender watched her round the pool and approach. "Most beautiful woman in the world, isn't she?"

I stared at the side of his face, remembering when he'd insulted Raven when she was right there, and I realized I knew exactly what she was talking about. He'd never remarked on the appearance of any woman I'd been with, but since Raven was Melanie's sister and they looked different from each other, he felt compelled to say something cold. "I disagree."

Fender didn't seem to hear me because his entire focus was on the woman walking toward him. He gently patted his thigh, and she came to his lap like a well-trained animal. He pulled her legs across his thighs and kissed her.

I stared at the pool.

Melanie helped herself to the cheese board and drank from his glass of wine.

I knew the conversation was over.

Melanie lifted her gaze and looked at me as she ate. "Is Raven okay? You two left abruptly."

"She's fine."

She drank from the wineglass, her eyes on me. "You're lying. You and Fender make the same face when you do that."

"I'm not lying. She's fine."

"Maybe now she's fine, but she wasn't."

Fender stepped in. "She wasn't feeling well. Supposedly."

Melanie set down the glass and ignored the gourmet food in front of her. Every glass of wine she had was from a vintage bottle, and the butler took care of every single need she had, she swam in a big pool in a mansion and sat in the lap of a man who adored her. Why would she jeopardize any of that? She wasn't like Raven whatsoever. She was superficial, dull, and weak. "Please tell me."

It was hard for me to deny her when I knew she genuinely cared about her sister's well-being. She couldn't just call and ask her herself. It might be months before they saw each other again. "One of my old lovers said something to her."

"What?" Melanie asked.

I shrugged. "That she doesn't understand why I left her for someone much less attractive, basically." It was untrue. Stasia had fake tits, plastic surgery, skipped breakfast, and only ate a hard-boiled egg for lunch every single day. She was worse than Melanie. "Which is completely untrue. She just said it to start shit."

Melanie erupted like a volcano, dormant one moment then explosive the next. "I'm gonna knock that bitch out! Who the fuck is this skank?"

Fender chuckled at her anger. "Come on, she's right. Stasia is sexy, and your sister is a swine."

Melanie turned to him and gave him a vicious stare. She was still for a second before she pushed off him and got to her feet. Then she stared down at him, so furious she didn't know what to do. Her palm slapped across his face so hard that an audible smack echoed over the grounds. "Don't talk about my sister like that, asshole."

My eyes were wide because I couldn't believe that just happened.

Melanie marched back to the house, her legs moving quickly because she wanted to get away from Fender as quickly as possible.

Fender turned to watch her go, but he didn't go after her. His hand moved to his cheek, and he rubbed the inflamed skin before he grabbed his wine and took a drink like nothing happened. "Kinda liked it." He looked across the grounds and swirled his glass absentmindedly.

I'd never really liked Melanie because she was so submissive and stupid. Respect was difficult to earn from me, and it took courage and guts to get my admiration. But she'd earned a little bit tonight.

I didn't return to the apartment until two.

I had other shit to do after leaving Fender's place. I had to drop in on my distributors to make sure they were following the guidelines they agreed to once we signed them on. My job was all about account-ability, both in and out of the camp.

I left my wallet and keys downstairs because I didn't lock up anything around Raven. There were guns stowed in every room of the apartment, and I had no doubt she'd uncovered at least one at some point in time. But I'd dropped my guard around her the way I did with one other person—my brother.

I walked upstairs and noticed the light coming from the bedroom. One of the lamps was on. I stepped inside and found her sitting up in bed, reading a book by the light of the lamp. She must have been at a really good part because she didn't look up at me right away. Her eyes trailed from left to right as she finished the page. Then she looked up at me. "Glad you're home."

I pulled my shirt over my head and tossed it on the floor. My shoes and jeans were left in the same spot on the floor. "Why are you still awake?" She was usually up early, going for a walk and getting a coffee and muffin.

"It's just too hard to sleep without you now." She set the book on the nightstand then turned off the lamp.

I got into bed beside her and turned on my side to look at her.

She scooted right up next to me, so our bodies were close, her face just inches from mine. One hand slid under the sheets and moved to my chest so her fingers could feel the warm skin over my abs. "How'd it go?"

I didn't want to tell her what Fender had said, but I wanted her to know that her sister had her back when she wasn't even there. "Melanie asked about you."

"How is she?"

"Living the life, frankly."

She smiled slightly. "Yeah…I picked up on that."

"She asked why you left the party early. I told her the real reason."

Her fingers stopped moving against me.

"Fender made an asshole comment about it. Melanie told him off and slapped him across the face."

Raven's eyes immediately widened in surprise. "What?"

"And she slapped him hard."

"Melanie?" She was incredulous at first but then started to laugh. "Oh my god, I cannot picture that."

"Well, she did." I smiled, loving the fact that she focused on the good part of the story instead of the bad.

"What did he do?"

"Just sat there. Said he liked it."

"Damn, she's got him wrapped around her finger."

"Big-time."

She chuckled again as she looked into my face. "You never smile…"

My lips slowly started to sink. "Not much to smile about."

"But you look so handsome when you do it." Her fingers moved to the corner of my mouth, and she gently brushed her thumb along my bottom lip. "I wish I could see you smile every day."

"I wish I could see you laugh every day."

Her eyes softened in a way I'd never seen before. "Maybe one day…we will."

TWENTY-FIVE
ALWAYS BE THIS WAY

OVERNIGHT, EVERYTHING CHANGED.

She was different.

Cold. Distant. Quiet.

When we passed coffee shops, she didn't have the same excitement she used to. There wasn't affection in her eyes when she looked at me, if she looked at me at all. I hadn't done anything to warrant her indifference, so I assumed it was a mood that would pass on its own.

The only time she was the woman I knew was when we made love.

When I woke up that morning, she had already gotten her morning coffee and muffins, and my cup

of coffee was sitting on the counter. I grabbed it
and took a drink, noticing she wasn't reading in the
living room.

I set the cup on the counter then walked into her
old bedroom.

She sat in the armchair and read her book, her
back angled slightly, earrings hanging down.

I leaned against the doorframe and stared at her.

She didn't acknowledge me.

"What did I do?"

She stilled at the sound of my voice, her eyes lifting
up to the window.

I waited for an explanation that never came.
"You've been different for days. I thought your
mood would pass, and it hasn't. I don't want to
spend our remaining time this way." My arms
crossed over my chest, and I continued to
watch her.

After a long pause, she closed her book and looked
out the window.

"Tell me."

She set the book on the table and got to her feet, finally looking at me for the first time in days, really looking at me. Her eyes took in my features, having that hint of emotion that had been absent for a while. She walked toward me then moved past me into the living room.

My heart started to ache. Our foundation was still there, rock-solid, but she was different…and I couldn't figure out why. Not knowing something about her scared me because I always knew every thought that came across her complex mind.

I dropped my arms and turned around.

She stood in the middle of the living room, her arms crossed.

The longer she stayed quiet, the more uncomfortable I became. "What did I do?"

She ran her fingers through her hair and shook her head. "Nothing."

"Then what's the problem?"

She lifted her gaze and looked into mine.

I waited, holding my breath.

"We can't do this for the rest of our lives." One hand slid up and down her arm, lightly touching her soft skin. "Can you do this for the rest of your life?"

I gave her a blank stare.

She stepped closer to me. "Because I can't."

I looked for further explanation in her eyes because I didn't understand her words. "I don't understand your meaning, *ma petite amie*."

Her eyes softened. "Look, if you want us to be together, things have to change. If you want to be with me, *really* be with me, then our lives have to be different."

My eyes shifted back and forth as I focused on her face. "If I want to be with you? What the fuck does that mean? What the fuck have I been doing since the moment we met? I've been with you, even when we were apart, even when I was with another woman, because my heart has always been with you."

She raised her voice when I raised mine. "And this will just be our lives forever?" she asked incredulously. "Going back and forth between here and the camp? Years will pass and we'll age, but we'll never really live? What about spending our lives together and having a family? How the fuck are we supposed to do that like this?"

"I've never spoken of marriage and kids to you."

"No. But it's a requirement to be with me, so you'll do it."

My eyes narrowed. "We're getting way ahead of ourselves here——"

"Shut the fuck up, Magnus. We've only known each other for months, but we've experienced more than couples together for a lifetime. The scar on my stomach will never go away, a reminder that I was willing to give up my life for yours. How many people can say that? We've suffered through unspeakable shit, and we're still together. If that hasn't pulled us apart, then what will?"

I clenched my jaw because I was furious and I didn't know why. "You're talking about a dream that I can't give you. You know that. So yes, this will be our lives indefinitely."

She shook her head, her eyes watery. "How can you watch *your girlfriend* go back and forth, almost be raped twice, be tortured—and you just allow it to happen?"

"I don't allow it. I've tried—"

"We'll never really be together until you change it."

I shook my head, my teeth clenched. "I will get Fender to release you eventually—"

"That doesn't solve the problem, Magnus. Even if he excused both of us, we'd never be happy. How could we ever forget what's happening at that camp every single day we're free? I could never forget it, so I could never really live. We could never have the life together that we want."

"What the fuck do you expect me to do about that?" If I could give her the world, I would. Tears had fallen from my eyes when I was pinned to the floor and listening to her scream my name. I hated that she had to be in that camp when I wanted her to have the freedom I'd already busted my ass to give her.

She turned quiet, breathing hard. "I expect you to stop it."

"Stop it, how?"

"Whatever way you can."

I shook my head. "We talked about this. I won't kill my brother—"

"Then convince him to do it in a different way."

"You know I've already tried. He won't change his mind."

"Then you make him change it," she snapped. "How can I spend my life with the man who's been part of such a horrible place?"

She'd just stabbed me with a knife.

"I need you to redeem yourself...fully."

"You said I'm not like them."

"And I stand by that. But for us to be together and move on, you need to make this right. You need to free those girls and not let new ones replace them—"

"In case you haven't noticed, there is terrible shit going on all over the world." I was pissed she was holding all this over my head, using my feelings for her as leverage. "You expect me to stop that too?"

"No, because you aren't a part of that."

I dragged my hands down my face, calming myself before I said something I regretted. "I do this, or you leave me?"

"No…I said nothing about leaving. I'm not going anywhere—*ever*." Her eyes filled with wetness. "But I'll never let you in further. We'll always be as we are…but never more. And you have no idea how much I want more. I don't just want my freedom, but I want to spend that freedom with *you*."

My hands moved to my hips, my eyes down.

She stared at me.

I ignored her look.

"Magnus."

I kept my gaze on the floor in defiance for minutes before I raised my chin and looked at her.

"I know you. I know your soul. And I know that you want to do the right thing anyway…" The emotion in her eyes changed into a look of longing, like I was the hero of her heart, I was the man who wouldn't just keep her safe, but everyone. She gave me a cape with only her eyes. "I know that's what you want, even if I didn't ask you to."

We walked together down the sidewalk, the cafes and bistros lit up with couples, friends, and family enjoying the summer evening in the most glorious city in the world. People passed us on the sidewalk as we made our way to the restaurant she'd chosen. We'd never gone out to dinner together, usually cooking in the apartment and having a quiet evening at the dining table. But she'd asked me to take her out—and I said yes.

She was in a black cocktail dress and heels with a small purse hanging off her shoulder even though she didn't have keys or a wallet. She only had a few bills inside, money I had given her and forced her to take.

She suddenly moved her hand to mine and interlocked our fingers.

I looked down at her beside me, still shorter than my height in her heels, and then I looked forward again. My hand gave her a gentle squeeze.

A soft smile moved into her lips, and she looked up at me.

I stared at her, seeing the way her eyes lit up in affection once more, brighter than the Eiffel Tower nearby, brighter than the Christmas trees in the windows during the holidays. She was the only woman who ever looked at me that way, who could make me feel special without saying a word.

We arrived at the restaurant and were given a table inside.

She sat across from me and looked at her menu, her makeup making her eyes stand out, her dress tight and sexy on her nice figure. Her brown hair was pulled to one side, and without realizing it, she bit her bottom lip as she tried to decipher the menu.

I stared at her instead of the selections.

She didn't notice. "Normally, I use Google translate for this, but I don't have a phone." She raised her chin and looked at me. "Any recommendations?"

"What are you in the mood for? There's beef cannelloni, citrus avocado with salmon, seafood pasta, roasted lamb, margherita pizza, steak and fries…"

"Ooh…that's a good list." She looked at the menu again even though she couldn't read it. "What are you getting?"

"Cannelloni." I set the menu at the edge of the table.

"I don't know if I want the pizza or the steak…"

"What if you get the steak and take the pizza home?"

"Can I do that?" She looked over her menu again, her eyebrows raised.

"Yes." A smile fought through my restraints and came on to my lips.

Her eyes softened when she saw it, like that was one of the things in the world that made her happy… when I was happy. "You're gonna get a blow job when we get back to the apartment." She set the menu at the edge of the table.

My smile widened. "We should go out to dinner more often."

I sat against the headboard and watched her move up and down slowly, taking my dick completely before she used her powerful thighs to raise herself once again. Her tits were in front of me, firm and sexy, and I just sat there and watched this incredible woman enjoy me like I was the only man in the world she wanted to be with.

My hands moved to her tits, and I squeezed them, listening to her breathe hard from both pleasure and exertion. She would close her eyes and let her lips part, releasing a gasp when my dick hit her in the perfect spot. I watched her with fascination, deep in the moment but also outside of it, watching this gorgeous woman make love to me in the sexiest way. She rolled her hips slowly, dragged her hands down my hard chest, cupped my face and kissed me with trembling lips. "Magnus." With her lips pressed to mine, she said my name.

My hands went to her ass and guided her up and down, knowing she was close. So was I. "*Ma petite amie…*" My face moved into her neck, and I felt my dick harden even more, knowing she was right at the edge.

She clawed my shoulders as she came, releasing a loud gasp followed by several more. "Yes…"

My arms wrapped around her waist, and I finished with her, both of us moaning and writhing as we hit ecstasy at the same time. My arms squeezed her harder than I should, but she never protested against the tightness, like she could handle a man's crushing embrace, even liked it.

As the crescendo of our passion faded, my hold slackened and my arms slid across her back as I pulled away, looking into her watery eyes and seeing the passion burn her all the way through. Just like always.

She moved into me and placed a final kiss on my lips before she got off me and lay in the spot beside me, her naked body coated in sweat, her hair in disarray. She closed her eyes and lay on top of the sheets.

I held my position and looked at her, watched her recover from the exertion because she was the one who'd done all the work for the last forty-five minutes. My hand went to her arm, and I gently grazed my fingers across it, feeling the dampness of her sticky skin.

Then she got out of bed, pulled on my t-shirt, and walked out of the room.

My head turned as my eyes followed her.

Her footsteps sounded on the stairs and then disappeared.

I grabbed my glass of water and took a drink.

When she came back, the pizza box was in her hand.

My eyebrows rose, and a gentle smile moved on to my lips.

She got back into the bed beside me and opened the top to grab a slice.

I just watched her.

"What?" She chewed a bite as she held the pizza box in her lap, her eyes on the contents of the box.

"I didn't say anything."

"You've never seen a woman eat pizza after sex?"

"No."

She opened the lid and turned the box toward me. "Want some?"

I shook my head.

"Come on, it's amazing."

I ate three meals a day and never snacked in between. I also avoided desserts because I didn't have a sweet tooth. In general, I wasn't much of an eater. I preferred to drink copious amounts of wine and scotch instead.

She took another bite and leaned against the headboard, her sexy legs poking out from underneath her shirt. "I want to eat as much of this good stuff as I can before we go back." She took another bite and ate closer to the crust.

When we stayed in Paris, it was easy to fall into this dreamlike reality, enjoying the city and each other. Sometimes I forgot about the camp altogether… until the departure date drew near. The feud with Alix had been resolved, or at least it seemed, so Raven wouldn't be in danger. But bringing her to that miserable place was getting more and more difficult.

She bit the crust in half as she watched me. "What?"

I shifted my gaze to hers, unsure what she referred to.

"You disappeared."

My eyes looked away again, staring at my dark bedroom and the shadows in the corners. "Nothing."

TWENTY-SIX

BACK TO THE BEGINNING

I DROVE DOWN THE STREET LINED WITH APARTMENTS in one of the upscale neighborhoods of Paris. People walked down the sidewalk with their dogs on leashes, their hands holding mugs of coffee. Shopping bags were in their hands, baguettes sticking out alongside the necks of wine bottles. It was still the quiet neighborhood I remembered.

When I recognized the house, I pulled over and parked in front of it.

Raven turned to look out my window, knowing we'd stopped for an important reason. We were on our way back to the camp, but I'd decided to take a detour. She held her silence and watched me look out the window.

I'd only come back to that house once. The city had repossessed it and sold it to pay off some of my father's debts. I'd watched the new family move inside—they'd gotten it at a cheap price because of the murders that had taken place.

There was a new coat of paint on the outside, but it otherwise looked the same.

Raven didn't ask any questions, picking up on my mood and my stare. "That's where you grew up."

I kept my gaze on the entrance, seeing the front door open and a teenage boy take the steps to the bottom. He turned right and continued on his way, oblivious to the two of us staring at him intently.

"Does it look different?"

I shook my head. "There's a new coat of paint on the exterior, but…" I remembered the Christmas tree that used to be in the front window every year. We would decorate it with ornaments we'd kept since childhood. The house would be filled with the roast turkey my mom would cook for hours, starting right in the morning. I remembered our family vacations to Italy and Switzerland. My childhood had been wonderful, with two loving parents and siblings I'd never forgotten. Money had ruined us, not because we'd lost it, but because my father thought it was more important than the most priceless thing he had—us. My brother seemed to have fallen victim to the same illness, chasing wealth like it was the answer to all his problems, like it would somehow prove something to our dead father, who'd been dumped in the ocean.

I liked being rich just like everyone else, but I also thought it was evil.

Her hand moved to mine as it rested on the center console. Her fingers moved in between mine, and she gave me a gentle squeeze, telling me she was there even though she didn't have the words to comfort me.

"My mother was a housewife. She kept that place perfect at all times, ready for any unexpected company that would stop by. Our meals were homemade every single evening. If she ever saw anyone less fortunate than us, she didn't hesitate to open her purse and hand over all her cash. She was really generous with her time, money, and her love…"

Her hand squeezed mine again.

"I have good memories of my father too. Before he pissed our inheritance away, he was a good man… for the most part. But he lost his mind when he lost his money." My father laughed loudest at the dinner table and was eager to take my brothers and me to sporting events. He loved us…at one time. "My eldest brother was quiet and studious. He went to university but chose to live at home because he wouldn't be able to survive without my mother's cooking. Can't blame him. And my sister…" I pulled my gaze away from the front door and looked straight ahead over the steering wheel. I could still hear her voice in my head sometimes, in my dreams, and she had the most innocent soul of anyone I'd ever known. Losing every member of my family was difficult, but her death was the worst. "She was my twin."

Raven released a quiet breath, a silent gasp.

"It's hard to explain, but when you're a twin, there's a different connection there. She was the hardest one to lose."

She pulled my hand to her lips and kissed my knuckles.

The feeling of her soft lips made me turn to face her.

Her eyes were wet, like my story had moved her down to her core. "I'm so sorry, Magnus."

I'd never talked about this with anyone before. Fender and I didn't even speak of it. The only conversation we'd had occurred when we hunted down our father and killed him. But once he was gone, that was it. We never spoke of that evening ever again. We never visited their graves. It was almost like it didn't happen at all…even though we both thought about it all the time. "It was a long time ago. But it's one of the things you never really forget…no matter how much time has passed."

She lowered my hand and held it on the armrest between us. "I know…"

I kept our hands joined for a moment longer, my eyes gazing down at our affection. My hand was twice the size of hers, with little scars. She had small scars too, from her time at the camp, from her battles to survive. They were almost the same.

Like we were the same person.

We arrived at the camp at sunrise.

The girls were being escorted to the clearing, and the guards stood along the perimeter, wearing their uniforms to hide their faces from the women, to engage an extra layer of fear to keep them focused on their tasks.

When I stepped into the clearing with Raven in tow, I could feel the change in energy.

I could even hear it, even though it had no sound.

I walked with her to her station, where she would pick up the boxes and distribute them to her table. Once she was back in that camp, it was back to work. Her freedom was gone. There were no long walks to the coffee shop near the tower. She was back to her empty existence, just another worker on the line.

There was nothing I could do about it.

She immediately got to work without saying goodbye or behaving like I was more than her guard.

I stared at her for a few extra seconds than I should have, thinking about that painful conversation we had about the future…about us. She was right—it was hard to leave Paris to work as a prisoner when she was more than that. But I turned around and departed the clearing, feeling the gaze of the guards right in my back.

It'd been a long night and I wanted to go to sleep, but I stayed awake and caught up on everything I'd missed. I needed to talk to my contacts in Colombia to begin the shipment to Spain so Napoleon could have a higher product quantity than our other distributors. I didn't agree with it, but I wouldn't defy Fender by purposely sabotaging his plan. I just hoped I was wrong…about all of it.

I walked into the communal cabin to find the guys playing poker, their favorite activity when the camp was asleep. It'd been two weeks since I'd left, and Alix's face was still a bit bruised—along with everyone else's.

Breaking the bones in his face wasn't enough satisfaction.

I was still angry.

I stopped at the table and looked down at them.

Alix didn't hide his raw reaction, the glimpse of fear that entered his eyes when he saw me staring down at them all with that furious look. He dropped his cards on the table. "You want in, Magnus?"

"No." I was angry at the other guys for their participation in the plan, but I knew Alix was the one who brainstormed the entire thing. I didn't need to waste my time interrogating them all to figure it out. "Trying to decide if I want to break your nose again."

The guys stilled at the threat, keeping their heads down as if they wanted to disappear, even the ones who hadn't been the problem in the past.

"Or your dick."

Alix held my gaze, but he wasn't the confident thug he used to be. "I thought we moved past this."

"I did too—the first three times."

Alix dropped his gaze, as if he knew this was entirely his fault.

"Come within twenty feet of her, and I'll kill you. Look at her…and I'll kill you." Her screams would haunt me for the rest of my life. They would play on repeat, even though she'd been spared from his ultimate cruelty. That feeling of pure helplessness, stuck to the floor while she begged for me to rescue her, was the worst experience of my life. It was somehow worse than listening to Fender tell me how our father had executed our family. "That goes for the rest of you, too."

Raven constantly possessed a somber mood while at the camp.

She wasn't playful or talkative.

I used to be the one who craved silence in the cabin, to work on my laptop without hearing the sound of her voice, but now that situation had been reversed. She was the one who craved the quiet.

She was also exhausted at bedtime because she worked in the scorching heat all day. Summer brought constant sunshine to the camp along with humidity, and the tarp over the clearing wasn't enough to combat the temperature of the sun.

Time seemed to pause.

We weren't living like we were in Paris…just existing.

The small bed didn't bother me anymore because we were practically one person during the night. The cabin had AC, so we weren't hot when we were close together, but we did sleep in the nude.

My eyes were on the window up above, looking at the moonlight as it poked through the curtain. It'd been a long day, but I couldn't sleep. She was in my arms, her hand on my chest and her cheek on my shoulder.

She started to shift in her sleep, moving like she couldn't get comfortable. Then her breathing escalated, a couple of suppressed whimpers coming from her mouth.

I watched her, wondering if she was suffering through a nightmare.

Then she jolted upright quickly, her eyes wide open and on the door, panting like she'd just sprinted a mile. When she realized the door was closed and there was no one in the cabin, she leaned against the wall and let her breathing return to normal.

I sat up and watched her.

Her hand moved over her chest like she had a stitch in the muscle. Her fingers slid through her hair next, taking a long time to bring herself back to a state of calm.

I didn't know how to comfort her. She was against the wall like she wanted to get as far away from me as possible. Her eyes didn't turn my way, like my existence didn't make her feel better either. After a final deep breath, she started to breathe normally, to drop her gaze from the door when the danger was really over.

Without having to ask, I knew exactly what her nightmare was about.

Alix had stormed in here and stripped all her clothes away before parading her outside, taking away all her dignity as if he had the right to claim it for himself. My power wasn't enough to keep her safe—not in that instance. If Fender hadn't randomly entered the camp and shown his loyalty to me, her fate would have been unspeakable.

A tear formed in the corner of her eye and streaked down her cheek, illuminated like a liquid diamond. She was calm now, so the tear must have formed previously but didn't have the weight to fall.

It was hard to look at her, hard to see the strongest woman I knew break down from her fears. "That will never happen again, Raven. You're safe."

She turned her body so her back was completely against the wall, and she crossed her arms over her chest like she was somehow cold in this summer heat. "As long as I'm here, I'll never really feel safe."

At nightfall, I waited at the gate.

The sound of approaching hooves announced Fender's arrival. One of his armed guards shouted over the fence to let us know they were there. They turned the lock on their side of the door, and then I turned mine.

I pulled both the doors open and let the horses pass through. Fender was in the center and in the lead. He was in his typical jeans, boots, and a long-sleeved shirt because it was a bit cooler that night than usual. The guys behind him turned off their flashlights once they were in the lit-up camp.

My brother got off his horse then removed his gloves. The men immediately moved in to take his things and lead his horse away to the stables without making a single noise. There was no greeting. No questions. Fender stepped farther into the camp and scanned his surroundings, as if a simple observation was enough to gauge the progress of the work happening in his absence. He looked at the clearing for a few seconds before he glanced at the edge of the fence, his paranoid mind needing assurance of safety with his own gaze.

I came to his side. "Do you want to talk tomorrow?" I noticed that he hadn't brought Melanie to the camp again. That seemed to be a one-time thing. I wondered what she was doing while he was away. Did she have the liberty to go anywhere she chose? Like Raven did?

"No." He moved ahead, crossing the space between the cabins toward his at the rear of the camp. The man was never tired, despite the long journey it took to bring him there.

I walked with him.

"Alix giving you any trouble?"

"No. I'm the one giving him trouble."

"Well, don't kill him. Executioners are hard to come by."

I suddenly felt sick. Men volunteered to do the dirty work because it wasn't the kind of job you could simply assign. You had to possess a special kind of evil to be able to stomach that kind of violence.

Fender asked me about production and our status with the shipment to Spain. "Were you able to negotiate a deal?"

"I did. But it's considerably more expensive to do it this way, which means we'll need to raise our prices."

"Done."

"But this will make it much riskier. Not sure if it makes sense to pursue it."

Fender stopped and turned on me. "It'll increase our revenue by fifty percent. Tell me, how does that *not* make sense?"

I stared at my brother's hard face, seeing a man so focused on the past and the future at the same time. He turned to money as the answer to all his problems, the cure to his nightmares. But it was driving him mad. "I think continuing an existing successful business takes precedence over higher profits. Fender, you're already wealthier than all other wealthy men—combined. What is it gonna take for you to be satisfied?"

He stared at me a bit longer before he continued forward.

I joined him.

He looked ahead as if I hadn't asked a question at all. "I will never be satisfied. Don't ask a question when you already know the answer." He reached the cabin and stepped inside. His meal was already on the table, along with a decanter of scotch and a glass. Everyone knew of his visit to the camp that evening, so they were all prepared.

Fender fell onto the couch and immediately started to eat.

I stayed by the door. "Goodnight." I turned to leave.

"No. I have something to say to you."

With my hand on the door, I stared at his back. His muscles shifted and moved as he ate his dinner, staring at the opposite wall. I could see all the good and all the bad instantaneously, and I knew my brother wasn't just the wealthiest man I'd ever known but also the stubbornest. I released the door and joined him on the couch.

Fender took a drink of scotch before he looked at me. He held my stare for a long time, processing the words in his head before he spoke them aloud. "Raven is free to leave the camp."

I heard what he said because there could be no confusion at all, but I continued my blank stare because his words entered my ears but not my brain. The stubbornest man in the world had changed his mind.

"Next time you return to Paris, take her with you. And leave her there." As if he had finished saying everything he wanted to say on the matter, he dropped his chin and looked at his plate so he could continue eating his steak and potatoes. After a long journey on the road, he always wanted a good meal on his table.

For a minute, I was speechless. I'd begged for her release many times, and every request was denied. I didn't want her to be here a moment longer, to wake up in the middle of the night and stare at the door like someone was about to break through it to take her. She was so joyful in Paris, and that was what I wanted for her every day. "Thank you." It didn't matter why he'd changed his mind. I got what I wanted, and I was grateful.

"I didn't do it for you." He finished chewing before he set down his fork and grabbed a drink. He tilted his head back and poured a good amount into his mouth before he set down the glass once again. "I did it for Melanie."

"Then I guess you two made up." Last time I saw them together, she'd slapped him across the face before she'd stormed into the house.

"I asked her to marry me."

With a non-blinking stare, I looked at my brother, never expecting him to say something like that. Time had passed strangely for the last few months, but that was all it had been...a few months. A woman he hardly knew had stolen his affection, and he was so obsessively blinded by her beauty that he became irrational and impulsive. It wasn't like him at all. Sometimes his greed made him do stupid things, but a woman had never made him do stupid things.

"She said yes." He stopped eating his dinner and rubbed his hands together, his eyes a little hazy like he was replaying the moment in his head. "But only if I let Raven go. She said she couldn't marry the man who kept her sister as a prisoner. I didn't have a choice, so I agreed."

Whether Melanie actually wanted to marry him or not didn't make a difference. I got what I wanted. It was such a relief, a load off my shoulders. I was powerful enough to keep her safe, but I would never make her happy…not here.

"But if she returns to this camp and pulls another stunt like she did last time…I'll execute her myself. If she does anything at all to interfere with business, I'll kill her. I suggest you make that very clear to her."

After everything we'd been through, I didn't think that would be a problem. Raven knew there was nothing she could do to change the situation. Even if she came back and burned the camp to the ground, it would just be rebuilt in a couple months, and the process would start all over. But I also knew that as long as this camp continued to function in this manner, it would haunt her until her dying day.

Fender grabbed his glass and took a drink. "I thought you would be more cheerful."

My eyes dropped for a moment, thinking about the best way to phrase my words, to give myself the best chance of success. "There are other ways of running this camp, better ways."

His gaze turned cold, like he already knew what I was trying to do.

"We could replace the girls with paid labor, and we could threaten—"

"No."

Damn, I'd barely gotten past the first sentence.

"If I won't do it for Melanie, why would I do it for you?"

At least Melanie had tried.

"I told her I would honor one of her demands, but not both. Raven will be free, but the camp will continue to run flawlessly as it has for years. There is no better system of operation—and we both know that."

The only reason I'd mentioned it to him at all was because it was important to Raven. But I knew it was futile. I wouldn't move against him, but convincing him with just words was ineffective. It didn't matter how strongly opposed I was to all of this; it would never change. I'd tried for years and years. When Raven was free, she might feel differently; she might learn to let it go.

Fender returned to eating. There were a few stalks of asparagus left, so he grabbed each one by the base and bit the tip, crunching the vegetable between his teeth.

I didn't agree with a lot of things Fender did, but he was my brother, and my loyalty would always be ironclad. That was why I started to feel guilty, harboring this secret from him when I should've told him months ago. "Melanie only came back to you to save Raven." I would've kept that information to myself, but now that my brother intended to marry her, I couldn't just look the other way.

He continued to eat, as if that information were irrelevant.

I studied him, waiting for some kind of reaction.

When he reached the bottom of the stalk, he tossed it back onto the plate. "You kept this from me."

"I didn't think it would matter to you. I didn't realize your feelings were so profound until now."

He rubbed his hands together as he looked at me, serious but not angry. "You're right. It doesn't matter. That woman is mine, and I will have her so no one else ever can. Whether she truly wants me or not, it doesn't change what I want. Together, we will make strong sons and beautiful daughters. She will be the woman in my bed every night, and every man who sees her on my arm will wish he were me. She serves a purpose, and she does that very well."

"If this is what you want, I'm happy for you."

He reached for his glass and held it at the top, his fingers resting down over the rim. "Maybe she did only return to me because she wanted something from me. I was foolish not to see it. But she fucks me so good that I really don't give a damn."

TWENTY-SEVEN

WHERE YOU GO, I GO

I DECIDED NOT TO TELL RAVEN.

If I told her this was the last time she would be in the camp, waiting for the week to pass would be excruciating. It would give her hope, and that would make every day at the clearing and every night in that small cabin all the more unbearable.

I also didn't want to tell her Melanie was marrying my brother.

I knew she wouldn't be happy about that.

I failed to understand my brother's fascination with that woman. I could understand the physical lust for a few months, but a relationship for a lifetime? That simply baffled me. Would you want to spend your life with a woman with no brains and no courage? Yes, their children would be beautiful, but they would also be idiots.

Raven's and my relationship was different when we were in the camp. Our connection was just as strong as ever, but there was definitely a lower level of joy to our interactions. As if a shadow passed over the sky and blocked out the sun, we were subdued and miserable. We were withdrawn from each other, not having deep conversations, just necessary words. We both seemed to count down the time until we got to leave.

Once the day arrived, we took the wagons with two other men and made it to the edge of the forest. Even on the seven-hour journey, she didn't say much. With melancholy in her veins, she just wasn't herself. Now that I knew a whole different side of her, it was hard to be in the presence of her sadness when there was a much better version of her.

When we got to the car, I drove down the country roads and headed toward Paris.

She immediately went to sleep.

I made the journey alone with the radio for company. I thought about my conversation with

Fender and his intention to marry Melanie. I never asked when this wedding was taking place or if there would be a wedding at all. Would it just be a bunch of papers to sign? Or would there be an actual ceremony? I didn't ask any of those questions because it had still seemed unreal at the time.

Hours later, we arrived in Paris.

She woke up and looked out the window, staring at the city near to her heart. She was instantly more relaxed, like she was on vacation. The corners of her lips lifted slightly, and she took in the lights of the city.

I pulled into the garage, and we went upstairs.

She made her way into the living room and immediately stripped off her clothes, as if they were chains that bound her body to that camp. She let them sit on the floor, even taking off her underwear and bra because she didn't want anything touching her skin. "You said you have other residences." She pulled her hair out of her ponytail and let the strands fall around her shoulders as she looked at me.

Even on her worst day, I found her beauty exceptional. "Yes."

"And is Rose at one of those residences?"

I'd kept my promise even when she'd betrayed me. "Yes."

Her eyes lit up like the moon on a clear night. "Can we visit her soon?"

We could do whatever she wanted, and she knew that. "Sure."

She bent down and picked up her clothes before she went upstairs and threw them in the hamper. Then she got into bed and lay under the sheets, ready to go straight to sleep after a long day of traveling.

I showered before I got into bed beside her.

I stared at the ceiling in the dark, thinking about how different my life would be very soon. I was happy that Raven would stay here while I was away, but I was also disappointed that I would be there for a month without her. I hadn't wanted to share my space with her initially, but now I couldn't imagine how that cabin would feel without her in it. I didn't know how I would sleep in that small bed without her on top of me. She was my only joy in that camp. And now I didn't know what to do without it.

When we woke up the next morning, she wanted to go out.

We walked to her favorite coffee shop, and she picked out a couple muffins. "I'll take a blueberry and a poppy seed." Raven watched the barista grab them from the glass case and put them into bags on the counter.

I already had my black coffee in hand. "I'm not hungry."

She turned to me and gave me a somewhat awkward expression. "They're both for me."

She was already completely different than she was yesterday at the camp. And I couldn't stop the smile from entering my lips. "Sorry. Should've assumed."

When she got her coffee and her muffins, she took a seat at one of the round tables on the patio and stuck her hand into the bag to pull off chunks to place in her mouth. Crumbs got everywhere, but she didn't care.

I enjoyed my coffee while watching her, seeing her appreciate the little things in life that were irrelevant to my brother. To her, happiness was as simple as a cup of coffee and a muffin, and sunshine on your face.

After she ate one, she moved on to the other. "I don't know how to choose a favorite. They're both good." When she was done, she wiped up the mess on her fingers and mouth with a napkin. "You want to go to the bookstore? I read all the books I took with me to the camp. I need something new."

"We can go wherever you want."

Her eyes softened slightly before she stood up and threw her bag away. She walked beside me with her coffee in hand, wearing a nice green dress Miranda had picked out for her. Her hair was in curls and over one shoulder, and when she did her makeup, her eyes really sparkled.

After we spent some time in the bookstore, we went window-shopping and then had lunch. She'd eaten two muffins just a few hours ago, but she had an appetite all over again.

In the late afternoon, we walked back to my apartment in the park and set our bags on the counter in the kitchen. She'd bought five books and a couple tops, and I'd brought home leftovers to have for dinner. The stress was gone from her shoulders, and she smiled to herself when she was happy, living in this dream with me.

But it wasn't a dream at all. It was real—and it would stay that way.

She flipped through each of her books as she stood there, like she wanted to smell the pages all over again. When she noticed my stare, she glanced at me to meet my gaze, as if I wanted something. But when I didn't speak or turn away, she knew I was looking at her for a different reason. Her smile faded, and she put the books on the counter.

I could get her attention with just my silence. That was how well she knew me. "There's something I need to tell you."

"Alright…"

"Fender has released you."

When she didn't speak, it was obvious she was struggling to understand the words I'd said. Her face tightened in a reaction, but she still failed to grasp the truth I'd spoken.

"You're free."

She bent her body farther toward me and crossed her arms over her chest. Instead of being happy, she was confused. "What…"

"You don't have to go back. You can stay here." I left out the part about her sister because it would just chase away her victory. "You'll never have to see Alix again. You'll never have to witness any of that ever again."

She shook her head slightly, in disbelief. "What about you?"

"What do you mean?"

"Will you still go to the camp?"

I nodded. "Yes."

"And I'll just…stay here? Alone?"

Why wasn't she more thrilled about this? "I can leave you money, and you can go to the bookstore every day, get your coffee and muffins, do whatever you want. If you wanna go back to school, you can do that too. You can have any life that you want." I'd assumed her freedom wouldn't change our relationship, but maybe it would. Maybe she would want to be with someone else, someone who didn't do the terrible things I did.

But I would never stop her from leaving, if that was her choice. "You could go back to America too…if you want."

Her eyes narrowed farther at my words.

I hadn't even given her the bad news yet, and she was acting like I already had. "I don't understand what's happening right now. I just told you that you never have to go back, and you're looking at me like that's not what you want."

She dropped her gaze for a moment and tightened her arms over her chest. "You're gone for a whole month every time you leave."

"And then I'll return for two weeks."

She shook her head. "That's not gonna work…"

I didn't understand what she was insinuating. Now that she was free, did our relationship not make sense anymore? I thought what we had was deeper than that, deep enough to survive being apart. "Then leave."

Now she turned angry. "That's not what I meant—"

"You talk about us like this shit is forever, and then I tell you this, and the first thing you wanna do is leave? What the fuck is that?"

She marched up to me and shoved me in the chest. "No, asshole. I'm saying I'd rather go with you than be here without you." The anger on her face slowly faded to a look of hurt. "You expect me just to be here by myself for a month while you're gone? What's the point of being here if I'm not with you? How am I supposed to sleep when you aren't beside me? How am I supposed to be happy in Paris when you're miserable in a camp in the middle of fucking nowhere?" She stepped back and tucked her hair behind her ears, shaking her head as she released a deep sigh, as if my reaction were a knife to her heart. She moved back to the counter and placed one hand on the surface, the other hand on her hip. She looked down at her fingers for a while until she brought herself back to peace. "Where you go…I go."

Instead of being embarrassed for making the wrong assumption, I felt warmth in my chest at her commitment to me. She'd rather go back to that camp, the place of her nightmares, instead of being in paradise without me. It was a kind of loyalty you couldn't buy. It was a kind of connection between two people that couldn't be severed.

She pulled her hand away from the counter and looked at me. She was calm now, only a tinge of anger in her eyes.

"It makes more sense for you to stay here. You can go back to university and finish your education. You can continue the life that was taken from you. You can even see Melanie. If you go back to that camp, you'll just be working all day in terrible conditions. You'll be much happier here." I didn't want to be apart, but I would never put my selfish interests before hers.

She straightened and crossed her arms over her chest. "Where you go, I go. That's final."

Now, I looked at her with new eyes, seeing the same woman I looked at every day somehow look different. Did I want to go back to the camp without her? No. But I would never be selfish and ask her to stay with me. She was stuck to me like glue. A lot of people said shit they didn't mean, made promises they couldn't keep, said they would be there, knowing they wouldn't show up, but not Raven.

She was different.

When she said something, she meant it.

It was easy for Melanie to go back to Fender because he gave her pretty things, gave her a life she could only dream of. It was easy to look the other way and ignore his crimes against humanity. But Raven voluntarily joined me in hell, walked away from her freedom to remain a prisoner with me.

Because it was real.

We were real.

We drove into the countryside and approached the iron gate between two tall trees with a brick wall that surrounded the property.

I rolled down the window and entered my code in the keypad.

The doors slowly swung inward.

I drove through and saw the gate close behind me in my rearview mirror. There was a large pond in front of the lawn of my home, filled with floating lily pads and fallen flowers. I drove down the path toward the two-story French estate and then pulled up to the front of the house.

She looked out the window and admired the two statues in front of the pillars, the traditional French architecture, the history of a place that had been around for centuries. "It's beautiful…"

It wasn't as large as Fender's, but it was still too big for one person. I bought it for seclusion when I needed a break from the city. Sometimes tourism was so rampant in the summer that I needed a place to retreat until they returned to wherever the fuck they came from.

We got out of the car and walked to the front door.

My butler greeted us with two glasses of wine, along with the perfect pairing of cheese. "Great to have you back, sir."

I took the glass off the tray and took a drink. "Thank you, Ramon. How have things been?" I spoke English so Raven could understand us.

"The house has been doing well. The stables—"

"I meant with you."

"Oh." He chuckled and placed his hand over his chest. "I've been doing quite well. Thank you for asking." He turned to Raven. "Lovely to meet you, mademoiselle. Please let me know if you need anything." He headed toward the doors. "I'll take care of the luggage."

Raven finished chewing her cheese as she watched him go. "He's nice. He just lives here all the time?"

"Yes." We moved forward and entered the large kitchen and sitting room. The back window showed the acres of land and the horses grazing in the pasture. "With an estate this size, it requires constant upkeep."

When she noticed the horses, she moved to the window and placed her hand against the pane. "Oh my god, I think I see her…"

I turned my gaze and watched her press her nose to the glass, watched her look at the horse that had carried her to the safety of my chateau. She had a connection with many things, whether it was humans or animals, because her heart was pure.

She turned to me. "Can we go say hi?"

When did I ever tell her no? "Sure."

We opened the gate to the pasture and walked across the grass to where the horses stood. Most of them were spread out and grazing, eating the fresh grass below their hooves. I kept horses as a hobby even though I rarely rode.

Raven walked out in front of me and cupped her hands around her mouth to shout across the field. "Rose!" She waved her arms in the air to get her attention. "Girl, it's me."

I didn't expect the horse to recognize her since their interaction had been so short. But I watched Rose lift her head and turn our way, looking at the two people who had entered her world. Her ears twitched a little bit, and she flicked her tail. Then she turned our way and came toward us.

Raven looked at me, bursting with emotion. "I think she recognizes me." She faced forward again. "Rose, I'm so happy to see you!"

Rose started to run, crossing the grass and coming close to Raven. She released a loud neigh as she approached. Then she dropped her neck so her nose could rub up against Raven's face.

I almost couldn't believe it.

Raven wrapped her arms around the horse and hugged her, chuckling but also crying in her emotional state. "You remember me…" She rubbed her behind the ears and moved her hand down the bridge of the horse's nose before she placed a kiss there. "You look so good. Have you been eating a lot of oats?" She laughed, like it was an inside joke between the two of them. "I wish I could bring you inside to sleep with me, but we both know how mad Magnus will get." She moved into the horse's chest and wrapped her arms around her neck, standing underneath her while rubbing her hands over her muscular shoulders. "Girl, I missed you…" She stood there with Rose, hugging her horse like she'd been the one to take care of her for years. There was a bond so strong that the horse could still recognize her even after months of no contact.

I'd never seen anything like it.

I watched their tender exchange and felt like I was in the presence of something truly special. It wasn't the relationship. It wasn't the horse.

It was Raven.

She was the special one.

After dinner, we took a walk outside across the estate, moving down the path between the flowers and bushes until we came back around and stopped at the pool.

"This thing is huge." She stood at the edge and looked down at the water. "Is this an Olympic-size pool?"

I shrugged.

"Do you wanna go for a swim?" She kicked off her sandal and stuck her toe inside to feel the temperature. "It feels really nice."

"You don't have a suit." It was something I hadn't mentioned to Miranda. I didn't know we would take a trip up here, and even if I had, I hadn't expected her to want to take a late-night swim.

"So?" She unzipped the back of her dress and let it come loose. "Don't the French like nude beaches?" She wiggled out of her dress until she was in just her strapless bra and thong.

"Ramon is probably in the kitchen right now…"

She dropped the rest of her clothing until she was in the nude. "He brings me wine and cheese…he can look all he wants." She jumped into the pool and disappeared under the water.

My gaze moved up to the windows to see if Ramon was looking.

He was.

Ashamed that he'd been caught, he quickly looked away.

I chuckled then looked down at the water again.

Her head broke the surface, her wet hair sticking to the back of her neck. She moved her hands to her face and wiped the water from her eyes. "Come on, get in." She lay back on the surface of the water then stuck her legs into the air so her head and torso were submerged in the water. When she came back up for air, she wiped her face again.

With my hands in my pockets, I just stared at her. "I'm not gonna walk up two flights of stairs to grab my suit."

"Then don't." She smiled at me before doing a flip in the water.

I smirked before I pulled my shirt over my head and tossed it onto one of the lounge chairs. My jeans, shoes, and boxers came next. When I was naked, I stood at the edge of the pool.

She came up for air and looked up at me. "Damn…" Her eyes were on my dick. "You aren't cold at all…"

I jumped into the water beside her and fell under the surface, bubbles surrounding me, the cool water comfortable against my warm skin. I saw her silhouette in the water as I rose up to breach the surface.

"See? Isn't this nice?" Her arms moved forward and back across the surface of the water as she stood in front of me, her chin at the waterline. "I always wanted to have a pool when I was little."

"You can use mine anytime you want."

"That sounds nice." She moved toward me then kicked from the bottom so she could hook her legs around my waist and her arms around my neck. Her naked body pressed against mine, her nipples cold and hard. She smiled as she brought her face close to mine, like she was happy to be with me, to be spontaneous with the one person she could be completely herself with.

My hands rested on her ass, and I lowered myself farther into the water so just our heads were above the surface. I hadn't used this pool for years, but it was always immaculately clean, like I could jump in at any moment. I didn't come to this estate often at all, and when I did, using the pool was not on my mind. The landscape lighting gave us enough visibility to see each other, but it was also dark enough that Ramon wouldn't be able to see our bodies under the surface. It was a clear night with a blanket of stars up above. It was just us…like there was no one else in the world.

Her smile slowly started to fade away when she saw the serious expression in my eyes, and she knew I was thinking deeply about a lot of things in that moment.

It was hard to believe this was the woman who'd run through the snow to get to safety, though the odds were stacked against her. It was hard to believe this was the woman I caught sneaking around the camp at night, trying to steal supplies. That seemed like a lifetime ago, and now we were swimming naked in my pool…as if none of that happened at all.

My future had always been an open book, even though I knew every page would contain the same words. The immediate future was the only thing on my mind—work and money. Romantic relationships were so far down the ladder they were barely even on the bottom rung. I searched for women based on a very specific criteria—appearance. But out of nowhere, this woman came into my life, and now I couldn't imagine the remaining pages of my book not having her name written in every sentence.

She was me. I was her. We were the same person.

I couldn't imagine my life without her.

My feelings were nothing like my brother's for his lover. He felt infatuation, obsession, for Melanie. It was superficial, lustful. Once her looks faded, what would they have left? But the way I felt for Raven was timeless.

She continued to look into my face and study my expression, like every thought I had was somehow transferred into her mind. She could touch me to know me. She could read my moods accurately. And she seemed to read me now. "Don't…"

My eyes watched hers, seeing the landscape lights reflecting in her eyes. Emotion was burning in her gaze, absorbing my feelings as if I'd just shared them with her.

"I won't say it back." She rested her forehead against mine and brought our bodies even closer, her tits pressed against my hard chest, her ankles locked together around my waist. "If you want me, you have to do what I asked you to do."

I pulled away slightly so I could look into her eyes better, see the emotion and conflict in her gaze, see the woman who put her integrity above her own desires. "It doesn't matter whether I say it or not. You already know how I feel."

Her eyes watered, the edges of her lids slowly filling with emotional wetness. She closed her eyes for a moment so she could take a breath and fight the urge to break down in front of me.

"And I know you feel the same way."

When she looked at me, there was resistance, like she wouldn't cave, no matter what. "Then that just gives you another reason to do the right thing. I am with you in this until the very end. You aren't just doing it for them. You're doing it for us. You're doing it so you can say those words to me and hear me say them back."

TWENTY-EIGHT

THE FUTURE COUNTESS

She sat on the floor in front of my fireplace, which was lit with roaring flames that filled the bedroom with light. It was the end of summer, so it was too warm to have a fire, but she seemed to enjoy it anyway.

A blanket was around her shoulders as she sat naked on the rug. It reminded me of a memory from the chateau, when she'd mimicked this exact scenario. It was wintertime then and she'd done it to keep warm, but the two instances were identical. I felt like I was back in time.

I got out of bed and pulled on a pair of boxers before I sat beside her. "It's a little warm for a fire."

She kept her eyes on the logs. "I just like to watch it…" She stared for a few more seconds before she turned and looked at me. Her makeup was gone and she was ready for bed, but she wasn't ready to sleep. We'd made love since we finished dinner, moving across the bed and getting tangled in the sheets. But instead of drifting off to sleep afterward, she made a fire and sat there to admire it. It'd been going for thirty minutes, and it probably only had thirty minutes left before it was snuffed out.

"Did you have a fireplace growing up?"

She nodded. "My mom would use it at Christmas-time. We would drink our hot chocolate in front of it."

"I can have Ramon make you some hot cocoa now, if you want."

She smiled slightly and shook her head. "Maybe another time." She turned her gaze back to the fire and watched it, silent a long time.

I stared at the side of her face.

"It's hard to believe so many things have happened. Rose and I lay in front of the fire at the chateau to stay warm, and it wasn't that long ago, but it feels like a lifetime somehow. That night I got into the car with those guys feels so far away that I'm not even the same person I used to be. I can never go back. Even when Melanie and I were living in Paris after you freed us, we still couldn't go back."

I listened to everything she said.

"She's different... I'm different."

I watched the flames light up her skin and give her a dreamlike glow. "There's something I need to tell you." It had left my mind because it didn't seem important at the time. I'd told her she was free, but she'd said she would rather be a prisoner with me. The news had faded into the background, but now I had to tell her.

She turned to look at me, her eyes now sharp and absorbed.

"Fender asked Melanie to marry him. Her answer was yes, but only if he released you."

Her eyes instantly hardened into a look of anger.

"She also asked him to stop running the camp in the way he does in exchange for her answer, but he said no. He would only let you go."

She shook her head slightly, her reaction so subtle but her distress so obvious. "I don't want my freedom, so she doesn't have to marry him."

I suspected that wouldn't change anything.

"I need to see her."

"Fender's at the camp."

"Even better."

I wasn't sure how Fender would feel about Raven and Melanie spending time together in his absence, but if he really intended to marry Melanie and have Raven be free, then he must know that the situation was unavoidable.

"Magnus, please."

I nodded. "I'll talk to him tomorrow."

I spoke to him over the satellite phone.

"What?" Fender knew I wouldn't call unless it was an urgent matter.

It wasn't urgent, which would probably piss him off. "Raven wants to see her sister."

He was silent.

"I already know how you feel about Raven, but that is something you're going to have to disregard. If you want to spend your life with Melanie, Raven is going to be a piece of that. Fight it, and you'll make your wife unhappy. So, I'm going to take Raven over there to spend time with her sister. I'm not really asking, just telling."

He was quiet for a long time, processing all the different things he could say in response. When none of those answers were good enough, he decided to hang up instead.

I put the phone down.

Raven looked at me, searching my expression. "What did he say?"

"It's fine."

We pulled up to Fender's estate and headed to the door. Gilbert greeted us and invited us inside. Fender must have informed the staff that our visit was permitted because there was no resistance at any of the checkpoints. "May I get you something to drink?" His English was getting much better, probably because that was how he had to converse with Melanie.

"Wine is fine," I said. "Whatever you have open."

Gilbert nodded. "I'll let Mademoiselle know you're here." He headed upstairs to the second floor.

I moved farther into the house and entered the sitting room. The energy of the house was different when Fender wasn't around. A lot calmer, more peaceful. When I looked outside, I saw the gardeners attending to the massive acres of perfectly sculpted landscape, trimming the bushes, watering the flowers, continuing to make it look like a picture in a storybook.

Raven sat across from me, wearing a pink dress, with her brown hair over her shoulder. She sat upright with perfect posture, but she fidgeted like she was nervous, afraid of the conversation she was about to have.

Melanie came downstairs moments later, her eyes on her sister, her affection knowing no bounds. She sat on the couch beside Raven then wrapped her arms around her.

Raven held her sister with the same depth of emotion, squeezing her tight.

The embrace continued for minutes.

Melanie pulled away and looked at her sister like she couldn't believe she was there. "You look good."

"But never as good as you." Raven gave her a slight smile showing she wasn't being disingenuous.

Melanie turned to me. "Could you give us privacy, please?"

I rose to excuse myself.

"He's fine. I'm just gonna tell him everything we're about to say anyway."

Melanie stared at her sister.

I lowered myself back to the couch.

Melanie didn't argue with her sister, but she did look surprised.

Gilbert came in a moment later and placed the glasses of wine on the coffee table. He also brought a cheeseboard with a sliced baguette for us to enjoy. He silently excused himself and left.

"Magnus told me that you agreed to marry Fender in exchange for my freedom." Whenever Raven talked to her sister, she had a different tone, a note of authority. Instead of being sisters, it was more like mother-daughter. Raven always filled the role of caretaker without thinking twice about it. "I really appreciate that, I do."

Melanie dropped her gaze and stared at her hands in her lap. "I tried to get him to free the girls, but he wouldn't. At least he gave me you."

Raven gave a slight nod. "I'm glad you tried. But I suspect his mind is so corroded and he doesn't understand how terrible he really is. He's lost all humanity…"

Melanie lifted her chin and looked at her sister.

"But you don't have to marry him."

She looked slightly confused.

"Because I don't want to be free."

Her eyes narrowed. "Raven, if you think you can destroy that camp from the inside, you're delusional. We tried to get rid of it and free all the prisoners, but it didn't work whatsoever. You need to let this go."

Raven shook her head. "That's not why. The only way that place is going to end is if Fender ends it… or he himself is ended."

"Then I don't understand…"

Raven took a long time to answer, like she knew how crazy she sounded before she even said anything. "I can't live apart from Magnus."

Melanie stared at her sister for a long time, realization slowly sinking in.

"Where he goes…that's where I go."

Melanie was still in disbelief. "But it's so terrible there."

She nodded. "I know."

"And if you're in Paris, we can see each other all the time."

"I know that too. But when Magnus goes to the camp, he's gone for a full month, and I just can't live with that kind of separation. All I'll be doing is waiting for him to come home."

Melanie clearly wanted to say more but held her tongue because I was sitting there.

"So, you don't have to marry Fender. I'm not choosing to go to the camp to protect you. I'm going because I want to be there…with Magnus."

I grabbed my glass and took a drink, feeling slightly out of place witnessing such an intense conversation that was about me, but that I wasn't actually a part of. I eavesdropped on everything they said, but this felt different. Raven basically told her sister I was the man she was choosing to spend her life with.

Melanie clearly didn't know what to say because she stayed quiet.

"You're off the hook."

I knew Raven was fiercely intelligent, but I also knew she couldn't think straight when it came to Melanie. She didn't see the truth because she thought so highly of her little sister.

Melanie looked at her sister again, trepidation in her gaze. "I'm going to marry him anyway."

Raven stared. She was still, absorbing those words with painful slowness. "Why?"

Melanie dropped her gaze like she was ashamed, too ashamed to look her sister in the eye. "The same reason you want to be at the camp with Magnus…"

"No…"

Melanie kept her head down.

"How can you feel that way for the man who subjects innocent people to a lifetime of imprisonment, and then a departure from life with a cruel execution? How? Melanie, ignore the diamonds and the gowns. I know you're scared to be on your own, but give yourself more credit than that. You can do it. You don't need him."

Melanie looked at her hands. "It's not like that. It's not about the money and the security."

"What is it? The sex?"

"No."

"Then what?" Raven started to raise her voice, unable to keep her anger in check.

"I know he's responsible for a lot of terrible things, but he's more than that. He's just so hurt by the awful things he's seen that he struggles to feel empathy and compassion for others—"

"Then *how* could you possibly care for a man who feels nothing for others?" Raven's eyes were big and raging, full of sheer disappointment for her sister.

"Because I believe he can change. I believe he can come back to the right side. I believe, in enough time, he will be who he used to be... He's just not there yet."

"Even if that is true, it doesn't change what he's already done. He's ordered his men to execute the weakest worker every week to keep the rest of them working like bees in a hive. He's done that for *years*, Melanie. He might not be the one with the knife or the rope, but he's the one with the blood on his hands. How the fuck do you feel anything for that monster?"

She dropped her chin again, her eyes slowly filling with tears. "That's a bit hypocritical, don't you think?"

"My man is nothing like yours." Raven kept her voice steady, but her rage was making her red in the face. "He's tried to stop Fender many times. He's tried to convince him to run the camp in a different way. He's tried to reason with him. They are not the same."

The moisture toppled over Melanie's lashes and dripped straight down her cheeks. "I know I can change him. I can…"

"You're still going to marry him without knowing for sure?"

"Yes. Because I have faith in him."

"Or is it because you know you have no choice?" Raven snapped. "Because if a man forces you to marry him, that's not love. That's cruelty."

"He's not forcing me." She lifted her chin and wiped away her tears. "He's never forced me to do anything. I can leave this place whenever I want. I stay because I want to stay. I'm telling you, he's not the barbarian you know him as."

"I don't care how you know him when you're living in this mansion and life is good. He chooses to execute innocent people. Period. Some of those women could be your friend. One of those women could've been me. The only reason why it wasn't is because Magnus saved me. Let *that* sink in."

Melanie inhaled a deep breath, more tears falling down her cheeks. "I understand… I do. I feel like I can feel both things at once. I hate him for the things he's done, but I've also fallen in love with the other side of him. You have no idea how ashamed I feel right now, having you look at me like that, knowing you're right and I'm wrong. But I also can't change the way I feel because I've never felt this way for a man in my life."

Raven had no sympathy whatsoever. "You're too young to know what real love is. You barely have had a long-term relationship with any man in your life. You've been traumatized by what you've been through, and you found a man who can protect you against all that. Stockholm syndrome. It's not real."

I actually felt bad for Melanie, loving her sister but also loving my brother. She felt so much guilt and shame, but she couldn't just walk away from Fender. It was too complicated. My relationship with Raven was still complicated.

"Raven…" She wiped away her tears with her fingertips and breathed until she was calm enough to speak. "I know it's wrong. I do. If I could just not feel this way, I would. I know Magnus and Fender are totally different people, but how are you going to be with a man who continues to work at the camp? Maybe he doesn't like it, but he still partici-pates. Fender doesn't like it either, but he feels like he has no other choice. Why can you be with Magnus, but I can't be with Fender? Magnus has never actually tried to stop anything."

Raven's gaze turned cold. "He saved us, didn't he?"

I hated seeing the two sisters pitted against each other when I knew how they really felt about each other. It reminded me of my relationship with my brother. "I will stop it."

Melanie slowly turned her head to look at me.

"I don't know how, but I will." It wasn't just about being with Raven; it was more than that. It was the right thing to do. Just because horrible things had happened to my brother and me didn't mean we were justified to do horrible things to other people.

Raven didn't look at me, but she inhaled a deep breath, and a look of pride came over her face.

"But I understand, Melanie."

Melanie's eyes slowly softened as she stared at me.

Raven looked at me, unsure of the meaning of my words.

I continued. "Fender is a good man. He's loyal like no man I've ever known. He's strong, refusing to break for anyone. He'd cut off his own arm and give it to somebody he cared about if that's what made them happy. He's just been hurt by what happened to us, and somehow, having all the money in the world will make our father pay for what he's done to our family. Hurt people hurt people… And Fender is so traumatized by what he had to witness in our childhood home that he's numb to the pain and suffering. It doesn't justify what he's done whatsoever. But he's not himself. He's never really been himself since that night. I believe he can see reason and change. I do. Yes, Melanie, I understand. I hate him for what he's done…but I still love him."

TWENTY-NINE
EVIL VEINS

WHEN WE RETURNED TO MY ESTATE, SHE WENT upstairs to my bedroom, but she walked quickly and with intention, like she had no desire to sleep. She walked inside and moved to the large window that overlooked the pastures. The curtains were open, so she crossed her arms over her chest and looked out, even though there was nothing to see in the dark.

I could feel her searing emotions, feel her anger. There would be retribution for what I had said to Melanie, and there would be retribution for what Melanie had said to her. I was willing to do anything for this woman except lie about how I really felt.

I stood behind her and watched her for a few moments before I removed my shoes and jeans. I pulled on my sweatpants and threw my shirt in the hamper in the closet. I gave her enough time to speak her mind, but when she didn't, I came up close behind her.

"I don't understand her…" She took a deep breath, her chest rising as her lungs expanded. "If she wants to marry a monster, fine. It's just another stupid decision like all her other stupid decisions. But I won't be a part of it."

I stared at her long brown hair as it hung down her back. As the months since I'd first laid eyes on her passed, it had grown longer and longer. It marked the passage of time when there was no other way to keep track of it. "You're all she has."

"I don't care. I can forgive a lot of things…but not that."

"I'll be there. I'm all that my brother has in this world, and even if I disagree with his decisions, I'm still his brother…and I'll be there for him. I know this is hard for you, but we have to remember that. Even if this is the worst decision of her life, you should still be there. She'll be unhappy if you aren't, and deep down inside, you know you will be too."

She slowly turned around to face me, her eyes angry. "This isn't some douchebag I don't get along with. This guy is evil."

"Alix was going to rape you, but Fender stopped it. He did it for me, but even after everything you did to make him hate you, he still did the right thing. His love for me was stronger than hatred for you. He's not evil." There were other times when Fender had shown his true colors, other moments of mercy he granted when it was unnecessary. "When you destroyed the camp, he could've tortured you and killed you, but he didn't. When I saved you from the Red Snow, he allowed it. When you took off with Melanie and tried to run, he let me spare your life. He's not as evil as you think he is. He's done a lot of shitty and unforgivable things, but he's done good things too."

Rage moved into her face. "I understand he's your brother and you feel conflicted, but I don't understand how you can defend him. He *kills* people."

"But he doesn't want to. He's never wanted to. He just couldn't find an alternative."

"And that makes it okay?" she asked incredulously.

I didn't know what I could say to make her understand, to understand why my brother was the way he was. "Imagine if your mother, the woman you hold a vigil for in your heart, came home one night and decided to kill you both. She squandered your family's wealth and, instead of living with that shame, decided everyone should die. How would that make you feel?" It still haunted me to this day, a grown-ass man about to hit thirty. "Could you imagine walking into your house to discover your dead sister executed in her sleep? Could you live as the sole survivor?"

Her eyes shifted back and forth slightly as she met my gaze.

"He lost all faith in humanity that night. He was never the same. He's obsessed with building wealth and strengthening our noble family name, as if that's the best way to spite our dead father. He's been obsessed with that goal to the point of insanity. He wants to bring honor back to our family, like that will somehow bring my dead mom and siblings back to life. He's mentally ill, to be frank. This doesn't justify what he's done at all, don't misunderstand me, but he's not evil like all the other men out there who get off on shit like that. He's just been so focused on his goal that he's ignored all the horrible things he's had to do to get there. I told you I would end the practices at the camp, and I meant that. I've never agreed with any of it, and I never will. But my relationship with my brother is never going to go away. I see more of him than you do, and I know that's hard to understand. I know I can convince him to dismantle everything and let the past go. It might take me longer than you want, but it will happen. But if this is a lifelong commitment like you say it is, Fender will always be a part of that. You will never escape him. So, you should be there for Melanie on her big day, if and when that happens, because everything you stand for will be honored. We will move on from this…and start over."

Her expression didn't change, but she didn't seem as angry anymore.

I knew our relationship was as strong as the bond I had with Fender because of everything we'd been through, so I wasn't afraid to watch her turn her back on me and walk away. But I was afraid she would think less of me because of the love I had for my only brother, the faith I still had in his soul. "We are the same. You've had to live with your sister's idiotic mistakes and have had to fix them, but you've never turned your back on her because you still believe in her. That's exactly how I feel about Fender, just in a different scenario. I believe in his redemption. I can't give up on him. I know you, of all people, can understand that."

The subtle rage left her eyes, and she started to calm herself once again. "I understand your perspective, Magnus. But you also have to understand mine. I've sat in that clearing with women who risked their lives to help me, and I had to watch one die every week...because of *him*. Melanie sat there in the clearing with me and witnessed the exact same thing. And that's why I don't understand. How could you fall in love with the man responsible for such a heinous crime?"

I was never in the clearing to witness it because it was too difficult to watch. My aversion to the practice was well known, so I refused to participate. Even if Fender wanted me to be the executioner, I would refuse.

Raven continued to look at me like she expected a counter.

Honestly, I didn't have one. "I guess she's witnessed enough of his other qualities to forget about that."

She wasn't angry anymore, just disappointed. "I have faith that you will end this, Magnus. But I'm not entirely convinced that your victory will happen because your brother has a change of heart. I just hope you have what it takes to do what is necessary."

It was a scenario I hadn't even considered because it was too repulsive. Even if my brother deserved to die, I couldn't be the one to take his life. I couldn't be like our father. But I also couldn't stand by and watch the killings continue. I would have to do something…no matter the cost.

When Fender returned from the camp, I went to his estate for a visit.

I didn't tell him I was coming, just showed up. Gilbert let me inside and escorted me to the living room, where I would wait for him to join me. Gilbert served me a glass of wine and placed a cheeseboard on the table even though Fender and I wouldn't touch it. Sometimes it seemed like he did those things just to make the place look nice.

I sat alone and tried to think of the right words to say, something that would persuade Fender to put all this behind us and move on. His greed made him stubborn, and his stubbornness made him greedier.

Footsteps sounded on the tile, but they didn't belong to Fender.

Melanie took a seat across from me, wearing an expensive dress with her hair nicely done. Now, she always looked like a modern French countess, with diamonds in her ears and jewelry on her wrists and fingers. On her left hand was a diamond ring that looked almost too heavy to wear.

She fidgeted with her hands before she looked at me. "Fender just got out of the shower. I thought I'd take the opportunity to talk to you."

I stared at her, seeing the similarities between her and Raven. They had the same color eyes, but Raven's had so much more depth to them. Melanie's timid nature annoyed me. She looked uncomfortable in her own skin; she didn't know how to have the confidence her sister possessed. It made her seem weak. I loved that Raven owned the room every time she stepped into it, and she stood tall and proud and commanded every ounce of respect that she deserved.

"I just wanted to thank you for what you said the other day...that you understood my feelings for Fender. I know it's going to be really hard to get my sister on board with this, so I need all the help I can get."

I shook my head. "I didn't do it for you."

She looked slightly stung by my honesty. She wore her feelings on her sleeve, and as a result, she was delicate. "I also wanted to thank you for being so good to my sister. She's always the one taking care of everyone else, but no one takes care of her. It makes me happy to know she has a man who will do anything for her. I just wanted you to know that."

That made me dislike Melanie less. She might be dull and weak, but she definitely loved her sister with all her heart.

Fender came downstairs in his sweatpants, his hair still damp from the shower. He stopped near the coffee table and looked down at Melanie, as if he were giving her orders in silence.

Melanie rose to her feet and quietly excused herself.

When she went back upstairs, Fender took a seat across from me. He stole my glass of wine and took a drink before he grabbed a slice of French bread and stuffed it into his mouth. It was almost dinnertime, so he was probably hungry. He relaxed back into the couch and stared at me as he chewed. "My fiancée tells me her sister isn't too happy about the news." He started the conversation with contentious hostility, so my odds of success were already low.

"Can you blame her?"

Fender stared me down like I'd insulted him. "I'm richer than the devil, I'm good-looking, I granted her freedom… I think I'm perfect." He grabbed the wine again and took a drink.

"Raven isn't impressed by money. And she doesn't want her freedom." I couldn't hide my sense of pride about her loyalty to me. She wanted me for me, not my money, not my looks. She'd rather go to that godforsaken camp to be with me than live a lavish lifestyle without me. It was something my brother couldn't say about Melanie. "She wants to be with me wherever I go."

He pulled the wineglass away from his face and held on to it as his arm rested over the edge of the couch. Seconds of intense eye contact followed before his eyes slightly narrowed. "Isn't that romantic?" He brought the glass to his lips and took another drink. "If the bitch wants to work, let her."

My eyes narrowed on his face. "Don't do that."

"What?"

"You know exactly what, Fender. I think Melanie is as dumb as a dog, but you don't hear me saying that."

My brother stared at me for a while before he set the wineglass on the table. "Sounds like this is getting serious…"

I held his gaze.

He didn't say another negative thing about Raven, and I suspected he never would. "I guess I'm gonna have to learn to tolerate her, aren't I?"

"She's more than tolerable."

"I disagree. And I'll always disagree."

The mood was already stark, and I wasn't sure if this was even worth doing anymore. I decided to move into more positive subject matter. "When's the wedding?"

He shrugged. "Whenever she gets a dress, I guess. We aren't having a big ridiculous wedding. We'll probably get married out on the lawn."

"I expected you to throw a big party."

He shrugged again. "She doesn't know any of those people. Prefers it just be us...and the two of you."

I knew Raven would attend, no matter how much she hated Fender. It was in her nature to take care of her sister, and no amount of resentment would stop her from being there.

"What do you want? I assume you have something else in mind besides discussing my wedding?"

I leaned back into the couch with my knees apart, regarding my brother with a steely gaze. "It's time to change things, Fender." I could list all my reasons, but none of them had ever changed his mind. It was always in the air between us, unspoken. It happened more often now because I was more determined than ever before to free the prisoners.

His gaze turned icy.

"Your fiancée used to be a prisoner there. Does that not change how you feel?"

He drank from the wineglass. "I know I've made that up to her."

"And what about the rest of the girls?"

He released a long and drawn-out sigh, as if he was fighting to keep his patience with me. "We've discussed this before, Magnus. If there was another way, I would do it. There's not."

"There's always another way. I will personally see to the project. I will personally vet every single person we hire. I will make sure they're loyal."

"There's no way to be completely certain of hired help. The girls that we have are completely certain —because they'll never leave."

My fingers automatically tightened into a fist of pure frustration. "You've accomplished everything that you wanted. You have the money, you have the woman—now live your life. Stop living in the past.

Stop trying to prove something to our decomposed corpse of a father. There is no reason to continue carrying on this way."

Fender's gaze shifted away like he didn't want to talk about the man who had assassinated our family. "I've heard your concerns before. The only reason you are vocal once again is because that woman has a grip on your spine and she's twisting it."

"I'm glad she's twisting it. Your fiancée wants the same. How do you expect to have a life with her when she doesn't respect what you're doing?"

"It's just business."

"But it's not *just* business. It's lives, Fender. I know you're better than this."

"Sorry to disappoint you, but I'm not." He suddenly sat forward with his arms resting on the insides of his thighs. He looked me dead in the eye as he spoke. "Our father murdered our family without any hesitation. He was a coward and took their lives in their sleep. He was a coward and didn't kill himself instead of claiming the lives of innocent people. And you know what? I'm just like him. The evil that ran in his veins runs in mine." He spoke in a different tone than ever before, sinister, cruel, terrifying. The demons he wrestled with came forth and started to pull him under the surface.

"That's not true."

"Yes, it is. When you see shit like that, you never recover. I'm not human anymore. I don't care about anyone or anything. And it's much easier that way."

I shook my head. "That's not true. You asked a woman to marry you because you love her. You would take a knife in the chest for me because I'm your brother. It's hard to carry the weight of the past on your shoulders, but don't let it define you. You still have a soul. I know you do."

His eyes looked empty, like he didn't believe that. "I've already done what I've done. If there's a heaven and hell, you know which one I'm going to. I'm damned, and nothing I do now will change that."

I could feel the energy of self-loathing around him, feel the emptiness inside his chest just from listening to his words. He thought he was destined to be this villain, and no action would change the fate that had been decided for him. "I believe all people can be redeemed. All people can earn redemption. You just have to try."

My brother stared at me for a long time, like he was thinking about something else instead of actually looking at my face. His mind was elsewhere. "You can be redeemed, Magnus. Your soul is still whole. You were still innocent. Me… It's too late for me, and we both know it. May as well make as much money as I can and enjoy spending it all while I'm still here." He set the glass down on the coffee table and rose to his feet as if this conversation was over.

I got to my feet and faced him. "Fender."

With a clenched jaw, he looked angry that this conversation was continuing when he wished it would die.

"We need to free those girls. Period." I pitied my brother because of the weight of his grief, the painfulness of his solitude, but it didn't change what needed to be done. "We can't do this anymore."

He stared me down, hostile.

"You need to stop this. Now."

"Or what?"

My eyes narrowed at the odd response.

"You going to kill me?" He took a step closer to me, rising to my unspoken challenge.

This entire conversation was offensive. I was pissed off that my brother wouldn't do the right thing because he thought so little of himself already. But I was also pissed off that he had no faith in me. "No. I'm not our father."

He was still angry, but slightly less.

"But this will happen whether you like it or not. I know there's still humanity inside you. I know you still have a chance. I just hope you find the strength to join me…instead of resisting me."

THIRTY
RED SNOW

When I returned home, Ramon informed me that Raven was in the stables. She spent a lot of her free time there, taking Rose for a ride or brushing her coat or scrubbing her hooves. There was a caretaker on duty to do all those things, but she took it on as a hobby.

When I walked into the stables, I found her standing in Rose's stall with the door closed. She had a bucket of oats on the shelf, and she fed Rose handfuls. "A lot better than that hat, huh?" She continued to feed her while she rubbed her other hand down the bridge of the horse's nose. "I'm gonna spoil you like crazy."

I came close to the door and watched her for a while, looking at her beautiful face while she had no idea I was there. When she felt threatened, she was so savage.

In her defense, most other times, she was gentle and kind, wearing her heart on her sleeve and filling every room she stepped into with light. I loved those things about her, that she fought like a man but loved like a woman.

Rose must've smelled me because she lifted her head and looked at me over the stall door. She let out a loud breath, making her nostrils widen.

Raven followed her look until she saw me. "Looks like we aren't alone."

I pressed my body against the stall door and rested my arms on the edge. I looked at Rose for a few seconds, seeing her be protective of Raven, even though I was more protective than she would ever be. I turned my gaze to Raven.

"Do you want to feed her?" She held up the bucket of oats.

I shook my head.

"Come on. I want her to like you."

"She doesn't like me?" I asked incredulously. "Who's the one who has been feeding her for months? Who's the one who got her out of that camp?" I shifted my gaze back to Rose and gave her a look of accusation. "Who's the one who let her shit in my house?"

Raven laughed loudly at the memory. "Oh my god, I'll never forget your face when you walked in there." She looked at Rose and continued to rub her snout, chuckling to herself.

I looked at Raven again, seeing the color in her cheeks, the light in her eyes, the joy in everything around her.

"Rose, he's right. He's been good to you." She turned back to me and beckoned for me to come inside. "You should still feed her. She loves her oats, so she'll love you."

I had no interest in feeding a horse or walking into the stable where her shit was in the corners, but I couldn't resist the woman who made the request. I opened the door and joined her.

Raven held out the bucket. "Get a handful and flatten your fingers."

Rose released a quiet snort, like she was telling me to hurry up because she was hungry.

I grabbed the oats then opened my hand wide to feed her.

Her teeth dragged across my palm, and her lips slobbered all over my skin. She ate them quickly and lifted her head to look at me, like she was ready for the next handful.

"Rose, you've had enough. I've already fed you too much as it is." Raven rubbed her hand down the horse's backside.

Like Rose could understand, she released a neigh.

Raven said goodbye before she walked out of the stall with me and put the oats away. We both washed our hands before we left and headed to the house together.

At my side, she walked down the pathway in her barn boots, looking cute in her jeans and plaid shirt. "How'd it go?" Her voice didn't carry her infectious happiness anymore. She was somber, like she already knew what my answer would be.

"I need more time." I kept my eyes on the lit pathway before us as we made our way back to the house. The conversation was painful for a lot of reasons, but Fender's resistance was the most painful of all. "I didn't expect to be successful on my first attempt anyway, but it was still shitty."

She didn't try to give me advice or rush me into a resolution. There was no reason to, when she had faith that I would fulfill the task I said I would complete. "Maybe I can talk to Melanie. Maybe I can get her to convince him."

I shook my head. "Unlikely."

"He wants to marry her, so he obviously values her opinion."

"I think Fender has a low opinion of himself, but there's no incentive to be good. He can't be redeemed, so what's the point?"

"It doesn't matter if he's redeemed or not. He should still do the right thing…even if he goes to hell anyway."

I slid my hands into my pockets and looked at the lit-up house. There were lights in the distance around us, but we felt isolated from the world. "He said he wouldn't stop. Then he asked if I would kill him if he didn't…"

Raven was quiet for a long time, the pause in her speech profound. "Would you?"

I wanted to do the right thing and amend all the wrongs, but my brother's blood on my hands would haunt me forever. "No. I would be no different from our father if I did. And I think telling him that…is what's going to bring him back to the right side."

"Are you sure about this?" I stood outside in the driveway in front of the pond. My car was there, my bag of essentials in the trunk.

She was in her gray work pants and black tank top, her hair pulled back and her makeup gone. There was less joy in her gaze because she knew she had to return to a life of misery for a month before she could come back here. "Yes."

"Because I would understand if you didn't want to come with me." I wanted her beside me every night, but what I wanted more than anything was for her to be happy. "It's a long time to be apart, but I know you'll be waiting for me." I knew she would be committed and faithful during those long stretches of time, and we would make up for what we lost every time we were reunited.

The resolution in her eyes didn't change. She was as determined as before, just a little morose. "I don't want to be at that camp. But I want to be with you, wherever that is."

The camp was as I remembered. It was a timeless place, where nothing ever changed except the seasons. The only way we knew how long we'd really been working there was by the subtle changes in our appearance as we aged. The girls only knew how much time passed by the weekly Red Snows. When a girl was executed, that marked the passage of time.

When we entered the clearing, Raven immediately got to work and took up her post. She never told me how the girls felt about her having a relationship with me, leaving the camp monthly, and returning after two weeks. If she had friends, she didn't tell me. We deliberately kept the girls apart from each other so they wouldn't be able to organize a coup.

I purposely walked up to Alix and put him on the spot. "Any news to share with me?" I got so close to him that he was forced to take a step back. Of course, I moved in again, just to make him uncomfortable. The beating I gave him was more than enough retribution for what he had done to me on so many occasions, but I would never forget the sound of my woman's screams, forget the way she woke up in the middle of the night and stared right at the door, like he was coming for her. I'd publicly humiliated him when I made him bloody and made him ask for mercy, but would that ever be enough after what he did to her?

No.

I didn't care about what he had done to me. I cared about what he had done to her. And sometimes I wondered if I would just snap one day…and kill him.

Alix found his answer. "No. Everything has been running on schedule."

"How's your nose?"

He didn't speak.

I spat right on his face, knowing I hit my mark when he jerked back slightly.

The other guards didn't react at all and kept their eyes on the girls.

"You're my bitch now, asshole." I walked off and headed to my cabin, knowing no amount of humiliation would subdue my anger. He'd provoked me too many times, and then he went after the one thing I actually cared about.

Raven and I fell back into our old routine. I worked late catching up on everything that needed my attention, and when I returned to the cabin, I sat at my desk and worked on my laptop.

Raven sat on the floor, leaning against the bed to watch the TV. She was quiet, rarely talking about her day and rarely asking me anything. I knew she wasn't upset with me. This place just infected her mood like a virus.

When she was ready for bed, she turned off the TV, brushed her teeth in the bathroom, and then got under the sheets. We no longer shared an oversize bed, but we didn't mind being pushed together into a single person.

My back was to her, and I continued to work on my laptop.

Her voice was low as she spoke. "How did you get into this business?"

I answered as I typed. "We started as distributors on the street. We would sell a few ounces so we could make rent and buy food. The older we got, the more ambitious we became. We eventually took control of the business we used to work for, and the rest is history."

"So, after the night when…everything happened… that was what you did to survive."

"We had no other choice."

"I can't even imagine."

I remembered everything like it was yesterday. "For the first few weeks, we lived on the street. Fender got pneumonia, and we couldn't afford to see a doctor, so I had to rob some guy…" It was wrong, but I didn't feel guilty about it. If I hadn't gotten my brother what he needed, he would've died. "We would eat people's leftover food from the garbage can. We would live outside in the elements, hot and cold. We couldn't go to the police or do anything else because we knew our father would hunt us down and finish the job. It was a rough two years... until we got into the drug business. We were desperate and ambitious, and the desperation led to the empire we have now. It's another reason Fender is so obsessed with money because he doesn't ever want to feel helpless again." A lot of other terrible things happened to us in that time period, but I chose not to disclose them. Everything I'd already said was heavy enough.

She was quiet, like she had no idea what to say to that.

"I don't agree with what we do to the girls here, but I'm not ashamed of everything else I've done. I don't feel bad for the people I robbed. I don't feel bad for being, first, a drug dealer and then a drug kingpin. I don't feel bad for the lies I told to good people because I needed something from them. When you're in survival mode, you have to do bad things to live to see the next day. Anyone who judges me can be damned." At this point, I knew there was nothing I could tell Raven that would make her feel differently about me. We were bound by the journey we both took to be together. We suffered greatly for each other, and that kind of loyalty was unbreakable. So, I told her everything without a filter, just so she could understand me a little better. Understand my brother a little better.

She still didn't say anything.

The silence stretched for so long that I turned around in my chair to look at her.

She sat up in bed, that pained look on her face, as if she were picturing those dark nights, the street fights, the tears Fender and I both shed when we were scared. "I don't judge you…at all. I think it's inhumane to judge someone for what they do to survive. The people who do have no idea what it's like to be hungry, to be scared."

I knew she'd lost her mother when she was a teenager, and then she had to take care of her younger sister when she probably didn't know how to take care of herself. So, she understood my story. Maybe she had never experienced it as intensely as I did, but she understood.

She patted the mattress beside her, telling me to join her in bed.

I still had a lot of shit to do, but work meant nothing to me when I had something more valuable just a few feet away. I shut the laptop then stripped out my clothes so I could join her. I slid into the sheets beside her and pulled her close, our faces almost touching.

She rubbed my chest with callused fingertips, looking at me with a mixture of sympathy and pity. But there was also something else there…admiration. "You're right."

My eyes shifted back and forth as I looked into hers, questioning the words she'd just spoken.

"We are the same person."

I stepped out of the communal cabin and noticed the torches. They were lit up around the perimeter of the clearing, less bright because it was still light out. In the summer, the light wasn't really gone until at least eight in the evening. But the symbolism of the torches was enough to instill fear in every woman sitting at one of the tables.

I never took part in the ceremony. I was either in my cabin or elsewhere. I was in charge of this camp when Fender was away, so I rarely busied myself with tasks that involved the prisoners. The only reason I had been Raven's guard in the first place was because we had lost a guard recently and we were shorthanded.

It was crazy how life worked out sometimes.

I stopped on the porch and looked at the torches. Alix wore the garb of the executioner, a mask covering the bottom part of his face while his hood was pushed down. He lit the final torch near the noose then began to stride down the aisles between the tables, looking for the victim they had already chosen.

It was cruel.

Alix kept moving and walked right past Raven. Whether I was around or not, he was smart and didn't look at her. He was afraid of me—always.

He should be.

He moved down a different aisle and stopped behind a woman who was probably approaching fifty years of age. I recognized her face because she was one of the first women to have come here, and when Raven liberated the camp, she was one of the few who didn't make it out. She started to tremble and shake, like she knew Alix was right behind her. Her eyes immediately moistened with tears.

Alix grabbed her by the back of the shirt and yanked her off the bench.

The sobs came next. "Please! Please don't do this to me!"

Alix dragged her across the ground to where the wooden pole stood, the ground still stained with the last victim's blood.

The woman didn't rise to her feet and, instead, dug her fingertips into the ground, clinging to life for just a few seconds longer.

I couldn't watch this.

I walked down the steps and turned my back to the clearing, heading to my cabin so I could close the door and shut out the sound of her screams.

"No! Please!"

I stopped walking.

My cabin was in front of me, just twenty feet away.

Why was I walking away?

"I work! I work hard every day!"

Why was I allowing this to happen?

Why was I trying to convince Fender to do things differently when I could just do things differently myself?

I turned around and walked back to the clearing.

The noose was tight around her neck, and she stood on the small box that would be kicked from under her at any moment.

When I moved past the line of torches, I saw Raven at the table, her head down, her eyes closed.

Alix pulled out his knife and prepared to kick the box from underneath her feet.

I walked past the tables and pulled out my own knife. "Stop."

Alix turned to me, his eyes narrowed.

"Cut her down."

A gust of wind blew through the clearing, making the lit torches flicker and almost go out. The energy was totally different now, even tenser than it had been a few seconds before I'd halted the slaughter.

Alix wasn't tentative with me like he'd been before. Now he was angry, unsure what act I was trying to pull.

When he didn't do what I said, I told him again. "Cut her down, or I'll cut your throat." I didn't care if I was outnumbered twelve to one. I wouldn't let this shit happen anymore, and I would kill anybody who got in my way.

Alix still didn't obey. "What are you doing?"

"The Red Snow is over." I pulled out my knife and aimed it at the wooden pole where the rope was tied. I threw the knife, and it cut the rope, freeing her from the noose. The blade embedded in the wood behind the platform.

The woman fell to the ground, praising God and digging her fingers into the soil as she cherished her good fortune.

Alix turned to the other guards to see their reactions even though their faces were hidden under their hoods. "What the fuck, Magnus?"

"We aren't doing this shit anymore." I stepped on the box and pulled my knife out of the wooden frame. I returned to the ground and turned my back to Alix as I walked away. I'd kick his ass all over again. "You got it?" I projected my voice so the other guys could hear without a hint of confusion. "The Red Snow is permanently prohibited. Anyone who tries will be hung themselves."

Alix's voice came from behind me. "Fender gave no such orders."

I turned around and faced him. I threw my hood back because I didn't care about hiding my face anymore. It was the first time I wasn't ashamed of who I was. "He's not the one giving the orders anymore. I am."

I sat in the chair in front of my desk, my body pivoted toward the door. My decision had been spontaneous, caused by a rush of adrenaline and guilt. I'd never planned on doing that, but now it was done, and I would face whatever consequences came to pass.

The door to the cabin opened, and Raven stepped inside. The girls were always excused after the conclusion of the Red Snow—or after the conclusion of whatever just happened.

She closed the door behind her then stood there and stared at me.

My eyes were on the floor, one elbow on the desk, while the other arm was over the back of my chair. My knees were apart, and I was surprisingly calm after everything that had just happened.

She stepped toward me until she was directly in front of me. "Look at me."

My head wasn't bowed in shame. It wasn't bowed with guilt. I just wasn't prepared to see her expression, to witness the look on her face that I would never forget.

Her hand went to my shoulder before it slid up my neck and then to my chin. Her fingers tugged at me slightly, forcing me to look up.

I met her gaze and would never forget the way she looked at me.

Her eyes were wet, and tears had fallen in rivers down her cheeks, creating two shiny streams of emotional release. Her bottom lip trembled once our eyes met.

It was hard to look at her, but I didn't turn away.

She lowered herself to her knees in front of me so our faces were level. Her palms cupped my cheeks, and she looked into my eyes like she never wanted to look away. She sniffled as more tears fell to her lips. "I love you…"

My chest tightened and my stomach did somersaults when I felt the heaviness of her words hit me like a ton of bricks. It wasn't just the words she said, but how she said them, how they were visible in every teardrop. It was the first time I'd really felt loved since I'd lost my family, since I'd lost my mother's warm embrace, since I'd had my last good Christmas. She was a new version of the family that I'd lost, all the love that had been taken from me. Now, it was back…and it was beautiful. "I love you, *ma petite amie*."

THIRTY-ONE

BROTHER

I STEPPED INTO THE CABIN CARRYING A TRAY OF food. I continued to eat in the communal cabin with the other guards just so I would be present within the camp, to hear their conversations and be part of them. After the Red Snow yesterday, it was definitely tense, but none of them opposed me.

Raven sat on the floor in front of the TV, and she looked up at me when I walked in.

I handed her the tray.

She took it and set it on the floor beside her, eyeing the cup of yellow liquid. "What's this?"

"Lemonade."

She took a drink and licked her lips. "I haven't had lemonade in a long time."

I took a seat in the chair in front of my desk. My shoulders hung with the heavy weight that no one else could see but me. My heart was having slight palpitations because of the dread in my veins. It was only a matter of time before I would come face-to-face with the consequences of my decision.

She listened to the TV with her eyes down on her food. She was always starving at the end of the day since she didn't get breakfast and had to work for hours straight.

I stared at the TV, but I really paid it no attention. There were only a few channels in English, so there was very little entertainment for her to enjoy.

When she was done eating, she turned off the TV and got up to place the empty tray on the table. She looked down at me, studying the consternation on my face. "What's going to happen?"

I kept my eyes on the dark screen and didn't answer her.

She leaned against the wall and crossed her arms over her chest, her eyes still on me.

"Fender will arrive tomorrow. And we will have words."

She rubbed one of her arms gently, taking a deep breath at my answer. "What do you think he'll do?"

I shook my head. "He'll be angry."

"Will he hurt you?"

Probably.

"Will he kill you?"

"We'll see."

"I don't want to be in this cabin when he arrives. I want to be there with you so I have your back."

It was one of the things I loved about her and despised about Melanie. Raven was fearless. "I don't think that will work. You're not exactly his favorite person."

"I'm not trying to be," she whispered. "But I'm not going to let anything happen to you."

Sometimes I wondered if I had fallen in love with a soldier instead of a gorgeous woman. "You can't help me. I don't need you to help me."

"But last time—"

"Last time, I accepted my punishment. This time, I do not. This time, I will stand by what I believe. I will look him in the eye and tell him he's wrong."

She kept her eyes on me. "I know he loves you. I've seen the two of you together. I know you are a weakness for him…"

I nodded. "I warned him I would resist him, so he shouldn't be surprised. That'll either help me…or hurt me."

When it was time for him to arrive at the gate, I left the cabin.

Raven was dressed as if she intended to come with me. She moved to the door like she planned to stand her ground and watch my back when I could only watch my front.

I opened the door and turned around and looked at her. "You can't help me with this."

Her eyes were both impassioned and furious, frustrated that she wasn't getting her way when it was so important to her that she did. "Where you go, I go… Remember?"

"I know. But not this time." I didn't want her there anyway. She couldn't help me, and I would be more worried about protecting her than protecting myself.

"Please…"

I shook my head. "He'll probably want to talk to me in private. There's no place for you. I'll be alright."

She started to breathe hard, overwhelmed by the frustration that sank her to the bottom of the ocean.

I left the cabin and locked the door behind me so she wouldn't follow me. Then I walked across the dark grounds and headed to the gate where his horse would approach any moment. Whenever I passed the other guards, they gave me a look of contempt, but they didn't dare oppose me. They were cowards, only showing their dislike but not actually doing anything about it.

I waited at the gate with the other guards.

It was dark and quiet. A long silence filled the space with only the distant sound of the forest. There were no clouds in the sky, so the stars were bright. It was unfortunate that such terrible things happened in such a beautiful place.

The sound of hooves became audible as the horses approached the perimeter. And then a member of his entourage yelled for us to unlock our side of the gate.

I removed the bolt that slid across the door and pulled the doors inward.

The formation of horses entered the camp, Fender in the lead. His eyes swept over his surroundings as he entered, but he took specific measures not to look at me.

He knew.

He climbed out of the saddle and handed the reins over to one of the guards. His bag was taken from the saddle to be carried to his cabin in the rear.

I approached him.

He looked me square in the eye, his eyebrows furrowed in subtle hostility. His brown eyes were cold and vicious, and the squaring of his shoulders and the tightness of his arms showed all the rage he was suppressing.

I didn't apologize. I didn't make excuses. I stood by what I did, and I would do it again and again. If he really wanted me to stop, he would have to kill me.

He spoke, his masculine voice deep and low. "If you want to have children someday, don't fuck with me." He turned away and walked to the cabin without asking for a report on the daily progress of our work. He'd just issued a violent threat against his own brother without skipping a beat.

I watched him walk away and couldn't hold back my retort. "You don't want to fuck with me either, brother."

He halted in his tracks, his muscular back rigid and tight. A few breaths made him expand and decrease in size, processing the rage I'd just provoked within him. Just when it seemed like he might turn around and face me, he walked off.

And blended into the darkness.

Fender didn't speak to me.

I worked the next day without seeing him or crossing his path. He must have been in his cabin the entire time, going over all the reports that Eric took for me and dropped off.

This had never happened before. Whenever Fender was angry with me, he charged me like a bull. He spoke his mind and engaged me directly. This was completely unlike him.

At the end of the working day, I approached the clearing to get Raven and escort her to the cabin, and that was when I noticed the torches.

They were lit.

Adrenaline dumped into my heart, and I jogged across the earth to get closer to the clearing and see what was happening.

There were three nooses set up now.

And the three women had already been chosen.

The girls struggled against the guards as they were yanked below the nooses. They screamed and cried, begging for God to help them. The woman I had spared days before was one of the three.

Raven immediately looked at me once I was visible, and the relief in her eyes showed her faith in me. I would put an end to this and spare their souls.

I marched past the table, with my eyes focused on Alix. "What the fuck are you doing? I made my stance on this perfectly clear."

Alix turned around and left the woman on the ground. The mask covered the bottom half of his face, but the shine in his eyes showed his hidden smile. "I don't take orders from you, asshole."

I pulled my knife from my pocket and held it at the ready. "Let them go, or I'll cut off your balls, your lips, and your nose."

Alix wasn't scared, as if he had a more formidable foe on his side. He looked behind me, like he saw someone standing there.

I already knew who it was.

I slowly turned around and met my brother's look. He was the only one in jeans and a shirt, never wearing the uniform. His focused stare was full of anger and disappointment. "Because of your fool-ishness, I will take three lives instead of one. The women can thank you for that."

We looked so much alike, had so many identical features, but in that moment, we couldn't look more different. The women and guards stared at us as the torches flickered in the breeze. "You're better than this." I dropped my voice, so only he could hear what I said.

"Sorry to disappoint you, *brother*." His eyes shifted back and forth as they looked into mine, his anger slowly fading to a subdued state.

"It doesn't have to be this way."

"Yes, it does." He looked past me and nodded at Alix, telling him to continue with the butchering.

I turned around and punched Alix so hard in the back of the head that he fell to the ground and didn't get up again. My knuckles burned at the contact with his hard skull, but there was so much adrenaline in my veins that I was immune to pain. I turned back to my brother and stared him down.

The two other guards with the women didn't move forward, having seen their enormous comrade collapse on the ground from a single hit.

I stood my ground and didn't back down. "I'm not going to let this happen." The line in the sand had been drawn, and there was no going back from this. I'd proclaimed my loyalty, and it wouldn't falter.

Fender took a step toward me, his expression starting to boil with rage. "You're weak."

"And you're deranged."

"Step aside, Magnus. I mean it."

"Or what?" I challenged. "You're going to kill me?" I asked the same question that he had asked me. I didn't believe he would, but I'd put him on the spot with a public audience, so he might have no other choice.

He looked slightly insulted, like the suggestion was offensive. But the anger quickly swallowed him again.

"The only way you're gonna stop me is by killing me. So, I suggest you pull out your knife and do it." I rolled the dice and waited to learn my fate.

My brother stared and stared, his feet planted on the earth and still. All eyes were on him, and he had to react. He had to do something to regain the power I'd just taken from him. If he didn't, he would forever be humiliated.

"We can do this another way. I promise you."

His eyes remained focused and didn't change, like he didn't hear a word I said.

"Don't be like Father. Be like Mother."

The mention of her made his eyes change slightly.

"Let's stop disappointing her more than we already have. Come on, Fender."

"We've already talked about this. It's too late."

"It's never too late. Stop this."

Silence seemed to last forever, and he didn't convey the thoughts in his mind. He didn't pull out his weapon or order the guards to continue the slaughter. "You win, Magnus."

I did my best to hide my reaction, but I felt so much relief in those words. My brother still had a soul... deep down inside.

"For now. When your rotation is finished, you'll be discharged from your service. You will never return here— and I will run this camp as I see fit."

My eyes fell as a new level of disappointment hit me like a ton of bricks.

"You called my bluff and won." He nodded to the guards to release the crying women and extinguish the torches. "I won't kill you. But we aren't brothers anymore. When you leave…I don't want to see you again."

THIRTY-TWO
THREE SOULS

Days passed, and Fender acted like I didn't exist.

The guards ignored me too, like there was no point in terrorizing me since I would be leaving soon... and never coming back.

I'd never expected Fender to counter with a threat.

To banish me.

Hearing him say he never wanted to see me again hurt—hurt deeply. The fact that he would rather lose me as his brother than do the right thing made me question who he really was.

Maybe I was wrong.

Maybe he didn't have a soul.

Raven sat on the bed across from me while I sat in the chair. Her feet were on the wooden frame so she could rest her arms on her knees. She was in one of my shirts with her hair pulled over her shoulder, tired and ready for bed. We hadn't spoken much since the incident in the clearing.

I hadn't wanted to talk about it.

"What are you going to do?"

I shook my head, my eyes focused on the window behind her. "I didn't expect him to say that."

"Me neither."

He didn't try to hurt me. He didn't try to kill me. He seemed to just abandon me instead. He got tired of listening to me push for justice, and it was easier to toss me aside.

It hurt because I knew we were more than that.

I just knew.

"How are we gonna stop this?"

I rubbed my hands together, my right knuckles still swollen and hot from when I'd knocked out the executioner with a single punch. I might be leaner than the bulkier guys, but I was fast and strong, and I could do a lot of damage. "I have no idea. I could hire a convoy of men to come here and dismantle the place, but unless I kill Fender, he'll just keep doing it...over and over."

Raven studied me, her thoughts obvious in the look in her eyes. She wanted me to kill him but would never ask.

It was something I would never do. Neither would he. "I'm gonna try to talk to him before he leaves."

"Do you think it'll help?"

"I've given him a couple days to cool off. I might get something done...but probably not."

I walked up to his cabin and saw Eric posted outside. I walked up the steps and approached the door.

Eric moved in front of me and placed his hand against my chest. "He doesn't want to see you."

"And he put you here to make sure that doesn't happen?" I asked incredulously. "Eric, if you want me to break your face again, continue to stay there. But if you want your previous injuries to fully heal, step aside."

Eric didn't move, but there was already defeat in his eyes. We both knew he stood no chance against me. Fender probably had different guards on rotation outside his cabin, and Eric just got the bad time slot. He stepped aside.

"Good choice." I opened the door and stepped inside.

Fender was relaxed on the couch with a bottle of scotch on the coffee table. The TV was on, and paperwork was scattered everywhere. "Eric's such a pussy." He grabbed the remote and turned off the TV, his back to me.

"You know none of the guards has a chance against me." I moved to the couch across from him and took a seat.

Fender sat up, shirtless and in his sweatpants. He tossed the remote on the table and stared me down, slowly growing angrier the longer he looked at me. "Say what you need to say. Then leave."

It was hard to look at my brother and see the lack of affection in his eyes. It was like he hated me. "I'm just as loyal and committed to you as ever. I don't want to leave the empire. You know I'm the only one you can trust fully. I just want to do things differently, that's all."

With his arms resting on his knees, he looked at me like he hadn't listened to a word I said. "Trust you? You made me look like an idiot in front of all my men. You know I could never stab a knife in your heart, and you used that against me. Maybe I trusted you before, but I certainly don't now."

"I did what I had to do."

"No, you didn't *have* to do it. Your dick is wet all the time because you can't think about anything except pussy. And pussy makes you weak."

"It's not about her."

"Bullshit it's not." He grabbed his glass and threw his head back to take a big drink before he slammed it down. "Ever since that bitch came to this camp, it's been fucking pandemonium."

"We needed pandemonium, Fender. We're better than this. I've had to look the other way for years, and I can't do it anymore. Just because we suffered unspeakable things doesn't mean we have to make other people suffer unspeakable things. You need to let this go. I am still with you all the way. We can still be the biggest kingpins in France. We just have to do it without including the innocent. That's all."

He shook his head as he rubbed his hands together. "And I already told you why we can't do that. If I could, don't you think I would've already?"

"We can. I give you my word."

He clenched his jaw and shook his head.

"I'm not gonna let this go, Fender. You can banish me from the camp, but I'm going to get back in here just the way I got into your cabin."

His eyes narrowed. "Are you threatening me?"

"I'm warning you."

"Sounds like the same thing to me."

"Trust me, you would know if I was threatening you."

He shook his head. "Don't make me do it when I don't want to do it."

"But you *do* want to stop killing the girls."

"No, I'm not talking about that." Both of his hands tightened into fists. "I'm talking about you. If you keep opposing me, you leave me no choice. Don't put me in that position."

This had just taken a dark turn.

"Take the girl and go live your life. Don't interfere with mine."

"Fender, why won't you even try?"

He shook his head. "Because I don't want to take the risk. I'll never forget how it felt to be powerless, to dig in a garbage can for food, to be at the mercy of someone bigger and stronger than me. I hate what we do to those girls as much as you do. But there is no other way. I care a lot more about my power than their lives. Yes, that means I'll be damned, but we both know I was damned a long time ago." He rose to his feet and left the sitting area. "I'm not having this conversation anymore. I made my choice, and you've clearly made yours. Come back to the camp, and I'll do what I have to do…and I guess you'll do what you have to do too."

THIRTY-THREE
LOYALTY

FENDER LEFT BEFORE SUNRISE.

I didn't even know he was gone until I went to his cabin and found it vacated. Our conversation didn't do anything other than solidify the breakdown of our relationship. Doing the right thing cost me my brother, but it wouldn't have had to cost me anything if he'd just left the darkness and stepped into the light.

I should be angry.

But I wasn't.

I was disappointed. Really disappointed.

I put him in a position he didn't want to be in, but he did the exact same thing to me. He wouldn't give any ground, when I wouldn't stop pursuing that same ground.

I didn't speak to Raven much because I was in such a sour mood. I felt the weight of the world on my shoulders, protecting strangers in the camp when I was about to lose access to it. I also had to protect my brother, because when I came back to put an end to the torture, I couldn't just kill him. There would be no hesitation to kill the other guards, but with him, I just couldn't do it.

Raven knew I didn't want to talk, so she didn't try to open me up. It was another reason why I knew she was the right woman for me. She understood exactly who I was and didn't try to change me. If I didn't want to talk, she let it be.

We were together almost every moment of the day, so we didn't always have something to say. We found this comfortable silence, unspoken camaraderie, and it made me feel less alone despite the loneliness in my heart. Ever since I became an adult, it'd always been Fender and me. Without him, I wasn't even sure who I was.

But having Raven made that a little easier.

She reminded me who I was. She reminded me what I was capable of. She reminded me what kind of man I wanted to be.

I lay in bed beside her with the moonlight coming in through the curtains over the window. Her hand was on my stomach, her cheek against my shoulder.

Without looking at me, she asked, "Are you okay?" She knew I was awake without seeing my face. She could tell just by the way I breathed.

We were supposed to leave in two days. Normally, I couldn't wait to get out of this place, but this time, I was afraid. What would happen when I wasn't there? People would die. Once I was free, I had to form a plan quickly because the longer I waited, the more victims would be hung on that noose. A plan had never felt impossible when Fender was my partner.

But now it was just me.

When I didn't answer, she propped herself up on her elbow and looked down at me, her hair all over my chest and shoulder. It was so long now, getting longer and longer with every month that passed.

"My life would be so much easier if Fender would just see reason."

She rubbed my chest then pressed a few kisses to my neck. "Maybe he will…before the end."

"I don't know…"

"You stood up to him and spared those three women, publicly taking away his power. He could've done something then, but he didn't. I think you're right. He's not evil as I thought he was. So, there's still hope…I think."

It was our final day at the camp. At sunrise, we would leave for the last time. I knew Raven would never return because I wouldn't bring her with me when I challenged my brother. It was too dangerous. There was too much at stake for me to risk the one thing I cared about the most.

I went to the clearing to retrieve Raven at the end of the workday, acting as her guard as if we were still in the midst of winter.

The sun was starting to fade over the horizon, tucking behind the tall trees, the clearing becoming shaded. There were long shadows across the ground, and the heat was starting to dissipate. Wordlessly, she left the table and joined me, her skin damp and shiny from the sweat. Not once did she complain about the tiring work she had to do. She did it every day just so she could sleep with me every night.

But as I turned to look at her, something happened.

One of the guards shouted. "A crew is headed this way!"

Raven's eyebrows rose as she stopped in her tracks.

I did the same and looked over my shoulder. "A crew? What does that mean?" I turned around the other way and jogged to the front gates.

Raven was right behind me.

Eric picked up a large board and dropped it into the slot across the gate, an extra measure to keep it closed.

"What the fuck is happening?" I shouted to Nathan, who was at the top of the ladder, looking over the edge.

"There's thirty guys on horses," he reported. "All dressed in black. All riding this way. They've got guns too."

There was no possibility it was any of our guys coming with the wagons or with a shipment. I didn't need to look over the edge to see for myself. "Keep them out as long as you can. We'll get the guns." Just as I turned away, I heard guns start to fire off and bullets pierce the wooden perimeter.

Nathan jumped off the ladder and landed hard on the ground. "Oh Jesus…"

Fear struck me like an ax to the chest. It was about survival, not just for the camp, but for our souls. I turned to Alix and gave an order. "Get all the guns out of the vault. Hand them out. Now." Alix took off at a dead run.

Another round of bullets struck the wooden fence around the camp. The only reason why I'd built it was to keep the girls in, not the enemies out. But now, I was glad I built that wall with my own hands.

"Who are they?" Raven's frantic voice came to my ears.

"I don't know. Stay behind me." I went up to another guard and gave an order. "Release all the prisoners. All hands on deck." He took off to get the keys.

I ran through the camp until I made it to the stables. I unlocked the doors and found a horse that was already saddled. "Here. Take her to the edge of the forest behind your old cabin."

She took the reins. "Why?"

"Does it look like I have time to explain? Just fucking do it." I left her side and ran back to the center of the camp.

Alix was handing out guns to the guards. When he saw me run up to him, he tossed me a rifle.

"I need a handgun too."

Alix pulled one out of his pocket and handed it over.

I gave other orders in the camp, but as the minutes passed, it became more chaotic. We'd never practiced for this outcome because no one ever knew about our existence. I had no idea who was marching on the outside.

The front doors started to creak as our enemies continued to slam into the wood and try to break it down.

We were outnumbered two to one without the girls, and we were unprepared, but we still had to do whatever we could to hold our ground.

A hand grabbed my arm.

I looked down at Raven, who was out of breath because she'd run all the way here from the tree line. I pulled the handgun out of my back pocket and gave it to her. "Do you remember how to get to the chateau? Ride there now—as fast as you can."

She took the gun but didn't even look at it. "What? What about you? Aren't you coming with me?"

"No. I have to stay here."

"Why? You don't owe these guys anything."

No, I didn't. But it still wasn't who I was. "I can't turn my back. This is my camp. I will fight to defend it. You have to go."

She stepped back from me slightly, her expression hurt like I'd just slapped her with my palm. "I'm not going anywhere without you."

The doors almost burst because their force was making the hinges split off. They would be in the camp any second.

I didn't have time for this, and the longer she argued, the angrier she made me. "I need you to go. Now. I will meet you there when I can."

She didn't walk away. "I'm not gonna leave you!"

I grabbed her by the arm and shoved her back, treating her like I did the first moment we met. "I told you to go! Now fucking go! I don't have time to babysit you. You don't even know how to use a gun. Get the fuck out of my sight so I can do what needs to be done." As much as it pained me to possibly end things forever this way, I turned away and moved to the gate the second it opened.

The men entered on horses, shooting their guns and aiming at anybody they saw

I looked behind me to see where she was.

She was gone.

It was a short-lived battle.

Battle wasn't even the right word for it.

More like a massacre.

The only ones who were spared were the prisoners. The crew obviously intended to use them for their own labor, so they returned them to the cabins and locked them inside.

The guards were executed.

One by one.

Men I'd known for almost a decade were killed with a bullet to the brain.

Our guns were taken from us, and we were forced to kneel on the ground in a line. Alix was on my left. Eric was on my right. Nathan was on the other side of him.

I wasn't the kind of man to give up, but most of the guards weren't trained for hand-to-hand combat, and they weren't great with a gun either. With a siege like this, they were completely unprepared, and they panicked the whole time.

I was only one man, and I couldn't do it all.

Now, I was on my knees, waiting for my execution.

A man stood in front of us, a cigar sticking out the side of his mouth. He was in black with a black leather jacket, boots covering the hem of his jeans. With his arms crossed over his chest, he stared at us. He sucked on his cigar and let the smoke dissipate from his mouth. He pulled the cigar out of his mouth to speak. "Which one of you is Magnus?"

How did they know my name?

Even though the guards hated me, they didn't rat me out.

I had no reason to hide. "Me." I was the one in charge, so my execution would be special.

He stuck two fingers in his mouth and whistled loudly. "Tell Napoleon to come over here."

My entire body went rigid when I heard that name.

Napoleon.

There was no point in spending my last moments angry, but I was furious. I didn't like Napoleon, warned Fender about him, and we'd only been working with him for a month... That was all it took.

He betrayed us.

He figured out where we operated. He must've followed Fender here and waited until he left.

I took no solace in being right.

I wished I'd been wrong.

Napoleon walked over from one of the cabins, taking his time while using his black pommeled cane. The tip dug into the soil and got dirty with every step, but one of his cronies would probably wipe it down when he was finished. For a man who needed a cane, he didn't seem to struggle getting around, riding seven hours on horseback to get to this camp.

The cane wasn't a crutch.

It was a distraction.

He joined our group and stood directly in front of me. I seemed to be the only person he was interested in because his eyes were reserved for me.

I held his gaze without blinking.

My back was to the rear of the camp, the forest where Raven had escaped with the horse. Her face was a blurry vision in my mind, the woman I found too late in life.

Napoleon stared for a while until a grin slowly moved on to his lips. "Looks like you were right."

"If you see Fender before I do, tell him I said I told you so."

He gave a slight chuckle. "You're brave. A lot braver than I would be if I were on my knees about to be executed."

"You'll find out when Fender gets to you."

"I highly doubt that. I've killed all of his men, taken his drugs, taken his partnerships…what's he going to do? His own brother warned him what I was, and he didn't listen. He's not a smart man."

"But he's a vengeful one."

"Alright." He lifted his cane and handed it to one of his men. "I'll pass on your message."

The guy took the cane and handed him a revolver.

"I'll start on the outside and work my way in." He pointed the gun at Alix's head.

Alix panicked. "Wait, no—"

He pulled the trigger.

Alix jolted backward and fell, dead before he hit the ground. I could feel the blood spray on my arms. I didn't hesitate at the sound, and I didn't feel bad listening to the gunshot that took his life.

He got what he deserved.

And I'd get what I deserved.

Napoleon pointed the gun at Nathan next.

An audible dripping sound hit my ears, and I knew he'd pissed himself.

Napoleon laughed. "At least one always pisses their pants…" He pulled the trigger, and Nathan collapsed just the way Alix had, this time falling face first.

I didn't look.

Eric shook violently, unable to keep himself upright.

Napoleon seemed particularly unimpressed with him because he shot him with no preamble.

Now I was the only one left.

Napoleon turned to me next. "I'll cut you a deal. Work for me, and I'll let you live."

I lifted my gaze and looked at him.

"Fender's mind is clouded by money and women. Yours isn't. And I'm sure you want nothing to do with your brother now that he didn't listen to you."

It didn't matter if I was right and he was wrong. He was my brother, and nothing would ever change my loyalty. "I'd rather die."

Napoleon stared at me for a few seconds, like my response earned respect, but also earned his anger. He lifted the gun and pressed the barrel against my forehead.

I closed my eyes.

I knew she was there.

I knew she wouldn't leave me.

I knew she was in the tree line and watching, her hand shaking as she held the gun I'd given her, hoping she would hit her target and save my life.

I had faith she was there, that she didn't go to the chateau without me, that she would only go where I went.

"*Ma petite amie…*"

And then I heard a gunshot.

Napoleon jerked back when the bullet pierced his body.

I'd been expecting it, so I got to my feet and grabbed one of his guards, bashing his face in until he collapsed. I grabbed his gun and shot the other guard. All the men were on the ground.

The other guards across the camp started to shoot at me when they realized what had happened.

I sprinted for the tree line, knowing she was somewhere over there, somewhere past the fence. My body pushed me faster than I'd ever run, somehow escaping the hail of bullets that caused clouds to form from the ground all around me.

When I approached the fence, I saw the rope drop down.

"Here!" Her voice was loud from the other side.

I knew she was holding the rope tight on the other end, so I grabbed it and pulled myself over, scaling the eleven-foot wall in just seconds until I dropped on the other side.

The bullets were loud behind me. Breathing hard with a pounding heart, I grabbed her wrist and pulled her with me. "Come on!" I got to the horse and climbed on first so I could help her up and behind me.

Her arms locked around my waist, and her chin moved to my shoulder, her heartbeat frantic against my back.

I kicked the horse and took off at a sprint.

Yells and gunshots were still loud behind us, still audible over our hard breathing and galloping hooves.

Her arms squeezed me tight like she was terrified, still traumatized by everything that had just happened. Her fingers dug into my shirt, and her breathing was loud against my ear.

I was an expert horse rider, so I held the reins with one hand and placed my other on top of hers.

And I squeezed it.

THIRTY-FOUR
TWO HEARTS AS ONE

I PASSED THE CHATEAU AND DIDN'T STOP. I BARELY had time to look at it. The sounds of gunshots and voices had stopped hours ago, but I didn't slow down. They wouldn't stop until they found me, so I had to get as far away from here as possible.

I kept riding until I reached a small home closer to the road, where I kept my car sometimes. I brought the horse to a stop then helped Raven off before I climbed to the ground.

Everything had happened so fast. I took a second to bring it all in, to remember the feeling of that cold metal against my forehead.

Raven didn't ask what the plan was next. Instead, she just looked at me, looked into my eyes like she was so happy I was there with her.

We didn't have time for this, but I couldn't look away. I wasn't surprised that she'd saved my life. I somehow knew she was there, having my back like she always did. But I couldn't describe my feelings in that moment.

Neither could she.

Even though I was sweaty and my hands were dirty, I moved into her and cupped her cheeks, bringing her face close so we could treasure this feeling of victory. "I knew you were there... I just knew."

"Because I told you I would never leave. Ever." Tears dripped from her eyes as she planted her hands against my chest, like she just wanted to feel my solid body, to feel the lack of bullet holes. "I'll never leave you for all my life. If you die...I die."

I cupped the back of her head and brought our foreheads together for a moment, embracing her in a way I never had. I finally told her how I felt, said those three words I'd never said to another woman, but now they didn't feel good enough, not strong enough. They were beneath what we had. I dropped my embrace and pulled away.

She sniffed and wiped her tears with her fingertips. "Now what?"

I grabbed the reins to the horse and handed them to her. "Put him in the stable."

"Just leave him here?"

"When we get to the city, I'll have Ramon fetch him and put him in the pasture."

"Good. Rose will have another friend." She took the horse down the path to the stables and got him situated.

I entered the code into the keypad so the garage door would open. Against the wall, there was a blue tarp over my motorcycle, so I pulled it off and rolled the bike out before I closed the garage again.

After she gave the horse hay and water, she came back to me. "Wow, are we going to ride that?"

"Yes." I kicked the stand down to balance the motorcycle before I retrieved two helmets from the garage. I handed one to her. "Don't be scared."

"Do I look scared?" She smiled before she pulled the helmet over her head. "They'll never be able to catch up to us now."

I got onto the seat and started the engine, making sure she was still good to run. "Hop on."

She got on the seat behind me and wrapped her arms around my waist. "What are we going to do now?"

"Get to Fender as quick as we can."

Hours later, we arrived in Paris.

I had no idea how far Napoleon would go to capture me. He might not care at all because he got what he wanted. He had the camp and the prisoners, so he could operate a drug empire and collect all the revenue. Fender and I were no threat to him now. Why should he care about us?

I left the city and drove into the countryside to his estate. After checking in with the guards, I made it to the entrance, and we walked to the front door.

Raven was still in the attire of the camp, tired and sweaty after the horrific day we'd just experienced.

Gilbert answered the door. "I apologize, sir. The count is not taking visitors right now, and he wanted me to tell you that he's not interested in your company—"

I pushed past Gilbert and walked into the house. "Fender! Get your ass down here right now!"

Fender's voice shot back immediately from upstairs. "Fuck off!"

"Napoleon took the camp, and I'm the only survivor. So, get your motherfucking ass down here right now."

Heavy footsteps sounded a moment later as he ran to the edge of the stairway and looked down at me, his eyes wide and fearful. He gripped the rail until his knuckles turned white.

"He hit the camp with men and guns, and he defeated us within an hour. He kept the prisoners and executed the guards. Raven and I escaped on horseback."

Fender was still speechless, processing all that nightmarish information in a single instant. He released the rail and came down the stairs, in just his sweat-pants like he'd been in his office upstairs. He reached the bottom and stared me down. "This all just happened?"

"About eight hours ago. We got to my motorcycle at the house and drove straight here."

Fender didn't know how to contain his anger, so he turned away and ran his hands over the stubble of his jawline. One hand was on his hip, and he paced in the entryway, his bare feet striking the tile with his movements.

Melanie emerged at the top of the stairs, in a dress with her hair in a braid over one shoulder. Her eyes were on her sister before she took the stairs and embraced her.

On her left hand was that enormous rock.

"Are you okay?" Melanie held her sister and pulled back to look her over.

"I'm fine," Raven answered. "Just a bit over-whelmed. But I'll get over it."

Fender continued to pace like he didn't know what else to do. "How did he know where the camp was?"

"I think he followed you."

He faced the opposite wall, his hands on his hips, breathing hard.

I stared at his back as I felt a swirl of many emotions. "One by one, they executed each one of us. I was with Alix, Eric, and Nathan while they were shot in the skull. I don't feel bad for what happened to them, but they didn't deserve that either. Your men died because you failed to listen to me."

Fender stilled.

"And the only reason I'm alive now is because Raven saved me. I was on my knees in the dirt, the last one to get a bullet in my head, but she shot him first."

Fender slowly turned around and looked at me.

"I am the sole survivor because of her."

Fender shifted his gaze and looked at Raven. While he was still cold and angry, there was a new look in his eyes.

He suddenly walked past us and into the sitting room. "Magnus, just you."

I left the women alone together and joined him in the other room. He sat on one of the couches. I sat on the other.

Fender rubbed his fingers through his hair and over the back of his scalp, taking deep breaths and letting out long sighs. "You were right, and I didn't listen."

I thought I would get a lot more satisfaction out of that, but I didn't get any at all.

"Now the camp is lost."

Men I'd known for years were dead, probably going to be burned in the woods somewhere.

He rubbed his hands together as he thought about everything. "We have to take it back."

My eyes narrowed in surprise. "Why?"

He looked at me. "Because we can't let him get away with that, Magnus. We don't let someone make a fool out of us."

"You mean make a fool out of *you*."

He didn't snap at me because he knew he deserved the insult. "We still have to do something. We have to take that camp back. We can't just let them overrun our business like this."

"So, after all this…you still care about money?" I shook my head. "Fender, you need to let it go."

"This man killed all my men and almost killed my brother. Do you think I'm gonna let that go?" He stared me down, turning angry.

"Do you want to take the camp back for revenge? Or do you want to take it back so you can run business as usual?"

He didn't answer.

"If your answer is the second one or both, don't expect me to help you."

Fender massaged his hands like he had broken knuckles.

"I will only help you if you run the camp differently. You set the girls free and hire people to do the labor. If we can't come to an agreement on that, I'll walk away." I knew Napoleon would do the exact same thing with those girls, make them work for the rest of their lives. He might not execute them weekly like we had, but he would probably do other unspeakable things.

Fender stared me down, silent.

"We do it my way. Or we don't do it at all."

After a long silence, he spoke. "Well, my way obviously doesn't work…"

I watched my brother finally come to his senses.

"And if we do nothing, those girls will never be free. They'll continue to be prisoners, just changing owners." He stared at his hands for a while. "I'm not sure if I'm fit for the drug business anymore anyway. I let greed get the best of me. I almost lost the most important thing that matters to me—you." He lifted his gaze and looked at me. "I want revenge for what Napoleon has done. He humiliated me. He took what's mine. He killed my men. And then he touched my brother. I want him dead."

I nodded in agreement.

"And if I rescue those women…maybe our mother won't hate me so much, won't be so disappointed in the monster I've become."

"She doesn't hate you, Fender."

"She should. I became a worse version of our father. I became everything that I hate."

"So, you're with me?"

"You know I'm always with you, brother." He watched me, his eyes unblinking. "I guess that means I'm about to retire. What do people do in retirement?"

"No idea. Have a couple kids? Go on trips? You're asking the wrong person."

"Well, what are you going to do?"

"I haven't thought about it." This had all happened so suddenly, and if I survived the attack, I had my whole life ahead of me.

"I guess we get old…and fat."

His joke made me smile. "I don't think the girls will stick around if we let that happen."

He stared at the floor for a while, his mood suddenly somber. "You've got a good woman, Magnus. She's earned my respect."

"Thanks. That means a lot to me."

"I owe her my life…since she saved yours."

THIRTY-FIVE

NOTHING BETWEEN US

WE KNEW WE HAD TO MOVE QUICKLY. WE COULDN'T take days or weeks to organize our crew and make a plan. The best chance for success was to hit them when they didn't expect us to come.

We rounded up the remaining men we had and made some calls. We had access to weapons and horses, so we had everything we needed to do this.

"You said there were thirty men?"

I nodded.

"We'll bring at least fifty. We'll have one man sneak ahead and attach a bomb to the front gate."

I had a better idea. "Then you'll announce to everyone that we are there, and also, exactly where we are. I think we should come from the rear."

"Come from the rear how?" Fender asked. "There's no road."

"Exactly. We'll sneak up on them, and they'll have no idea. We can make it by horse. We don't need to bring wagons or anything else."

"I guess that could work…"

"I know the way. We can move in the dark. When we reach the fence, we can climb over. They won't even know we're there."

He sat across from me on the couch and looked down at the maps. "Was Napoleon killed? Or just wounded?"

"No idea. I'm not even sure where Raven shot him. I didn't have time to look. I just got out of there."

"We'll assume he's alive, then. But if he was bleeding badly and couldn't get to a doctor, he probably wouldn't have survived. Did they kill the physician at the camp?"

"As far as I know, they killed everybody."
Except me.

"Will you be able to do this tomorrow night? You can go home and get some sleep, and we'll leave tomorrow afternoon."

"Yeah, that works." I just needed a few hours of rest, and I would be recharged. There was so much adrenaline and vengeance in my veins that I was so pumped, I might not be able to sleep at all.

"I have a couple horses. Can we use yours?"

I nodded.

"Alright." He stacked his maps and paperwork and closed his laptop. "I'll let you get some sleep."

I walked into the other room and found the girls sitting together on the couch in the other living room. I stepped inside and looked at Raven. "Let's go home."

She hugged her sister, and they both got up and joined us in the front room.

Fender turned to me. "Just in case things go south, the girls should stay at your apartment. Napoleon knows where I live."

I nodded in agreement.

Raven's expression quickly changed, looking at me like I'd betrayed her. "What does that mean? What's happening?"

"Fender and I are taking a group of men back to the camp tomorrow night. We're gonna kill them all, free the girls, and then walk away from the business."

Even though I was finally giving her what she wanted, she didn't seem to care. "And you expect me just to wait here for you? I'm coming with you."

It didn't surprise me at all, but she would never talk me into it. I turned to Fender and said goodnight before I headed to the front door.

Raven walked behind me, chasing after me. "I'm coming with you. That's final."

I walked down the steps to my bike in the round-about. "Raven." I turned back around and gave her my focused stare.

She halted when she saw the look in my eyes.

"You can't come with me this time."

She shook her head, her eyes furious. "I want to free those girls as much as you do."

"It's too dangerous."

"You think I care? After everything I've survived at this point, you think *this* is too much? I protect you, and you protect me. That's how this works. That's how this has always worked."

I appreciated her loyalty to me, but without proper training or experience, she wouldn't be able to assist. "We're going to sneak into the camp with fifty men. We'll be armed and prepared. You don't have the skills for this."

"But I had the skills to shoot that asshole from a hundred feet away, and I've never shot a gun in my life. Come on, give me more credit than that."

I wanted to lose my temper and scream, but I knew she deserved better than that. "Nothing you say will change my mind. Fender and I are the best fighters in our crew, and we will destroy those assholes. I won't be able to focus if I'm worried about you the entire time. You need to trust me."

"And what do I do if you don't come back?" Her voice broke. "It's not like I can just move on. You are the man I'm supposed to be with, and without you, I'll be alone…forever. If you die, I want to die with you. If you're going to risk your life, I risk mine too."

"I will come back."

"You can't promise that."

"Did I promise?"

Her eyes fell. "I want to save these girls too. I belong there."

"And you did save them…because you saved me."

She inhaled a deep breath, her eyes watering.

"They're not going to expect us to hit so hard and so quickly. It will be an easy defeat. I'm not arrogant and won't be complacent about it so my guard will drop. I will finish this, and I will come back to you. You need to have faith in me."

She continued to breathe hard, like I'd just asked her to do the impossible.

"I'm not bringing you. I'm sorry, but I'm not. Instead of spending our last night arguing about it, we can go home and be together. That's how I want to spend our time. What about you?"

She inhaled another breath, her eyes watering more. After a loud sniff, she nodded. "Are you riding to the camp?"

I didn't expect such a question. "Yes."

"I want you to ride Rose. She'll take care of you."

My heart softened as I heard her offer. "Okay."

We slept on and off. We made love many times then went to sleep. We would wake up again and be together once more before drifting back into our dreams. When we woke up the next day, it was past noon.

After I showered and got ready, I went downstairs to see a coffee waiting for me. There was also a muffin, even though I wouldn't eat it.

I grabbed the cup and took a drink.

She stood there, in a nice dress with earrings in her lobes, terror permanently in her eyes. She was like a wife watching her husband go off to war.

I stood in front of her and looked into her face, seeing the invisible tears behind her eyes. "In a few hours, those women will be free. There will never be another Red Snow. They'll go back to their lives and find peace. Just think about that while I'm gone."

She looked down at her hands. "I care about those girls, but I care about you a lot more. You're the one I'm worried about. I need you to come back to me."

Watching her love me was the most beautiful thing I'd ever seen. It was a kind of love that was far beneath the skin, deep in the heart. It was unconditional and passionate. I'd been with a lot of beautiful and interesting women in my lifetime, but I'd never had anything like this, something so special. I wasn't sure what I did to earn the undying affection of such an incredible woman. I knew I would treasure it every single day as long as I lived. "I will do everything I can to come back to you, *ma petite amie*."

"I know…"

My hands cupped her face, and I pressed a kiss to her forehead.

Her arms wrapped around my waist, and she rested her head against my chest. She held me tight like she didn't want me to go.

I didn't want to go either.

But I knew, once it was over, it would just be us.

Just us forever.

The sound of the elevator rising to our floor was audible from where we stood near the kitchen.

"It's Fender."

She pulled away but kept her arms around my waist. "I've never been so scared in my life. It's far more terrifying to lose the life of someone you love than your own. I never thought I would fall in love like this. I never thought I would have a man like this. I just got you… I'm not ready to let you go. You're supposed to be my husband. We're supposed to make babies. Please don't take that away from me."

All those things didn't scare me. I'd never thought about having a family of my own. I never thought about having a wife. But once Raven and I were committed to each other, all of that seemed natural.

I never even told her I wanted those things. She said she wanted them, and then I did too. "I won't."

The elevator doors opened, and Fender and Melanie joined us in the living room.

I pulled away from Raven and regarded my brother. "Are you ready?"

He nodded.

Melanie looked as pale as a ghost. Her cheeks had no blood, her lips were the same color as her skin, and her eyes were dull. Her gaze was on the floor as if she didn't want to look at the scene before her.

"Alright." There was nothing left to do but say goodbye.

Fender turned his gaze on Melanie and studied her for a few seconds. His gaze was cold and hard, like he wanted to make this a clean break. But his eyes remained on her face like he would never be ready to look away.

She whispered to him. "I'm scared…"

He moved into her and cupped her cheeks with his big hands, cradling her face so her gaze was locked on to his. "You'll be safe."

"That's not why I'm scared…"

He regarded her for a long time before he leaned down and kissed her. "Beautiful, I love you." He pulled his hands away and stepped back without waiting for her to say it back.

She grabbed his arm and pulled him back. "I love you too." She wrapped her arms wrapped around his neck and hugged him tightly.

I didn't want to say goodbye to Raven. But the sooner I left, the sooner I would be home. This was the last thing standing in our way. We could bury it in the past and move on.

She came in close to me. "Kill anyone who stands in your way. I don't care who they are. Don't let anything come between us."

"I won't."

She leaned in and kissed me on the mouth. It was the kind of kiss she gave me when it was just the two of us alone in bed, full of passion and desire, warm breaths and wet lips. "I love you." It was only the second time she'd said those words to me, but it felt like she'd been saying them to me since the moment we met. She never really needed to say it at all to show how she felt. It was almost redundant.

But I liked hearing her say it anyway. I like watching her say it. I liked feeling her say it. "I love you too." I gave her a final squeeze before I turned away and walked off.

Fender joined me, and together, we took the elevator to the bottom floor and got into the car. He was the one behind the wheel, and he hit the gas to take us away from the apartment.

We didn't speak to each other for a long time. We got on the main road and joined the other guys with their cars hooked to the trailers with the horses, including Rose. We had a couple hours before we got to the drop-off point.

With one hand on the wheel and his eyes on the road, he said, "I never understood what you saw in her. But now I do."

THIRTY-SIX

REDEMPTION

In a single-file line, we made our way through the terrain and approached the camp from the rear. With the light of our flashlights, we made it through, crossing the river and getting closer and closer. It was a few hours before sunrise when we approached the wooden fence.

We turned off the flashlights.

We got off the horses and tied them to the trees.

As Raven requested, I took Rose. She was a good horse, well trained, handled the dark without any reluctance. She crossed the river like it wasn't her first time…because it wasn't. I opened a bag on the saddle and grabbed a handful of oats. I opened my hand wide and fed them to her. "Thanks for the ride."

When I joined Fender, he already had the ropes ready. "I'll help you over. We should be near the stables, so the water pipes will be on the other side. Tie the rope there."

I nodded.

He leaned against the fence and cupped his hands together for me to step into.

I held on to his shoulders, stepped into his hands, and then he lifted me up until I reached the top of the fence. He gave me an extra boost from down below so I could pull myself over and drop down again.

The camp was quiet.

I was still as I searched the grounds, to see if they had guards on duty. The only ones I saw were near the front gate. Two were at the top of ladders looking over the edge, as if they did expect us to show up. There were two other guards down below, both holding rifles.

But they were all looking the wrong way.

Fender threw the rope over the fence.

I caught it before it slammed against the wood and made a noise. I secured it to the water pipes by tying it in a triple knot. Then I gave a few tugs so he would know it was ready to bear the weight of the men.

One by one, they climbed over.

Fender was the next one to join me. He kneeled and looked around, seeing the men posted by the front gate. "Good thing we came from the rear. Good call, Magnus."

When our men were over the fence, we fanned out and spread throughout the camp, ready to take each cabin silently. We didn't want open gunfire if it could be avoided. We would rather save the bullets anyway.

Fender went to one cabin to take out the guards, and I kept moving to the rear. I suspected Napoleon was staying in Fender's old cabin since it was the largest on the premises. I wanted that man dead, and I wanted to be the one to do it.

But I never made it.

An alarm sounded, blaring so loud that it would wake up everyone in the camp. It wasn't ours, so it was something they must've installed when they settled.

I turned around and watched chaos explode.

Men ran out of the cabins with their guns and shot at our men. They were still outnumbered, so our guys were shooting most of them down. My first instinct was to check on Fender, but when I looked across to the cabin he had entered, he stepped out and glanced around, and no one came up behind him.

He must've killed them all with his knife.

I'd wanted this to be a simple takedown, but I'd underestimated Napoleon.

He knew I would get away. And he knew I would come back.

I was about to join the fray and kill as many men as I could, when something heavy slammed down into the back of my head.

I hit the ground, and my arms couldn't break my fall. I hit the earth, blood dripping from my skull and mixing with the dirt. My vision blurred for a moment before I could turn over and look at my assailant.

Napoleon stood with his cane held in his hand, and he looked down at me with an unforgettable sneer. "You little rat." He raised his cane and prepared to slam it down on me again.

Raven's words came into my mind.

Kill anyone who stands in your way.

I rolled out of the way, and the cane missed me by a few inches. I stumbled to my feet, still disoriented, and pulled out my gun.

He smacked it away with his cane, and it flew across the ground, out of my reach. "You could've just lived your life. You could've accepted your surrender gracefully. Instead, you chose to come here to get beaten with a stick by an old man." He swung his cane again, moving with a speed that defied his age. I backed away so he wouldn't crack my ribs. But I tripped in the process and fell on my back. Gunshots and screams rang through the night as the camp was filled with pandemonium.

My gun was far away in the other direction now, so I reached for my knife.

But he was quicker because he didn't have a head injury. He struck me with his cane, hitting me in the chest and making me cry out.

"Scream like a rat!"

I kicked him in the shin and made his knees buckle underneath him. I tried to crawl away.

"Magnus!" My brother's angry voice came from across the clearing.

Napoleon got on top of me and put his weight on my arm so I couldn't stab him with my knife. He slammed his knee into my leg and made me cringe while he banged my wrist into the dirt so I would lose my hold on the hilt of the blade.

Heavy footfalls came my way, my brother coming to rescue me. "Get the fuck off him!"

Napoleon slammed his head down into mine and made me see stars. Then he seized the knife out of my hand and turned it at the right moment.

Stabbing my brother in the stomach.

My brother stilled, immediately went weak, couldn't speak, and then fell back and collapsed in the dirt.

Everything happened in slow motion. It also happened at double speed. I heard my scream come out of my mouth, mixed with angry tears. My body was so weak from the kicks and the hits, but a sudden jolt of energy came out of nowhere and cleared away my blurry vision, the throbbing headache behind my eyes, all the aches from the injuries Napoleon had caused.

Napoleon spat on my brother. "The two for one special."

I slammed my boot into his chest and hit him so hard, he flew back.

I rolled onto my stomach and crawled for his cane.

Just when I snatched it, Napoleon grabbed me by the ankle and dragged me back.

I turned over and slammed the cane straight down on his head.

Blood burst from the wound in his skull.

I kicked off his hold and crawled on top of him.

I slammed the cane down on his head again.

Again. "Die, motherfucker!" I beat him again and again, splashing blood all over myself, delirious in my anguish, screaming and crying out in pain and rage. I kept hitting him when there was nothing left, until his skull was open and his brains were mixed with the dirt. By the time I was done with him, it looked like a semitruck had run over his head.

I leaned back on my heels and caught my breath, seeing the damage I had caused, the vengeance I'd finally gotten. I threw the cane down on his body and went back to my brother. "Fender!" I moved over him and saw the blade still stuck in his stomach, blood everywhere.

He was still awake.

"I'm here." It was one of those moments when I shut off all my emotions and became a selfless vessel for the other person. His wound was so bad there was no chance he would survive. The blade was too big, it was too deep, he'd already lost too much blood. "You're gonna be alright." I looked over my shoulder. "I need a medic! Satellite phone! Get over here!"

Fender looked up at the night sky, so calm it was like he'd just had a glass of scotch and was ready to drift off. "No, I'm not." He shifted his gaze away from the stars and looked at me. "But thanks for lying."

I pulled my shirt over my head and looked over my shoulder. "I need a few guys. Now!" I grabbed the hilt of the blade and pulled it out of his stomach, ignoring the way he cringed in pain. I wrapped my shirt around his injury and put the pressure on. "Fender, you can get through this. I need you to stay with me, alright?" I kept my voice steady even though I was so fucking scared. There were already tears in my eyes because I wasn't ready to say good-bye. I wasn't ready to lose the only family I had left.

His voice was still calm. "Magnus."

The guys came over, one of them bringing a suture kit and bandages, while the other had a satellite phone. The battle was still going, but the victory was ours. I took the bandages. "Call our pilot. Tell him to bring the chopper here now. Fender needs to get to a hospital."

The guy stepped away and made the call.

I knew he had a lot of internal bleeding, and there was nothing I could do to stop it. All I could do was keep the pressure on and hope he made it.

His voice came again, weaker. "Magnus."

I couldn't look him in the eye. I just couldn't do it. My hands pressed against his stomach, putting pressure on the wound that was supposed to be mine. I was the one who was supposed to be stabbed. Not him.

He placed his hand on mine, becoming soaked in his own blood. "I deserve this."

I shook my head. "Stop it."

"You know I deserve this. The girls are free, and I'll be dead. That's how it should be."

"You aren't going to die! Stop it!"

"Brother."

I struggled to keep back my tears. "Please don't…"

"Look at me."

I breathed hard as I felt more blood stick to my hands.

"Magnus."

I turned my gaze on him, feeling the tears in my eyes. It was so hard to look into eyes identical to mine, to remember everything we had been through together. He was my friend, my ally, my everything.

"You are the man I could never be but always wanted to be. You said I was the one you looked up to, but it was always the other way around. You're a good brother...and I love you."

Tears fell down my cheeks, and I couldn't breathe anymore. "I love you, brother."

He squeezed my hand. "Tell Melanie...nothing would've made me happier than to see her in that white dress and make her my wife. Tell her to forgive me...but I did what I had to do. And I would do it again...even if I knew what would happen."

I squeezed his hand.

He started to grow weaker, like he didn't have the strength to talk anymore.

I kept the pressure on his stomach even though there was no hope. My brother was dying right before my eyes, the shouts dwindling in the background, the world becoming quiet as I waited for his soul to pass. All I could do was sit there...and watch my brother die.

THIRTY-SEVEN
TRUCE

NONE OF THE MEN APPROACHED ME. THEY LET ME sit with my brother while they took care of the camp. They unlocked the cabins to release the girls and let them out into the clearing. I had accomplished what I'd set out to do, but it felt meaningless now.

My brother closed his eyes and went still, his skin becoming pale and gray. My hands remained on the wound, even though it was pointless. There were tears on my cheeks, and they continued to flow because I knew the loss would never stop hurting.

The sound of propellers sounded in the distance, and it grew louder and louder as the chopper approached. When wind started to blow my hair into my eyes, I knew they were landing behind me.

But it was too late.

The helicopter landed, the engine shut off, and then the wind died down. The medics left the chopper and ran to us to start their procedures.

As hard as it was, I let go.

I stepped back, my hands dripping with his blood. I turned around to embrace Raven, but then I realized she wasn't there. I was alone. I'd thought I would always have my brother, but now I didn't. I watched the guys stare at us from a respectable distance, assuming the worst.

That the boss was dead.

They placed Fender on a stretcher and lifted him from the ground to carry him into the chopper. I walked at the rear, assuming all they could do was take him to the morgue at this point.

They placed all the equipment on his body, taking his blood pressure, his pulse, putting oxygen into his nose. They got the monitor working. One of the medics said, "He's got a pulse."

I stilled at the announcement.

"It's weak. Probably won't make it to the hospital. If we can give him some blood, he might hold on."

The engine started, and the propellers started to spin.

The medic turned to me. "Are you coming?"

I turned around and gave the orders to the men before I climbed into the helicopter and shut the door. Fender looked dead, looked like there was no hope, but there was still a chance...even though it was so small. "What can I do?"

The helicopter lifted from the ground and rose above the forest on its way back to the city.

One medic got an IV line going, while the other pulled out vials and medications.

"Do you know what his blood type is?" the medic asked.

"Yeah," I answered. "A positive." I only knew that because mine was the same.

The medic turned to the cabinet and searched the packets of blood. "We're out."

"Take mine."

The medic turned to me. "You have the same?"

I shouted over the engine. "Yeah."

"Alright. Take a seat. We have to do this fast."

I sat down at the table and extended my arm, directly beside my fading brother. "Stay with me, alright?"

The medic started the process. "Don't get your hopes up. I don't think he's going to make it."

When we landed at the hospital, the medical team rushed him into the operating room right away. No one said anything to me. No one gave me false assurances. He was just taken away.

All I could do was sit in the waiting room and stare at the floor.

For injuries of this magnitude, we couldn't use our own medical team. We needed surgeons and equipment to get this done. It wasn't a simple bullet in the arm that could be pulled out with tweezers and an old-fashioned suture kit.

He would probably die on the table.

I didn't know what to do. The girls didn't have a cell phone, so I had no way to reach them. I could call Miranda and have her go by the place and bring them here, but by the time they arrived, he might already be dead. Raven wouldn't care less about my brother's demise, but she would care about my sorrow. And Melanie would care, obviously.

I couldn't bring myself to talk on the phone, so I texted Miranda and told her what to do.

Then I waited.

I hadn't moved from my spot in over an hour, staring at the floor and remembering the final fight with Napoleon. That man had always been a liar. He'd purposely made us underestimate him. There was no mistake; he was a force to be reckoned with. He was savage, brutal, straight-up evil.

I wished Fender had believed me. I didn't know Napoleon was all those things, but I always knew I didn't like him.

It was a hunch. It was instinct.

I heard a distressed voice coming from my right. "Please help me. I'm looking for my fiancé. I guess he's in surgery?"

I rose to my feet and walked over to the check-in counter. "He's here. Just waiting for news." I'd washed the blood off my hands, but there were still drops on my shirt. My clothing was black so it was hard to see, but it was there, like drops of rain.

Melanie turned to me, her eyes already overflowing with tears, terror in her gaze, looking like she'd lost everything that mattered to her. "Is he going to be okay? What happened? Did you kill the mother-fucker who did this to him?" Raven stood behind her, her hand on her sister's arm but her eyes on mine. She wanted to move into my chest and embrace me, but I was the one clearly uninjured, and her sister needed her right now.

I wouldn't lie. It would just hurt more. "Melanie, I'm sorry… He's probably not gonna make it."

The pain on her face was indescribable. Her whole world crashed down around her, the horror and heartbreak conveyed in the expressions she made. Her hand moved over her mouth, and she stifled a sob she couldn't control.

I'd already shed all my tears at the camp. I didn't have anything left.

Raven turned her sister into her chest and let her cry against her, holding her the way a mother held her daughter. She cupped the back of her head and rubbed her back, letting her fall apart.

I wanted to be with my woman, to feel her comfort me because I'd already lost a part of my soul, but I knew she was pulled into two different directions and she had to choose.

She made the same choice I would've made.

I turned away and gave them their space. I went back to the chair, sat down, and stared at the floor once again.

They stood together for fifteen minutes, Melanie cycling through sobs and hysteria before she turned quiet. But then the whole thing would start all over again. She eventually excused herself and went to the restroom to clean up.

Raven came to me.

I was on my feet so fast and moving into her like we were two magnets that were unable to oppose the forces that attracted our souls. My arms held her body, and I brought our faces in close together, reunited with the woman I'd worked so hard to come back to. I was covered in bruises and scars, but nothing that would change my life.

"Are you okay?" Now it was her turn to shed tears, to release happy tears that I had returned to her. It easily could've been the other way around, with me on the operating room table dead, but Fender had made sure that didn't happen.

"Yes."

She examined the cut on my head where I'd been hit with the cane and saw the bruising emerge from underneath my shirt. She looked me over, visibly in pain at my discomfort but still happy that I was there and whole. "I don't know what I would've done if you didn't come back to me."

"But I did come back."

Raven's eyes watered as her hands moved to rest on my neck.

"Napoleon was gonna kill me. Fender saved me. That's why he's in there…and I'm not."

Her eyes watered. "I'm so sorry…"

She understood exactly how that would make me feel. Instead of wanting my happiness at being safe, she focused on the guilt and the pain that I must be feeling, knowing the cost of my life was his. It was another reason I loved her so deeply, that she understood my feelings so easily without my having to explain them. "Yeah…"

"There's still hope, Magnus."

I shook my head. "He's lost too much blood. There's too much damage. I'm surprised he made it until the chopper got there."

"Then don't be surprised if he makes it out of surgery, too. That man has a lot to live for, and I know he will fight his hardest to live for you." She cupped my cheeks and watched my eyes water like hers without any judgment. "Don't give up on him."

"It's just easier to assume the worst because if I get my hopes up…" I shook my head. "I know he's done bad things, but he's a good man. He's always taken care of me, ever since we were kids. He told me he would sacrifice his life for mine all over again. Doesn't matter how much we fight, how

much we disagree, his love has always been unconditional. I have no idea how I'm going to go on
without him." That was something she could
understand because she'd refused to leave Melanie
in that camp. Raven never took the easy way out
because she was always committed to being at her
sister's side. Raven and I were two sides of the same
coin, two people of the same soul.

"Fender is the kind of man you should never underestimate. Let's not underestimate him now."

Melanie wasn't able to sit the entire time. She
would pace in the waiting room, take a walk
through the hospital, just kept moving because
sitting still was too difficult.

Raven sat beside me and held my hand. "It's been
six hours. That's a good sign."

I turned to look at her.

"That means he's still alive. If he's lasted this
long…"

Maybe there was hope.

"What happened to the girls?"

There was another couple in the waiting room, but they sat on the opposite side, and the woman had fallen asleep on her husband's shoulder. "They were released from the cabins. I told the men to walk them down the trail to the end of the road. Trucks will pick them up and bring them back to the city. They'll get some money and some clothes. Then they can do whatever they want…"

She nodded. "I wish I could've seen it."

"Me too." But my place was here, next to my brother.

"What will become of the camp? Will Fender continue to run it with hired labor?"

I shook my head. "He decided to retire."

She couldn't hide her surprise. "Really?"

"It's time for both of us to move on."

"I just can't picture a man like that in retirement."

I shrugged. "We'll see how it goes."

"What about you?"

I stared into her face and admired her blue eyes. She was both brave and innocent. She was such a small part of my past, but my entire future. "I think I'll settle down with a wife…have some kids. Walk to a coffee shop and get a few muffins in the morning. Read in bed. Go horseback riding…"

Her hand squeezed mine as a beautiful softness filled her gaze, like I'd just described a dream come true. "That sounds nice."

A doctor in a white coat emerged and headed straight toward us. Our tender moment was ruined once reality announced itself.

I rose to my feet and prepared to hear the worst news of my life, but also still hoping for the best.

He got right to the point. "He's stable. He had a lot of internal bleeding, but I think we addressed everything. His blood pressure is back up, his pulse is strong, and I think he'll make a full recovery… eventually. We're gonna keep him in the hospital for a couple days just to monitor him before we let him go. Do you have any questions for me?"

I couldn't speak because I hadn't expected him to say any of that. I'd expected my brother to die on the table; I'd expected to be the last one to carry the family name.

Raven spoke for me. "He's just overwhelmed right now by the good news you delivered. When can we see him?"

"He'll be under for a few more hours, but when he wakes up, you can visit with him. We're gonna put him in a room soon."

"Thank you," Raven said.

The doctor walked away.

I didn't realize how long I'd been holding my breath until my lungs started to ache. I finally released the air and felt tremors all over my body. Just hours ago, I'd watched my brother bleed out into the dirt and stare at the stars until he couldn't keep his eyes open anymore. But he was going to survive.

Raven moved closer into me. She wrapped her arms around me and held me tightly. "Everything's going to be alright."

I squeezed her to me and rested my forehead against hers. I somehow came out of the darkest moment of my life with everything I wanted. I got to keep my brother, and I grew my family by finding Raven. She gave me another reason to live, to aspire to be a good person, to be better than I was before. "Yeah, I think it will be."

I let Melanie go in first since she was the most unhinged. She was an emotional wreck, sobbing her eyes out before she even saw him. They were alone together for over an hour.

I waited in the hall with Raven, anxious to see my brother but also patient because Melanie was a part of our family now. Now, I didn't care that she was dumb and dull once I witnessed the sincerity of her feelings. She really loved my brother. I could see it. So, I could forgive her for being a lesser woman than her sister.

Melanie eventually stepped out, her eyes puffy like she'd been crying in there too. "He wants to see you."

I moved to the door with Raven's hand in mine.

She pulled away and stepped back. "It should just be you. He's been through a lot, and the last thing he wants to do is see my face."

"He's moved on." I grabbed her hand again and pulled her into the room with me. Even if Fender still didn't like her, he would have to get used to her because she was the other half of me.

He sat up in bed wearing a hospital gown with an IV in his hand, a monitor beeping next to him. As he looked at me, an emotional look subtly passed across his face. But then there was a smile. "You thought I was a goner, didn't you?"

I came closer to the bed instead and stood over him. "Well, you kept saying you were dying, so…"

He chuckled. "I was just giving you shit."

I moved my hand to his and gave it a squeeze.

His smile dropped.

"I'm glad you're okay. I wasn't sure what I was going to do without you."

"You don't have to worry about that…for now. I think Melanie might kill me. My fiancée is pissed."

I gave a slight smile and took a seat.

His eyes shifted to Raven next. Instead of looking at her with hatred, his expression was subtle and impassive. "Truce?"

She came closer to the bed. "Truce."

"Any woman who saved my brother's life twice can't be that bad."

"And a man who rights his wrongs and sacrifices his life for someone else…" She struggled to get it out, like there would never truly be forgiveness for what he'd done. "Can't be that bad either."

He extended his hand to shake hers.

She stared at it for a few seconds before she placed her hand in his palm and shook it.

I didn't expect Raven to ever love my brother, ever really forgive him for what he had done, so her tolerance was enough.

"I'm glad you're okay." She pulled her hand away.

"Really?" he challenged. "I thought nothing would make you happier than if I died."

"You're the man my sister loves. You're the man my man loves. So, no, it wouldn't make me happy. What makes me happy is knowing that those girls have been given their lives back, that the camp will no longer be the setting for such terrible things, that even the most terrible men can change. I don't think you've redeemed your soul because you can never give back the lives you've taken, but you turned back on the darkness and decided to step into the light...and that does count for something."

THIRTY-EIGHT
GIVE IT ALL AWAY

WEEKS PASSED.

Didn't take much for us to get back into our old routine, going for walks in the morning, making dinner at night, sleeping together in the master bedroom upstairs. Now, without the sense of dread weighing on our hearts in anticipation of our return to the camp, it did feel different.

Part of my life had ended, but it didn't quite feel over.

I still dreamed about it. I could still feel the dry wood under my fingertips from the railings down the steps. I could still hear Alix's voice even though he was dead. I could still smell the trees, feel the breeze, see the Alps every time I closed my eyes. My time at the camp was so dark that I felt like it would never truly leave me. Horrible things that I'd seen would always be a part of me.

Raven was happy, but there was always a hint of melancholy to her presence. It seemed like she had left the past behind her.

I called my brother to check in on him and his progress, and he said Melanie had taken good care of him and he was now back on his feet, just without a purpose. Retirement didn't serve him well, and unless he got a hobby soon, he would go crazy.

I wasn't sure what to do with my time. Being with Raven felt like enough for me. She read in bed beside me, and I did the same. *The Count of Monte Cristo* was epically long, so I was still reading it, while she powered through books ten times quicker.

The two of us had dinner in the city, and after we were finished, we took a walk down the sidewalk toward the Eiffel Tower. It was lit up like a Christmas tree, a beacon of hope for all Parisians. I knew it was particularly special to Raven because she never got tired of making a visit and walking down the path with the lit trees.

We reached the grounds and walked side by side, passing other couples in the dark, enjoying their late-night decaf coffees. The first day of fall had arrived. It was hard to believe that I had known Raven for almost a year. It had passed so quickly because of all the chaos.

She suddenly stopped in front of one of the benches while staring at the tall structure rising into the darkness, its brilliant luminescence like star fire.

I stopped beside her. I was so deeply in tune with her moods and body language that I knew she had something to say, that it'd been on her mind for weeks. I didn't rush her to share because I knew she would come to me when she was ready. Now, I looked down at the side of her face and watched her eyes light up as they reflected the tower.

She finally turned her head and looked at me. "There's something I need you to do."

I stared, focused on her blue eyes, and waited for more.

"All your wealth comes from their labor, their sacrifice. I can't enjoy it, I can't spend it, not when I know how you earned it."

My hands remained in my pockets, and I stared at her with my unblinking gaze.

"I want you to give it to the surviving girls. I want you to give it to the families of the girls who've passed. I want you to pay reparations for what the camp has done to them."

She'd just asked me for the world. "You can't expect me to give away all my money. Some, yes. But not all."

Her eyes were focused on my face, saying more in her silence than she did with words.

"If I gave it all away, then what? I won't be able to take care of you anymore."

She shook her head slightly. "I've never wanted you to take care of me. We take care of each other. That's how this works."

"We'll have to get jobs."

"That's fine. I'll go back to university and finish my education. I'll get a job as a professor there."

"And what will I do?" All I knew was drugs.

"You can build things. Be a contractor."

I sighed loudly because I didn't want to do that. "I don't like people."

She nodded slightly. "What about horses? You're good with horses. You could be a trainer, caretaker."

It wasn't the worst idea in the world. "If I give all my money away, we won't be able to keep Rose."

The statement really made her emotional. "We can pay to keep her in a stable. In the meantime, we'll work and save to buy our own land. We'll have a house, pasture, place to raise a family. We'll do it the right way."

I couldn't believe I was entertaining this idea, to give up all my money that I'd spent a decade earning...just like that. "You worked in that camp for almost a year. A portion of the pot is yours too."

"Then we can use that for an apartment or something."

Fender and I had worked so hard to earn back our wealth after our father pissed it all away. We were supposed to have an inheritance, have something to pass on to our kids. Now, I would have nothing... again. "You'll leave me if I don't do this?"

She shook her head. "No. It's a request, not an ultimatum. But we'll be fine, Magnus. We don't need money to be happy. We just need each other. Let's leave the past in the past and move into the future. Wash your hands of this completely and start over."

All that money never really made me happy. I liked my fancy car and my estates, but I felt lonely. Raven came into my life, and all of a sudden, I was actually happy—during the times when I could be happy. Maybe she was right. Maybe I could give it all away…and be happy with her. "Okay."

She looked at me in a way she never had before, like she fell in love with me all over again, deeper this time. She moved into me, wrapped her arms around my neck, and kissed me on the mouth as her fingers dug into the back of my hair. "We'll live well. We'll be happy."

THIRTY-NINE
I DO

THE GIRLS WERE UPSTAIRS GETTING READY.

Fender and I sat together in the sitting room, both of us wearing tuxedoes and shiny shoes. There was a bottle of scotch on the table, and we refilled our glasses and continued to drink, the sort of thing he did well in his bachelor life.

Fender swirled his glass before he looked at me. "You gave it all away. I'll never understand that."

I'd slipped the girls' checks underneath their doors. To the family members who'd lost their daughter, wife, or mother, I did the same. It would never bring back the person they'd lost, but maybe it would make their life a little easier. After I gave away the first check, I realized it was the right thing to do. It made me feel sick, so I didn't even want the money anymore. "We don't need it."

"Where do you live now?"

"In her old apartment. The tenant moved out, and we moved in." It wasn't a fancy place, but it was close to everything so we didn't need a car, and we had a great view of the tower. It was also the place where I grew closer to her, where I had one of the most spiritual moments in my life. Maybe one day, we could buy it.

"And you're okay with that?"

I nodded and took a drink. "It feels right."

"Our goal was to retire. And you're working again."

I shrugged. "I like horses. As long as I don't deal with people, I'm fine."

"You could start the business again. Just do it the right way."

I consider that so I could earn back my wealth, but it was still a dangerous business, and all I wanted was a peaceful life. I wanted simplicity. I wanted to go to work and then come home to the woman I shared my life with. "I'm not interested in that anymore."

He looked at me over the glass as he took a drink. He didn't seem to agree with what I had done, but my money was gone, so there was no point in making an argument. "Are you happy?"

I thought of our little moments, doing dishes in the sink, watching her teach me how to do the laundry, the smile in her eyes when she woke up and saw me next to her. It was a life I should've had in the first place. I should've grown up with my family, went to university, settled down with someone special, and had a great life. "Yes."

He gave a slight nod, like that was all he wanted to hear. He raised his glass to me.

I lifted mine and tapped it against his.

We both took a drink.

Fender turned to look across the house to the staircase. "What's taking her so long to get ready to marry me?"

"Maybe she's come to her senses."

He turned back to me, his eyes narrowed. "She knows there's no other man who's man enough for her."

"I don't know…" I liked to tease my brother. It was easy to get a rise out of him.

"I'm sure she just wants to—"

Melanie reached the bottom of the stairs and came into view, Raven behind her and helping with the train of the dress. "Be careful. Don't step on it."

"I am being careful," Raven said.

Melanie turned around and faced her sister, her hands moving down and smoothing out her dress. "That took forever. Do I look okay?"

Raven came close and fixed her sister's hair before bending down to adjust her dress. When she came back up, she grabbed both of her arms and gave her an affectionate look. "You look perfect, Melanie."

I knew Raven would never truly be happy with her sister's decision to marry Fender, but she put on a smile and was there for her. There was nothing she could say to make her sister feel differently, so she let it go.

Fender stared at Melanie the whole time, ignoring both me and the scotch like we didn't exist. His eyes were laser-focused, like he'd never seen anything so magnetic in his life. "Yes, she does." He got to his feet and stepped away from the sitting area to get closer.

Melanie turned to look at him, and the sincerity of her gaze was unmistakable. Fender was truly the man she wanted to spend her life with, and her love was stronger than his sins. She gathered the front of her dress and lifted it slightly as she walked to him, her eyes taking him in like there was music playing and she was walking down the aisle. When she reached him, her arms circled his neck and she hugged him.

His powerful arms wrapped around her body, and he held her close so he could embrace her, so he could stick his hand into her hair and kiss her deeply, even when the woman wasn't even his wife yet.

Raven emerged from behind them, wearing a pink dress the color of rose gold, with flowers in her hair. She watched them together for a moment before her eyes shifted to me. She wore a slight smile, like she'd somehow missed me in the few hours we'd been apart.

I knew I'd missed her.

The four of us stood with the priest on the grounds as the ceremony took place. Fender and Melanie looked at each other like no one else was there, and with their hands held together, they pledged their love and loyalty for a lifetime.

Melanie was facing me, but instead of looking at her, I looked at Raven. I could see the conflict on her face, see how happy she was for her sister, but also upset by the man she'd chose to be her husband.

Her brown hair was in curls up and over one shoulder with a row of flowers in her hair. Her makeup was heavier than usual, accentuating her features and making her lips look so plump. The tight dress was beautiful on her, and I wondered how my brother could be so fascinated with Melanie when Raven was so much more than her sister could ever be.

The priest ended the ceremony, and the two of them kissed—again.

Raven and I clapped.

Fender took Melanie's hand and pulled her away, walking with her across the large estate where they would live for the rest of their lives. Her white dress trailed behind her, and she walked close to him as if normal proximity wasn't quite enough.

The priest followed them.

They left the two of us to stare at each other.

I stepped closer to her until my face was just inches away. "Beautiful."

She smiled in a special way, the tenderness in her eyes more than her lips, but the compliment meant the world to her. Her sister's beauty could never outshine her own, at least not when it came to me.

"Doing okay?"

She released a sigh and gave a subtle nod. "He's the man she wants. Nothing I say will change the way she feels. We can't always choose who we love. Sometimes, love chooses you." Her hands moved to mine, and she interlocked our fingers. "Just trying to move on and leave the past in the past. We've done everything we can to make it right. Fender has done everything he can to make it right. Suffering and guilt won't change what's been done. So, I know we need to find happiness when we can."

I loved her pure heart, her integrity, and her morality. I loved that she stood up for what she believed in, no matter the adversity. She was strong, brave, fierce. This was the woman I wanted to raise my daughters to be the same way, to raise my sons to look for a woman who didn't need a man at all, but wanted one all the same. I'd had no idea what I was really looking for in a partner until I found it. "You make me happy."

Her eyes softened.

"I didn't just give away my money. I gave away my rage, my vengeance. I gave away my broken heart because a whole one took its place. I didn't just find happiness with you, but also peace. You gave me peace."

EPILOGUE

RAVEN

I UNLOCKED THE DOOR AND STEPPED INTO THE apartment. My bag was over my shoulder, full of textbooks and my notebook. I locked the door behind me and set the bag on the counter. The dishes were done, the apartment was clean, and there was dinner cooking on the stove. "I'm home!"

His voice came from upstairs. "Just got out of the shower."

I took a peek at dinner and even stuck my fork inside to get a few bites before I grabbed a couple plates and set them at the small dining table near the window. It was a cold night, Christmas just a few weeks away. Our tree was in the corner, decorated with white lights and shiny ornaments.

He came downstairs a few minutes later, in jeans and a long-sleeved shirt.

"Thanks for making dinner. Smells great."

"And tastes great, right?" He gave me a playful stare, like he knew I'd snuck a bite.

"I mean…I was just checking to see if it was done."

He chuckled and came in close to wrap his arms around me before he gave me a kiss.

My arms wrapped around his neck, and I held him tightly, feeling those lips convey all his love.

He pulled away and turned to the stove.

I knew how happy he was every day. He didn't explicitly say it, but it was obvious in his features, in his lovely smile. It was a side to him I never knew at the camp, never knew outside this apartment.

He served dinner, and together we set the table and ate. We shared the events of our day, his time at the ranch taking care of the horses, me discussing my classes in my graduate program. I was trying to learn French since I intended to become a citizen here at some point, but it was difficult. Sometimes I had Magnus speak to me in French to speed up the process, but it was frustrating most of the time.

When we were finished, he said, "Do you want to take a walk?"

"It's pretty cold outside…" I looked out the window and saw the frost in the corners.

"We can get some coffee on the way."

"Can we walk to the tower?"

He smiled as he got to his feet and cleared the plates. "I was hoping you would say that."

He went upstairs to retrieve something, and when he came downstairs, he was holding his hardback copy of *The Count of Monte Cristo*. It was the French edition, so different from mine. Instead of leaving it on the counter, he brought it with us.

"You're gonna carry that heavy book the whole time?"

"I just finished it. But we could talk about it."

It had taken him forever to finish that book. It was massive, at least nine hundred pages, but I read much quicker than he did. It was one of my favorite books, so I didn't mind having a conversation about it. "Sure."

We left the apartment, got a couple coffees, and walked together down the sidewalk, discussing his favorite parts of the book. He would open it sometimes to find a favorite quote and read it to me.

He was already so sexy, but a man who read was even sexier.

We reached the grounds of the tower and walked together, our coffees almost finished because we'd drunk them too fast to stay warm.

"What was your favorite part and why?"

He looked ahead as he considered the question, the book at his side. "How determined he was to escape. He was fueled by vengeance rather than desire, but it still gave him the extraordinary ability to be patient and determined. Reminded me of you."

I smiled as I looked up at the lights of the tower, remembering the way we met and treasuring the way we fell in love. It was a story no one else would ever have.

He moved to a garbage can and threw away his coffee. "Are you done with it?"

I took a final drink until it was empty and handed it over.

He tossed it inside and kept walking.

"Now how will I stay warm?" My hands moved into the pockets of my jacket.

His arm went around my waist, and he held me close as we walked. "Like this."

My arm hooked around his waist, and I smiled up at him as we approached the base of the tower. And we stood there together, our warm breaths escaping as vapor into the dry air. We stood there together for a long time, just enjoying the moment.

I'd wanted my freedom so much, but the freedom with him was so much better than my solitude. He was the other half of my soul, the only person in the world who truly understood what I'd been through, the only person who really saw me. "I love you." We weren't one of those couples that said those words every time we parted, every time we went to sleep. We said it very rarely, but in those isolated moments, those words had more meaning.

He looked down at me but didn't say it back. But he didn't need to.

He dropped his arm from my waist and held out the book.

The trees around us were wrapped in white lights, and the cold kept other pedestrians away. We were the only people there, in the most romantic city in the world. It was like it belonged to just us.

I took the book from him and lifted my eyes to his face.

"I want you to have it."

My eyes softened.

"I know I saved you. But you saved me too."

My hand squeezed the book before I looked down at it, seeing the words in French that I could mostly translate. The story had been a beacon of hope in that small cabin, had been my guiding light in the dark. It meant the world to me.

I opened the book and saw the words in French. But as I flipped the pages and moved to the middle of the book, the weight felt different. It was much lighter, like the pages didn't carry the same weight.

I continued to flip until I noticed the square hole cut into the second half of the book.

There was a box fitted inside, the lid removed.

And in the center was a ring.

I hadn't experienced a jolt of adrenaline like that in a long time. My breathing went immediately haywire, like I was about to run. My pulse raced and pounded in my ears. I hadn't expected this at all, so it really took me by surprise.

It was a single band, white gold. There were no diamonds. After giving away all his money, we didn't have much left, let alone enough to buy a fancy diamond ring like what Melanie had.

That was what made this ring so special.

I pulled it out of the slot and closed the book. It reflected the lights from around us, reflected the emotional expression on my face. I turned the ring in my hands and saw the engraving on the inside.

Ma Petite Amie

I finally lifted my gaze and looked at him, my eyes wet and about to break like a dam.

His expression was focused and stern, but there was a special softness to his eyes, like he could feel how happy he'd just made me. He took the ring and placed it on my left ring finger, sliding over the knuckle until it fit in place. He didn't ask me to marry him. The gesture itself made his feelings incredibly clear.

My arms wrapped around his neck, my hands still gripping the book, and I moved into him to kiss him in front of the Eiffel Tower, finding a family that I never really had. I'd never felt whole, never felt complete, and then I found this man, the hope in the dark, a man who had endured unspeakable pain for me.

He squeezed me and held me close, kissing me like he loved me, kissed me like I was the one thing he'd been waiting for. He loved me without having to say it, was the man I needed without having to ask. He was the one and only man I could spend forever with. And I knew I was the only woman who could ever make him happy.

Apart, we were both broken. But together, we were whole.

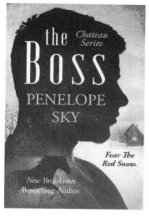